CAIRNAERIE

For Mark—
you know why

Cairn: A mound of rough stone left as a memorial

Aerie: A hiding place built high

PROLOGUE

Baltimore 1827

Silver Watch

The boy startled when the door latch clinked before his uncle entered the small, smoky room. He quickly placed the silver watch back on the shelf and turned. "I finished bringing in the wood, sir," he said, pointing to the hearth. "Is there anything else you want me to do?"

"You kin set about upstairs. See that your sisters are ready to go. They'll be here before the high sun."

And with the high sun came change.

The boy would remember that week as a beginning and an end. For the rest of his life, it would seem as if a watch had been stopped and reset to a different life, as if all that came before were something merely imagined. First, on that Monday, Franny and Susannah had left in a fancy barouche with a buxom woman from Philadelphia and her slight husband who, in their charity, had agreed to take in two young girls. Franny was seven and Susannah was nine. The couple had neither room nor inclination to accommodate a boy. Besides, a boy his age was old enough to take care of himself, or so said common sentiment.

Still, as he had waited with them he hoped for equal charity, but by the end of the week, he knew his path would veer a different way.

On Friday, as he, himself, walked away, he wondered if he would ever see his sisters again. For him, adventure lay ahead—adventure by necessity—and he would make the best of it. Up to this point, his life had not been his own. Now it would be, in a way that every man—every boy—takes charge of his own destiny.

Behind him the heavy door thudded shut, and he turned for one last look. The afternoon sun like a thick marmalade glazed the modest doors and brick facades of the houses lining the cobbled street. Anne, his youngest cousin, pressed her puzzled face and a small hand against the cloudy window pane. From now on, she would fight with the others alone, standing straight-legged, arms crossed, eyes narrowed to challenge her siblings. They would ignore her or tease her, as they always had, but he would not be there to take up for her. Never again. He waved, although it was he who needed the most encouragement. She left the window, disappearing back into the fold, leaving behind only a smudge on the glass and a glint of sunlight. At that, a rush of fear cut through him like pain, fear for Anne, and Franny, and Susannah, but mostly for himself.

He gripped his sack, his ten fingers equal to his years, and slung it over his narrow shoulder. The silver watch, wrapped in his few clothes, hit the middle of his back.

"Since this was yer grandfather's, I'm givin' it to ya," his uncle had said after the barouche had trundled away. "Yer ma—God rest her soul—would of wanted ya to have it." Standing in his modest front room, the uncle had cradled the timepiece the way one might hold an egg as he initiated his nephew's necessary parting. Then he had placed it in the boy's hands, folding his fingers around it. "Not right me keepin' it. Hold onto it. But if ya have to sell it…." His uncle had looked away and not finished his sentence. He wished the boy could stay—he was a kind man at heart. But with an ailing wife and five children of his own to feed, he had little choice. "No sense starvin' with a silver watch in yer pocket. Find ya a job, son. Save what ya can. You're a resourceful lad. Yer da and me—we made it across the ocean. We did. You'll find yer way." He cupped the boy's tender hands in his own, and they lingered eye to eye, the way men share affection. "Of course, ya will," he added, as if to reassure himself.

The boy had expected more instruction, but none had been forthcoming, so he left, feeling lost in a way that maps and directions would not help. He walked down Commerce Street toward the harbor, a destination that seemed reasonable and, if nothing else, familiar. The sky above him looked limitless, but near to earth, the city closed in around him. Cattle-drawn drays and carts, horse-drawn curricles, phaetons, and jostling masses of people crowded the streets of the bustling city. Sunlight poured over rooflines and saturated streets and alleys, but its warmth was short-lived. Evening shadows would soon carry in cool darkness.

He passed the basilica, an architectural papacy, its spire the single structure high enough to reach heaven. It overshadowed the lesser buildings—rows of conjoined houses huddled side to side with windows adorned in crucifixes and candles, and marble stoops overrun with frolicking children. Last week, he had been one of those children.

At the docks, he watched the horizon dissolve into the bay's waters, and across it he saw hundreds of vessels. There were showy clipper ships with luffing sails and swinging lanyards, efficient four-masted barques with gunwales draped of lashings like broad-throated matrons, and smaller schooners that rocked, and modest dinghies that bobbed. Everywhere seagulls squawked and soared, and some walked jauntily along the piers, snaring bits of food like tiny, feathered busboys tidying the wharves.

The boy slid down next to a bollard and tucked his sack beside him. Sailors shimmied up riggings, rolled barrels down gangplanks, and lugged heavy wooden crates onto the docks. He looked down at the boots his uncle had cut down for him—square-toed, thin-soled, and too big for his feet. He rubbed the ground, gritty and white from crushed oyster shells. It was solid. He liked the feel of it.

When a chill rain rolled in with darkness, he lifted his sack back onto his shoulder and headed toward the canal bridge. Soon, the sky and waters blended into one black canvas, broken only by occasional flashes from shipboard lanterns and the ghostly glow of restless sails, like luna moths darting in and out of lamplight. All night he stayed awake, listening to the shouts of boatmen, the rhythm of the lapping water, and the creaking and groaning of wooden docks pitched by the tide.

In the distance, a fog bell rang.

—

Autumn faded into a sustained season of damp cold. Under a bridge abutment, the boy huddled against the seawall, where he was sheltered by a makeshift tent he had built from pieces of driftwood and from discarded sailcloth that he had scavenged. He adjusted one side of the tent to shield the wind, securing it with a large stone, and then he pulled his blanket around his shoulders. For more than a month, he had forsaken a day's food here and there until he had saved enough money to buy the blanket from a merchant on Bay Street. Occasionally, a shopkeeper had tossed him a broom or traded him a coin for an errand. He had stolen food when he had to, even though the act lay on his conscience like an earned grudge.

He slipped a hard, stale roll from his pocket and lifted a dented porringer he had picked out of a trash heap and kept perched on a bollard to collect rainwater. Chewing the bread into a bland mass, he held it in his mouth to prolong his meager meal. He fingered the watch, now secured in his pocket with a crude fob fashioned from a strand of rope. Trousers that fit him a few weeks ago drooped, and his coarse belt, cinched tight, rubbed his protruding hipbone. He finished the roll and picked crumbs off his coat. Shifting to get comfortable, he wrapped his blanket tight around him and closed his eyes. The bay churned. Clouds blew cold.

A wind gust and the sound of his porringer clattering across the dock woke him from a deep slumber. Lightning crackled. Thunder boomed. The wind howled as if demons possessed the night. Rain blew through his shelter, quickly saturating his blanket. He cast if off. Clutching his sack, he bolted from underneath the bridge as his shelter collapsed. He ran as fast as he could through the deluge up toward the city. Hatchets of rain chopped muddy rivers into the street. Sallow light glowed from rain streaked windows.

He found an alcove fronting a building and squeezed into its recessed doorway, but the furious rain followed him, running down his face and chest and chilling him to the bone. Crouching close to the door, he felt a hard lump pressing against his stomach. *No sense starving with a silver watch in yer pocket.* Despair descended on him as mercilessly as the storm. No family. No fortune. No future. The boy began to cry.

A few souls scampered through the storm, their boots splashing through puddles and hammering across wooden walkways in a strange timpani. No one noticed the dirty, hungry boy until a small, wizened man shuffled passed. He stopped, listened.

"What's wrong, son?" said the man, stepping into the alcove and leaning down. The boy, fearful of the shadowy face rendered invisible against the black night, cowered. "What's wrong? Why you cry?" The voice was kind and comforting.

The boy looked up.

"You come on with me, son. Les us get outta dis rain." He grabbed the boy's elbow and helped him to his feet. "Son, my name is Ezekial."

1927

CHAPTER 1

Autumn 1927

Cairnaerie

Thursday was the kind of day that could crumble in his hands, so crisp and clear, like skim ice. John Klare killed the engine of his Nash Ajax and pushed open its door, which caught at the bottom and required a gentle prod with his foot. Wind rolling over the wooded hills that stretched as far as he could see rustled across the running board of his automobile as he stepped out. Leaves skittered by, dancing along the rutted road and catching in an iron gate where more than a few summers of wilted honeysuckle had interlaced the gate's rusted bars, all but obscuring them. Brittle stems of moonseed and sumac rattled on the breeze, and long red tendrils of Virginia creeper twined through the tangled brush like a little girl's lost hair ribbons.

Almost hidden among the weeds, a weather-beaten sign hung askew on a hand-forged hinge. He pulled aside a knot of leaves to read the faded letters: Cairnaerie.

"Ha. Found it," he said, delighted with his path-finding skills. From his childhood, he had yearned to be an explorer, religiously following Shackleton, Amundsen, and Scott on their journeys. He had read enviously of Nelly Bly and her travels. But education had been the pragmatic choice for the young man with wanderlust, and education was an opportunity he could not afford to squander. Adventuring would have to wait.

He tore back more brush to push open the gate, and he stepped through. Pausing, he buttoned his wool Chesterfield, slipped a pair of leather gloves from his pocket, and peered up at the sun that was idling behind the whitewashed sky. His trip up the mountain had taken longer than he had anticipated, and he had papers to grade before tomorrow. But they could wait, too. He leaned into the breeze.

Like the gate, the fields were clotted with weeds and seedlings, splattered muddy and rust-colored from the raw dirt beneath. He followed a narrow path, freshly pressed-down through the grass—as if a short log had been dragged along it. Going westward, he kept to the path that paralleled a wall of stacked fieldstones. The wall, in need of repair, was randomly broken and toppled here and there by scrubby cedars and pokeweed. Less than a quarter mile in, the path dipped into a marshy swale where frozen grasses reflected the morning's light. He stepped gingerly through the half-frozen muck. He regretted that he had not thought to bring his galoshes. Still, the blustery air was invigorating, and he relished being out of his office, away from the banging radiator and stuffy, dry heat. He had forgotten how much he enjoyed a good, brisk hike—even though he would pay for it later. His leg was beginning to ache, but he ignored it.

When the terrain led upward again and he reached a knoll, he paused to turn up his collar. He was thin and angular with an aquiline nose, a hollowed face with long bones, and black hair. A few strands of premature gray gave him a mature look, but his overall appearance was youthful.

In the distance, he could see a steeply pitched roof tucked in a thick grove of bare-limbed trees. Had it not been early December, he could not have seen it at all. Scattered around it were the dilapidated outbuildings of an abandoned farm. Farther beyond, undulating hills rose until the landscape blended into banks of blue mountains, all together resembling a rumpled quilt on an unmade bed.

As he approached the house, dry, stubborn oak leaves spun high overhead like semaphores, and twigs crunched under his shoes where seasons of winterkilled vegetation covered what had once been an expansive yard. It was flushed with weeds, many taller than his shoulders, and altogether unkempt and neglected. In one more season, he thought, the weeds and the walls of boxwoods and ivies would consume the house altogether. If it had not been for the peculiar path leading him first through the fields and now through the yard, he might have turned back.

He stopped just short of the porch to view the full house. Chimneys punctuated the steeply pitched slate roof and rose as if large birds were perched atop. Ornate cornices and dentil moldings framed red brick walls. Long windows stretched from the floor to the ceiling of a wide, wrapping porch where faded paint was peeling from decorative balusters. At the far end of the porch, an empty swing, animated by the breeze, squeaked as it swayed on rusted chains. In the pungent autumn air, it looked rather forlorn. Only smoke curling from one chimney and the light from a single window suggested the house was occupied. Otherwise, he might have thought it abandoned.

As he mounted the seven steps to the porch, he reached into his breast pocket to touch the letter that had brought him.

Cairnaerie
November 18, 1927
Dear Professor Klare,
    I am a distant relative of General John Breckinridge, distinguished Vice President of the United States and a brave and

decorated soldier who fought valiantly for the Confederacy during the War of Succession.

I am assembling some family documents—my reason for writing. As they may be of some historic value, I hope to enlist your assistance in assessing them.

I feel quite fortunate that you, reputed to be a studious and conscientious historian, have come to Hyssop recently by your appointment to the faculty of Haverston College. I am hopeful you will be able to pay me a visit. If you are able to do so, kindly let your intentions be known by mail to Mr. Zephyr Elias, Hyssop, Virginia.

With great anticipation of your reply, I am—
Sincerely,
Miss Geneva Snow

John had replied immediately, and a second letter with a hand-drawn map followed shortly.

Driving out of town early in the morning, he had wondered if he had embarked on a wild goose chase—or if he might just find something to impress his dean.

He knocked on the door. Momentarily it opened, and through a tight crack he heard a woman's voice: "Professor Klare?"

"Yes. John Klare."

The hinge whined, and a small, elderly woman, dressed neatly with a single brooch pinned to a high collar, appeared in the threshold. She seemed timid at first and then warmed quickly as if a kind of ingrained hospitality took over.

"Do come in," she said with a rolling drawl that sounded lyrical to him, a Midwesterner. Smiling up at him, her eyes were the color of nightfall, a dark and penetrating blue. She examined him carefully and said, "You are so kind to come."

"It's my pleasure." He shed his overcoat and gloves and smoothed back his windblown hair as his eyes adjusted to the dim light. She took his coat in two arms and held it high to keep from dragging it on the floor—she was not tall—and laid it across a long bench.

John marveled at the cavernous foyer. On one wall, a tall gilded mirror hung from a picture railing that rimmed the room. On the opposite wall, a huge and brooding seascape overwhelmed a collection of smaller paintings, mostly landscapes. The floor was patterned with alternating light and dark planks running diagonally from the room's perimeter toward the center where it formed a striking, six-pointed star. Directly above it, an immense crystal chandelier with a cascade of pendalogues held tiny candles, some straight, others leaning as if they had long ago surrendered to the heat of repeated summers. Beyond the foyer, a second hall with a winding staircase opened into a dining room with a long, banquet-sized table. Except for mansions along the Ohio River near his boyhood home, he had never seen a house quite so grand—or one so out of place. In the westernmost parts of Virginia, utility, not opulence, generally prevailed.

Miss Snow led him into a parlor off the second hall. In contrast to the house's unkempt exterior, this room was bright, clean, and perfectly appointed—a comfortable room filled with carved tables, chests, and richly upholstered seating, albeit a bit worn. The walls were papered with a muted blue and yellow pattern that reminded John of small ducks. Two brass oil lamps and a fire burning in the hearth warmed the room. Altogether, especially after his trek, he found the yellows and soft lights of the room inviting.

Like the foyer, paintings covered the walls—large landscapes in heavy, gilded frames and smaller still lifes. But the focal point of the room was a portrait above the mantel—a young man dressed in a high-collared coat with black hair. Piercing eyes made him appear stern, almost regal, yet in his face there was a distinct and endearing kindness.

"A stunning portrait," said John, nodding toward the painting.

"My father. My mother painted it."

"Handsome man—and she was quite an artist."

"Yes, she was. As a girl, she was very fortunate to have a tutor who cultivated her talent. She loved to paint and did so prolifically—as you may have gathered."

"Yes, I noticed," he said, smiling. "These are all hers?"

"Yes. And what you see hanging is a fraction of what she did. Her studio is full of paintings. My father's portrait has always been my favorite. It's an oil—but I loved her watercolors, too, particularly of the farm. She was quite versatile. Please, Mr. Klare, make yourself comfortable."

John chose a settee near the hearth—a decision he quickly regretted. Wire springs covered with horsehair and damask made him feel as though he were sitting on a fencepost. He shifted to find a comfortable position as Miss Snow settled herself across from him in a platform rocker. Her dress barely rumpled at her tiny waist when she sat down primly as if onto a seat of roses rather than a threadbare, chintz-covered chair. She ran a hand across her cheek, checking her hair, which was pulled back into a bun and neatly secured with two silver combs. It struck John that her hair and the house's slate roof were the same color.

"Tea?" she asked, lifting a silver pot. Before he could refuse, she handed him a blue and white teacup filled to the brim.

"Thank you," he said, balancing the dainty cup and saucer in hands too large for bone china. He took a sip, swallowing quickly to keep from grimacing. John despised tea.

"I do so appreciate you coming. I hope you did not think me too forward in inviting you here, but I..." She paused and lifted her cup. "I never go out, but I was eager to make your acquaintance." She blew on her tea before taking a sip.

"I always enjoy a good walk. Finding your house, though, was a challenge."

"How so, Mr. Klare?"

"The road up the mountain wasn't easy for my automobile. Quite an adventure. But here I am—and I enjoyed the trip."

"An adventurer, are you?"

"I'd like to be." He bent forward to set his cup on a small marble-top table next to a vase of dried hydrangeas. "I am curious, though. I'm the most junior faculty member at the college. There are far more experienced historians there. Why me?"

"I thought a younger man was more likely to come. A more eager man." He thought he saw a twinkle in her eye. "Or shall I say a hungrier man?"

He laughed. "Yes. I am indeed. My dean terms me 'wet behind the ears.' "

"Well. I have faith in youth. I always have."

As they talked in the room that seemed to have been lifted out of another time and place, the oil lamps made a "srrrring" noise, and the hearth fire crackled. He took up his teacup again to be polite and thought: *If this is a wild goose chase, at least it's interesting.*

"Can you guess my age?" she asked.

He choked on another swallow of tea.

"Did I surprise you?" she said, smiling.

"Yes, you did," he said, clearing his throat. "I'm afraid I don't often hear that question from a genteel lady."

"Well?"

"You want me to guess your age?"

"Yes. I do." She tipped her head to the side in a manner slightly teasing. "I do indeed."

John set down his teacup again—happily—slid to a more comfortable position on the settee and crossed his arms. During his time in the commonwealth, he had learned to respect the circuitous routes conversations often took. Southerners didn't always appreciate his directness, so he parried.

"Guessing a woman's age—a perilous task. How is that done with impunity?"

She laughed. "There is no peril in my request, Mr. Klare. I promise you. Please. I want you to guess."

Leaning forward, he dug his elbows into his knees and out of habit rotated his signet ring. It had belonged to his grandfather—a man he would never stop missing.

"Why don't you give me clues? Historical clues. I'll be solving a problem—less perilous."

"Wonderful." She clapped her hands together and stared straight through him with child's eyes, with the same eagerness he had seen in his nieces—a zeal uncommon for a woman of her years. After a few moments, she said, "All right. I'm ready. I was born before the country was a century old—the year saw the seeds of a growing conflict. The president was Franklin Pierce. The Kansas-Nebraska Act had passed and the Mexican War had ended about seven years earlier. There. Now, tell me. How old am I?"

The quickness with which she had summoned these facts astonished him, but he tried to hide his surprise and think.

"You're not making this easy."

"Life is not easy, Mr. Klare." She said this with a certain sobriety, as if she knew it firsthand.

"True," he said, his own history bubbling up uncomfortably.

He slipped a small notepad and a stubby pencil from his vest pocket, items that he, a perpetual note keeper, always kept with him. He scribbled down numbers, screwed up his mouth, and contemplated the ceiling, brooding with a smidgeon of drama, which amused Miss Snow.

She waited, watching him.

Finally, he posited. "Seventy-two?"

"You are correct." Holding her cup and saucer level with her chin, she stared pensively across it into the fire. "Seventy-two. I was born right here. In the spring of '55, April the 17th—the day the lilacs bloomed. That's what my mother always told me. I have lived here all my life. All of us—Mama, Daddy, and my brothers." She breathed deeply, fortified by her memories. "I am the last."

"You live alone?" he asked, surprised. He didn't want to be indecorous, but his curiosity got the best of him.

"Oh, yes. For many years."

"How do you manage?"

Now it was her turn to parry. "Oh, I manage fine. I am quite resourceful." She lifted the teapot and smiled. "More tea?"

"Oh, no." He held up his hand. "But thank you."

"Now tell me all about you, Mr. Klare. I know you are an assistant professor of history. You graduated from the university. And I believe you taught at St. Ballard College before coming here."

At the mention of St. Ballard, John blanched. He wasn't interested in discussing that part of his life.

"Tell me more," she said.

Before he could begin, a longcase clock began to strike the hour. Standing in the curve of the staircase, it sounded as if it were speaking for the house. Pausing, John noticed a pair of pince-nez glasses resting on an open book. But it was the small, gilt-framed picture of a girl beside it that caught his eye—a beautiful girl who seemed strangely out of place in an antebellum home.

"Lovely, isn't she?" said Miss Snow, noticing his observation as the clock's tones decayed.

"Yes. Quite."

"Her name is Joly. She is…." She hesitated. "She is a special friend."

"Joly. Pretty name for a pretty girl."

"Yes, she is lovely."

John sensed she wanted to say more, but she did not. Instead, she moved the conversation forward.

"Now, Mr. Klare—about you. I do want to know all about you."

"Well. Let's see. I took my undergraduate degree at a small college in Indiana, then I was drafted…"

"…A veteran."

"Barely. I served a month and was headed for France when I fell off a horse and broke my leg. Instead of Europe, all I saw was a state-side barracks in Texas and the inside of a hospital ward. I headed back to school and then to the university for graduate school."

"Do you still ride?"

"No, I don't, I'm afraid. A month in traction cured me. I enjoyed it—riding, not traction—but I prefer wheels over hooves these days." Unconsciously, he rubbed his thigh that had begun to ache. "My sister says I have wanderlust. I guess I do. My car sure made it easier to move to Hyssop—and to get here today."

"I'm sure it did. I remember riding to Hyssop with my father."

"You must know the way well."

"I did. A long time ago. I'm not sure I'd know the way anymore. Now, Professor Klare—more about you. What drew you to study history?"

"My grandfather." Instinctively, he touched his ring again. "When I was a child, he would entertain with me all sorts of stories. He made them exciting—much more than academic."

"History *is* so much more, isn't it?" she said enthusiastically, as if they had struck a rich vein of agreement, and with this, she seemed to relax. "What about the rest of your family? Tell me."

"Very small. My parents are still in Ohio, where I grew up. I have two nieces and a sister—Kate. I had a brother, but he died in the flu epidemic."

"I'm so sorry. I'm sure that was difficult."

"Yes. Ten years ago—hard to believe. I had just gotten off crutches and was back at school. He was only fourteen."

"To lose a brother is so hard—so unexpected. Even a child feels such a loss."

The room was very still for a moment as if their similar memories appeared for each to acknowledge.

John broke the silence. "Well, that's about all there is. I've had a rather uneventful life."

She smiled at him dubiously. "When you reach my age, you may think differently."

"Then I will defer to your wisdom," he said, glancing at his wristwatch. "In your letter, you mentioned General Breckinridge. He was a relative?"

"Yes. But I am afraid he was not a very close relation. Rather distant, in fact." She sounded almost apologetic and paused in the rocker that she had unconsciously begun to move back and forth. "He was my fourth cousin—twice removed. We were distant relatives."

"A cousin is a cousin," he said diplomatically. "You also mentioned documents."

She brightened. "Yes. Letters, among other things. My two eldest brothers served the Confederacy. Grayson wrote to Mama faithfully. I came across them recently—more than sixty letters. Mama must have hidden them. I had not seen them for years."

Now John was intrigued. Original sources were a historian's holy grail—and he suddenly had a mental picture of handing a bundle of letters to his dean.

"Is this the family history you mentioned?" he asked, wary of being presumptuous.

"Yes—and no," she said, a bit flustered. "Part of it. But I am not quite ready to give them up. I wanted to meet you first. I hope you understand." She reached one hand toward him to underscore her sincerity. "My age, I suppose. I have to do things one step at a time."

"Certainly. I'm happy to wait," he said, though in truth he was a bit disappointed.

Leaning back, she sighed deeply and closed her eyes. "I am feeling rather tired all of a sudden."

"I should be going." He moved to rise.

"One minute more," she said, perking up. "Please."

He resettled himself. In truth, patience had never been his strong suit, but something about this woman, this house, gave him pause. He needed to be patient—and step carefully.

Miss Snow placed her hands together in a prayerful gesture, touching the tips of her fingers to her lips. "I must ask you one great favor, Mr. Klare. I must insist that you keep our visit and correspondence secret—just between the two of us. You must tell no one about me—or my house. It is very important. I can't tell you why quite just yet. Discretion, you see. It is terribly important. In due time, I will explain, but for now, I must insist."

The ticking of the clock filled the room, and as if on cue, the sky clouded and the room dimmed. She looked directly at John, her eyes deep blue pools. "Will you trust me? Can I trust you?"

1860 — 1864

CHAPTER 2
1860

Petulance & Duty

G en-ee-va!" Vivvy yelled a second time, her voice rising the way it did when she called a pig. "Gen-ee-va Snow! I ain't calling you again. Get yourself in here."

The child hiked up her wet, muddy skirts, raced up the stream bank, and ran toward the house. She knew if she dawdled any longer, Vivvy would notify her father.

"I'm here," shouted Geneva, bursting through the kitchen door that bounced hard against the wall and then back into the frame with a bang. "Stop yelling at me, you ol' peacock. You're not the boss of me."

Vivvy raised her hand, but the girl slipped by her. Neither heights nor depths—and certainly not the displeasure of most adults—fazed Geneva Snow.

"Your Daddy, he tol' you to take care of them mangy cats. Not me," Vivvy said. She shook a bowl of gelatinous scraps toward the girl. "I ain't doing your job for you. I got too much to do all by myself. I'm already a heap of distraction, and them cats jes makes me worse."

Geneva glared at the bedeviled cook and grabbed the bowl, setting it down for the cats that were whining at the door. Vivvy turned around to finish paring potatoes, muttering, "Those mangy cats oughta be throwed in the Cleary and drowned to death."

Steam billowed from a large copper kettle atop the cookstove, and the salty aroma of ham saturated the room. Geneva pushed open the door to let the cats in and squatted down to rub their soft butter-colored fur. She had found them in the barn one morning while Lightner was milking. Lightner, a kind soul, was the eldest and the most respected slave on the property—a gentle and earnest man with a dignity that everyone respected. He would balance on a milking stool and squirt milk into a bucket. Occasionally, he would aim a stream of milk from a cow's teat into a hungry mouth—cat, boy, or girl. Geneva had gathered up the weanlings, carried them in her pinafore into the house, and plopped them unceremoniously onto her father's desk.

"I want to keep them, Daddy," she had petitioned with a look he found hard to resist—the way he found most of her requests hard to resist.

"Where is their mother?" he asked, continuing to write, ignoring the yowling mass, but moving a bottle of ink to the other side of his desk.

"She wasn't nowhere around."

He raised a brow. "Geneva. Don't you mean anywhere?" He replaced his pen in a large brass standish. "She was not *anywhere* around."

"That's what I said."

"No, you did not. You said…"

"I know. I know." Geneva huffed and then parroted her father. "She was not *anywhere* around."

He suppressed a smile. "You're certain?"

"Yes, sir. Ask Lightner. The mama cat was *nowhere* to be found," she said and looked at her father with a little gleam.

He leaned back and clasped his hands behind his neck. One kitten teetered along the edge of the desk. Geneva put her hand up to keep it from falling.

"Aren't they sweet, Daddy?"

"I'd prefer if you brought me puppies."

"You already have a dog. You have Blue. I want these. Just for me." She cocked her head, pleading with him. "Please, Daddy. Please."

Bertram Snow fell silent as the kittens wiggled and mewed. He sat forward and rubbed their necks. Geneva was used to waiting on her father. They were closer than she would ever be to her mother.

"Please." She moved close, nuzzling her father. He felt her long black eyelashes brush his cheek. "Please, Daddy?"

"Oh, Little Bird." *Where in the world did you come from?* he thought, never failing to be amazed at his daughter's will. He put his arm around her and squeezed her shoulder. "How about you ask me in French?"

She wrinkled up her nose and spoke slowly: "Avoir...un... chat?"

"You want one cat?" he asked.

She looked perplexed. "No. All of them."

"Then say 'chatons'—kittens. You asked me for one cat. Say, 'Puis-je avoir des chatons.' "

"Avoir...des...chatons?"

"Close enough. You may keep deux."

"Only two?" She started to pout, but the negotiation was over. "Thank you, Daddy—I mean, Merci, mon cher pere." She kissed him on the cheek and tried to wink at him, but it was a skill the five-year-old hadn't mastered. It came off as a blink.

Amused, he raised his forefinger and touched her chin. "Little Bird, you must take care of them. You. Do you understand?"

"Yes. And I will. I promise. I'll feed them every single day."

"And keep them out of my study? Your mother and Clarissa have enough to do with you and your brothers."

"I will." Geneva scooped up the kittens. "I love you, Daddy."

Bertram watched his daughter skip out of his study. She had always reminded him of Anne.

While the kittens ate, Geneva pushed the basket closer to the stove. Lightner had climbed up in the loft of an outbuilding and dug around to come up with the old split oak basket with a missing handle. It was perfect for kittens. Clarissa, Lightner's wife, had given Geneva leftover cloth from her sewing box to line it.

"You take these," Clarissa had said, handing her the scraps. "These'll make them litt'l kitties a good sof' bed."

Geneva had thanked her and then placed her hands against Clarissa's warm black face, pulling her close. "Daddy said I can't keep them all. Simmy can have one."

"She'd like that, Miss Geneva. Like it a lot," Clarissa had said. "Next time she comes in, you tell her. Maybe her Daddy can find her a basket, too."

Vivvy, who hated the cats, resented the intrusion into her kitchen. As sour as the milk she would set aside for the slop bucket, her disposition shone on her broad face. She was nearly as wide as she was tall, and every part of her was fat. Geneva had once announced—loudly and in front of guests—that four Clarissas would fit into one of Vivvy's dresses, an observation her father had quickly hushed. The cook's wrists bulged from the ends of her sleeves, and her ankles and feet, always swollen, lipped over the edges of her flat shoes. In the hottest part of summer, she often dispensed with them altogether and flapped around the kitchen's brick floor in her bare feet. But the most remarkable thing about Vivvy, other than her cooking, was her speed. Despite her rotundity, she could explode like a racehorse, catch hold of Geneva, and jerk her to attention. The two were constantly at odds—their spats often refereed by Clarissa or Clarissa's daughter, Simmy.

The cats provoked the cook even more. Adding to Vivvy's irritation, Geneva had soon grown bored with their care but refused to give them up, in large measure to spite Vivvy. It was a war of wills.

Geneva's mother walked into the kitchen to see her daughter hunched over the cats. "Where have you been?" she said, observing her daughter's clothes.

"At the creek. Watching water spiders."

"Striders, not spiders, Geneva," corrected Thomas, her eldest brother, who breezed through the kitchen, grabbing a handful of chinquapins and shoving them into his pocket.

"*In* the creek more likely," said Caroline Snow, exasperated with her daughter. "Look at me, Geneva."

Geneva cut her eyes up toward her mother.

"Go upstairs right now, and change your clothes. Then give your dress to Vivvy to wash."

"But I…"

"Don't argue with me."

"Yes, ma'am," she said, continuing to attend to the cats.

"Simmy," Caroline said to the thin, dark girl standing in the hall—the girl who smiled perpetually. "Go help her. Make sure she doesn't get mud all over her room."

Clarissa, working in the kitchen's far corner polishing silver, nodded for her daughter to go. Simmy moved toward the door while Geneva dilly-dallied.

"I mean now, Geneva!" Caroline said.

Geneva jumped up. When her mother turned her back and the riled-up cook's hands were wrist-deep in biscuit dough, Geneva stuck her tongue out at Vivvy before she disappeared through the dining room. She ran up the stairs with Simmy close behind and slammed her bedroom door. The room shook and the chandelier in the hall tinkled.

From downstairs, her mother yelled: "Geneva Snow! Stop slamming doors!"

"I hate Vivvy," said Geneva, opening her wardrobe and grabbing another dress. She threw it onto her bed and slipped out of her muddy one.

"You ought not hate," Simmy said quietly, running her hand over the soft quilt covering Geneva's tall elegant bed. "And Vivvy's not so bad. She's jes grumpy."

"She's hateful."

Wearing her chemise and pantalets, Geneva tiptoed into the hall and dropped the muddy dress over the banister, watching it flutter down through the curve of the winding stairwell. She knew full well Vivvy would come get it. She pictured the large cook folding her girth and grunting to pick up the dress. Simmy, accustomed to Geneva's mischief, stood at the bedroom door with her arms akimbo.

"One of these days you're gonna make Vivvy so made, she'll beat you silly."

"No, she won't. Daddy wouldn't let her," said Geneva petulantly, leaning over the banister. "Simmy, you wanna watch?"

"No, I don't wanna watch one bit. I don't want Vivvy mad at me. You oughta come back in here."

Vivvy didn't appear right away, and Geneva tired of waiting. The girls went back into Geneva's room and closed the door, this time softly.

"You even got mud in your hair. Mercy!" Simmy said. "Where's your hairbrush?"

"In my bureau. I'll get it." Geneva drew the brush through her thick chestnut hair, wincing when it came to the muddy tangles.

"Lemme help you," Simmy said. "Stand still."

"No." Geneva jerked away. "You'll pull my hair."

"No, I won't." Simmy took the brush from her hand. "You got the tenderest head."

Geneva held her hair close to her scalp while Simmy pulled the brush slowly through the hair, which fell across tanned and freckled shoulders. Her mother always sent her out properly covered, but more times than not, Geneva would strip down to her undergarments to romp. Her mother never knew. And Simmy, who helped Clarissa with the laundry, never tattled.

"When'd you go down to the creek?"

"This morning."

"All by yourself?"

"Of course not."

Simmy did not need to ask more. "Mercy. I surely do hope Zeph ain't this muddy."

"He's not muddy. He's just wet."

"Wet? Why's he wet?"

Geneva, suddenly wide-eyed, clammed up.

Simmy tossed the brush on the bed and put her hands on her hips. "What'd he do?"

"He told me not to tell." But she would tell Simmy—she told her everything.

"Tell me! What'd that brother of mine do?"

"There was a big old snapping turtle," Geneva said sheepishly.

"And you was poking at him, wadn't you?"

"Maybe."

"What'd you do, Geneva? Zeph's too smart to mess with a snapping turtle."

Geneva huffed. "Well, he had my pantalets."

"You took 'em off?" Simmy slapped her hand over her mouth.

"How else was I going to swim? The stupid turtle pulled them off the bank. But Zeph got them back—and the turtle almost got him. He had to jump the creek, and he missed."

"Zeph's gonna be in trub-ble."

"I said I wouldn't tell, so you don't tell him I told you. You hear me?" Geneva wagged her finger in Simmy's face.

"I won't tell him. I swear. You know I won't."

———

The house was still and the night, calm. As his four children slept, Bertram pulled rockers onto the porch for himself and Caroline. He sat down beside her, handing her a sherry. The fluted edge of the pressed glass caught the soft light from an oil lamp. At her feet sat her mahogany paint box, an elegant carrier for her washbowls, blocks of ink, mixing pans, and the finest sable brushes he could buy. She had spent part of the afternoon in the yard painting on hot pressed paper, her favorite kind, clipped taut onto a stretching board to keep the paper from cockling. Bertram could never decide which was more beautiful, the landscapes around Cairnaerie or the watercolors of them his wife created.

Nearby, the porch swing dangled lopsided from a single chain, the result of two boys using it to catapult a third. He could not help but smile. In the morning, he would get Lightner to help him fix it.

He reached over and took Caroline's hand. A full moon over the mountain bathed everything in milky light. It had been eighteen years, and all his dreams had come true. He remembered the first time he had seen this land...

He stood in the broad meadow, surrounded by dense forests rising like palisades, and he watched the surveyor ride across the field, dragging the iron

*chain as it clanked along rocks protruding from the mountain soil. At in-
tervals, the surveyor stopped, made notations, and repositioned the chain,
stretching it out to its standard sixty-six feet. He recorded each geographic
mark: to the east, an outcropping of rock overlooking the valley; to the north,
a line of cedars and hemlocks that masked a waterfall descending through a
steep, impassable gap—a gash in the mountains as if a giant's ax had fall-
en; to the south, acres of dense hardwood forests; and to the west—ascending
tables of land ideal for raising crops and cattle. The chain had rattled as it
snaked through the dormant grasses chewed down by deer and elk plentiful
throughout the wild lands where he stood.*

*Bertram had found the acreage at a good time, when land was dispensed
for a price far less than properties to the east. The mountain land overlooked
a dozen young towns strung along the rutted wagon road, running north to
south in the valley below. He had filed the warrant the month before, leaping
up the steps of the Richmond courthouse to deliver it, eager to purchase an
initial four-hundred-acre tract. As a newly married man, he had imagined
the land bringing hope, prosperity, happiness.*

*The surveyor twisted in his saddle: "How far you want me to take it,
Mr. Snow?"*

*Bertram cupped his hands around his mouth: "I want the house near
the spring." The surveyor signaled his understanding with a wave and
turned his horse toward an artesian spring that bubbled up on the property
and ran into a small creek.*

*The two men had traveled on horseback from Richmond, camping over-
night on the eastern ridge before the long ride across the valley. It was the
spring of 1843. They stopped in Hyssop to scout out an office for Bertram
and suitable quarters for Caroline and him to use while their house was being
built. Throughout the valley, new courthouses were underway, businesses were
sprouting, and weekly mail delivery arrived by stagecoach. Railroads had come
as far as Winchester. It was only a matter of time until they came south. In a
few years, the roads would be graded and planked and some macadamized.*

He had looked out across the valley as the surveyor worked, taking in the air so different from either the salty harbor air of Baltimore or the swampy humidity of Richmond. He had inhaled the pure mountain air. If optimism were currency, Bertram Snow knew he had already become a wealthy man.

Out of the darkness, cows lowed. Caroline, her eyes closed, nodded off. Gently, he took the glass from her hand and let her rest. Bertram had seen his future that day with the surveyor, and now, as he paused with his wife, his children sleeping, he savored his life. His law practice was thriving, and he had recently been appointed a circuit court judge—the youngest ever—and here on the mountain, he grazed and wintered Angus cattle, a diversion from his legal duties that he enjoyed immensely. The mountain winters made his cattle hearty; the proximity to stockyards in the northern valley made them profitable. His good fortune had come indeed.

In quiet moments like tonight, Bertram often thought of his friend Ezekial. How he wished he could tell Caroline about him, but he believed she would not understand. She had come from a different world, and some things were better left unspoken. Only the present mattered—but still, the past would always echo for Bertram Snow.

Yes, he thought, *I am a blessed man.*

———

Standing at the back of the house chopping wood for Vivvy, Zeph watched for the Judge to return from town. His palms were sweaty. He set his jaw so tight his teeth began to ache. What he was about to do was dangerous—unheard of—but he had to ask. He wanted this.

His young arms strained as he lifted the ax high in the air. When it fell, the wood cracked and chunked open and the split log thumped onto the ground. After each chop, he would stand up straight to look for the telltale dust that enveloped the road whenever a traveler approached Cairnaerie.

Zeph had a pleasant manner. He was also clever for his age, earnest, and confident enough to make decisions when others might stand back and wait for orders. When he had heard about a school for coloreds—both free and slave—in a local church, he had raced back home to Cairnaerie to ask his father.

"Ain't my place to say," Lightner had told his son. "You got to go ask the Judge. Up to him, not me. Some things you got to do for yourself, son. I be doing you no kindness if I do for you what you oughta be doing yourself." Lightner thought he knew what the man would say, knowing Bertram Snow as he did, but he didn't tell this to his son. Instead, he encouraged him. "You be brave. No harm done in asking."

Zeph almost lost his courage right then and there—but not his desire to go to the school. It took him most of two weeks to muster the gumption.

He upended another log on the stump, wiped his hands on his pants, and gripped the ax.

When he saw the Judge's horse canter over the hill, he quickly rehearsed again what he planned to say. Balancing another log on the stump, he tried to keep his mind quiet while he listened for the horse to near the house. He heard hooves clop into the yard. He heard the horse whinny and snort. He heard the leather saddle squeak as the Judge dismounted.

"Hello, Zeph," said the Judge, stepping into the yard strewn with split logs. "Looks like you've been working hard." The Judge smiled and handed the boy the reins.

"Yessir. I'll have all this finished by suppertime."

Zeph laid down the ax, preparing to take the horse to the stable. His mouth was dry and his courage, all he had, was flagging.

The Judge untied his satchel and set it on the ground. But instead of heading into the house, he propped his foot up on a runner of the fence.

"Zeph?"

"Yessir?" The boy stood up straight. "You want something, Judge?"

"I have a question for you."

"Yessir?"

"I understand they've opened a new school."

Zeph's eyes widened, and in spite of himself, a grin popped up on his face. "Yessir. I think I heard about that."

"You think that's something you might like?"

Zeph could hardly believe his ears—and barely kept from shouting. "Yessir," he said, trying to be calm.

"Now, I understand you must be on time and work hard," the Judge said. He dipped his hand into his pocket, took out his watch to check the time. "Do you think you could do that?"

"Yessir. I b'lieve so."

"All right then." The Judge moved to leave. "You can start next week." As he walked away, he was smiling. Ezekial Coker would have been pleased.

Inside the house, Bertram was brushing dust off his coat when Caroline cornered him in his office.

"What were you talking to that boy about, Bertram?"

"Zeph?"

"Yes. That one. I heard about the school for coloreds. I hope you're not thinking of letting him go."

"Well, as a matter of fact, I am," he said, opening his satchel and removing papers.

"Oh, Bertram. I don't think that is well advised at all." Caroline put her hands on her hips. "They don't need school. Besides, I don't have enough help around here as it is. That boy is just getting to where he's quite capable, and I honestly don't think…."

"…Caroline," he interrupted. "Zeph works hard, and he's never asked me for a thing. I can't see anything wrong with him learning to read."

"But they're not like us, Bertram. They're different. They're un-refined and…"

"…Oh, Caroline," he scoffed as he emptied his pockets. He dropped a handful of coins on his desk and then scooped them into a drawer where he kept loose change. He sat down.

"You didn't grow up with the kind I did," she continued. "They're dirty—and some are lazy and shiftless."

The tone of her voice set his teeth on edge, but he tried to un-derstand her point of view. Early on, he had learned to listen—not to trust solely in his own counsel. It was one of many lessons he learned from Ezekial. He would freely admit some coloreds were worthless—but he could say the same for some white farm hands he had hired. Bertram heard her out patiently, but he was unmoved.

"You cannot encourage this, Bertram. It could lead to trouble, I'm afraid," she said, trying to be diplomatic—as diplomatic as Caroline could be, given that her attitude toward those she considered lesser differed from her husband's. "I have always tried to be kind to them, but I can't imagine why these colored children deserve the same con-sideration as our own."

His patience was wearing thin, and this comparison made him cross. "Zeph has a heart of gold and a mind of considerable worth—just like Lightner," he said. "He wants to learn, Caroline. So you need to stop this. Do you understand? My decision is made."

Caroline, dismayed, looked at her husband, who rarely spoke to her harshly. Tears welled up in her eyes. Bertram, a tenderhearted man to his core, stood up and embraced her.

"I didn't mean to upset you—and I don't want to disagree with you. But that boy wants to learn. I won't stand in his way. I can't stand in his way. What harm could it do?"

"But we've given him everything—a home, food, a job...."

"Everything?" He pushed her away gently and held her at arm's length to look straight into her eyes. "Everything except education." He spoke kindly but forcefully, aching for her to understand. *And freedom,* he thought but did not voice.

"Oh, Bertram. To stand in his way is one thing. I'm not suggesting that," she said. "But to promote education. I think that's a very dangerous step. You simply don't know where it will lead."

He pulled her close again. "Then we shall have to agree to disagree, my love," Bertram said. "Will you trust me?"

She put her head on his chest, tucking under his chin. "Do I have a choice?"

"No."

"All right then," she said. She stood up on her tiptoes and kissed her husband. Caroline knew where to pick her battles. If her husband wanted to let the boy do this, so be it. She wouldn't argue any more this time. But she would keep her eye on things.

Caroline always kept an eye on things.

CHAPTER 3

Summary 1861

Rings & Misgivings

Caroline walked into the back hallway and froze. High above her, Geneva was sliding backwards down the curved banister over the two-story drop to the basement. She had been dared by Thomas and Grayson, who on seeing their mother evaporated into their bedrooms. Geneva was halfway down before Caroline could even speak. When the girl reached the bottom, her mother grabbed her under one arm, hauled the flailing child into Bertram's study, and sat her down in a chair next to his desk.

"Ouch," the child protested, hitting her elbow on the arm of the chair.

"This is no way to welcome your father home," said Caroline, red-faced and fuming.

Bertram looked up from his desk, fully prepared to hear another story of Geneva's exploits. "What happened this time?"

"Your daughter slid down the banister. From the top," said Caroline, and then she turned to her daughter. "Do you know how dangerous that is, young lady?"

"It's their fault," Geneva said.

"Your brothers? It's their fault? They put you on the banister?"

"No. I climbed up." The girl crossed her arms and huffed. "All by myself."

Bertram repressed a laugh and cut his eyes at his wife. Caroline threw up her arms in surrender.

"You deal with her, Bertram. I can't." She stormed out, bequeathing the task of discipline to her husband.

Bertram smiled at his daughter. "What am I going to do with you, Little Bird?"

"It was fun, Daddy." She pushed two little fists against her cheeks and grinned. "It was really fun."

"I bet it was," he said. "Shall I try it?"

"No, Daddy. It's too high and you're too big. You might fall off."

"I might fall off? What about you?"

"I'm careful."

"I see." He lowered his voice, trying—but failing—to be stern. "Don't do it again. It scares your mother."

"But…"

"No buts, Geneva. Don't do it. I don't want to have to spank you."

She pouted. "Yes, sir."

Geneva left, skipping.

"Find something else fun," he shouted after her. "Something not so dangerous."

Bertram stood in the stairwell the next morning and called his children to breakfast. Geneva, hungry, came first, wearing her favorite dress, a red cotton jumper thoroughly faded and torn, with no bows or flounces. It had only a single line of white buttons, a few missing, running down the front.

"As soon as we finish breakfast, Geneva," said Caroline, seeing her daughter's attire, "I want you to change your dress."

"But I want to wear this," she argued until she saw her father raise an eyebrow. "Yes, ma'am."

Her father always deferred to his wife on matters of dress and etiquette. She was a woman of style and refinement—traits the daughter had not inherited naturally and not yet learned. Unlike dark-haired Geneva, Caroline Snow was fair-skinned, almost ruddy, with thick and often unruly auburn hair—her finest feature—framing a heart-shaped face and pale blue eyes.

"You'll change after we've eaten," her father said as they waited for the rest of his family to gather.

"Yes, sir." Geneva picked up her fork and stabbed it through the cutwork of the tablecloth.

"Put your fork down, Geneva," Caroline said. "You'll scratch the table."

Geneva sneered—slightly so that her father would not notice—and laid down the fork. Her mother always seemed out of sorts with her.

The three brothers skidded into the dining room, buttoning their collars. To be late for a meal was frowned upon in the Snow household, though on most occasions, Geneva was the late one. Vivvy waddled in from the kitchen to serve ham, gravy, grits, scrambled eggs, applesauce, and beaten biscuits, one of Geneva's favorites. On Bertram's cue, the family bowed their heads.

"Heavenly father. We bow to acknowledge your goodness and to offer our thanks for the bounty before us…," he began.

Geneva tried to be still, but her feet were restless and she was famished. She swung them back and forth and rolled the edges of the lace tablecloth between her fingers. She tried to listen to her father, but the smell of bacon distracted her and steam rising from the grits only intensified her hunger. Her father's prayers seemed to get longer and longer. She opened one eye and stole a glance

at Hayes sitting cherub-like across the table, his hands pressed together under his chin. She eyed her fork, ready to grab it.

"…. And have mercy on our nation as it struggles through the
war. Bless our sons and bring them home safely. In Jesus Christ, our
Lord, we pray. Amen."

Home safely? Geneva's head shot up and her mouth popped open,
but she stopped short of spitting out the question on the edge on
her tongue because tears were running down her mother's cheeks.

That evening, Bertram Snow stood as his family filed by him into
the fourth pew of the Hyssop Presbyterian Church. Geneva hated
sitting through church twice on Sundays. She looked forward to
the morning service and visits in town when there were other girls
to play with, but by Sunday night she was tired and bored. Sitting
still was a challenge. To pass the time, she invented stories about
the people around her. It was a fine diversion unless she giggled—
a transgression earning a raised brow from her father and hushes
from her mother.

Occasionally, she could catch Hayes' eye. A few years older, he
was the closest to her in age and the most companionable in temper-
ament within the family, which was divided into younger and older
parts by a sad series of miscarriages. Graced with his mother's auburn hair and fair complexion that betrayed every emotion, Hayes
was quiet and sensitive. He often suffered under the regiment of
discipline in the Snow home because he was not rough-and-tumble
like the older boys, Grayson and Thomas, uncanny copies of their
father, nor was he strong-willed like Geneva. He was Geneva's con-
fidante and spent hours playing with her. Often it was Hayes who
covered up her misbehaviors. Only Simmy was closer to her.

The Presbyterians represented the valley's prominent families,
and not a single dark face graced their gatherings, a fact Geneva

found wholly unjust. She didn't understand why Simmy and Zeph had to sit in the buckboard outside the church or store or any place the family visited. Since the trio played together at Cairnaerie, why couldn't they go to church together? She was never satisfied with her elders' explanation that they had their own church. Nor was she shy to ask why the Elias family couldn't sit with them for dinner, instead of at the farm table in the kitchen, since such an assemblage made perfect sense to the six-year-old. *A distinction you will grow to understand,* her mother assured her. *Listen to your mother, Little Bird,* was her father's standard reply.

Geneva's dress clung to the backs of her legs, and the seams rubbed her underarms. She hated the dress with its scratchy crinoline. She fidgeted. Try as she might, she could not seem to train her attention on the sermon of the Reverend Calhoun, a willowy man with a somnolent voice, pale, oniony skin, and a severely receding hairline. Geneva watched him scrunch up his nose to raise his spectacles, which slipped perpetually down his nose. When Geneva tired of watching him, she watched other congregants. Several rows in front of her, one man slept upright. He was drooling, a long line of spittle dangling from his partially open mouth, and his head bobbed as small snored crescendos escaped.

"Look." She nudged Hayes and snickered. "He is going to wake the dead," she said, repeating a phrase she often heard from Vivvy.

"Stop," Hayes whispered.

She crossed her arms and reared back against the hard pew, bumping her head. Her father gave her a stern look. Tears squirted from her eyes, but she blinked them away and began counting the candles on the communion table. She followed milkweed seeds floating through the side door left open to ventilate the sanctuary. She wanted to catch and keep them for Clarissa, who stuffed them into her mattress, but she dared not move—now her mother was eyeing her. Geneva watched a pair of elderly sisters sniffle and wrestle with lacey handkerchiefs. Through the window, she saw horses harnessed to buckboards or tied to hitching posts. In foul weather, Geneva would sit in empathetic misery as rain pounded the tethered animals. Tonight, though, was pleasant.

While the minister murmured on, she gestured for her father's wedding ring, which he gladly gave her—anything to entertain the wiggly child. She slipped it on and off her fingers. As the setting sun flickered through the leaves of a dogwood tree, she held up the ring to look at the sun through the gold circle and found she could reflect it onto the side of Hayes' head.

"Stop," whispered her father, disturbed by a flash of light.

Geneva drew her mouth up in a moue. Soon, though, her eyelids grew heavy. She slumped against her father, who pulled her into the curve of his arm. Sometime before the closing benediction, she fell asleep. Bertram pried open his daughter's hand to retrieve his ring before he carried her to the waiting carriage. He held her in his arms during the trip home, letting Thomas take the reins.

"Grayson, carry her up to her bed," Bertram said when the family arrived back at Cairnaerie. He handed his drowsy daughter to his son. "Thomas, you tie up the rig and help Lightner with the horses."

"Hayes, you get to bed. I'll be up directly," Caroline said before following her husband into his study and pulling the heavy pocketed doors closed.

Bertram lit an oil lamp that bathed the room in sallow light. He sat down at his desk and ran his hand across the dog-eared pages of a large open Bible. Caroline, her skirts brushing the floor, crossed the room to his desk.

"Can't they wait until after Thanksgiving?" she pleaded, voicing her petition one more time.

Bertram stiffened. "It's their duty." His tone, usually gentle, was more like a general's tonight. "Duty knows no seasons. It doesn't obey a calendar." He rose and walked away from her to the window.

She followed him. "I understand duty, Bertram. But I do not want to give up my sons for a lost cause."

"Nothing is lost until it is tested. Nothing is lost."

"Can you promise me? Can you?"

As Bertram stared into the night, a night as black as Caroline's worry, he didn't answer. He could not promise.

She watched her husband's reflection in the darkened window for any change in the strong disposition she relied on, but tonight wished she could temper. When they first met, he had taken her breath away—when he, a handsome and confident young lawyer, had approached her, the shy daughter of a Richmond planter. Now his hair was grayer, his frame thicker, but he had lost none of his bearing. Age had enhanced it. She cherished him with all her heart and on love alone had left the comforts of her eastern plantation home to live in the mountains.

"I worry for my boys," Caroline said.

"I know," he said. "I do, too." Bertram found it hard to resist her pleas. He had his own misgivings, but for him duty and responsibility marked manhood itself. Men did not shy from loathsome tasks. "I'm sorry, Caroline. I'm sorry there is a war at all. I'm sorry Thomas and Grayson are leaving us, but our duties must come before our wants and desires. Duty is the price we pay for our lives."

"I understand that." She spoke with vehemence bordering on desperation—because she would never truly understand. "But they are only boys."

"No, Caroline. Thomas and Grayson are men now. Young men called to duty."

Caroline winced, unable to stave off the heartache she suffered. How she wished she could persuade her husband to intervene. But knowing her appeals were futile, she turned away and left him alone.

As she closed his study door and stepped into the hall, melancholy swept over her, the same emotion she had fought since the war began in April. It was almost too much to bear.

"Mama." From above her came a small, sleepy voice. "Are you coming?"

At the bottom of the staircase, Caroline saw traces of mud dotting the floor and ran the toe of her shoe across them. Even in her black mood, she smiled, grateful tonight for even the smallest distraction. She would never understand Geneva. She would never understand war. She would never understand.

Geneva's door was open, and the child lay half asleep in her tall carved bed, a furnishing Caroline had ordered made for her—the child who was both blessing and vexation, the headstrong and precocious daughter who knew her own mind, who relished climbing along creek banks in the low pastures and exploring the natural world surrounding their home. While most young girls her age were already well on their way to a proficiency in domestic skills, Geneva was wholly uninterested. She knew what she wanted—and she knew how to get it.

Her mother found her independence irritating, but her father delighted in her spirit. Any traditional opinions he held about a woman's role collapsed under his daughter's curiosity. She was intelligent and loved to read, a skill she had learned by age five with her father's eager help. Bertram planned to send his sons to college after the war ended. His daughter would be educated at the Presbyterian Female Seminary or another suitable institution for young women. Though he hoped nature would take its course and his daughter would grow to be a proper young woman, her desire to learn was precious to him. He believed Geneva's intelligence, as all good things, proceeded from God and should be encouraged.

Snow, himself, was a scholarly man, driven by a solemn duty to improve his mind—a duty as important as living an upright life and a lesson Ezekial Coker had drilled into him. Unable to afford a formal education, Bertram had worked his way up from a position as a janitor for a law establishment, catching the notice of the partners who saw promise and granted him access to their libraries. In addition to law, he had tackled classic literature, languages, history, mathematics—whatever he could find to satisfy an insatiable desire to learn. Eventually, he had become a lawyer through sheer hard work, but even though he was self-taught, he never lost a sense of awe at his own success.

In a division of labor both traditional and practical, Caroline Snow ran the household with grace and artistry. Her duties often consumed her. Born and raised on a large tobacco plantation, she had been groomed to be the wife of a man of stature, so she had fallen effortlessly into her role, though life on a farm with fewer rather than abundant slaves had been difficult at first. Over time, however, Caroline grew to love their mountain home. In what spare time she managed, she closeted herself in her studio, a small, second-story room on the north side of the house where she painted. The studio had been a gift from Bertram when he built the house. Painting was her avocation and her escape.

She pulled the covers over her daughter's shoulders and stepped to the window to pull down the sash half way. The night air was cooling.

"Mama?"

"Yes? What is it, Geneva?" She sat down on the side of the child's bed and put her hand on her daughter's head.

"Are Thomas and Grayson leaving?"

Caroline did not answer. She pulled up the coverlet and tucked it around the child. "You go to sleep, now. We'll talk about it tomorrow."

As the mother stroked her daughter's hair, the child yawned and closed her eyes.

"Pray for them, Geneva," Caroline whispered. "Pray for them."

But the child was already asleep.

CHAPTER 4

Autumn 1861

Lavender & Tatting

Caroline struggled to remain composed as she gripped the balustrade, the knuckles of her delicate hands twisted and tight. Leaves covered the yard, and the sky was visible through the branches that grew more barren each day. The whish of each crisp leaf as it tumbled across the porch grated on her nerves, and the bright sun seemed impudent. To Caroline it all felt sad, this change in the seasons, especially today. It was not a happy day.

She watched as Thomas and Grayson led their horses up from the barn. At her feet lay two rucksacks, each filled with warm clothes: extra knitted socks and heavy wool shirts. A newly hired girl had made them, and Caroline had fussed at how they had turned out. No one had made clothes better than Clarissa, and she hated that her sons would not have the best garments she could provide. Caroline didn't trust the Confederacy—or anyone for that matter—to care adequately for her boys. She worried about them—two boys itching for adventure. She had mail-ordered long johns, an extravagant purchase, but they had not yet arrived. When they did, she would send them on.

Grayson's horse snorted and shook his head. Grayson rubbed its forehead, and the horse quieted. The second son had always had a way with animals.

Thomas grabbed the rucksacks, handed one off to his brother, and strapped the other one behind his own saddle. Hayes, who was sitting in the swing, pulled his knees up to his chin and watched. He wanted to go with them, but the eleven-year-old could not pass for older, as did other boys who had enlisted too young. Grayson barely qualified, having turned seventeen in late summer. Had he not, Caroline was sure she could have kept him home with her. She hated the war.

Geneva was still asleep upstairs. They would wake her at the last moment.

Vivvy came around to the front of the house, rocking on her old thick legs and carrying two parcels of food: thick hunks of fried bacon, hard chunks of smoked venison, cornbread, and bags of dried cherries.

"Dis'll git y'all far as Lynchburg," she said, handing one to Thomas and the other to Grayson. "You boys take care of yourselves, ya hear?"

"We will, Vivvy. Thank you," said Thomas, taking his bag and giving her a peck on the cheek that she playfully brushed off before turning to leave. Vivvy believed it was bad luck to watch them go. As she walked away, she lifted her apron to wipe her eyes. Although she would never let on, she was fond of the boys.

Bertram checked the cinches on both saddles and ran his hands over the horses' hocks, checking their fetlocks and hooves. He had hired a local farrier to shoe both horses, two of Bertram's best mounts. He didn't want a horse throwing a shoe.

Lightner came up from the barn with two muslin pouches filled with dried lemon balm and lavender, which he tied to the saddles.

"This'll keep 'em in line fer you," he told the boys as he scratched each animal's pall. Lightner, tall and willow thin, bent down and whispered to the horses, "You carry 'em boys good." For Lightner, too, the boys' departure was hard. He would miss their help and their company. He hoped Thomas and Grayson's absence would be a temporary departure—unlike the sad one he had suffered in March.

Bertram turned toward the swing. "Hayes. Run get your sister." The boy jumped up.

Shortly, a sleepy-eyed Geneva appeared in the front door threshold. Barefooted, she was still wearing her nightgown, and her hair, matted from sleep, resembled a bird's nest. Hayes pushed her out onto the porch before reclaiming the swing.

"Are they leaving now?" she asked her mother as she rubbed her eyes.

Caroline bit her lip and tightened her grip on the railing. She looked at Bertram, pleading with him to answer for her.

"Yes," he said. "Tell your brothers goodbye."

Geneva ran down the stairs and jumped into Grayson's arms. "Don't go," she said, hugging his neck. "I don't want you to go. Promise me you won't leave."

"I have to, but I'll be back. Won't be long. You'll see. We'll have those Yankees licked faster than you can say jackrabbit."

She reared back in his arms, cupping his face in her hands, and pulled him nose-to-nose. "Promise?"

"I promise."

"Say it again."

"I promise," he said, laughing.

Grayson put her down, and together he and Thomas stood at attention and gave their sister a little salute. Their excitement was apparent.

"Godspeed, boys," Bertram said. "We will keep you in our prayers. Write to your mother."

Caroline hugged her sons and could barely let go of them. She did her best not to cry, but the moment they disappeared across the hill into the swale, she ran from the porch and locked herself in her studio for the rest of the day.

"When are they coming back, Daddy?" Geneva asked as she hung off the porch before jumping down across a short hedge and running back up to the swing. "Move over," she said, shoving Hayes aside with her hip. "When, Daddy?"

Bertram stood silently with his arms crossed, looking toward the road.

"Not for a while, Little Bird," he said.

"I'm hungry," she whined.

"Me, too," Hayes said.

Their father continued staring down the empty road.

"Daddy, I'm hungry." She brushed her feet on the porch floor as Hayes pushed the swing. "I'm hungry!"

Finally, he stirred and smiled at Geneva and Hayes. "Well then, let's go see what Vivvy's cooking. Come on." Extending his arms, their father took their hands and led his remaining children into the house.

———

Caroline slipped into Geneva's room to check the child's window. The temperature had dropped, and the wind was kicking up. She knew her daughter had a penchant for opening windows no matter the weather. Seeing the stiff breeze blowing the new yellow curtains, her mind, never far from Thomas and Grayson, wondered if they were warm. She pulled down on the window rail to lower it.

"Don't close it," said Geneva, rolling over. The bed creaked, and the curtains snapped.

"I thought you were asleep." Caroline bent down and pushed a strand of hair out of the child's face.

"I want to sleep with the wind." Geneva yawned. "It talks to me." She closed her eyes and drifted back to sleep.

Outside, the wind blustered, a dry sullen wind, and an occasional gust rattled the window and drew a moan from the flue. Caroline could not help but think it was blowing something hard into their lives. By the light coming from an oil lamp in the hall that reflected off a tall mirror, she looked around her daughter's room. Scattered everywhere—on tabletops and across the floor—were collections of rocks and thistles, assortments of sticks and dried bones, and tiny medicine bottles tied closed with scraps of yarn and fabric, each holding captured bugs. How many times had Geneva rushed into her father's study with an insect trapped in her hand, breathlessly wanting to know what it was, where it came from, or where it lived. Her endless questions, though, too often came with mud and dirt. Caroline had almost given up trying to keep her clean.

Books were strewn about, too, some held open with rocks, others marked with feathers or dried leaves. Caroline and Geneva were so very different, but they had one thing in common. She understood her daughter's fascination with nature; as an artist, she saw it with her own keen eye. But while the mother was neat and tidy, the daughter was wild and adventuresome. She sighed, looking at the tall wardrobe filled with pretty dresses, none of interest to the girl. On the floor, dropped in a heap as if the occupant had suddenly vanished, lay a pair of muddy pantalets, a stained pinafore, and a pair of girl's boots, unhooked and coming apart where the worn leather bottoms met the uppers. Geneva stubbornly refused to part with the shoes, even though a brand-new pair waited for her at the foot of her bed.

As Caroline stood up to leave, she rubbed her hand across a dresser scarf spread on a chest of drawers. With a pang of sadness, she smoothed it out. She had always been impressed by Clarissa's needlework, almost jealous. The woman's skill with a needle or a shuttle was artistry—not unlike Caroline's own with a paintbrush. Clarissa had tatted the scarf for Geneva, and then she had wrapped it in a piece of discarded burlap tied up with kitchen twine and presented it the morning after Caroline had given birth—one of many deliveries Clarissa had faithfully attended. Caroline remembered the pure joy radiating from Clarissa's face over the birth of a girl, coming a few weeks after Simmy's birth. She had, in her own humble way, shared in the celebration. "We finally got us baby girls," she had said with a kind of thrill that mothers alone can share. She had cared for Caroline and tiny Geneva while she cared for her own newborn daughter. The dresser cloth brought back a sweet memory....

Clarissa was shelling peas by the hearth when she walked into the warm kitchen. A pot hung over the fire on a wrought-iron crane, and puffs of steam escaped from beneath its heavy cover.

'Clarissa, tell Vivvy to serve dinner a little early this evening. Mr. Snow won't be back until tomorrow, and honestly, I am so hungry I could eat a horse. It smells so good.'

Thin and dark, Clarissa smiled up at Caroline with an uncluttered kindness.

'You like me to fix you a little bowl now? It's plenty cooked. Jes waiting for Lightner to bring me some chard in from the garden.'

'Yes, please.'

'You go on in the dining room and set down. I'll bring it in to ya.' Clarissa put down her work beside the low slung, rush-bottom chair and checked her own daughter, who was sleeping in a basket at her feet. Tenderly, she pulled the blanket over the small exposed shoulder before getting up.

The dining room table was covered with a linen cloth. All the breakfast dishes had been cleared and the crumbs, swept away. It was empty except for a large vase in the center, overflowing with Queen Anne's lace whose small black seeds dotted the table. As Caroline settled into a chair, she heard her young sons squealing in the side yard where Lightner was pushing them in a rope swing he had secured high in the branches of an oak tree. From where she sat, she could see the shadow of the swing arcing back and forth across the yard. When the boys weren't swinging, they followed Lightner around the farm like ducklings. He was as much playmate as teacher; from him the boys were learning valuable skills. Caroline smiled, picturing Lightner's strong hands pushing the boys; Clarissa might have to wait a while on the chard.

Clarissa carried in a tray with a spoon, a glass of buttermilk, and a steaming bowl of Brunswick stew—a mixture of squirrel, root vegetables, and stock. 'I'll cut you a slice of Vivvy's bread after it cools down a mite.'

As she set down the tray, they heard a tiny wail coming from the upstairs nursery. Caroline started to stand up, but Clarissa put her hand on the young mother's shoulder.

'You jes sit and eat, Miss Caroline. I'll go...'

In the dim light, Caroline fingered the line of perfectly tatted picots and rings. She wondered what had happened to Clarissa's tatting shuttle. Maybe Lightner would know. In one of his fits of generosity, Bertram had bought her the ivory shuttle inlaid with mother-of-pearl. The gift—Caroline told him at the time—was an unnecessary indulgence and a dangerous precedent. But her husband had been as delighted to give the gift as Clarissa had been to receive it. *I suppose Simmy should have it now,* she thought. *I'll find it and save it for her.* A soft pain gripped her. *Oh, Clarissa. You've left us too early. You had promised to teach me to tat.*

As she left the room, Caroline propped the door open with a chair so the wind would not blow it closed. Tonight, she fought melancholy.

CHAPTER 5

1864

─────◆─────

Porch & Belvedere

The sky over the valley glowed an ominous dirty orange as Bertram stood looking eastward. Awakened before dawn by echoing volleys of cannon fire, he had taken up his post on the porch hastily. The air held the acrid scent of burning, carried like a pestilence on the prevailing wind. The war seemed to be everlasting, and it had already taken a great toll. All day rumbles of cannon fire and the muffled, sporadic pops of gunfire haunted from the east. For weeks, rumors had circulated about Yankee marauders and militia moving through the valley. Now it appeared they had marched to Hyssop. He wanted to ride to the ridge to see if what he had imagined—what had been their great fear—had indeed come to pass, but he would monitor from his porch, a provisional sentry box. Propped up against the balustrade was his Sharps carbine, loaded, cocked, readied.

Inside the house, Caroline struggled to maintain a calm ordinariness, a masquerade for her son and daughter—and for herself. She pretended the fury from the valley below was of no consequence, yet she worried for her sons, fighting somewhere within the bleeding state.

Geneva raced down the staircase, through the foyer, and toward the front door. "I want to swing," she said, tugging on the heavy, double front doors; funeral doors they were called, built wide enough to accommodate coffins.

"Don't open that door, Geneva," said her mother, coming out of the parlor.

"Daddy's out there. I want to go out."

"I said no."

"I want to swing." Geneva stomped her foot.

"Your father is busy," she said and waved her away. "Go upstairs. Find Hayes."

Geneva ran to a window to peer out. "Daddy's not busy. He's just standing there." She ran back and gripped the doorknob. "I want to swing."

"Do not argue with me, young lady," said a frustrated Caroline. She grabbed her arm and pulled her from the door. "Go upstairs. Right now! I'll call you down for supper in a little while. Now go."

"Come on, Geneva," Hayes said. He was standing at the top of the stairs and recognized fear in his mother's eyes. Begrudgingly, Geneva obeyed, but she moved and moaned as one greatly inconvenienced.

When her children were out of sight, Caroline slipped out to the porch. She took Bertram's arm and laid her head against his shoulder. For several minutes, an eerie and blessed quiet settled on their ears.

"Are we safe?" she asked.

"Not yet, but soon. I hope."

"How long?"

"I don't know. I'm waiting until they move south of here. It looks like they're burning everything, Caroline."

"Will they come this way?"

"I don't think so. Small bands, if they do. Or looters."

"Why would they come here?"

Bertram shifted his weight. He pulled her closer and kissed her hair. "They're hungry, Caroline."

Behind them the door opened, and Geneva appeared.

"Geneva!" said an exasperated Caroline. "I told you to stay inside."

Ignoring her mother, she ran to her father, who lifted her up. "Your mother told you to stay inside. It's not safe out here."

"I tried, Mama," Hayes said. Standing behind her, he had stopped at the threshold.

"I love you, Daddy." Geneva hugged her father's neck.

"I love you, too, Geneva, but you must stay inside."

She opened her mouth to protest, but he put a finger to her lips. "Not now, Little Bird." His voice was tired, but unyielding. "Go back inside with your brother. Your mother will be in soon." He set her down with a thump.

"Oh, Daddy, look at the sky."

"I see it. Now go."

He grabbed her shoulders and directed her toward the door. Reluctantly, she obeyed, but Geneva was undeterred. She raced up the stairs with Hayes following. At the top, he opened a drawer to get out a board game, Mansion of Happiness. "I'll play with you, Geneva."

"I don't want to play a dumb game!"

Before he could close the drawer, she grabbed his hand and pulled. "Come on."

"No, Geneva. We have to stay inside."

"We're not going outside. Come on."

She yanked on her brother until he followed. Quietly, Geneva opened a small door at the end of a corridor off the upstairs hall, and they climbed the narrow stairs leading to a small empty room used to ventilate the house in warm weather: the belvedere. Circled with windows on all sides and shaped like a small turret, the room provided panoramic views of the farm and mountains. It was Geneva's favorite room—and she had all but claimed it as her own.

"I don't think we're supposed to go up here."

"Oh, hush! I come up here all the time."

"All right, but be quiet."

Even before they reached the top of the stair, bronze light soaked the small enclosure. The setting sun magnified and distorted the smoke, turning the sky into an inferno. Even fearless Geneva was shaken by the reflected war scorching the sky.

"What is it, Hayes?" asked Geneva as they knelt together in front of the eastern windows. "It looks like hell."

"It's the war. It is hell."

The children were quiet.

"Hayes?" Geneva's voice held the barest hint of worry.

He preempted her question. "Don't worry. Thomas and Grayson are far away."

Long past midnight, long after the furious sounds of the war had moved south, Bertram finally left his post. He stood alone in the night air still rife with the caustic smell of smoke. The balmy darkness, full of invisible sounds, soothed him like a lullaby after the cacophony of destruction his ears had been trained on since dawn. Mercifully, he had not had to raise his rifle to any man. He bowed his head and whispered a prayer of thanks for the protection his land afforded his family.

He sat down in the swing and gazed at the sky, still partially obscured by spectral billows of smoke. Stars scattered across the horizon shone like embers from a dying campfire. He wished he could tether his absent sons and reel them back to Cairnaerie. With each passing day, his faith in their safe return dimmed. Of late, he had prayed, asking not only for their safety but for assurance of their eternal lives. They had moved beyond his protection, beyond the sanctuary of Cairnaerie, but not—he knew with certainly—beyond God. With stalwart faith, he gave his sons into the hands of the Almighty.

Bertram rested his head against the swing's cool, metal chain and watched as an ant strode effortlessly along the balustrade. For the first time since before dawn, his shoulders relaxed. A barn owl hooted from high above. A cricket chorus rose and fell in a slow, weary heartbeat. He rested until sleep began to overtake him, and then he picked up his rifle and went inside. He turned the key in the brass lock. Tonight, he locked all the doors.

———

Chimneys of smoke and ash curled along the blackened landscape below him as Zeph lay on his stomach on top of a ridge overlooking the broad valley. Hidden by the night and tall grasses silvered by the moon, he thought about Simmy. She was sleeping back in the cabin with Prudy, her beloved doll—a worn stocking stuffed with leftover wool that their late mother had made for her. Simmy was oblivious to the world that was turning upside down. But Zeph knew—some things at least—and he wanted to know more. His daddy never said much about the war and what it meant, but he had listened to the talk. Zeph had wanted to see for himself. Now he knew. And it worried him.

He rolled over onto his back, rustling the grasses, and opened his eyes wide to take in more of the night. Above him the sky seemed endless with a depth of pointed lights—the moon's scattered children winking at him from the mottled blackness. He picked up the forage cap he had found and traced the buckle on the head-band with his fingers. Angling it toward the moon, he let the re-flection illumine the bloodstains on the brim. His mind could not let go of the image—the soldier with half a face. He prayed for the Snow boys. He wished Thomas and Grayson would come back, but until they did, he—Zephyr Elias—would look after Simmy and the Snows, all tucked safely away at Cairnaerie.

Night was almost over. Across the valley, a ribbon of color traced the eastern mountains while mourning doves, close by, cooed from the brush. Very soon, the morning would roll over and awaken. He had to get home before his daddy woke. Zeph stood up and put the cap on his head. He soldiered his way back home, hands braced at his sides, shoulders squared, chin in, marching in cadence to an imagined drum.

Until Thomas and Grayson returned, Zeph promised he would protect Cairnaerie.

CHAPTER 6

1864

Letters & Locks

The longcase clock in the hall struck three as Geneva dashed up the stairs after her cats, who naughtily veered into her parents' bedroom and hid underneath their tall sleigh bed. On her mother's desk, a walnut box—always kept locked—was open. Next to it lay the key and a stack of letters. Curious, she looked and immediately recognized Grayson's handwriting. She read the top letter.

December 10, 1861
Dearest Mama,

The weather has turned foul this week. A storm blew in Sunday right after chapel and brought snow, which continued into Monday. I'm mighty glad for the extra socks and underclothes you insisted I take. Some of the other boys have had to put scraps of paper or bark in their shoes to cover worn-out soles. My boots are holding up well so far. Some of these fellows are facing the winter with cloth coats. The wools they gave us ran out before all the boys got them. I'm mighty fortunate....

Geneva heard her mother mount the stairs. Quickly, she put down the letter and dove under the bed to pull out the cats.

"I told you to keep those cats out of my room," her mother said, scowling, her hands full of a stack of linens, which she placed on the bed.

"All right," Geneva mumbled.

"What did you say, young lady?"

"I mean, yes, ma'am."

Geneva left the room with a cat draped over each arm. At the top of the stairs, she glanced back to see her mother lock the box and hide the key in a small desk drawer hidden behind a piece of decoration.

The next afternoon, while her mother and father were away in town, Geneva slipped into their bedroom and found the key. Closing the bedroom door, she unlocked the box and lifted out a handful of the letters. Covering them with her skirt, she carried them to the belvedere.

The high room was stuffy, so she cracked several windows. When the draft rattled the door at the bottom of the stairs, she scurried down and locked it. Then she spread out the letters, reading them one by one.

January 21, 1862

Dearest Mama,

I got the package you sent. I'm sure God sent angels to carry it since we moved our camp last Friday—yet your package reached me. Now I know how the children of Abraham felt—your package was like manna from Heaven. My socks were wearing thin, and the union suit you sent is the best thing I've seen in a year. I'm sure I'm the warmest soldier here now that winter has set in.

If you can see any way to send several more, I know my friends would be grateful. One fellow has gotten so thin and coughs terribly—we're concerned he might not make it through the winter, especially if it continues to be as cold and damp as it's been up till now. Also, I'm getting low on writing paper, if you could send some my way....

April 12, 1862
Dearest Mama,

I expect Hayes and Daddy are cutting the winter rye about now. I see farmers cutting and stacking hay, and the fields lying covered with shocks remind me how nice it will be to get back to Cairnaerie.

Tell Hayes not to get any ideas about enlisting. This is an exciting life all right, but I could do with a lot less excitement. I suppose nobody knows what a good life he has till it's taken away. I promise you, I'll never complain about farm work again. Nothing is harder than soldiering....

December 9, 1862
Dearest Mama,

The bolt of my rifle jammed today, and the barrel blew up right beside my face. My ears were ringing all afternoon, but seem better tonight. I'm awfully fortunate since the metal breach went flying away from me instead of into my face. The barrel hit me in the mouth, though, and broke off one of my front teeth about half way. It was painful initially, but the Captain—a fine fellow by the name of Jay Mildred—gave me some persimmons to chew on—that eased the pain considerably. When I think about the arms and legs some of the fellows have lost, I'm happy to be giving up a tooth. Tell Geneva she's now got a snaggletooth brother....

January 21, 1863
Dearest Mama,

My unit has a day of rest today, and it is welcomed by every one of us. We marched hard yesterday—nearly twenty miles.

Our captain—I've mentioned him before—is a young fellow from Mississippi, and he's a fine leader, who is most considerate of his men.

Our rations are slim, and no one should worry about us becoming fat. I think often of Vivvy's delicious meals, and when I chew hard tack, I pretend it's a slice of Daddy's good country ham.

If Mr. Pascal still has any apples stored, and you can find a way to send a bushel our way, I would be most thankful.

The weather has not been too unpleasant most of the month, and I look forward to our annual February warm spell. I hope Lightner can get out some early peas and onions. I wish I could be there to help.

I am fit and missing everyone at Cairnaerie....

Gradually, the war that Geneva had known only through the referential conversations of adults came very near. Sitting in the belvedere with the sun streaming in, she felt safe—yet at the same time unsettled. She wanted her brothers home with her. She counted on her fingers: Thomas and Grayson had been gone for three of her birthdays. Surely they would come home before she turned ten next April.

When the clock struck three, she gathered up the letters, tiptoed downstairs, and slipped them back into her mother's box. But as she opened the desk to replace the key, it slipped from her hand and fell through a seam in the floor. Horrified, she dropped to her knees, but the key was lodged beyond her reach. She ran to find Simmy.

"I need you," she whispered to the girl wielding a feather duster in the parlor.

Simmy laid down the duster and looked at Geneva. "What'd you do now?"

"Come on."

As they ran up the stairs, the clock struck the quarter hour. A little panic rose in Geneva. Time had slipped up on her. Vivvy stuck her head out of the kitchen and yelled for Simmy. Without breaking her stride, Simmy shouted, "Comin', Vivvy. Be there in a spit."

Kneeling head-to-head over the crevice, Geneva pointed to the key. "You see it?"

"I can see it, but I can't reach it." She sat back on her knees. "When's your mama coming back?"

"Soon." Geneva looked strangely rattled.

"You wait here."

"What about Vivvy?" Geneva asked.

"If she hollers again, tell her I had to visit the privy."

Simmy rushed out of the room, down the stairs, and slipped through a side door to avoid Vivvy. She ran to the carriage house where Zeph was oiling a saddle and started poking around.

"What are you looking for?" he asked. He scratched his nose with his wrist as he turned to look at her.

"Nothing," she said. She pushed around some tools and dug in a box of odds and ends. "I need a little piece of wire."

"What for?"

"Nothing."

Zeph put down the cloth and wiped his hands.

"So you need a piece of wire, but you don't need it for anything." He laughed at her. "Geneva's done something, hadn't she?"

"'Course she has. She dropped a key down a crack. I need to get it out before her mama gits back."

"Here," he said, finding a long nail with a bent tip. "This work?"

"Maybe." She reached for it, but Zeph held it up high.

Simmy jumped. "Give it to me, Zeph. Give it! Her mama's gonna be back soon."

"I'll help."

Geneva scooted aside when Zeph and Simmy returned. Simmy went to the window to watch the road while Zeph fished the nail down through the crack.

"Move back, Geneva. I can't see," he grumped. "You're blocking the light."

Geneva scooted over with an uncharacteristic meekness. Watching nervously, she held her breath.

"Got it," he said, and he lifted the key.

Relieved, Geneva grabbed it out of his hand and slipped it back into her mother's desk just as Simmy saw a team of horses come onto the road past the swale.

"They're comin'," Simmy said.

Zeph stood up and brushed off his pants. "We can't be always fixing your problems," he said.

"Yes, you can," Geneva said, condescendingly. "It's your job."

Zeph narrowed his eyes, but he held his tongue, as his father had taught him to do.

CHAPTER 7

1864

Reapers & Responsibility

Alone in his study, Bertram pored over his books. Near the window, sleeping in a pool of sunshine, Blue, his faithful hound dog, snored softly. Bertram relished the time and the opportunity to work uninterrupted.

The war had suspended time—and most of his law practice. What little legal work he still had, he accomplished from his study at Cairnaerie, but jobs were few and far between. He hoped when the war ended he could reopen his office in Hyssop, but nothing was certain. No one had imagined the conflict would drag on so long—or that Lincoln would suspend the right of habeas corpus, a decision that offended Bertram's bedrock belief in justice.

Adding to his woes, he hadn't been able to sell his cattle for three springs. It was too dangerous to drive a herd through the valley where either army might confiscate the animals. Bertram and Hayes, nearly fourteen, had considered driving them northwest through the mountains toward Cincinnati, but the risk was too great and the travel too difficult. They had eventually decided against it.

Still, the Snows were luckier than most. Abundant wild game on the property—elk, deer and turkeys especially—and a pond full of geese sustained them. Lightner, with a few farm hands, tended a large garden that fed the Snows and their staff. More and more Bertram leaned on Lightner, Zeph, and Hayes. He missed the help of his eldest sons, but he hoped at war's end, he would have them back. Caroline sewed until her fingers bled. She also churned butter that she packed into firkins for sale in town—and she painted feverishly during her few spare moments. Vivvy was masterful at turning a little bit of not much into a hearty meal. Briscoe Robinson, her young nephew, often brought from town any supplies she needed—those that could still be had.

As Bertram dipped the nib of his pen into a bottle of ink, he heard someone yelling. Blue stirred and raised his head.

"Father! Father!" Hayes was running toward the house.

Alarmed by his son's tone, Bertram stepped out onto the terrace.

"Lightner's hurt. Come quick."

Every nerve in Bertram's body fired. He lumbered across the terrace. "What's happened?" he yelled as they rushed toward the barnyard.

"Horse spooked—reared up next to the reaper—pushed Lightner into the knives. He's bleeding bad."

When they reached the barn, Zeph and two farm hands were hunched over Lightner. Zeph, bare chested, held his own shirt against the wound in his father's side, trying in vain to stem the bright red blood soaking through.

Lightner turned his head. "Judge, I had me a little accident." He tried to smile, but winced.

"Be still, Lightner." Bertram, his heart in his throat, knelt beside him and stripped off his own shirt. He handed it to Zeph. "Use this."

Blood gushed from three gaping wounds as Zeph switched the garments.

"We've got to stop that bleeding," Bertram said. "Get him to the house."

Hayes and Bertram with the help of the farm hands lifted him while Zeph kept pressure on the wound. Lightner's strength was waning fast. His face was drawn.

"Oh, my Lord Jesus," Vivvy said, throwing up her hands as they brought Lightner through the kitchen door and laid him near the hearth. "What in the world happened?"

"Get some cloth, Vivvy," Bertram bellowed while he cradled Lightner's head. She hurried out and returned with an armful of rags and her own pillow, stuffed with straw and milkweed seeds. Gently, she helped lift his head. Dark sticky blood covered Lightner's entire side, and fresh blood began to pool under him.

Simmy, drawn by the commotion, walked into the kitchen and stopped, stunned at the scene.

"Simmy!" Zeph yelled at his sister. "You get outta here. Go!"

Wild-eyed, the girl fled. Zeph turned back to his father, who had passed out halfway to the house. Zeph rubbed his face to roust him. "Pa?"

"Bring him to the guest room," Bertram said, shattering all decorum.

Under her breath, Vivvy muttered thanks that Miss Caroline was gone for the day as she followed the men upstairs with the rags and a bucket of water. She filled the washstand bowl and rung out a fresh rag while they laid Lightner on the bed that was covered with starched linens and sumptuous quilts.

As best they could, they bandaged the wound, but a large and ominous bulge was beginning to form. Vivvy brought a cup of water to the bedside, but Lightner had not revived. Bertram sent the farm hands, loitering downstairs in the foyer, back to work. He, Zeph, and Hayes stayed with Lightner.

That evening, when Caroline and Geneva returned, Vivvy met them at the door with the news. Geneva, hysterical, wanted to go straight-away to Lightner, but Vivvy barred the door on strict orders from the Judge: "You keep her out, Vivvy. She doesn't need to see this, and it won't do Lightner a lick of good."

Caroline, dismayed at the thought of losing another servant, took her supper in her room and retired early.

The next morning, before the light had washed out the night's shadows, Bertram came into his bedroom quietly, walking as if he were carrying a burden too heavy even for him. Caroline stirred. Looking up at her husband, she whispered. "Bertram?"

"He's gone, Caroline." His voice broke. "Lightner's gone."

She climbed out of their bed and slipped on a dressing gown. "I'm so sorry, Bertram. I know he was special to you."

Her husband made no reply as he removed his bloodied clothes, rolled them into a ball, and threw them to the floor with a motion that dispensed both pain and anger. Caroline poured water into the washbasin for him to clean his face and hands. Wisely, she said nothing more, but offered what sympathy she could without fully understanding the depth of his grief. To her, this event was little more than a sad inconvenience.

For a long time, Bertram did not speak. Lightner's death echoed of sorrows he had known long ago. A flood of emotion over deaths and separations washed over him—when his parents died, when his uncle had sent him out. He could almost feel his grandfather's silver watch in his pocket. Reflexively, he reached down to touch it, to join this pain with the pain of the past, but he had left it in his study for safekeeping.

He took comfort in remembering the help given him by Ezekial and the wisdom of his wise friend's words. *You work hard, Bertram. You'll have troubles, but you do what's right. And you'll see. You'll be alright. D' good Lord. He'll take care of you—carry any burden you got.* Bertram would cling to that counsel. Losing Lightner broke his heart.

Sitting by the window, as morning light crept up the wall and flooded the room, he stared into the rising sun. He thought about Clarissa and Lightner—how faithful they had always been—how pleased they were with the cabin he had built for them—how grateful they had always been for any kindness. He remembered Lightner taking him aside and, with tears in his dark eyes, thanking him for letting Zeph go to school. He could see his face still, the delight in it—and the trust he vested in Bertram. How happy he himself had been to suggest it—and how glad he was that he had done so. He remembered the care Clarissa and Lightner had given his own children. Lightner had been his employee, but also his friend.

Bertram wiped his face and continued staring into the sun. For this man who had been like a brother, he would repay his debt to Ezekial: He would take care of Zeph and Simmy as if they were his own.

Finally, exhausted and spent, Bertram came to bed and, sobbing, fell asleep in Caroline's arms.

Geneva stretched out on her bed with her journal open. The house was strangely quiet, a concert of muted whispers and scuffling feet. Lightner's death left a void in Cairnaerie as indelible as the blood stains on the kitchen floor and in the bed where he died.

Three sharpened pencils lay in the fold of her book. She stared at them, examining the crisp, perfect points. Two days before,

Lightner had sharpened them for her. She could still see him grinning, taking his penny knife from his pocket and shaving two sharp points. He had done it a hundred times for her. Lightner had the strongest hands she had ever seen. She had watched him wring a chicken's neck in no time flat, take off a wagon wheel, pick up a barrel of soap, slice through the belly of a hog—and cradle a little orphaned kitten as gently as a moonbeam. Now his strong brown hands were stilled. Geneva did not know exactly what had happened because no one would talk to her except Vivvy. "Lightner— he gone on up to Heav'n, chile," she had said with a hitch in her voice. Heaven, though, was a vague concept to the nine-year-old. It left her sad and confused.

She asked questions, as she always did, but instead of giving answers, her mother had sent her to her room. Still Geneva wanted to know. She had slipped up to the belvedere to watch her father, Hayes, and two farm hands lift Lightner's body onto a wagon. Someone had dressed him in one of her father's finest coats, and he appeared to be merely sleeping. Hayes had climbed onto the seat to take the reins. She could not see her father's face, but in his shoulders and manner she had clearly seen his distress.

Geneva picked up one of the pencils and held it up to the light. A perfect point. And then she wrote…

I saw Vivvy wiping up blood in the kitchen. Lightner is dead and no one will tell me what happened. I know Thomas and Grayson will be sad to find out—maybe they won't tell them, either. I wish I could talk to Simmy …. July 12, 1864

She put down her pencil. *Where is Simmy?*

Sneaking out of her room barefooted, Geneva tiptoed down the stairs and out the back door, keeping an eye out for Vivvy.

She stood at the door of the cabin and whispered, "Simmy?" There was no answer. Slowly, she opened the door. "Simmy? Are you in here?"

The young girl looked up, her eyes wet and swollen. Balled up in the corner of her small bed, she clutched Prudy. Geneva closed the door and stood awkwardly, not knowing what to say or do. Dust floated on sunlight pouring in through the window. The light shimmered and settled on wet lines running down Simmy's cheeks as if God himself were trying to comfort her. Geneva bit her lip and shifted from one foot to the other.

"He's dead," Simmy said, and she began to whimper.

Geneva crossed the small room. She curled up with Simmy, and together they cried.

Alone in the orchard, Zeph lay on his back, beside himself with grief. His clothes were crusted with dirt and mud from the grave he, Hayes, and the Judge had dug—and filled after laying Lightner to rest. Even though Bertram and Hayes had planned to do the job themselves, Zeph had insisting on helping.

He picked up a shriveled apple and threw it as hard as he could, trying to keep from crying. It smacked against the bark of a tree and exploded. He ran his fingers through the grass and jerked handfuls of it out of the dirt. Above him clouds drifted. He thought about heaven and about the reunion taking place there. Despite his sadness, that one thought made him smile—his gentle and kind mama looking up to see his daddy coming, seeing them embrace. Maybe heaven was the only hope that was sure.

He focused on the mountains, wondering as he so often did what was beyond them. He had gone there in books, never even dreaming he would travel there—although there had always been some small spark of hope. But it was gone now, that hope—never spoken aloud and never realized—gone forever.

His late father's words echoed in his head: *Some things you got to do for yourself, son. I be doing you no kindness if I do for you what you oughta be doing yourself.*

He stayed there alone and away, until the moon rose in the sky like the rounded edge of a tombstone. Without a word, he stood up. Zephyr Elias stepped into his father's role, as best a fourteen-year-old boy could.

1928

CHAPTER 8

1928

Loss & Librarians

John Klare rummaged through his office, looking for the letters from Miss Snow. He pulled open every drawer and searched every nook and cranny, but the letters were not to be found. All he could find were a few crude sketches he had drawn after his visit to Cairnaerie.

His first semester at Haverston had ended. Christmas had come and gone, yet he had received no more correspondence from Miss Snow. He re-checked the pockets of his overcoat hanging limp on a spindly coat rack behind his door, and he scoured his desk drawers a second time. He looked under his blotter. Nothing.

His visit to Cairnaerie—and especially the request for secrecy— had left him with nagging questions. After he made a few careful and surreptitious inquiries in Hyssop, he had even more. No one, it seemed, had ever heard of a local family named Snow. It was as if they had never existed. *Maybe I dreamed the whole thing,* he thought cynically.

Moving aside a pile of books stacked on the floor, he got down on his hands and knees to look underneath his desk. He pulled out the drawers again, all the way out of the desk, to see if his letters had slipped down behind them. Nothing. He smacked the side of the desk—he hated losing things.

Leaning up against one wall was his framed diploma, exactly where he had put it when he arrived the prior summer. Propped up in front of it was a folder of clippings about Lucky Lindy and a book on Admiral Peary. He picked up the folder and rifled through it. Nothing. Blowing out his frustration, he gave up. He had other things to do.

He sat down to finish his new lecture notes. This term he was teaching World Expansion, which gave him a chance to discuss the great explorers: Vasco da Gama and Drake and Magellan. He enjoyed it, but he wasn't sure about his students. His small office was sparsely furnished with a desk, two straight chairs, one barrister bookcase missing the lowest two glass doors, and the rickety coat tree. Across his desk, books, papers, pencils, and a large Art Deco inkwell—a graduation gift from his sister—were assembled seriatim. He filled his fountain pen, and then he picked up his papers and squared them. Behind him, the radiator clicked and hissed like a one-man band.

He loosened his collar and flipped open the textbook. *If this were any drier, it could be used as talcum powder.* He had made the remark earlier to another professor who was—unbeknownst to John—the book's co-author. John was learning to be more circumspect about his opinions, a lesson he should have already learned. He shut the book and stretched his neck.

John loved history, but teaching it had turned out to be a different animal altogether. During graduate school at the university, teaching had seemed glamorous—the kind of career he would enjoy. Rufus Smalley, his former professor, had made it look appealing. Reality, however, was proving different. He had quickly realized he preferred research. Even better, he would love to explore real history. Maybe in Europe. Maybe the Orient. Maybe later. For now, his job at Haverston was his focus, his fresh start.

He finished scribbling one page of notes, but he wasn't in the mood to write a lecture. He gave up. Leaning back, he stared out into an anvil sky. A gray gloom hung over the mountains. His job, coupled with the visit to Cairnaerie and the lost letters made him irritable. *Why can't things just go smoothly?*

Through his window, the white stone portico of the courthouse caught his eye. He jotted a note to himself on a scrap of paper: 'check court records.' And then he began to scribble on his blotter: a shutter, a large ornate door, a swing in need of paint, a sign hanging on an iron gate. Opening a drawer, he took out more paper as he recalled more details: the carved lintels, the high ceilings, the crown molding in the parlor, and the striking floor with the center star. *Was the house really this magnificent? I may never know,* he mused ruefully.

At the far end of the hall, a telephone jangled. Moments later, a young secretary appeared at his door. "Professor Klare, you have a telephone call." She batted her eyes and smiled, gestures he didn't catch.

"I'll be right there," he said. Quickly, he added to his note— 'architecture books'—and speared the note onto a small statue of Mercury standing on the top of his inkwell. He hurried down the corridor lined with oak-framed doorways, narrow benches, and portraits of stern-looking former faculty members. Taking the telephone from the secretary, he pressed the receiver to his ear. She smiled sweetly at him. He did a quarter turn.

"John Klare," he said.

"Helen Van Soren here."

"Pardon?" he said, the name not registering.

"Helen Van Soren—from the library."

"Oh, the library." He still couldn't place the name. "Yes. May I help you?"

"I'd like to help you. I've found something I think you'll want to see."

"And this is about?" he said, wondering if she were selling something.

"I'd rather show you than tell you. Will you be coming by here anytime?"

He glanced at the wall clock about to strike four.

"How about now?" he said, happy for an excuse to get out of his office.

"Fine. I'll watch for you. I'll be at the front desk."

John set the receiver in its cradle and walked back to his office. He stuffed a pile of notes into a double-strapped leather briefcase he had picked up at an auction for practically nothing, and he grabbed his coat, leaving his homburg swinging, as he often did. Hats were a nuisance to him and only benefited the local haberdasher. As an afterthought, he picked up his sketches of Cairnaerie, stuffed them in a folder, and tucked it under his arm. He snagged the note off the inkwell and hurried out of McKuin Hall.

His shoes clicked down the stone steps. Wind rattled the bare limbs of trees along Fisher Street. The clouds had lifted, and the brightened sky was the same blustery one that he remembered from Cairnaerie. It improved his disposition considerably—as did being out of his stuffy office. But he couldn't stop wondering about Miss Snow. It was like an itch.

Deep in thought, he headed down the sidewalk toward the library. *She said she'd invite me again. But she hasn't. Why?* His steps slowed. *Didn't she like me? Trust me? Was I too forward? Does she know about St. Ballard?* He stopped. *What if she's dead?* This thought caught him off guard at the same moment a wind gust grabbed his folder.

Before he could react, his sketches flew off into the breeze like a flock of startled birds. He watched them zip through the tree branches and sail off into the winter sky. Disheartened all over again, all he could do was shake his head.

John pulled open the library's door and approached the front desk. The library was an old cottage with an addition that had been pressed into service ever since the college first opened its doors. The lobby, such as it was, had polished floors, a large counter, and that aroma peculiar to books. It echoed with a kind of bustling silence. A dour-looking woman, peering over a pair of heavy spectacles, scrutinized John.

"Miss Van Soren?" he inquired of her.

"That's me," answered a much prettier librarian sitting behind her. "Professor Klare?"

"Yes."

"You're fast. I didn't expect you quite so soon," she whispered. Standing up, she gestured for him to follow her. "This way."

For a moment, John forgot all about Miss Snow as he walked down a short hallway behind the willowy librarian who wore a smart brown skirt, a wide-collared blouse and a long, belted sweater bouncing behind her like a puppy.

She led him into a workroom lined with shelves and cabinets. Opening a drawer, she took out two letters and handed them to him. "These belong to you, I believe."

"Where did you find these?" he said, delighted to have Miss Snow's letters again.

"Under a stack in the 900s. I noticed them the other day when I was re-shelving." She stuffed a curl behind her ear, an uncoopera-tive lock in a head full of brown waves that were forced into a stylish Clara Bow bob.

"I've searched everywhere for these," he said. "They must have dropped out of my coat when I was here." He slipped them into his pocket.

Crossing her arms, she leaned against a cabinet. "Who is Geneva Snow?" It never occurred to Helen not to ask—a boldness that had gotten her in hot water more than once.

"You read them?" he asked, a bit surprised.

"I had to know whom to return them to," she said, sounding a bit miffed. She had expected at least a modicum of gratitude. "I don't customarily read other people's mail."

"I'm sure you don't. I'm sorry. Of course—you had to look. I'm glad you did. Thank you for finding these. For calling me."

That's better, she thought. "So, who is she?"

The question hung in the air. John, on the spot, was a bit flummoxed.

"That's a great question," he said evasively.

"Well?"

It was clear she wasn't going to let this go.

"Honestly, I'm not completely sure."

"Honesty is a good start." She was teasing him now.

"Well, the truth is I really don't know anything about her." He tried to change the subject. "How long have you worked here?"

"Long enough to know when a professor is being evasive." She turned around and opened a drawer. "Why don't you sit down? I have more to show you. Would you move those books?"

John stacked up several books and pushed them aside.

As he sat down, she handed him a long leather tube, four inches in diameter. "Open it. You'll like this. I promise."

Eyeing her suspiciously, he slid the cylinders apart.

"When I found your letter and saw the name—Cairnaerie—it rang a bell. I racked my brain until I remembered coming across these several months ago."

John unrolled a bundle of yellowed papers. Written in florid script along the top was 'Cairnaerie,' and below it was a bold signature: Bertram Snow, Esq. John was speechless. He pushed back his chair to stand and reached over the table to help Helen slide books onto the four corners to hold down the curling edges.

"Was I right?" she asked.

"Where did you find these?"

"In a box in the attic. They'd been there a while—judging by the dust."

"But house plans? In the library?"

"You'd be amazed what you find tucked away here. Scrapbooks. Newspapers. Ledgers. People must think libraries are depositories—like museums. I even found a box of shoes."

"Shoes? You're kidding?" he said.

"Not a bit. A pair of satin shoes. Pink. I've also found petrified mice, wigs, uniforms, scores of pipes, and—I kid you not—a set of false teeth."

John shook his head.

"If you ask me," she said, "the college needs to clean it all out or build a new library."

John ran his hand across the plans, trying to take in what seemed like an amazing coincidence—or a bit of good fortune. He thought about Shackleton.

"I went in right here," he said. "There's the foyer and the parlor."

"You've been there?"

"Only once."

"Where is it?"

Engrossed and suddenly transported back to Cairnaerie, John didn't answer right away as he pored over the plans. "I saw a winding staircase. Yep. Right here." He tapped his finger on the spot.

"Where is the house?" Helen asked again, and when he still did not answer, she put her hand down in the middle of the plans. "So where is it?"

John looked up. Helen, eyebrows raised, waited. "Where is it?"

Suddenly Miss Snow's words echoed: *You must tell no one.* John swallowed and quickly debated his choices. *Should I spill? Would I break my promise? She found these herself—but I lost the letters.* Weighing his integrity against her questions, he straightened up. *What do I have to lose?*

"Would you mind if we closed the door?" he asked.

"Sure." She pushed it shut with her foot.

"I'll tell you what I know—which, believe me, is not much—if you'll keep it between us."

"A secret?" she quipped. "I love secrets."

"No, I'm serious. I promised." He felt like a child apologizing for his conscience.

"Promised who?"

He pointed to the plans. "The woman who lives there. Miss Geneva Snow."

"So she lives there? All right. I'm game. But why all the secrecy?"

"I don't know. And that's the truth."

"I respect that," she said. "So you met her?"

Your persistence is impressive, John thought as he looked at her. "I guess you deserve an explanation." He pulled out a chair for Helen and then sat down next to her. "The first letter came out of the blue. She asked for help compiling some family history. I was curious, so I went. The second letter had the map. The house is west of here—up the mountain. But when I got there, she didn't tell me much at all—and then she asked me to keep our meeting secret." John took the letters out of his pocket and handed them back to Helen to read. "If you can figure out more, I'm listening."

Helen was intrigued. A longtime fan of mysteries, she sensed one here. She would have made a good detective had that been a choice at her small New England college, but teaching and library science were her only options.

John eyed the plans again. "Do you have some paper?"

"Sure." She pointed to a drawer. "Pencils are on the counter." He pulled out several sheets.

Helen laid the letters down and took the paper and pencil out of his hands. "You talk. I'll write."

While John examined the plans, Helen jotted notes, employing a skill she had honed as a secretary working her way through school.

"Front porch—supported by columns—surrounds two sides of house. One, two, three floors. And an enclosed belvedere. Main floor: dining room—bay windows off the back and one side of the house, two parlors, and the foyer." He turned his head and squinted to read some small script. "This note says walnut and ash. Makes sense—the floor is striped. And there's a star in the center of the floor. Looks like a study adjoins this front parlor. Second floor—I count eight bedrooms. There's a second staircase at the back of house and another small one on the third floor and into the attic."

"This is not your run-of-the-mill house," she said, writing fast to keep up. "I'm amazed no one knows about it. You're sure?"

"As far as I can tell."

"That's odd."

"Not really. It's not easy to find—well off the beaten path."

"And she lives there?"

"Yes—and apparently alone—at 72."

"How do you know her age?"

"She told me." He gestured toward the plans. "Can I take these with me?"

"Sure."

As he re-rolled the plans, the older librarian tapped on the door's glass panel and motioned for Helen.

John left the library with the plans—and his curiosity rekindled.

CHAPTER 9

1928

Swope Chapel

Joly Jennings fingered a gold locket around her neck as she rested against the heavy pitchfork she had pulled from the ground. A handful of bulbs were scattered at her feet. Her coarse, black hair, drawn back in a ball, was tied with a faded bandana, and a calico apron covered her clothes, a plain cotton dress and a worn sweater. Her grandfather, Zeph, sat on the porch, humming. The spring air was fresh, the way it smells after a good winter cleansing. Emerging violets and squirrel corn peppered the ground surrounding the modest homestead she kept with her grandfather. Their yard, a ragged piece of ground carved out around an old chapel, was hidden deep in the Soot Woods and surrounded by armies of black jack oaks and hickories, chestnuts, walnuts, and hundreds of pines. Deceptively close to Cairnaerie, the chapel's location was convenient for Zeph, who after decades still looked after his childhood friend, Geneva Snow.

Zeph spent many mornings pushing back leaves from the chicken coop so the hens could scratch. In early spring, he planted a garden in a nearby meadow. In summer, he would sit for hours shelling peas or snapping beans while Joly got jars cleaned and a fire going to put them up for cold weather. They stored their larder under the house where decades ago Zeph had loosened the floorboards and dug out a root cellar.

"Churches don't come with cellars," Zeph told Joly every time he lifted the floorboards. "If I was gonna live in a church, I had to go dig me a root cellar." He stored root vegetables, potatoes, apples, cured meats, and canned goods, all lined up on shelves built against dirt walls whitewashed with lime.

The chapel had made a fine home for Zeph and his family for a long time. More than a half-century of weather had robbed it of paint, but all the original windows drew heavenward like hands pressed palm to palm in prayer. As a young man with a strong back and hands the size of dinner plates, Zeph had built a kitchen onto the back of the sanctuary. He had furnished it with cast-off fixtures and a wood stove thrown out of a schoolhouse. In the mornings, especially in winter and spring before the thick growth of leaves came out, sun tumbled through the tall windows, erasing the color from the walls.

From pews, he had built two benches and a trestle table; one end of the table was pushed up under the window. Over the years, he had cut up more pews for shelves, cabinets, and beds, and he had scavenged whatever he could to make it a home. He had left one pew and the pulpit intact to serve as their own private church for times when weather kept them in, which it often did during the mountain winters. Zeph slept in an alcove off the west side of the long, narrow sanctuary, and Joly slept closer to the kitchen, as she had since she was an infant, in a second alcove on the east side. Heavy draperies, castoffs from Cairnaerie, enclosed each alcove for privacy and warmth.

"Your cradle—it rocked right here," Zeph reminded her every morning, as he had done for as long as she could remember. "Look at those grooves in the floor. Simmy rocked you till you fell asleep every night, right here near the stove where you'd be warm."

Joly missed Simmy, her great-aunt who had raised her with Zeph. She had never known her own mother. She had died in childbirth, and her father had disappeared shortly after. They had left before Joly's memories began to form. But Simmy was always there, always with her, so she felt her absence acutely—now that she was planning to marry. How she wished Simmy could be with her for the wedding. She had been gone for a handful of years, but it seemed a lifetime.

Standing in a column of filtered sunshine, listening to her grandfather humming, Joly's thoughts transported her back in time...

"You be careful," Simmy called to her. Joly waded into the creek, the shallow water, graceful as a waltz. "Some of them rocks is real slippery. You be careful, honey."

"I will, Simmy." Joly held her arms out for ballast and guided her thin brown legs through the water. Flickering sunlight warmed her face while the cool from the night forest lingered and the creek tossed dampness into the air.

Simmy sat watchfully on the bank with a bushel basket and an apron full of string beans. Just after dawn, she and Joly had walked to a meadow near the chapel and spent a good two hours picking beans. The six-year-old was her great-aunt's shadow, her constant companion.

"You want me to come help you?" Joly called.

"No, honey, you jes have you some fun. You done enough work for one morning. You can help me cut some fatback later, before we cook these up."

When Simmy snapped the last of the beans, she scattered the pile of tips and strings along the creek bed and shook out her apron. "Come on, Joly. Time to git back."

Joly made her way back across the creek, her bare feet shuffling through the water. "The water tickles, Simmy."

Her great-aunt smiled and picked up the bushel basket, balancing it on her hip, as she grabbed Joly's hand at the water's edge and pulled her up.

"Look," said Joly, pointing toward a patch of white, star-shaped flowers. "They're like Miss Geneva's star."

"Starflowers."

"Can I pick some?"

"Sure can. Jes don't take 'em all. You gotta leave some for the animal folk to enjoy."

Joly knelt and gathered a handful of flowers. "Can I take these to her?"

"'Course ya can. We'll put 'em in water soon as we get back. We'll go up and see her this afternoon." Simmy brushed dirt from the child's hem.

"Simmy?"

"Yes, honey?"

"Does Miss Geneva get lonesome?"

"Don't think so. Why you thinking about that? She's got us, don't she?"

Joly paused thoughtfully, touching the flower pedals. "We're her good Samarians?"

Simmy smiled. "You mean good Samaritans."

"Yes. That."

"Joly! Joly!" her grandfather hollered, interrupting her reverie. She jumped, and he laughed at her. "Quit your daydreaming."

"You got me, Grandpa." She propped her pitchfork up against the split-rail fence running along the flowerbed and bent down to collect bulbs.

The path, leading through the woods from the chapel to Cairnaerie, was part of the secret Simmy, Zeph, and Joly had kept always. When she was a child, the path, and Cairnaerie, and the friendship of Miss Geneva had been a private jewel, a gift Simmy and her grandfather had bestowed on her. Joly could not remember the first time she had walked the path with Simmy. Her earliest memories were shadowy, but so sweet they burrowed into her heart—into a place where secrets nestle down for safekeeping. Simmy had always told her that if you keep a secret, you own it, but if you tell it, it's lost. Forever. *You cain't ever get it back again,* Simmy would say, *jes like a broken egg or a soap bubble.* As Joly grew up, the secret became a favor to honor the wishes of their reclusive friend.

She rubbed the dirt off a bulb and shook her head. "We won't have irises next spring," she said, renewing the perpetual argument she had with her grandfather.

"Oh, they'll be fine," he said. "You gotta get the bulbs out of the ground 'fore they rot or some varmint up and eats 'em. Moles like 'em—better'n I like your biscuits. And you know how much I like your biscuits." He grinned.

"I still think we're months too early, Grandpa. Simmy used to wait till fall."

Her grandfather was a clever man who could grow any kind of vegetable, but flowers had been Simmy's talent.

"They're up early this year—had plenty of time to feed," he said.

Joly pushed her sweater halfway up her forearms. "I guess we'll find out next spring, won't we?" Gathering the corners of her apron together, she filled it with bulbs and carried them over to the porch. "Here's more, Grandpa."

"Put 'em in here," he said, tapping a straw basket perched beside him. Zeph scrutinized each bulb, pulling them close to his Cheshire face and clear black eyes that twinkled between grinning crow's feet. "I can tell you what color these will be, girl."

"Oh, shush," Joly teased. "You cain't tell what color they'll be."

"I sure can. When we put 'em back in the ground next fall, we oughta mark 'em by color. Then you'll see."

Joly went about her chores, smiling, while Zeph sorted the bulbs.

"Purple. This one's purple."

"I don't know how you do that," Joly said as she bent down to pull a stand of chickweed out of the fence line. "I smell bulbs—and I jes smell dirt."

"You gotta learn how to smell color. Purple—it's a clear, smooth smell—like a cool breeze. And yellow, it's right strong. Yellow's easy to smell."

"All I ever smell around here is chicken dumps and mud."

"That's brown," he said, slapping his knee and laughing.

"Then I can smell brown jes as good as you."

Joly watched her grandfather. His wiry hair was powdered with gray patches. His large hands were those of a craftsman. How good he had always been to her. He had taken care of her—he and Simmy—and now it was her turn to look after him.

Her earliest memory was of frying eggs on the woodstove with Simmy—eggs they had gathered together. In her mind's eye, the skillet was at face level, and she had to hike up her shoulders to keep from burning her arms. When the three of them would sit down to eat, her grandfather would go on like it was the finest meal he had ever eaten. It was how he approached most things—looking for the best in people and in circumstances. It was how he had survived life's bitterest disappointments.

Joly went back to digging. The spring air was soft as a veil. Squirrels and birds chattered in the trees.

"Grandpa?" Joly said, sitting down next to him, dumping another handful of bulbs in the basket. "Do you think Miss Geneva will come?"

"You ask her yet?"

"Yessir."

"What'd she say?"

"Said she was thinking about it."

He rubbed a bulb with his thumb and seemed to ponder. "Well, you jes let her think. You've done all you can by asking." He brushed off his palms and put a hand on his granddaughter's shoulder. "But honey, don't you get your hopes up too high. It's been a long time. An awful long time."

CHAPTER 10

1928

———————◆———————

Puzzles & Hunches

Sitting in a spindly chair that squeaked every time he moved, John balanced a ledger on his knee as he made notes. The ledger's spine was broken, and its pages were singed. He brushed dust and flakes of paper off his pants leg.

"It's all I could find this morning," the clerk had told him, as he handed him two deed books, a ledger, and one box of records. "Fires got most everything else."

"Fires?"

"Yessir. Yankees set fire to everything they could find in '64. And what they couldn't burn, they stole. Course, I don't remember it, but my granddaddy does. He watched 'em burn his barn to the ground. Burned everything they could get their hands on. Didn't matter if it was important or not. Didn't matter who owned it."

John closed the ledger and set it on the floor. He brushed off his pants again and blew dust off the box at his feet before he opened it. Inside he found a mishmash of death certificates, contracts, and receipts.

Emboldened by the return of the letters and the discovery of Cairnaerie's plans, he had been sure there would be something else to discover. He had spent most of the morning searching, but in spite of his earnestness, nothing he found mentioned Cairnaerie or the Snows. No deeds. No bills of sale. No licenses. The best he had come across were a few ledger entries from a local business for farm supplies purchased by a 'B. Snow.' It was becoming clear that whatever evidence once existed was long gone.

He checked the clock at the end of the hall—fifteen minutes until his next class. It would take him seven minutes to get from the courthouse to McKuin Hall. He closed the book to return the materials to the clerk.

"Thanks," he said as he lifted the stack across the counter.

"Yes, sir. You come on by anytime. I'm glad to get out anything for you. Wish I had more to show you. You lookin' for anything specific?"

John was tempted to explain more about his search. The man was local. Maybe he knew something about the Snows. But he decided against it, for the time being at least. He had already told one person. That was enough for now.

As he hurried out of the courthouse, the wind picked up and the sky was clouding over. He heard a rumble of thunder. John never carried an umbrella. Like hats, they were more trouble than they were worth—and Shackleton wouldn't have carried one.

Passing McClanahan's Diner, he smelled brisket and remembered he had not eaten lunch. He would eat later. He didn't want to be late for his class. Dean Rollins frowned on tardiness.

Walking at a fast clip, he pondered one more clue he could follow. He pulled out the letters and examined the name in the return address. *Zeph Elias.* He wished he had thought to ask Miss Snow.

A thunderclap and a sudden downpour sent him running down the street, stuffing the letters back into his pocket and hugging his briefcase to move faster. He leapt up the steps of McKuin Hall, three at a time, and charged through the front door where he ran right into Dean Albert Rollins, who was opening his umbrella. The umbrella and several books went flying. The dean staggered and caught himself on a railing. John slipped on the wet floor and fell flat. Scrambling to his knees, he picked up the books and umbrella, and stood up, apologizing profusely. "I'm so sorry, Dr. Rollins."

The dean eyed John, who stood dripping like a dunked cat. "You're in quite a hurry, Mr. Klare." He gathered himself and adjusted his rumpled coat.

"I am so sorry. The rain, you see. My class. I didn't want to be late."

"Then you need to plan better."

"Yes, sir," he said, trying not to grovel, but failing. "I do, sir. Yes, sir. You're right, I do—I will. I am so sorry." Sheepish and rattled, John handed him the books and his umbrella.

"Shouldn't you go? Your class?"

"Oh. Yes. Yes, sir."

Soaked through to his underclothes, John turned and hurried down the hall. He tossed his waterlogged coat across the back of an empty chair and took his place behind the lectern in front of a roomful of snickering young men—all in dark coats, white shirts, and neckties. He ran his fingers through his wet hair, smoothing it, and tried to sound dignified. "Good afternoon, Gentlemen...."

—————

Sun streamed through the large front windows of McClanahan's as a whirring ceiling fan clicked overhead. Above the sound of clinking tableware, diners conversed in booths and around small tables. Except for a lunch counter at the local drug store, McClanahan's was the best place to eat in town. It had opened the year before, along with a new school and several businesses. Times were good in Hyssop. Plus, the college had increased its enrollment by nearly fifty, bringing a surge of new people to the community.

"I played a hunch." Helen, who had suggested John meet her for lunch at noon, leaned forward. Her green eyes crinkled with excitement.

"A hunch?" he asked.

"Yes." She set down her grilled cheese sandwich and wiped her mouth. "Think about this: If Cairnaerie is as grand as you say it is, then the money to build it couldn't have come from the valley. No one here was that wealthy. It would have come from somewhere else."

"Good point," he said, impressed with her reasoning.

"You said Miss Snow is seventy-two, right?"

"Yes."

"So—if she's lived there all her life, then it had to have been built before 1856." She pushed her plate aside and took a letter from her purse. Smiling, she slid it across the table.

"What's this?" he asked.

"I did a little sleuthing."

"You're a regular Sherlock Holmes."

"I am, aren't I?"

"No wonder everyone asks for your help in the library."

"Someday, I'm going to run it—or maybe the Library of Congress."

"The Library of Congress?" He laughed.

"Why not?" she said, but she blushed. "Don't laugh. I could do it."

"I bet you could," he said, smiling as he opened the letter.

"I called a friend in Richmond to see if any records there listed the name Snow."

"And?"

"Apparently, a Bertram Snow bought four hundred acres in 1843 when land was first offered here. He bought more later—fifteen hundred acres in all. It's in a trust set up decades ago. But..."

"...The trail runs cold?"

"Yes. Unfortunately, it's sealed. The trustee is a man named Anderson Goodwin."

"And let me guess," John posited. "Nobody knows who he is."

"That's right. And apparently, he's not local. I checked. And I'm afraid he's not listed with the state's attorneys, which means finding him is going to be next to impossible. My friend suggested talking to the local bank."

"Good idea," John said. "I'll do that."

The waitress refilled their coffees and asked if they wanted anything else. "Pie? Cake?" she asked cheerily, smiling particularly at John.

"No, thank you," he said without looking up. "Just the check."

As John fished in his pocket for his wallet, out of the corner of his eye, he saw a girl crossing the street with an older man. He had a curious sensation and wondered where he had seen her before.

"What are you looking at?" Helen asked.

He gestured toward the street. "Do you know them—the man with the girl?'"

"The colored ones?" Helen asked, and she craned her neck to look down the street. "Passing by the newspaper office?"

"Yes."

"No. I've never seen them before."

"She looks familiar. But I can't place her."

"Maybe you've just seen her around. It happens. Happens to me all the time."

John shrugged it off as he paid the check and tucked his wallet back into his vest pocket. "You're probably right."

Late that night, though, he did remember: The girl on the street was the same one whose picture he had seen on Miss Snow's table. He was sure of it—but for the life of him, he could not remember her name.

CHAPTER 11

1928

Penance & Rivers

John smiled broadly as he slipped through the library's front doors. He caught Helen's eye. "Can you take a walk?" he asked quietly.

She gestured that she would ask. Helen approached the head librarian and whispered to her. The older woman looked over her spectacles at John, and he made a point to smile, a gesture she did not return.

"Let me get my coat," Helen mimed. It had been a long morning, and she was ready for a break. She grabbed the sandwich she had packed for her lunch.

As they headed down the library stairs, John reached into his vest pocket and handed her a letter.

"What's this?"

"Came yesterday. Read it."

"Ah! From our mysterious Miss Snow?"

"Yes, it is," he said with a hint of victory.

"No wonder you're so cheerful."

"I was beginning to think I'd never hear from her again."

They followed a boardwalk toward the back of campus. The air was still cool for spring, but the sun was warm. John welcomed winter's end. Even with his Midwestern upbringing, he was averse to cold weather.

"Another invitation?" she said, slipping the letter from the envelope. A long strand of beads swung and clinked against the buttons of her coat.

"Yep."

"Are you going?"

"Of course I am," he said, looking mischievous.

Helen eyed him suspiciously.

He motioned toward the letter. "Go ahead. Read it—Read it out loud."

> *Dear Professor Klare,*
>
> *Please forgive my tardiness in extending you an invitation, but I have had numerous matters to attend. I would like to have you join me for tea on the afternoon of April 1, around two o'clock. I hope that is convenient for you. I look forward to continuing our conversation. Please bring your wife, as I would love to meet her.....*

"Your wife?" Helen said, looking bewildered.

John laughed.

Helen did not. Her face reddened. "John Klare, you're a cad." She stuffed the letter in the envelope and shoved it back into his hands. "What gave her that idea? Or are you married—and forgot to tell me?"

"No, I'm not. I promise. She must have misunderstood when I mentioned Kate—my sister."

"Really?" she answered curtly, quickening her pace.

John realized his little joke might have been unkind. "Helen, I didn't mean to embarrass you."

"You didn't embarrass me," she said. "You surprised me, that's all. And I don't like surprises. Secrets, yes. Surprises, no." She gathered herself—and not to be outdone—stopped, and with a sly smile placed a finger on the center of his chest. "You'll have to make it up to me."

"Agreed. How?"

"Take me with you."

As if to let the little tiff fade away, they walked in silence up the limestone stairs behind McKuin Hall, stopping at a terrace on the highest point on the campus. From this vantage, the view overlooking the river was splendid.

John stood, eyeing the vista. His mood grew serious. Helen took a seat on a stone bench and picked some lint off her skirt as she waited for him to speak—something she was becoming accustomed to.

"What do you know about erosion?" he asked.

"Erosion?" Helen said, amused at the odd question. "That's quite a conversation starter. First you pretend you have a wife—and now you think I'm a geologist."

"No, seriously. Erosion." Looking at the river hundreds of feet below, John remained pensive and stuffed his hands in his pockets, staring as if transfixed.

"Librarians don't know everything," she said, watching him from behind. "What are you looking at?"

"Come here." He motioned to her. "Look." He pointed to a wide stretch of the river where it spread out into the valley. "Do you see a bend? Anywhere?"

"No."

"There isn't one," he said, and then he pulled out the letters and unfolded the map. "Look at this. She drew a distinct bend in the river. Right here. See it?"

"Maybe she just can't draw."

"I don't think so. This is too deliberate. But I think I know why." He thumped the map.

"Let me guess. Erosion?"

"Aha!" John whispered.

Helen, sitting across from him at a small table in the library's reference room, pushed aside a stack of books and leaned forward. "Aha, what?"

"I was right. Listen to this," and he read: "During September of 1896, the western half of Vassel County sustained more than a week of hard rain. The deluge followed an unusually wet summer that left the ground saturated. Worst hit was the area west, which caused a break in the Sawmill dam. The Cleary River rose more than twenty feet above flood stage and engulfed the area called Finley's Bottom. The flood caused a permanent change in the river's path."

John closed the book and angled it for her to read the spine: 'The History of Vassel County.'

"She thinks Finley's Bottom is still there?" Helen said.

"She must."

"But that was more than thirty years ago."

CHAPTER 12

1928

Journals & Clocks

Sitting near the bank of long windows in her library, a spot with the best light for reading, Geneva slipped off her pince-nez and rubbed her eyes. She closed her book and laid it aside. Assorted others were strewn on the table next to her; each one had a different shape, color, or covering. Several had wooden covers laced together with strips of leather, but most were tied in small signatures and bound with cloth in various prints and fabrics. She picked up one covered in faded yellow chintz and thumbed through it. The boxy, printed words were from her own childish hand. She came across a cornflower, pressed flat, and a Queen Anne's lace, still holding its seeds. "All these years. The promise of life," she whispered. Lifting it gently, she twirled the dried flower between her knotted fingers, watching it unleash its tiny black seeds, which fell back down into the fold of her journal. She remembered pilfering it from a bucket of flowers her mother had cut for the dining room table.

She leafed through the rest of the yellow journal, finding rose petals that had long lost their scent, a four-leaf clover Lightner had given her once, and a tiny tatted piquet she had made when Clarissa had tried patiently to teach her to tat. But she had never mastered this art of making lace, even using Clarissa's ivory shuttle. The truth was she had never had much interest in learning it, even from her beloved Clarissa.

She touched each item and turned each page tenderly as she read her own words written so long ago.

Daddy brought us candy from Bristol. I like the cherry, but Daddy and Hayes like the horehound. I think horehound is nasty. I will save some for Simmy. Simmy loves cherry, too.... February 27, 1861.

I got caught playing dolls with Simmy in her house. Mama took Baby Bea away from me and told me I could not have her back until I learned to behave. I know Vivvy told on us because she saw us when she emptied the slop. Vivvy's as mean as Satan. Mama gave me a switching and told me to never go in there again. But Daddy said Simmy could come to my room and play. I want Baby Bea back. She'll be lonely without me.... May 30, 1863

Simmy is my best friend. I do not care what Mama says about being proper. I want to give her my silver hair combs, but if Mama found out, she would be mad. Maybe I'll give her one of my dolls. She can have any of them—except Baby Bea.... August 23, 1863

Yankees burned down the town today. Daddy wouldn't let me go out. We can't even go to church because we must hide from the Yankees. I hate Yankees.... September 30, 1864

Today is Simmy's birthday. I gave her my locket, but she would not take it. I told her it was still hers. I will keep it for her.... April 3, 1866

I am eleven today. Daddy says I am old enough to learn to read. How silly he is, since I've been reading and writing since I was five. Simmy is the one who needs to learn to read. Zeph told her girls are stupid and cannot read, but I think he is the stupid one. All boys are stupid—except Hayes and Daddy.... April 17, 1866

Reading through her journals, Geneva relived her life as she had done so many times over the years. Occasionally, she dabbed her eyes with a handkerchief she kept tucked in her sleeve.

The room was still except for the faithful ticking of the long-case clock. It had been a favorite of her father's—an extravagant purchase he made shortly after his marriage to Caroline Hampton. It was tall and majestic with a changing face featuring a sun or moon. Although the clock's walnut casing was plain and lacked the elaborate carvings of other furnishings in the house, it was a beautiful piece. As a child, the tall clock had fascinated her. Every Sunday morning, she watched her father turn the key in each of the three winding points to make the heavy bronzed pinecone-shaped weights rise. Now it was Geneva who wound it every Sabbath with the key she kept in his desk drawer—the same place her father had kept it. Only once did she recall not hearing the clock's ticking, but at that moment, everything—even time—had seemed to stop.

Carefully Geneva closed the book and placed it on the table. She sank back in the chair to rest her eyes. How long ago her childhood was, but her own words still ferried her back in time, stirring up the same feelings, the same frustrations, the same arches of pain and joy.

The sun, like an incoming tide, crept across the wide plank floors from the south window until the full width of the room was flooded with light. Next to the belvedere, which she frequented less and less lately, the spacious library was Geneva's favorite room. Thousands of volumes filled its shelves as did bundles of periodicals bound together with string. She had read every one of them and some, multiple times. Pushed to the back of the room, the librarian's ladder, anchored to a high metal gutter, stood idle. She remembered when her father had had it installed, just before the arrival of the first shipment of books from Mr. Fendell, the bookseller. She smiled, seeing herself scampering up the ladder when her mother wasn't looking to run her hands along the gilded letters on her father's most valued books. She no longer climbed the ladder. She had promised Zeph she would not. Now Joly scaled it in her stead when the need arose.

Lying on the table next to Geneva, two journals were set apart from the rest. The smaller of the two, bound with faded red silk and tied with a red satin ribbon, was dog-eared and worn. The larger one was new and freshly covered in a bright pink calico.

Geneva heard footsteps outside the library and a small tap on the window pane. She looked up to see Joly motion that she was coming in through the kitchen.

"Sweet Joly." She hugged the girl. "It's so good to see you. Can you stay for a spell?"

"Long as I get back to get Grandpa's supper on."

"How is he?" said Geneva, taking the girl's hand and leading her into the parlor.

"Ornery as ever. Stays too busy. You'd think nobody in Hyssop could do anything for themselves. He's working up at the college some. They got him building shelves and painting. Jes about anything."

"How are his eyes?"

"About the same. He's not seeing too much worse."

"Has he seen a doctor?"

"Yessum, but he says he can't do much unless Grandpa will wear spectacles—and he won't. He does all right, though. Not much keeps him down."

"He's always been like that. Now come and sit down with me." Geneva took Joly's hand and led her to the settee near the hearth. The two sat next to each other like schoolgirls. "Tell me now, how is your Mr. Oden?"

Joly beamed. "Oh, Thatcher's wonderful—this much taller than Grandpa and strong. He can split a cord of wood faster'an I can peel a peach. And he's a fine carpenter, too."

"Just like your grandfather."

"Someday he says he's gonna build us a place up near Sherd's Knob. It's gonna look out over the mountains. Says it'll be right on the crest of the hill, so when the sun's shining, it'll come in every window. And the wind—it blows all the time up there—so I told him: 'Thatcher Oden, you ought to call it Windy Hill.' But he says he wants something poetic."

"How is the wedding coming?"

"Miss Gladiolus is helping. I've told you about her—she's a character—but always willing to help anybody. She's fixing up wildflowers for me. Nicodemus is such a pretty church." Joly's face, as firm and smooth as a buckeye, glowed with excitement. Geneva recognized true love, and her own heart stirred.

"I'm still hoping you'll come, Miss Geneva."

"I'm thinking, dear. I'm thinking," she said. "We will see."

Joly was silent for a moment. "It's gonna be hard without Simmy. I miss her."

"I know. I miss her, too."

Listening to the girl, Geneva imagined it could be Simmy sitting with her. Everything about Joly was graceful like her great-aunt, long fingers, long face, long legs. She had Simmy's gestures and the same lilt and quake in her voice. But Joly held her head slightly downward, a concession to shyness.

"Oh, I almost forgot," Joly said. "I brought you some iris bulbs. I'll go get 'em. I put 'em out on the steps. We can plant some in Simmy's garden come fall if you want to. I don't know if they'll do much since we dug 'em up so early—you know how Grandpa does—soon as the flower fades, he's wanting to dig. But we can see."

"Would you mind spreading them out in the shed for me? The first one, before you get to the smokehouse. It's plenty dark and cool in there. I've got some newspapers stacked inside the door."

"Be glad to," she said, and she hopped up. "I'll be right back."

The memory of Simmy's gardens sparkled in Geneva's mind like a full-color dream—the yellow and purple irises, the golden jonquils, the lavender hydrangea, the cascading peonies that only lasted until it rained. She and Simmy had played there, often dodging cantankerous Vivvy or Geneva's mother. Geneva wanted to close her eyes and merge time. How excited Simmy would have been at the wedding. How she would have delighted in all the preparations.

While Geneva found Joly's excitement contagious, her request was unsettling. Could she find a way? Could she leave Cairnaerie after such a long time?

Joly came back into the room, brushing off her hands. "I put 'em on that first shelf, right by the door. I'll turn 'em when I come next time."

"Thank you. Now I have something for you," she said. She picked up the pink calico book from the table, the new one. She handed it to Joly, folding the girl's hands around it. "This is a place to pour out your deepest feelings. If you do, you'll always remember how happy you are today. It is so good to remember your happiest days."

"Thank you," said Joly, tearing up. "I will—and I am happy."

Geneva touched a locket at the girl's throat. "This is so lovely."

"It was Simmy's."

"I know. I remember it. It was a birthday gift."

Geneva put her hand to her own throat over the necklace she always wore: a gold chain holding a single gold band. *Someday,* she thought. *Someday I must tell her.*

CHAPTER 13

1928

Ships & Cups

Absentmindedly, John twirled a pencil back and forth through his fingers—a trick his grandfather had taught him—as he read through a stack of student essays. He yawned, partly in response to the text and partly because his office was insufferably hot. He had tried to turn off the valve on the radiator, but it was frozen. Even though he had made repeated requests, no one from maintenance had fixed it.

The spring term was half over, but already he eagerly anticipated its end, a time when he would be free of academic protocols and unmotivated students. What he would give for the means to travel to France or Hungary or Scotland—or even sail to Antarctica like Shackleton. But these days, he didn't even bother to dream about it. After the fiasco at St. Ballard, he was thankful to have a job. He strongly suspected he was employed because of the intervention of Rufus Smalley, who had helped him patch up the pieces of his career and move on. If nothing else, he owed it to Smalley to do well. The mystery of Miss Snow would have to wait, he supposed, for the time being at least. He had work to do.

Dean Rollins ran a tight ship. An imposing figure—tall, rotund and hairless—he ruled with well-cultivated intimidation. Shortly after John's arrival at the college, an English professor and the bursar's secretary had been dismissed in a flurry of hushed conferences and secreted memorandums. Long after their departure, rumors of indiscretion lingered like the smell of cigars. Thereafter, the faculty—John included—was dutifully circumspect.

On his first visit, he had found Rollins aloof—the very antithesis of Rufus Smalley. A mousy secretary had ushered him into an expansive fan-shaped office lined with mahogany wainscoting. The room's walls angled toward a bank of eight curving casement windows set with heavy beveled glass. The positioning of the windows made the room appear to bulge outward. A mammoth desk straddled the midpoint so when Rollins arrived after some twenty minutes, he was backlighted, becoming an imposing bared-domed silhouette with a stentorian voice.

John had answered his few impassive questions as best he could and left the interview convinced he had wasted his time. Surely his past troubles had doomed him. But a week later, an offer had arrived in the mail. He accepted it promptly. With a two-hundred-dollar loan from his father, he bought a second-hand, slightly dented touring car—a 1926 green Nash Ajax with a winged radiator cap—and headed east.

He marked the last essay, tossed his pencil down, and checked his watch. Rain mixed with sleet pecked on the window. After a few weeks of spring-like weather, a cold snap was a disappointment. So was the newest letter from Miss Snow. He picked it up and stuffed it into his pocket. Inexplicably, she had cancelled his second visit. It was all beginning to feel like a good old-fashioned mystery, and it annoyed him.

"Better get moving," he said out loud, pushing away from his desk. He didn't want to keep Helen waiting. He grabbed his coat from the wobbly coat tree that was beginning to list badly. He turned it into the wall to keep it from falling over.

McClanahan's was nearly deserted, and a dull sun sneered through leftover rain clouds. John, lost in thought, stared out the window. The newest letter lay on the table between him and Helen.

She stifled a yawn and wrapped her hands around her coffee cup. Her thick green Bakelite bracelet clanked on the table. She slipped it off and set it down. Sipping her coffee, she watched John. With his dark hair and lean build, he reminded her of Abraham Lincoln or Edgar Allan Poe. *Poe, too morose*, she thought. One corner of her mouth rose slightly. *Lincoln. Noble. Definitely Lincoln.*

Until her discovery of Cairnaerie's plans, she had not met any men who interested her since she had left home to study library science at a small women's college in upstate New York. John was different—but that was neither here nor there, because Helen had plans. Already she had established herself as a valuable member of the library's staff. Faculty sought her out. To herself, she wondered how long it would take the board to appoint a woman as head librarian. When they did, she wanted to be that person. It would be a good steppingstone to the Library of Congress.

Helen set down her cup. "What's bothering you?" she said. "I know you're disappointed, but you've hardly said a word."

"Oh, sorry. I didn't mean to be rude." He picked up the letter, bent down a corner, and retreated into his thoughts every bit as much as if he had gotten up and left the restaurant.

Helen smiled. *Yes. Pensive Mr. Lincoln.*

"I don't get it," he said after a few moments. "She lives by herself, says she doesn't go out—yet she knows things. How? She knows what's going on in the world. There's something here I'm not getting. She knew I'd been hired at Haverston. How did she know? It was hardly front page news."

"She must have contact with someone. A caretaker?" Helen speculated. "How else could she live alone?"

"Surely there's someone else—but then why doesn't anyone know about her or the house?"

"Maybe you haven't asked the right people."

"Could be."

Outside a car passed with a whoosh over the wet street. The waitress refilled their coffee cups. Helen ran her finger around the edge of her bracelet.

"Maybe she wants it that way, John. Did the letter say anything about meeting later?"

"No. She just cancelled. No reason." John reached in his pocket for a tip.

"What if you wrote to her?" Helen suggested, putting her bracelet back on and gathering up her purse. "You still have the address. Why don't you ask her if you can pay her a visit?"

John slid some coins underneath his plate and smiled at Helen without a word. *Why in the world didn't I think of that?*

1866 — 1868

CHAPTER 14

1866

Man & Child

The sun languished in the August sky as Zeph stood in the open door of the loft, heaving pitchforks full of hay down to Bertram and Hayes, who, in turn, threw it inside where two hands raked it throughout freshly swept stalls.

A breeze blowing all morning had died, and the hot air was as close as skin. Dust and chaff choked the air—and it was teeming with the aromas of manure and fodder. Throughout the barnyard and feedlot, flies buzzed and cicadas sizzled, adding heft to the rising temperature. Farm work was hard, especially on summer days when work stretched out like a hammock between the dawn and dusk.

Sweat steamed from Zeph's body as his hands and arms rhythmically shoveled and pitched. He exhaled as he stopped to break apart another shock. Barn swallows darted in and out of the rafters.

The war was finally over, but the struggle was not, especially for the farmers whose barns and houses had been burned and looted and whose livestock had been confiscated. The war had left behind a tattered society. Families worked hard to reconstruct their disrupted lives.

Even though the Snow family had been spared the property devastation many of their neighbors suffered, they had not been left unscathed. Grayson had died late in 1864, months before the war ended. The last letter to his mother found him struggling to overcome fever and diarrhea. The family—none more fervently than Caroline—had prayed for his full recovery, but before the month was out, notification came in a letter from a fellow soldier that Grayson had died of flux and was buried in a Confederate cemetery outside Petersburg.

The company he and Thomas had joined in Lynchburg split, and while Grayson's group had marched east, Thomas remained in the valley, joining the Stonewall Brigade—the exploits of the company reaching legendary proportions, which had bolstered the family's hope. Perhaps it was such hope which made the news so hard—news of a stray bullet exploding in the back of the head of Corporal Thomas Snow, killing him instantly. Three of his fellows, given leave, had loaded his broken body in a wagon and carried him to Cairnaerie, a homecoming that had crushed Caroline. She mourned for her sons and threw herself maniacally into her work, keeping busy and painting obsessively, steeling herself against the pain that would never leave her.

Standing in the yard below the loft where Zeph was working, Bertram took a handkerchief from his pocket and mopped his reddened face. Over the course of the war, his hair had turned snow white, and his shoulders had grown more stooped as if he carried a permanent burden. He yelled up to Zeph: "How much more hay's up there?"

"Half dozen shocks."

Bertram had built his barn into the side of a hill. It was supported below with walls of chiseled limestone blocks set by itinerant masons and above, by timbers covered with clapboards—all beneath a cantilevered roof for protection from hard winters. The loft on the top level made it easy to pull a wagon in; on the lower level, stables opened into a fenced barnyard.

"Let's see if we can finish this before noon," Bertram said as he shouldered a pitchfork.

"Yessir," Zeph answered.

Together, they pressed into the work.

Zeph's voice was deeper now, assured—no longer the voice of the child who had come to Bertram at the end of the war and pledged his loyalty to the Snows. At sixteen, he was broad-shouldered and strong, and he had stepped into his late father's role on the farm bravely, without so much as a word. The Judge had worried about saddling him with so much responsibility, but Zeph never flinched, never doubted his job was to do as his father had always done. While Hayes or the Judge started the machinations of the farm, Zeph kept the engine steady. He supervised both white and black—displaced Southern soldiers and freed slaves, both desperate for work, and who were often directed to the Snow place by other farmers with no work for them or no inclination to hire them. While an occasional hire would bristle at Zeph's leadership, few bucked it. Usually, they were in no position to object—and any who did, Bertram sent packing.

Many itinerants wanted little more than to earn a hot meal. Caroline or Simmy would send them to the back stoop where Vivvy would give them a job in exchange for a meal or two. Some stayed long enough to chop wood or to haul water before they would be on their way, some going north, some going south—all part of a mass migration in the war's aftermath.

Bertram, himself, had not hesitated to take up the plow. With the help of Hayes and Zeph, he supported his family, not as a gentleman farmer, but as a dirt farmer whose sunburned, wind-burned face and calloused hands put food on his table. His judgeship had been invalidated as all in the South were at the war's end, and his law office in Hyssop had been burned to the ground, leaving a limestone foundation and chimneys rising from the charred rubble. When he had first stood seeing his primary livelihood reduced to ashes, the fears he had known on the wharves of Baltimore crept into him like an insidious disease. But he resolved to rebuild his practice, even though the sight had shaken him to his marrow.

While on the surface the Judge and Zeph maintained the pretense of farmer and farm hand, necessity demanded a reversal of roles. Zeph taught Bertram in an unspoken tutelage that neither acknowledged but both understood. On the surface, all propriety—the backbone of their society—remained intact. But in purpose and effect, Zeph became the farm manager. Unlike Hayes, who sometimes struggled to fill his role, Zeph handled the tasks with ease, the same ease of his late father, Lightner. Next to Bertram, he shouldered the greatest burden for Cairnaerie's survival. Had he been blessed with other opportunities that were unthinkable in 1866 Virginia, Zeph might have become a fine lawyer or a successful merchant. Clearly, he had no deficiency of intelligence. Instead, though, he labored alongside the Judge—two humble men so different, yet so alike.

What Zeph understood of the war and its aftermath, he had learned in the community of his church, lessons heavily seasoned with duty to God and family. Though under the law he had been free to leave—a clarification made generously and sincerely by Bertram Snow at the war's end—he chose to stay at Cairnaerie. It had been an easy choice, beneficial for all involved. Zeph had a job, a roof over his head, a home—all he and Simmy had ever known. His devotion to the Snows was familial. Privately, Zeph had wept over the deaths of the Snow sons. Privately, he had shared their burden of grief. Privately, he had comforted Simmy and Geneva. At Cairnaerie, Zeph and Simmy were separate—but integral—and need was a worthy calling for him, which he accepted with grace.

"That's a good place to stop," Bertram yelled, looking up and shielding his eyes from the sun. He shoved the tines of his pitchfork down into the feedlot's soft dirt. "I don't know about you fellows, but I'm hungry as a bear."

"You ain't the only one," Zeph said. "Judge, you want me to close these doors up here?"

"No, leave them open. We've got one more wagonload coming. I'd like to get it put up before dark."

Vivvy stood in the kitchen preparing the noon meal, waiting for the men to come in from the fields. She was scolding Briscoe, who grinned at her like a mockingbird, unruffled by a single word of her raving. His face, shaped like an upended pear, had bulging eyes spread too far apart across a wide nose that dropped severely to a sharp point, making him look like a little brown owl.

"Briscoe, if I tol' you once, I tol' you a thousand times, don't bring me bad flour."

"I swear, Vivvy, it's all the man had. He's getting more sometime next month, he thinks, but for now that's all I can git."

"Well, you jes take it back to him and tell him I don't want it. It's so full of weevils—even the hogs ain't gonna eat it."

"All right, Vivvy. Keep you pantyloons on," Briscoe said, flapping his arms and grinning.

Despite her aggravation, Briscoe's high-pitched voice coming out of his little owl-shaped face made Vivvy smile. She turned away.

"I'll see what I can do fer you first thing in the mornin'," Briscoe said. "Don't want you mad at me. You're my most loveliest auntie. Yes, you are, Vivvy. You know you are."

She shooed her nephew out the back door with a swat from a broom. He did a little jig for her and left the same way he had come in, grinning. He loved needling Vivvy.

"I be back to fetch you for church Sunday," he hollered, stepping backwards and waving at her. "You be ready now. Put on your fancy petticoats. I might jes take you dancing."

Vivvy suppressed another smile and harrumphed. Stowing the broom, she bent down to lift a mortar and pestle from under the table. "Grindin' my own wheat. Never thought," she muttered.

Vivvy had started a pan of spoon bread when Caroline came into the kitchen. "Do you know where Geneva is?"

"No, Miss Caroline. I got no inklin'," Vivvy said. Steam rose from the stove, and sweat dripped into the brown folds of her neck. "I cain't keep up with dat chile."

"I b'lieve Miss Geneva's gone up to the orchard," Simmy said as she collected plates from the china press.

"Where's Zeph?" Caroline said.

"Jes come up from the barn. He's out back," Vivvy said.

"Simmy, run tell him to go get her."

Simmy slipped out the door.

When Zeph saw his sister walking through the yard, he knew exactly what she wanted—finding Geneva was a task as habitual as the rising of the sun. "She's gone up in the orchard," Simmy said.

Even after pitching hay all morning, Zeph sprinted. Simmy, watching him run, thought: *They named him right—runs like the wind.*

The war had robbed Geneva of two brothers, but little else had penetrated her protected world. The change she noticed most was her father's aroma. It was the finest discernment of an eleven-year-old. He had always smelled of musty law books and fine cigars; now he had the tang of the farm hands—the sweat, the dirt, the pungent smells of harvests and horses. But if she were greatly influenced by the changes, she rarely let it show. She kept busy, her fascination with learning and the natural world occupying her. Youth, naïveté, and an overly-protective father sheltered her from the outside world as if a fortress had been built.

After his sons' deaths, safeguarding his family had become an obsession for the Judge, borne out of guilt and a wish to block further sadness. As hard as it had been to lose his sons, seeing Caroline's suffering had been almost as painful. When he and Hayes were required to be away from Cairnaerie, usually for business, he entrusted Zeph to look after the women.

Geneva was an exhausting charge—and having someone to entertain her was a relief to her mother. On some occasions, Geneva could persuade Simmy—and occasionally Zeph—to ride horses with her or hike the hills behind Cairnaerie. More often than not, it was Zeph rather than Hayes or Geneva's father who retrieved the girl from the creek or pulled her out of the limbs of a tree. Although Caroline assured her husband she was training their daughter properly, she did not always succeed. She wanted to teach her but was no match for the child's own self-determination.

"Your mama's looking for you," Zeph yelled when he saw Geneva straddling the low branch of an apple tree.

"I'm right here," she said, not bothering to look up.

"I can see that." Perspiration beaded on Zeph's forehead. "She wants you back at the house. Vivvy's almost got y'all's dinner ready."

"Zeph, come here. Look at this." Geneva carefully pulled back the leaves where five hungry mouths opened and closed like bubbles on a pancake. "Watch this." She buried her hand in the pocket of her skirt and pulled out an earthworm. She dangled it over the hungry birds. "They gobble them up." She looked down at Zeph with a mixture of delight and amazement.

Zeph grabbed another branch and pulled himself up high enough to inspect the nest. "Their mama's gonna come back and feel helpless," he said.

"No, she won't, Zeph," Geneva argued. "I'm helping her. They're hungry."

"I 'spect you getting hungry yourself."

"A little," she admitted.

"Well, come on now. Let's go," he said, dropping down and then pulling on her arm. "You don't want to get your daddy riled."

Zeph helped Geneva out of the tree, both taking care not to disturb the nest. "Take those worms outta your pocket," he said. "Vivvy'll have a conniption fit if you bring 'em in the kitchen."

"Wait a minute." Geneva squatted at the base of the tree and pulled three long night crawlers out of her pocket. With her fingernails, she scratched a hole in the dirt, laid the worms down and spread the dirt over them. "There," she said, and she gently tamped the soil before wiping her hands on her skirt, leaving brown trails.

Zeph pointed to her soiled dress. "No wonder Vivvy gets aggravated with you."

Geneva ignored him and screwed up her nose. "I should keep the worms and put them in her shoes. That'd fix the old cow."

He reached down and pulled a knot of her hair. "You better not. Vivvy'll git ya."

"Stop!" she said.

"Besides—that's mean."

"Well, Vivvy's mean. A whole lot meaner than me."

"You sure?" he said, teasing her.

"Yes. She's a lot meaner."

As they traipsed back through the field, the sun slipped past its zenith. Zeph, towering over the animated child, listened patiently to Geneva's endless questions and inflexible opinions.

Late in the afternoon, Geneva, sitting cross-legged near a stand of lilacs next to the house, hunched over a book. She barely heard her father and brother pass by and knock the mud and straw off their shoes before going into the house. But when Zeph came by, she shut the book and followed him.

"You were right," she said.

"Right? About what?"

"The birds. That the baby birds won't eat. How'd you know that?"

"Don't know. How'd you find out?"

"I looked it up. It's right here. See." She opened the book, and Zeph squatted down close to her.

"Oooo. Zeph, you stink." Geneva pinched her nose.

"I 'spect I do. I been pitching hay." Zeph straightened up and laughed as Vivvy came out the kitchen door.

"Gen-ee-va!" the cook yelled. "Where you at?"

"Hateful woman," said the girl, running off. "I'm coming!"

Zeph watched her disappear around the corner of the house and heard a door slam. She was gone, but his thoughts lingered after her. He could barely remember his own carefree days as a child, when the two of them played throughout the farm. He smiled, thinking about the time he had hauled her out of the creek when the snapping turtle took her clothes.

He filled a bucket of water from the cistern, and standing in the side yard, stripped to his waist. He threw handfuls of water on his face where rivulets of dirt and sweat striped him. As best he could, Zeph washed away the sweat, dirt, and smell.

CHAPTER 15

1868

Books & Crates

Fall changed the focus of work on the farm. The fields were stripped bare, the barns and cellars were filled, and the pantry was well stocked for winter. The air, fuming with decaying leaves and drying crops, also held tangy aromas that seeped out of the smokehouse where a dozen hams were hung to cure.

For the first time in months, Bertram found daylight to work on his accounts. Sitting at his desk, gnawing unconsciously on his knuckles, he pored over his ledger. He hoped to sell one more load of cattle. Outside rain fell steadily but gently. *A perfect rain*, Bertram thought. He looked up and sat back in his chair as the study door opened and Caroline carried in a tray. "I thought you might be ready to have a little break," she said. She set it down and poured him a cup of tea.

"Thank you." He stretched his back and pulled a chair up close to him. "Sit down. I've been thinking about your suggestion."

"And which suggestion is that?"

"About finding a tutor for Hayes."

"Oh, yes." A familiar ache tore through Caroline, but she hid her pain—another burden she knew her husband shouldered. How much he had wanted to educate his sons. Now two were lost. And she knew a tutor might keep Hayes at Cairnaerie a little longer.

"I'd like to enroll him in college next year. He's bright—he'll do well. But I want to make sure he is prepared. Geneva would benefit as well."

"I have tried, Bertram," she said, seeming dismayed.

"I know you have." He took her hands and with his thumbs, gently rubbed them. "Our Geneva is not easy. She has a mind of her own."

"That's an understatement," she said with a sigh. "But you seem to have no trouble at all with her. She tolerates my instruction—but gives so little effort."

"I know. I suspect learning to sew and such is not enough for her."

"It should be for any girl, but you're right, it isn't." Caroline looked down. "I worry what will happen to her if she doesn't learn. She's so far behind. How will she ever run a home?"

"Be patient with her. She's only thirteen. She has plenty of time."

After wasting several months trying unsuccessfully to find a competent tutor, Bertram finally gave up and set upon a plan of his own. He had learned law through his own diligence. Why couldn't his children be similarly educated? He knew of an excellent establishment in Winchester he had visited over the years. He would travel there to acquire suitable books.

———

"I wish you'd take the train, Bertram," Caroline said, standing with him in front of Cairnaerie as he packed his saddle. "I worry about you traveling alone." Wrapped in a lavender shawl, she shivered in the foggy morning chill.

"It will do me good to ride. It's been too long since I've stretched my legs, and it will give my mind a rest. I'll try to be back before the end of next week."

She smiled. "I'll be waiting for you."

"Then I'll be eager to return," he said, taking her in his arms and kissing her. They lingered in an embrace. "I love you, Caroline. Never forget that."

"I love you." She buried her faced in his chest. Having anyone she loved depart from Cairnaerie was difficult. "Come back, my love."

Bertram mounted his horse and rode toward the swale. Turning in his saddle, he looked back. Bravely, Caroline waved.

Bertram rode for several days, going north along the valley turnpike, drinking in the scenery and noting progress in the towns strung along the road. From newspaper reports, he knew many towns had been devastated during the war, but as he traveled north through the valley that sloped down toward the Potomac Basin, it was evident much rebuilding had occurred

When he arrived in Winchester, he made his way along the cobbled streets that were strewn with building materials—and optimism. Donations from Baltimoreans and others had supported repairs to the town.

Arriving at Fendell's Bookshop, Bertram was relieved to see it still standing and open for business. A bell attached to the door tinkled as Bertram stepped in. Looking up, the bookseller initially appeared puzzled and then he smiled broadly. "Is this my friend, Bertram Snow?"

"It is indeed. A bit older and grayer, I'm afraid."

"But richer and wiser as well, I'm sure. It is good to see you, my friend." The two men clasped hands. "What brings you?"

Bertram smiled and slipped a long list of titles from his pocket and held it up. "This," he said.

Much to the delight of Mr. Fendell, Bertram placed a large order and requested it be shipped to Cairnaerie. He left detailed instructions—as well as his desire for haste. He was eager to begin his children's formal education.

Several weeks later, books arrived in eight sealed barrels that had traveled by train as far as the railroads were intact and on wagons when they were not. When they had reached the depot in Hyssop, the barrels were loaded onto a dray and tied down for the bumpy ride to Cairnaerie. Having rarely, if ever, had a single order this large and given the uncertainty of transportation, Mr. Fendell accompanied it to ensure the books' safe arrival.

The delivery was widely anticipated, especially by Geneva who for days had positioned herself on the porch, usually reading in the swing. She had finally outgrown her penchant for climbing trees and wading in the streams, though she would never lose her love of nature. She wanted to know about the world beyond Cairnaerie and had asked her father to include books with illustrations of faraway places like Persia and Siam and Greece.

"If I never visit them, I can at least dream about them with some semblance of accuracy," she had told him. She had not added—out of respect for her father—that she doubted she would ever go anywhere, given his determination to protect her.

When the books arrived, the mood was celebratory. One by one, the heavy barrels were unloaded, hauled to the terrace outside of the study, and emptied. Stacks of books were carried through the exterior doors, which were exact matches to the double-leaf front doors.

Mr. Fendell rolled up his sleeves and sorted the books while Bertram directed him where to place them. "Start them here," he said, indicating a spot on the floor-to-ceiling shelving recently installed. The shelves had been built to Bertram's exact specifications, as was the ladder fastened at the top to roll along a metal track.

Geneva, itching to dig into these treasures, stood nearby as Mr. Fendell dusted each volume and meticulously organized them alphabetically by author.

"Bertram," Caroline said, looking in briefly. "Have them carry the barrels and stack them next to the smokehouse when they are emptied. I can use them for butter or salt."

After the books were shelved, the barrels removed, and the room returned to order, Bertram and Mr. Fendell left Geneva to browse while they retired to the porch to share a toddy.

When the bookseller left a few days later, it was with the promise to send Bertram lists of recent publications. "I would appreciate that very much," Bertram said as he bid his friend safe travels.

For the rest of the year—and for years after—smaller cartons of books arrived regularly until Bertram's study had become, in the best definition of the word, a library.

1928

CHAPTER 16

1928

Opportunity & Civility

Tobias Jebson unlocked the post office, kicked open the door, and rolled up the shades. Two months before he had arrived in Hyssop, attracted by its commerce. In addition to the college, the thriving town boasted a tanner, a feed store, a small music school, a printer, several churches of varied denominations, a newspaper office, and a mercantile, owned by W. D. Proffitt, who also owned the bank.

To his good fortune, Tobias had fallen right into a job the morning that Moss McKinney, the longtime postmaster, died while hauling a sack of mail to the train station. Moss, a burly man with a shock of white hair and the ruddy face of a child, had come up the hill with the mailbag slung over his back ready to clip it on the hooks for the engineer to grab when he fell over dead, face first, right into the dirt. As it happened, Tobias came along at that very moment and had the presence of mind to relieve the dead man of the mail and flag down a truck to carry Ol' Moss back to town.

Moss McKinney's funeral had been a community-wide affair. He had opened the post office long before the Great War, and nobody could imagine getting mail from anyone else. During the war, the post office had been a lifeline for families of soldiers serving overseas, and Moss, a kind man sometimes bearing bad news, had earned their respect and devotion.

In the midst of the public grieving, Tobias—who never saw an opportunity he didn't consider—appointed himself the new post-master. And with people so stunned at Mr. McKinney's passing and grateful to be getting their mail, no one objected. Tobias Jebson had a job.

He also assumed the mantel of homeowner when he moved into the house Moss had occupied—a stumpy white clapboard with a thinly pitched roof and a crooked stoop that hung off the front like a hangnail. The house doubled as the post office, a long-standing arrangement Moss had with the government. When official papers came, Tobias simply signed them "Julius Mossback McKinney," as the late postmaster had done, and sent them on their way. And when Moss McKinney's government checks came, he cashed them farther down the Valley where—as far as anyone knew—he was Mr. McKinney.

The mail came twice a week, thrown out of the mail car onto the wooden platform when the engineer of the hulking Roanoke slowed down to snag the outgoing mail hung high on a hook above the platform. When the train had passengers, it stopped long enough to take on water and supplies before lumbering off, with the piercing whistle and rhythmic rumble of the forty-ton engine filling the valley.

Tobias had settled himself on a stool behind the mailroom's counter window when he heard dogs begin to whine. "Train's a-coming, Pete," Tobias said to the stray tomcat who had adopted him. Pete, stretched out in a band of sunlight, ignored him. Momentarily, Tobias heard the train's whistle blow, followed shortly by a rumble—his signal to head to the station. He jumped up and grabbed his coat.

Halfway down the street, he passed Zeph Elias, one of the many customers whose acquaintance he had made in his new position.

"Good morning, Mr. Jebson," Zeph said pleasantly, tipping his hat.

"You're early. I ain't got the mail yet this mornin', but you go on up. Door's open. Have you a seat. Pete's up there keeping warm."

"Yessir," Zeph said.

Tobias turned around and walked backwards calling to Zeph. "Hey! You get bored, you go 'round back and see if you can find where my roof's a-leakin'. It got to dripping last night after the rain and kept me up like an ugly woman."

"Yessir, Mr. Jebson. I'll see what I can do." Zeph was the town's all-purpose handyman. People called on him for small jobs that required more skill and patience than the average homeowner possessed: stopping a leak, building a shelf, moving a sideboard, repointing bricks, or fixing windows. There were few things Zeph couldn't do, and there was nothing he would not at least try. All the years he had spent working at Cairnaerie had served him well.

Zeph was also known for his friendliness, honesty, and frugality, which had allowed him to provide for his family. After years of saving, he had accumulated a respectable bank account that teller Betty Louise Perfader oversaw. Every week Betty Louise would hand Zeph a receipt and a friendly greeting. She was the kind of woman who treated everyone the same, regardless of their age, their color, or their status in the community. She never asked Zeph about his money; she was tightlipped, accurate, and friendly—the marks of a good banker. As Moss McKinney had done with the post office, Betty Louise had helped open the town's bank before the turn of the century and had stayed there ever since. She was the teller and the only full-time employee.

Betty Louise was also an astute judge of character and had reservations about the new postmaster, but she kept her opinions to herself. Tobias Jebson had quickly acquired a reputation for things clandestine, and she, like the rest of Hyssop, suspected he was a bootlegger. Most of the men said nothing, hoping to be the lucky beneficiaries of his wares from time to time. The women didn't say much, either. He seemed harmless enough and, more importantly, he kept their mail coming. It was not their business, anyway, and townsfolk felt no great compunction to help the government police an industry that may have been illegal but certainly not immoral.

The bank's president, W.D. Proffitt, came around every few days to check on things, but most of his time was spent running his mercantile, which offered everything from postage stamps and garden implements to work boots and canning supplies—and his most popular item, cold Coca-colas.

Zeph was waiting in the post office, sitting on a splint-bottom chair that had seen better days, when Tobias got back with the day's mail. The postmaster came up onto the stoop and pushed open the door. "Cold as a witch's tit out there," he said. "I don't b'lieve spring's coming this year." His whole body shuddered.

"You might be right," Zeph said, standing up. "One day's warm, next one's cold as blue blazes. Never can tell."

Tobias dumped the mail onto a table behind a partition with a small service window. "I'll have this mail put up in a minute. You take a look at my leak?"

"Looks to me like rain's blowing in above the window—that's all. I'll go by the mercantile this morning and get you some caulk. I'll patch it up for you when I come back by this way."

"I'd appreciate it, Zeph. Just tell W.D. to put it on my tab."

Tobias sorted the mail, sticking letters into cubbyholes and holding out Zeph's.

"You git more mail'n any nigra I ever seed," he said, handing him a stack of magazines and letters. "Can't see why anybody'd need to read all that."

"Yessir," Zeph said politely. In all the years he had picked up mail, Moss had never commented on it.

"Looks like you got you 'nother one of them letters, too," he said, picking up a brown, official-looking letter with a Baltimore postmark and waving it. He laid it on the stack and drummed his fingers on it before he handed the bundle to Zeph. "I b'lieve you got you a sugar daddy up north."

"Oh, it's jes my pension check," Zeph said.

"Pension check? You done work for the government?"

"No, sir." Uncomfortable with the question, he tried to change the subject. "You got you a garden, Mr. Jebson?"

But the postmaster wouldn't bite. He narrowed his eyes. "How come you getting pension checks?"

"Oh, that's from work a while back," he said, tucking the bundle under his arm, eager to be gone. "I'll be seeing you next week, Mr. Jebson."

Zeph stepped toward the door and away from the questions the way a peacemaker slips away from an argument. As he left the post office and headed into town, a little worry niggled his mind, but he dismissed it. Zephyr Elias was an optimistic man.

CHAPTER 17

1928

Welcomes & Introductions

I owe you," John said as he turned onto Main Street, heading out of town. The Ajax puttered along like a giant pull toy.

"For what?" Helen said, tucking a small leather clutch purse beside her and smoothing her skirt.

"For suggesting I write Miss Snow."

"Glad it worked. Did you find out anything at the bank?"

"No. Nothing," John said casually. He did not want to recount the banker's rude rebuke and hoped Helen would not press him for details.

All he had managed to do was raise the hackles of W.D. Proffitt, the short, corpulent man with massive growths of black hair on his head, chin, and neck. "Matters of clients," Mr. Proffitt had said condescendingly, "are the business of those clients, not nosy college professors. When you have legitimate business to discuss with me, I'd be happy to talk with you. But since it appears you don't, I have work to do. Good day, sir."

Mr. Proffitt had pirouetted like a top on his spit-shined oxfords, flaring the jacket of his three-piece suit, and disappeared into his office, leaving John to suffer the stares of a half-dozen customers in the bank's resonant lobby. Betty Louise Perfader, ever discreet, attended to her customers and didn't look up. John exited the lobby quickly, almost expecting the banker to follow him, wagging a fat finger.

The conversation had haunted him all week, but another invitation from Miss Snow had buoyed him considerably.

"What time is she expecting us?" Helen asked.

"Two o'clock."

"You told her I was coming, didn't you?"

"Yes, I wrote her."

"And you explained about your 'wife'?"

"Actually, I didn't," said John, still feeling a little guilty about tricking Helen. But she had apparently forgiven him. "I thought I'd explain in person."

By the time they reached the house, Helen was glad she had taken John's advice to wear sensible shoes. Their trek along the path from the road to Cairnaerie had been longer than she had expected. For John, tinges of spring green and his traveling companion made the journey more pleasant than it had been the prior December.

"Professor Klare. Welcome," Miss Snow said. "Do come in."

"Miss Snow, I would like for you to meet Helen Van Soren."

"My pleasure," the older woman said tepidly, eyeing Helen with an anxious look. "I thought you were bringing your wife."

"No. I'm not married. I think you were thinking of my sister, Kate. Helen is a librarian at the college."

"Oh," she said, brightening. "A librarian—perfect. Then, it is my pleasure to meet you."

As they entered the parlor, Miss Snow, looking a bit nervous again, turned to John: "You have not told anyone else, have you?"

"No. I promise."

"And he has sworn me to secrecy," Helen added quickly. "As a librarian, he finds me useful."

"Useful? Oh, Mr. Klare—a librarian is far more, I'm certain." She smiled at Helen. "A library is a wonderful place, and librarians...."

"...You're right, of course," John interrupted, thoroughly embarrassed. He did find Helen useful, but he also enjoyed her company. "And I have a very good reason for bringing her. We'll explain."

"Do tell, Professor Klare. And make yourselves comfortable. I have mint tea and orange blossoms in the kitchen."

Miss Snow slipped out of the parlor that appeared to have been freshly dusted and straightened. A vase of wildflowers adorned the table.

"Did you say orange blossoms?" Helen asked when Miss Snow returned and set down a silver tray filled with tall glasses and a plate of delectables arranged on a crocheted doily.

"Yes, orange blossoms. My mother's favorite. Try one, won't you?"

Helen lifted a small gooey cake the size of a silver dollar and took a bite. "Mmmm. Delicious."

"I use an extract I order from Florida."

"That's exotic," John said.

"Oh, you'd be amazed what you can order through the mail these days. I understand you can order an entire house. I find that hard to believe."

John ate one orange blossom and sipped the mint tea, which he found less disagreeable than ordinary pekoe.

"Honey is even better than sugar to make these with," Miss Snow went on. "I used to keep bees, but they got to be too much. I have not been able to get my orange extract lately, though. But I had squirreled away one little bottle for special occasions. And this is a special occasion—to have guests."

Miss Snow was fully in charge and as gregarious as John had remembered.

"Tell me about yourself, Miss Van Soren. I've often thought what a wonderful place a library would be to work. As Professor Klare may have told you, I am fond of reading. It is my favorite pastime."

"Actually, he has told me very little," Helen said.

Miss Snow smiled at John, as if to acknowledge his trust.

"I'm a research librarian."

"And good at it," John added. "In fact, we brought something I think you'll find interesting. Helen found it—it's why I took her into my confidence." He handed Miss Snow the tube with Cairnaerie's plans. "It's a long story, and I won't bore you with all the details. Suffice it to say, Helen found these in the library. The plans for your house."

"Cairnaerie? Oh, my! I cannot imagine," she said, as Helen helped her unroll the plans. "Where in the world? Oh—it's Daddy's signature." She ran her fingers over the letters. "His house—he loved it so. What a treasure. Thank you. I cannot tell you what this means to me."

Just then, a door opened at the back of the house, and they heard footsteps. "Do I have more company?" Miss Snow said, as if cued. She set down the plans.

Through the parlor door came a young woman and an elderly man whose face was as friendly as black-eyed Susans. It was the pair John had seen on the street near McClanahan's. He caught Helen's eye and nodded toward the small portrait on the side table.

"Oh, Joly, Zeph, come meet my new friends," Geneva said. "Miss Van Soren, Professor Klare, I'd like you to meet my friends. This is Zeph Elias, and his granddaughter, Joly Jennings."

To Helen, the scene seemed rehearsed. For John, pieces began falling into place. *So this is Zeph Elias*, he thought, recognizing the name on the original correspondence. He stood and extended his hand, a gesture his hostess took special note of. "It's a pleasure to meet you," John said.

"Miss Van Soren is a librarian at the college. And Mr. Klare teaches history."

"I'm right proud to meet you both," Zeph said, his voice like black strap molasses. "But call me Zeph. Most folks do. Don't matter a bit to me—jes so long as they call me to dinner." He chuckled at his own favorite joke.

Helen addressed the girl: "And you're Joly?"

"Yes, ma'am."

"What a lovely name," Helen said.

"Thank you," Joly said softly.

"Won't you join us?" Miss Snow offered—an invitation that shattered propriety. "I have orange blossoms."

"No, but thank ya anyway," Zeph said. "We jes walked up to bring you some watercress and spring onions—awful good this year. Joly fixed us up some onion soup last night. Mmmm. Mmmm."

"I left them in the kitchen for you," Joly said.

"Thank you both."

"Well. We need to be on our way. Pleased to meet you folks," Zeph said.

They departed the same way they had come in.

"Zeph and Joly are very dear to me," Geneva said.

"Do they live nearby?" John asked, finding it impossible to bridle his curiosity. "I didn't see any other houses."

"Near enough." She smiled. "Did you wonder how an elderly woman manages here alone?"

John raised his brow and smiled at her astuteness. "Yes. I did."

"Zeph has helped me all my life—an indispensable help. He was born here at Cairnaerie. His father and mother, Lightner and

Clarissa, came here when Cairnaerie was built. Dear people. Very devoted. They were..." She seemed to choose her words carefully. "...a gift. Yes, a gift from my grandparents."

"I expect it took a lot of people to run a large farm?" said John, fishing.

"Yes. There were many servants. And friends." She smiled cryptically. "Most came from other farms. My father took in abandoned slaves like lost children. He never turned them away—he never bought them, either. He did not believe in the institution of slavery. My mother did, but not Daddy. He hired, never bought." She poured more tea. "Let me see the plans again."

Geneva lay awake for a long time that night, unable to sleep. The day's events played over and over in her mind, as did worries and questions John's visit was meant to answer: *Will he help me? Can I trust them?*

When Joly first invited her to come to the wedding, she had thought it all quite impossible. How could she leave Cairnaerie after so many years? But a little germ of hope—and Joly's wish—had egged her on until she had made her decision to at least try. She could hear Joly's voice as clearly as if she were standing in the same room: *Will you come?* She had to try—and now, she had taken steps. Yet one question left her sleepless: *Am I courting disaster?*

She climbed out of bed and stared into the moonlit sky. Beyond her window, crickets gnawed on the darkness, and an occasional night bird stirred the air. She pulled a throw around her shoulders. Perhaps a cup of tea would help her sleep. She lit a candle to walk down the stairs. In the kitchen, she found water in her iron kettle still warm. She filled a silver infuser with loose tea and dipped it into her cup. While her tea steeped, she walked out to the terrace. Standing in the night, the flagstones cold to her bare feet, she tried to imagine leaving and being at Joly's wedding. But she could not visualize it. No specific plan had come to her, only this first step. How would it all play out?

Once before, Geneva had succeeded in going to a wedding. It had taken courage—and a large measure of deception. She had found the courage then. Would it escape her this time?

Geneva walked back inside, took up her tea, and went into the parlor. The light from the dying fire cast shadows around the room. The clock ticked in a rhythm as comforting as a lover's heartbeat. By the light of an oil lamp, she read for a long time, until somnolence came. She blew out the lamp and walked by moonlight and memory back to her bedroom.

Perhaps tonight she would have pleasant dreams.

CHAPTER 18

1928

Mail & Malice

It was May, yet an early morning snow had blanketed the valley, turning fields of shocks into congregations of angular snowmen. Late snows were common in the mountains and sometimes they followed days as warm as those in mid-June. A fine, light snow was still falling. It stuck to trees and buildings and flew in their faces as Zeph drove his rig to the post office. Joly held a satchel for the mail and huddled close to her grandfather; specks of frozen snow blew around them like tiny bits of glass. Claudine clopped along, swinging her head side-to-side, shaking snow from her russet mane. Zeph had supplies to pick up at the mercantile, but his first stop was the post office. W.D. Proffitt rumbled past in his cream-colored Packard on his way to the mercantile. Zeph waved. "Someday, Joly, I might have to buy me a motorcar."

"You'd love that, wouldn't you, Grandpa?" She squeezed his arm.

"I surely would. A big ol' red one."

"Red? I thought you wanted a yellow car."

"Color's no matter, is it?"

"Sure idn't, Grandpa."

Zeph stomped the snow off his boots before he opened the door and held it for Joly. Another customer was at the counter mailing a package, so they hung back. Without thinking, he steeled himself. When the window was free, Zeph stepped forward.

"How you, Zeph?" Tobias twisted on his stool behind the counter and grabbed a bundle of mail. "Saw you coming by the window there. See you gotcha a helper today. Who's this pretty little thing?"

"My granddaughter, Joly."

"Howdy do," he said, ogling the girl standing by the door.

"Pleased to meet you." Joly nodded politely.

"Well, what you think of this snow?" Zeph asked. "I was awful surprised when I got up this morning."

"You and me, too. Damn. What happened to spring? I sure wadn't expecting snow."

"Good to see the sun this morning, though. This'll all be gone 'fore the middle of the afternoon. Pro'bly be hot by the end of the week. This time a year, you jes never know."

"I 'spect you're right," Tobias said.

"You got 'ny mail for me today?"

"Jes what come earlier in the week. The train musta got holt up. Habn't heard it yet this morning. Here you go, Zeph." He handed him a stack of mail secured in the fold of a thick magazine.

"Thank ya, Mr. Jebson."

Joly opened the satchel. Zeph dropped in the mail.

Eyeing Joly, Tobias said, "You oughta let her come get your mail for you. I'd be glad to do business with this one."

"Oh, Joly's too busy planning her wedding."

"You getting married? Well, I be damned. He's a lucky man. You a pretty thing."

Tobias leered at Joly, who, clutching the mail sack, had moved close to the door. His eyes stroked the undulations of her body, starting at the well of her neck, slowly passing over her full high breasts and down her tapering waist to the flare of her hips. For a split second, he caught her eyes and held them lecherously until Joly looked away, a surge of embarrassment clawing its way up her neck and face. Tobias, a man unashamedly possessed of no thoughts other than those of his own pleasure and welfare, would lust over this dark beauty for the rest of the day.

In the distance, a lone train whistle echoed off the blanket of snow.

"There's the train," Tobias said. "I better git up there and git the mail." He slipped on his coat and walked out of the post office alongside Zeph and Joly, and they parted. Tobias made his way down the road in a kind of goosestep to keep the snow from overtaking his fancy alligator bluchers, which he had lifted off a corpse in a funeral home in his prior location.

Zeph stood on the porch for a minute and rifled through the mail. He was looking for the brown envelope that came every month. It was not there, but he thought nothing of it. It had been late before.

Zeph's weather prediction had been wrong. It was snowing again by the time Tobias closed the post office for the night. He went out, shut the front door, and walked around to the back of the house. Inside the cold room, he loaded the stove with firewood and newspapers and tossed in a match. The fire caught with a whoosh. He settled into a chair directly in front of it and propped up his feet on an old milking stool. The room, furnished by the prior owner, was dirty and unkempt, having had little attention since Moss McKinney's unexpected departure. Tobias' stomach growled. He rummaged around the room for something to eat.

Flopping down in the half-dark on his cot, he stared at the fire as he chewed a stick of jerky while the room warmed up. *That Joly's a good looking nigra,* he thought, a little shiver of excitement juicing his body. He closed his eyes, letting his imagination take a little jaunt. He was beginning to doze off when Buster started barking. Buster was a hound dog that lay in a heap of skin and bones tied to a cedar tree behind the post office. He, like the house and the post office, had belonged to Moss. Tobias kept him for one reason—he was a good sentinel. He jumped up and peeped out the door—straight into the face of Cletus Jurden.

Cletus, who was known around town as a simple and harmless fellow, had quickly attached himself to Tobias when he first arrived in town. Tobias had put him to work—an arrangement of mutual benefit.

"Shit, Cletus. You scared the hell outta me. What d'ya want? Post office is closed."

Cletus lowered his face, eyeballing Tobias from under scruffy eyebrows. "I come to let you know I might have you a new customer."

"You do, huh. Who?"

"Well, now I don't say for sure—but I might."

"Quit it, Cletus. You either do or you don't."

"Why don't you invite me in to sample some of your merchandise? I might be able to recommend it."

"All right, Cletus, you lying son of a bitch. I know what you're up to." He said this with a wry smile. "Come on in. And bolt the door."

Long past midnight, Cletus slithered out the back, setting off Buster for a full ten minutes. Before he got home, he had relieved himself three times and puked in front of the Episcopal parsonage.

Tobias, able to hold more liquor than a French whore, got hungry again and heated up a can of pork and beans and some black coffee. He brushed off mouse droppings and picked mold off the back of a hard piece of cornbread before sitting down to eat it with his beans. The room was warm now, almost stuffy, so he stripped down to his shorts and stretched out on his cot, but he could not sleep. The cot's chainmail squeaked, and the calamus of a feather poking out of the worn tick mattress stuck him in the back. He cursed, pulled it out, and settled back down. He had another little jaunt with his black beauty and then thought about those brown envelopes that came in her grandfather's mail every month. He realized the mailbag was still sitting the middle of the post office floor. He could get up and sort it.

He pulled on his trousers and a worn leather aviator jacket he had found in the Baptist Church clothes closet. It was cold against his bare chest. He shivered. In a pair of mud-caked milking boots, he clumped outside around to the front part of the house where he slung the bag over his shoulder before returning to his warm room.

He dumped the mail onto his cot and picked through the pile of letters and magazines until he found the brown envelope. Holding it up against the light of the stove, he fingered the Baltimore postmark. He pushed back the pile of mail, put the brown letter down alone, and went to pour himself another shot. He sucked it down in two gulps, never taking his eye off the brown envelope. His arms went a little weak and his courage rose. He set a teakettle on top of the stove and waited for the stale water to make steam.

It took no time for the glue to release. Carefully he pulled back the flap and bent the envelope open to find a check. The National Bank of Baltimore: Pay to the order of Zephyr Elias. Fifty dollars.

"I'll be damned," he said, and he slapped his knee. Then he carefully resealed the envelope.

CHAPTER 19

1928

Heat & Hesitation

John closed his book and checked the time: 12:18. *I need to sleep,* he thought, dropping his book on the floor beside his chair. He cracked his neck and stretched. *Why am I still wide awake?*

When John had moved to Hyssop, he brought little more than his clothes, an assortment of books, his tennis racket, his U.S. army-issued rucksack, a pair of boots for hiking, and two sets of linens Kate had given him. Everything had fit neatly into the back seat of his car, so his room was rather sparse and utilitarian, which suited him fine. On a meager salary, John had decided that having an automobile was more important than fancy accommodations. Along with three others, his monthly rent supported the long-widowed Armenia Grubb, whose rambling house had more doors than windows. Outside his window, the air was not moving, and his room was uncomfortably warm.

He stared at the ceiling and watched a spider walk across it from corner to corner as he wrestled with a worry he could not shake. His last visit to Cairnaerie had been congenial, but meeting Zeph and Joly had dredged up memories of St. Ballard. He had replayed what had happened there a thousand times, not once doubting that he had stood on the noble side of right. But being right had not mattered at all.

"Being employed does," he said to the empty room.

From down the hall, he heard a door open and a man cough. Apparently, he wasn't the only one who couldn't sleep. *Maybe it's the heat.* John had longed for warmer weather. Now he had it. He had always thought Midwest weather was difficult, but the capricious mountain weather rivaled it. He wished Mother Nature would make up her mind.

He got up and found the folder with the letters from Miss Snow and sat down on his bed, kicking off his shoes. His big toe poked through one of his socks. He was glad his mother had insisted he learn to darn. Making a mental note to pick up some yarn and a needle from the mercantile, he pulled out his darning egg from the bedside drawer and set it on the table. He smiled. *Thanks, Mother.* She had given it to him on his twelfth birthday and ever after the job had been his.

Settling back, he re-read the correspondence from Miss Snow for the umpteenth time. Whatever she wanted in exchange for her brother's letters, he could probably provide—although during his last visit, she still had not explained fully. No matter the nature of the task, he hoped her history might also be a catalyst for his own career. He could use a catalyst. Thus far, his stint in academia had been lackluster.

He turned the envelope over and examined it carefully. Outside, a streetlight flickered and bugs pinged against the glass shell of his lamp. Some historians were ruthless, but if nothing else, Geneva Snow—by plan or providence—had picked a historian with a conscience, a costly one, but a conscience nonetheless.

John went to the rolltop desk that consumed a quarter of his room because—as Miss Armenia had explained—it had been her uncle's, and she could not part with it, and would he mind having it in his room? He rather liked it because he could organize his business.

The top rattled as he pushed it up. He placed Miss Snow's letters into a cubbyhole and pulled up a chair. He smiled at two crayon drawings propped up in front of a bank of small drawers. One vaguely resembled an elephant. The other was a house on a hill, a man standing next to it with black hair and grossly elongated legs and arms. He presumed he was the man. Opening a drawer, he took out a sheet of stationery and primed his fountain pen.

Dear Kate,

Please tell the girls I love the pictures they sent, and I'm glad they like the crayons. I hope I earned some brownie points for remembering their birthdays this year......

CHAPTER 20

1928

Memories & Emotions

Beside a cold hearth at Cairnaerie, Joly mended a curtain, thinking how nice a fire would feel. The afternoon had turned chilly, and the fragrance of rain wandered through the room like a lost child. As Joly worked, Geneva dusted a collection of china boxes crowded into a tall and intricate curio. On the table nearby lay a stack of newspapers and magazines that Joly had brought with her, along with a bundle of rhubarb and a box of freshly dug bulbs sent by Zeph.

"There," Joly said, shaking the fabric and then inspecting her tiny stitches. "I'll hang it back and be done with it."

"Thank you. My hands shake so, I don't get much mending done anymore."

"Glad to do it. I love to sew."

"You're just like Simmy. She was a good teacher, wasn't she?"

"Oh, yes. She was so patient with me—did everything by hand. Grandpa wanted to buy her a new fancy sewing machine, but she didn't want any part of it. Anyway, she could sew better'n any machine."

"She tried her best to teach me," Geneva said, "but I'm afraid I wasn't much of a student." She finished her chore and propped the duster in a corner to sit down. "Come. Let's have some tea." She lifted a cozy from a small, brown pot.

Joly joined her on the settee and took up a cup.

"Tell me what your Mr. Oden is up to these days."

"Right now, he and his brothers are working on a house for a man at the college. He took me to see it last week—showed me all around. There's a pantry big enough to put a piano in. The setting room's got windows—long ones—that look down the valley. You can see for miles. They're building a bed and a washstand and a big walnut table for the dining room. Grandpa helped them pick out the wood."

"He's always been good with any kind of wood."

"Oh, I know. He built my cradle. He reminds me every single morning—like I'd gone to sleep and forgotten."

Geneva laughed. "He built it for your mother. His little girl. He was so proud of it."

Joly lowered her eyes. In a soft voice, almost a whisper, she said, "I wish..."

"I know," Geneva said, reading her mind. "I wish you had known her, too. She was a sweet girl."

A breeze blew through the windows and captured their attention the way an unexpected visitor might.

"Someday," Joly said, watching the wind jostle the curtains, "I'm gonna have a big house like that with a big porch looking out at the mountains—and I'm gonna set there and rock my babies."

Geneva swallowed hard and took a quick deep breath. She was happy for Joly, but the girl's hopes and dreams stirred deep emotion in her. More and more lately, these spells had come over her. To her relief, Joly didn't seem to notice.

"Oh, I almost forgot," Joly said. "I put the baking powder and the alum you wanted in the kitchen."

"Can you stay for a little supper?"

"I'd like to, but Grandpa..."

"...I know, honey." She patted Joly's knee. "Have you talked to him about our conversation?"

"Not yet. But I will. It's in my mind to do it soon. I promise. Anything else you need before I go?"

"No, I don't believe so. Thank you for bringing my mail. Would you carry a letter to your grandfather for me? It's on the kitchen table with a tin of cookies. Take them, too, if you would.

The clock struck four as Geneva stood at the kitchen door, watching until Joly disappeared into the woods. Alone again, she closed the door and went to the library. From a shelf filled with her handmade journals, she selected several and sat down to read.

I am 15 years old today and Daddy told me Leroy Whitcomb wants to come and visit me. He is a nice boy but has a bovine face and whiskers that stick out like a walrus. How can Daddy expect me to find a husband when all the boys in the county are as ugly as Leroy? The best are dead, like Thomas and Grayson. I still miss them so much.... April 17, 1871

They tell me Sally Purvis is engaged to a Mr. Waltham from Boston. I would rather marry a horse than a Yankee, but Daddy reminds us that the war is over and behind us. But a Yankee is a Yankee—and I find them insufferable, haughty and arrogant.... November 12, 1871

I found an old abandoned church this morning while I was riding. It's beautiful, sitting all by itself in the middle of a growth of

trees. It looks like nobody's been there for years. Zeph was there....
August 20, 1872

I stayed in the belvedere all afternoon trying to read, but I spent
most of my time watching Zeph and the men hauling hay into
the barn. Simmy told me she will probably have to take care of
him her whole life. She is probably right. All Zeph does is work....
September 4, 1873

Daddy is pressing me. Effie Armstrong's boy, Brill, wants to ask
for my hand, but I will never marry anyone if I must marry some-
one I hardly know. Mama says I do not know what love is—that
you decide to marry and love grows. She might be right about love
growing, but not about Brill Armstrong.... January 2, 1874

I do not believe I can endure much more of Mama's pushing.
Vivvy tells me everyone already regards me as a spinster, which
upsets Mama far more than me. She tells me perpetually that all
the other 19 year olds have already married. I remind her that
is simply not true. If I ever marry, it will be because I want to.
Honestly, an occupation interests me far more than an ugly or
boring husband—I could become a teacher or maybe a famous
writer.... February 18, 1874

Geneva paused and watched the last rays of sun slip down and
hover at the bottom of the sky. She remembered her emotions with
such clarity, and it stirred her like a resurrection. She dabbed her
eyes with her handkerchief. Picking up the worn and faded red silk
journal, she untied the frayed ribbon.

I will be 20 next spring and have finally admitted to myself that
all the suitors I have entertained are a tedious lot—either full of

awkwardness or so taken with themselves they should simply marry themselves. Mama worries that I find none of them attractive, but not one is the least appealing. I hear her whispering about my solitary state, yet I cannot bring myself to fulfill her wishes. I am burdened by another thought altogether—one I dare not shape into words..... September 17, 1874

Geneva closed the book. Remembering and stirred by Joly's request, her nagging worry persisted—the same one she had struggled with for so long. *When do I tell her?*

1870 — 1878

CHAPTER 21

1870

Losses & Promises

Geneva sat on the edge of Hayes' bed sulking as her brother placed the last of his traveling clothes into a leather grip his father had bought for him. The rest of his belongings had been packed in a trunk and sent ahead with all the supplies he would need for the year. Though he was going to school and not to war, Geneva was struck with a sense of loss, the kind that made her mouth dry and kept her awake at night, watching the moon inch across the sky. Already a handful of years had passed since Grayson and Thomas were lost, but the morning of their departure still haunted her.

"You don't want to go, do you, Hayes?"

"Geneva…," he began, pausing to roll the collars and cuffs Vivvy had starched and pressed. "I've put Daddy off long enough."

"You didn't answer my question."

"Don't make me."

For a moment, neither spoke. Instinctively, she patted down his clothes. From downstairs rose the sound of dishes and silverware clinking as Vivvy cleared the table following their meal. *"Our last supper,"* Geneva thought dryly.

Hayes was not in a mood to argue with his sister, yet she persisted. "You sound like Zeph," she said. "You go along with whatever Daddy says. Why don't you tell him you don't want to go?"

"I'm going, Geneva. He wants me to." Hayes turned toward the window. "And maybe I want to go."

"No, you do not, Hayes Snow." She stood up and jabbed his shoulder until he faced her. "I know you. You'd rather do anything than leave Cairnaerie."

"I'll be back."

"Will you? Are you certain?" Her voice was defiant. "Can you promise me you'll come back?"

"Listen," he said. He placed his hands on her shoulders and tried to sound reassuring. "I'll go, get my education, and then I'll be back. It's that simple. You don't have to worry. There's no war."

But Geneva would hear none of it.

"How are we going to manage without you? How is Daddy going to run the farm? Especially since he's reopening an office in Hyssop. He can't do both without you here."

Hayes shrugged. "He has Zeph. He doesn't need me." He slipped a Bible into his bag and closed it. "He's trying to do something good for me—to give me a chance to be something more than a farmer."

"There's nothing wrong with being a farmer."

"I know, Geneva. But he has his reasons. You don't remember. You were too young."

"I remember more than you think, Hayes!" She was tired of the endless assumptions everyone made about what she knew and what she didn't know.

"He loved his work, especially being a judge, and it was hard when he had to give it up. Do you remember, Geneva? Do you?"

She hated being challenged and looked away.

"After the war," Hayes continued, "he couldn't serve as a judge anymore. But he never complained. He did what he had to do. How can I do differently? It's my turn. This is my duty."

"Hang duty! It cost Thomas and Grayson their lives. And for what?"

Hayes pushed his dresser drawers closed. The lamp atop the dresser shook. She knew him too well. "Listen. You're the one who should be going to college. We both know that. You're the one who likes to study so much. Be patient. You'll be sixteen next spring. Maybe he'll send you then. But I'm the one now. The decision is made." He smiled, trying to reassure her—to defuse her. "I'll be back before you know it. And I'll bring you all my books. That I can promise."

Geneva refused to watch Hayes leave. She had watched as Thomas and Grayson left—and it was the last time she ever saw them. Now Hayes was going, and she could almost hear fright whispering to her. After tucking a letter in the bottom of her brother's bag, she fled to the woods, running until she was exhausted, and fell in a heap, sobbing.

Simmy saw her leave. "She was awful upset," she told Zeph. "I think you best go after her. No tellin' what she'd do."

Zeph found Geneva asleep, lying in a bed of pine needles in a familiar copse of white pines—a spot where they had often played together as children. It was nearing dusk. He stood at the edge of the small clearing, encircled by the trees. He didn't wake her, but waited.

Zeph had known Geneva all his life, but this girl seemed different, distant and unfamiliar, not his childhood companion, not the girl he had pulled out of trees and rescued from snapping turtles, and not the girl who had climbed on her father's shoulders to watch farm hands skinning hogs, and not the girl who had made steps out of stacked books in the library after her father had forbidden her from climbing up the shelves.

As she slept, he noticed the curves of her body, the shape of her mouth, the texture of her alabaster skin. In the fading light, her face was no longer childish at all. Her hands and arms were slender, her bust full. He saw her, as if for the first time, with a kind of innocent voyeurism. He struggled to reconcile his lifelong history with the girl he had known and the woman he now saw sleeping.

When she stirred, he stepped quickly out of the shadows so as not to startle her. "Geneva, it's me. Zeph."

"What are you doing here?" She pushed herself up and brushed pine needles out of her thick, dark hair. Every nerve in her body was raw. Her face was striped from tears.

"Simmy saw you run off. Sent me to find you. You all right?" he said with a gentleness that stood in stark contrast to his strength and size.

"I'm fine, Zeph." She paused. "Hayes is gone."

"I know." Zeph sat down on a heavy root protruding from a tree and picked up a flat stone, turning it over and over in his hand. On the fringes of his mind were thoughts he had never had before, unsettling thoughts. They seemed unnatural, illicit. He fought to keep them from overtaking him. He examined the forest floor and the forest's depth of trees and the stone in his hand, focusing anywhere except on Geneva. The woods, still and cool, became uncomfortably quiet. It was a long time until either of them spoke, and it was Geneva who broke the silence.

"When Thomas and Grayson left, Hayes promised he would never leave. And now he's gone. Daddy sent him away. He didn't want to go, Zeph. I'm all alone now. There's nobody for me. Mama's busy. The farm consumes Daddy. And you and Simmy—you work all the time."

Zeph listened. He would also feel Hayes' absence.

"We need him here. Daddy can't run the farm without him, and Mama and I depend on him. You'd never go off and leave Simmy. I know you wouldn't."

"I don't think I would, but I can't know everything in the future. Your daddy means well."

"That's what Hayes said."

"You're afraid he's not coming back."

Not trusting her voice to answer aloud, Geneva nodded as tears welled up.

"Your daddy wants Hayes to be something, maybe be a judge, like him. You got to be happy about that—happy for him."

"Hayes does not want to be a judge!" Her words were like a drawn sword.

"Are you sure?"

"I'm sure, Zeph." She pounded the ground with her fist. "He didn't want to go to college in the first place. He was told to. Hayes always does what he's told."

Zeph turned the stone over and over in his hand while he let her anger dissipate. He understood the passion behind it. "Sometimes, Geneva, the wise thing ain't always the right thing," he said.

"What in the world does that mean, Zeph?" In the moment, she had little tolerance for reason.

"Maybe he doesn't want to go—but maybe Hayes doesn't want to disappoint your daddy either."

Geneva smacked the ground again. "So he disappoints me instead!"

Finally, Zeph faced her directly. He considered his words. "I guess he thought you'd understand."

His words pierced Geneva. She turned away from him. She wanted to be angry with Hayes, but she could not. Zeph was right.

She couldn't hold onto her fury any longer; it drained out of her like a punctured bag of sugar. "Maybe he was wise," she said, "but it is not what's right for Hayes. I know it's not."

"Time'll tell."

"Yes, I suppose it will. Time, the one thing that seems endless."

"But it's not, Geneva."

"No, it isn't, is it?" She sighed deeply and leaned back on her arms. "It just seems that way."

Zeph and Geneva sat together as the moon rose. Silver light pooled like mercury on the forest floor, and a night fog was rising.

"It's late," Zeph said, finally. "Don't you think you best be getting back? Your mama and daddy'll be back from the train soon, and your mama won't be too happy if she's gotta go looking for you."

"She wouldn't do that. You know she wouldn't. She'd send you, Zeph."

They laughed together, rekindling for a moment the playfulness of their younger selves.

Zeph helped her up. She brushed the remaining leaves and needles off her dress. And then she touched Zeph's arm, looking up into his eyes. "I hope you never leave. Promise me, Zeph. Promise me you'll never leave Cairnaerie."

Something deep and frightening stirred within Zeph.

CHAPTER 22

1872

Sisters & Suitors

Caroline tilted the letter toward the window for more light. She was interested in her sister's speculation—a reply to her own recent correspondence describing her frustration with seventeen-year-old Geneva's failure to find a husband. Of all those she might have turned to for help, it was her sister's council she valued most.

> .... *He has an adventuresome spirit, and I must tell you he is a handsome and intelligent young man of 24 who could possibly be a suitable husband for your lovely Geneva—but how I presume. My friends have warned me continually against my incessant matchmaking, but having no daughters myself, I find it a temptation I cannot resist. So forgive me, dear sister, if I am being presumptuous...*

When Caroline heard Bertram coming into the bedroom, she quickly folded the letter and stuffed it into her bodice. She knew he disapproved of matchmaking, especially for their daughter.

Bertram took off his coat and sat on the side of the bed to remove his collar and cuffs. Caroline rose from her chair and joined him. She rubbed his neck.

"You are working so much you need some help. Do you think it might be the right time to take on an associate?"

He looked at her with a half-smile. "Interesting that you would suggest that." Bertram had always intended to pay in kind the favor of his own mentoring. "My practice is growing again, and I could use a clerk." He reached over and pulled his wife closer to him and planted a kiss on her lips. "You are always one step ahead of me, aren't you?"

"I try to be," she said. She snuggled closer to him. "I have a new letter from sister, and she mentioned a young man. His name is Edwin Waite—from a very respectable family. His grandfather was a business associate of our father. Sister recommends him highly. He's just out of law school and is eager for work."

"Interesting," Bertram said. "Let me think about it."

Caroline did not mention the possibility of a match with their daughter. On this point, she was sure Bertram could not be persuaded. For her part, though, she could create opportunity and from opportunity perhaps fate would intervene. Sometimes nature needed assistance.

The subject broached, Caroline let it drop, but as she left the room, she was buoyed. Later, she wrote:

> *...It is all I can do for now, dear sister. As much as I understand the ancients' tradition to make such decisions for their children, I am up against a child who is determined to have her own way. I shall have to be patient and hope nature takes its proper course. If your young man could write to my husband, I think it might move the matter forward in a beneficial manner.*

CHAPTER 23

1872

Names & Acquaintances

Simmy was stationed by the front door to watch. She ran her fingers along the grooves in the carved front doors, each one wiped clean of road dust and wiped down with linseed oil. The house, with windows flung wide open, was filled with flowers, and a pitcher of mint tea was cooling in the springhouse. Caroline had tried her best to get lemons, but the train hadn't come in time. A little oil of lemon might have substituted, but she opted for mint, which was abundant near the kitchen door. A still-warm apple pie, covered with a linen cloth to keep off flies, waited on the sideboard in the dining room. Simmy could smell it from her post; Vivvy had promised to save her a piece. Caroline's finest bone china, a blue and white English pattern—a wedding gift—graced the table with sterling silver flatware and hollowware, all polished to a luster.

Vivvy lumbered around the kitchen preparing the meal. At Caroline's request, she had killed a goose, gutted it, and stripped the pinfeathers before stuffing it with apples and potatoes for roasting. Alongside the goose, Vivvy would serve country ham, beaten biscuits, assorted jellies, and an array of vegetables—chards and beets and whatever else the garden gave up. It would be a feast intended to impress.

Geneva found the preparations bothersome and stayed out of the way. "I will have my nose dusted and my face shined if I stay too still," she had told Zeph as he saddled her horse, Dally. Zeph smiled but made no comment. Geneva was right. Simmy had told him as much.

When Simmy spotted the coach coming over the rise, she ran to tell Caroline.

"Go find Geneva and tell her I said to come out and meet Mr. Waite."

"I b'lieve Miss Geneva's out ridin', Miss Caroline."

Caroline's eyes flashed. "I could throttle her. I told her to stay here."

"I'll go tell Zeph to find her, Miss Caroline."

"Thank you, Simmy. And make sure she's dressed properly."

When Edwin Waite stepped out of the coach he had hired to bring him to Cairnaerie, Simmy wondered if a king had arrived, so lofty was his bearing. He wore the finest clothes she had ever seen: an overcoat with a wide velvet collar over a frock coat and waistcoat. At his neck a silver stick pin secured an ecru tie. He wore leather gloves and carried a top hat made of beaver hide that had suffered a few dents during his travels. Edwin Waite was impressive—in an grandiose sort of way. Even Caroline felt a bit dowdy.

"Welcome to Cairnaerie, Mr. Waite. We are so glad to meet you," Caroline said, flowing down the steps, her hands extended.

Edwin scrutinized the house. It was much more than he had expected to find in the mountains, a location considered wild and untamed by Eastern Virginia standards. He was delighted. With Caroline's urging, Bertram had agreed to consider taking him on as a clerk, and the opportunity awaiting him appeared quite promising. He envisioned himself building his own grand house.

Geneva returned to the house and stepped into the foyer still wearing her riding clothes. Her hair was windblown, and she smelled of leather, saddle soap, and horses. Simmy, who had watched her trudge discommodiously out of the fields, came behind and pushed her out the front door.

"Geneva. There you are," Caroline said. If she were disappointed with her daughter's appearance, she didn't let it show. "Mr. Waite, I'd like for you to meet my daughter, Geneva."

"Edwin Armand Waite," he said with a pretentious tone. "I am pleased to make your acquaintance, Miss Snow." He bowed, keeping his eyes fixed on Geneva, who was clearly inconvenienced.

"Mr. Waite is from Richmond," Caroline said, as if Richmond were a magical place.

Geneva suspected her mother was up to more than cordial introductions, which compounded her lack of interest in this visitor.

"Good day, Mr. Edwin Armand Waite," Geneva said, stepping no further onto the porch.

"My mother is French," he said, explaining his unusual middle name. "Most people are curious about it."

"Herman," Geneva said.

"Come again?" Edwin asked.

"Herman. It's French for Herman. Didn't you know? That makes you Edwin Herman Waite."

Caroline winced. Edwin, though, appeared amused—and intrigued.

"I shall call you Herman." She then flipped around. "Goodbye, Herman." And she was gone.

Embarrassed by her daughter's rudeness, Caroline took the young man by the arm. "Let me show you around."

Edwin, however, was impressed with Geneva, despite her disdain—or perhaps because of it. He liked a conquest. Immediately, he wondered if this spirited girl might make a suitable wife. Isn't this what his aunt had implied might be Caroline Snow's ulterior motive? The girl was certainly attractive enough, even in her disheveled state.

To Caroline's aggravation, supper that evening was an awkward repeat of Edwin's prickly introduction to Geneva. In spite of the sumptuous meal and the obvious effort to be welcoming, for every action Caroline took, Geneva seemed intent on countering.

Bertram, tired from a long day, busied himself serving plates from the array of dishes concocted to impress young Edwin. This had all been Caroline's idea, and Bertram had reservations. To be fair, though, he would give the young man a chance.

"Do you ride?" Edwin asked Geneva, who was seated across from him.

"Doesn't everyone?" she said.

"Geneva," her mother scolded under her breath, giving her daughter a sidewise glance that said *mind your manners.*

Geneva ignored her as she buttered a piece of her roll.

"I trust you also read, judging by the fine library your father has assembled," Edwin said, still focused on Geneva.

"Yes," Geneva said. She took a mouthful of baked cottage cheese, one of Vivvy's specialties, and gazed out the window while she massaged the cheese in her mouth the way a cow chews cud. Caroline shot her husband a pleading look. Bertram finally stepped in.

"Edwin," Bertram said, "tell us about your family."

As their guest rambled on about second cousins twice removed and a lineage that included an English Duke and a governor, Geneva's mind drifted. Occasionally she caught a word or two, but the moment Vivvy served dessert, fruit compote with apple pie, Geneva excused herself. Caroline was relieved.

Edwin retired to the guest room. Taking a bit of snuff he kept in a small, jeweled box, he curled it into his lip, and then he took out a fountain pen, similarly boxed, and a sheet of fine engraved stationery embossed with his family crest and ornate initials: "E.A.W."

May 2, 1872
My dear aunt,

I have arrived at Cairnaerie to find your description of the house and grounds quite accurate. I must confess my initial skepticism when you told me of the Snows. I presumed, as many do, these western counties are backward. That is true of the town, Hyssop, but as for the Snows, the assumption is erroneous.

Judge Snow is a pleasant man, and Mrs. Snow has welcomed me graciously. The only one who did not seem pleased at my arrival is Miss Geneva Snow.

The Judge will take me to his office in the morning, and if he and I agree on a suitable apprenticeship, I will find more permanent lodging. Nothing, however, will quite compare to Cairnaerie.

I promise to keep you apprised of my plans. I am indebted to you for arranging this opportunity for me.

Please give my kind regards to Uncle Ephraim.
Your devoted nephew,
Edwin A. Waite

Several days later, Geneva was sitting next to the window in the library so absorbed in a book she didn't hear Edwin enter. He crossed the room, watching her. He faced the wall of books, but he kept her in his frame of vision.

When she looked up and noticed him, she was annoyed. "What are you doing in here?"

"I've come to look up a case for your father."

She glared at him and then angled her body away from him, boring into her book.

"What are you reading?" he asked.

She didn't answer. He selected the volume and carried it toward Bertram's desk where he deposited himself, shoving aside a stack of documents.

"Hey! That's Daddy's desk," she said icily.

"Well, he's not here."

"He will be." Geneva slammed her book shut, huffed, and headed for the door, but as she passed the desk, Edwin caught her arm and tried to grab her book.

"I'm interested in what you're reading, Geneva."

"It's none of your business!" She jerked away, adding under her breath as she stormed out of the library, "You are such a bother." Geneva had no reason to dislike him, except that he interrupted her life and his opinion of himself irritated her.

For the rest of the week, she avoided Edwin so skillfully that he, at one point, asked if she had left to travel. She skipped breakfast most mornings to stay in her room until she saw him leave for town with her father, where the Judge had reopened his law office. As soon as the wagon pulled away, she would race to the kitchen, famished, where Vivvy would give her some late breakfast. Despite their own history of conflict, Geneva and Vivvy agreed wholeheartedly when it came to Edwin. Neither liked him.

Caroline, however, fawned over Edwin. "I feel as though he's brought a little of the feeling of my home here," she told her husband. "Sometimes I miss Richmond."

"You're not thinking of going back, are you?" Bertram said, teasing.

"Of course not. My home is here," she said, and she kissed him. "I could never leave you—or our beautiful Cairnaerie. Besides I know of no Richmond wives whose husbands build them their own studio for painting." Caroline grew serious and teary-eyed. "What a kind and generous man I married."

Bertram beamed and pulled her close.

"By the way," he asked, "how is my portrait coming?"

Weeks passed as Caroline watched Geneva for any spark of interest in Edwin, but to her dismay, she saw none. Instead, her daughter seemed dead set against having anything to do with him.

"Mama," Geneva said, strolling into her mother's studio one afternoon. "I thought he was going to find lodging in town."

"Edwin?"

"Of course, Lord Edwin, the pompous. Who else has invaded Cairnaerie?"

"Geneva! We are his hosts. And to answer your question, I don't know."

Edwin had quickly, or perhaps deliberately, lost interest in finding other lodging, Caroline admitted to herself. But she would not discuss her doubts with her daughter.

"Apparently, he has found nothing to his liking."

"Oh, what a surprise," Geneva said caustically as she toyed with her mother's tubes of paint, arranging them into the letter "G."

"Stop that, Geneva." Caroline abruptly put down her brush and straightened her paints. "He is a nice young man, and I think you should be kinder to him."

"He is an arrogant donkey, Mama. You don't see the way he looks at me when you're not around—or the way he treats Simmy. Yesterday he ordered her to wipe his boots."

"She can do that for him."

"Mama! Simmy is not his slave—and she is not yours, either!"

"Stop it, Geneva!"

"Then I suppose I can ask the great Herman to clean *my* shoes? Since he works for Daddy?"

Caroline reached up and slapped her daughter. "Do not be insolent, young lady. Edwin is your father's clerk. You may not like him, but how you treat him is a reflection on you, young lady. If you're not going to be courteous, you can at least be civil. That's the end of it. No more!"

"Yes, ma'am." Stung but unbending, Geneva touched her reddened cheek. "I'm going riding." With no remorse and no intention of obeying, she left.

As she walked away, her mother called after her. "And one more thing. Stop calling him Herman."

Caroline picked up her brush, stewing. *Most girls would swoon over a man like Edwin. What is wrong with my daughter?*

———

"I've found several small rooms to rent," said Edwin, lounging in the parlor with his boots propped up on a low table. He was holding a small glass of claret and chewing on a biscuit he had lifted from Vivvy's kitchen. Crumbs tumbled onto his shirt. He brushed them onto the floor. "The rent is reasonable."

Caroline, sitting at a small desk and writing a letter, looked up, hopeful. Edwin had lived at Cairnaerie for most of the summer and even she was beginning to tire of him.

"But they're all second-story rooms above noisy businesses. And they're insufferably hot." Edwin sighed theatrically. "I want to do everything I can to perform my duties to your kind husband, so I need to work with as rested a mind as a good night's sleep can provide. I am concerned such accommodations might hinder my usefulness."

"Have you tried the livery stable, Herman," said Geneva, stumbling into the conversation as she entered the parlor to retrieve a book she had left on the mantel. "Or perhaps the stockyard?"

"Geneva Snow!" Her mother shot her a withering look. Geneva ignored her and tripped out of the room with a little too much glee. "Good day, Mama. Herman."

"Edwin, you'll have to excuse Geneva. She often speaks before she thinks." And as if obliged to offset her daughter's insolence, she added: "You're welcome to stay here for as long as you need."

Standing at his bedroom window late that afternoon, Edwin watched Geneva ride up the hill toward the orchard. He smirked. He was more determined than ever to win over Geneva Snow. She was beautiful, educated, and spirited. She would make a feisty but fine wife—and she was a fine horsewoman. Fully assured of his own appeal, he knew it was merely a matter of time until she recognized his charm—of that he was certain. Perhaps they would take a wedding trip to France.

When Geneva was out of sight, he flopped back on the unmade bed in the middle of his unkempt room, kicked off his mud-caked boots, and pondered what might impress the proud Miss Snow.

CHAPTER 24

1872

Whips & Partings

Geneva slipped on chamois breeches underneath her skirts and rolled them up around her ankles so her mother wouldn't see them. She was eager to get outside. After a long summer, the air was crisp and the leaves were turning. It was a perfect day to ride. Grabbing her riding crop, she slipped out the back of Cairnaerie and headed for the barn. Perhaps she could persuade Zeph or Simmy to ride with her today.

As she walked toward the barn, she saw Zeph leading Dally, already saddled for her, out into the lot. Behind him strode Edwin, dressed in jodhpurs and a showy red jacket, looking more hunt club than farm. She stopped. He was carrying a saddle. *Hell's bells. How inconvenient!* she grumbled, and she dove behind a tree to think.

Avoiding "Herman" had become more and more difficult. She had hidden behind the kitchen door more than once and spent hours in the belvedere while he roamed the house looking for her. Another time she had volunteered to help Vivvy pluck chickens, a task she despised, when he all but insisted she go walking with him. Vivvy had rescued her, handing her a wriggling chicken whose neck had just been snapped.

Geneva was tired of eluding Herman Waite. Now here he was again—invading the one place she had so far completely escaped him. If he planned to ride, she would find something else to do.

She looked up into the perfect blue sky on a perfect day to ride. *Why should he keep me from riding? I can outride him, anyway.* She stepped forward.

Except for the two men, the barnyard was deserted. Dally snorted and dipped his big head as Zeph checked the bridle and reached up to adjust it before taking the reins.

"Boy," Edwin yelled to Zeph. "Get me a horse." He tossed the saddle on the ground in Zeph's direction, spooking Dally.

"Whoa, whoa," Zeph said, soothing Geneva's horse.

"I said get me a horse."

The saddle lay in the dirt as Zeph led Dally toward the fence. "Yessir. Be glad to, Mr. Waite. Just as soon as I tie up Dally."

"I said now, boy. Are you deaf—or just stupid?"

Zeph kept walking, pacing the horse. "Be just a minute, sir."

"Now, boy," Edwin raised his arm and yelled again. "I said now!"

"Yessir," Zeph said, quickening his pace. "Just as soon as I..."

Geneva watched as Edwin raised a whip and planted a stinging slap on Zeph's back. She gasped. Zeph flinched, but he didn't cower or let go of Dally. Stunned, Geneva could hardly comprehend what she was seeing.

Zeph set his eyes on the horizon and kept walking.

"You hear me, boy? I said get me a horse." Edwin was yelling now like a maniac, and he raised his arm. The whip cracked again.

This time Zeph faltered and bloodstains appeared on his shirt. Geneva wanted to vomit. She had never seen a man treated like this. Never. It had never happened at Cairnaerie.

Suddenly and without thinking, she was running. As she approached Zeph, their eyes met, and she tried to convey all the apologies and sympathies one gaze could transmit.

"Dally's ready," Zeph said calmly when he saw her, but she ran past him and flew at Edwin, pounding on his chest, unleashing the anger that had smoldered all summer.

"You cannot treat him that way. You horrible, horrible." She pounded furiously, screaming. "You have no right to..."

Edwin caught her wrists and held her. He was laughing at her. "Whoa, little lady. You're a spitfire, aren't you? You worried about your boy?"

She kicked at him furiously, breaking his grip, and so angry and shocked she could no longer speak.

"Why don't you come riding with me, Miss Geneva?" Edwin said with an insouciance that infuriated her even more. He tried to grab her again, but she backed away and ran toward the house. Edwin stood alone with the horses, wondering how one young woman could have so much spirit. When he turned around, Zeph had disappeared.

Geneva barreled through the kitchen door right past Vivvy, who spun around like a top but could not get a word out before Geneva had run straight through into her father's library, wild-eyed and out of breath.

"Oh, Daddy," she said, and she broke into uncontrollable sobs.

As the sun went down, Geneva hid in the belvedere with her journal.

Herman Waite is the most despicable person I have ever known. He parades his superiority like a pompous pig, and yet he is an inferior breed. He is a pig. This sad episode has awakened a sensibility in me I can barely express. How can any man treat another, even a colored man, with such cruelty? Daddy promised me he will talk with him. Mama wants to believe it wasn't so bad, but she is wrong. She did not see what I saw. I saw the evil in his eyes, and I will never, ever forget it. …. September 1, 1872

Two mornings later, Edwin's gutta percha trunk with leather straps and brass fittings sat on the front porch of Cairnaerie. Its sullen owner, dressed as finely as his luggage, slouched in the swing with one heel propped up on the balustrade. He picked at his thumbnail and waited impatiently for the rig.

Zeph had said nothing to his employer until asked to verify the attack. Bertram had winced at the marks on Zeph's back. Then he had talked to Edwin, but he could not convince him his actions were wrong. Instead, Edwin had insisted it was "merely a friendly tap, a tease," and he tried to laugh it off.

Caroline, also, tried to explain it away and pleaded with her husband to give Edwin a second chance, but Bertram's mind was made up. Had there been an ounce of remorse, he told her, he might have reconsidered, but there was none. He dismissed Edwin Waite.

Alone in the parlor, Caroline pulled a chair up to a desk and dipped the nib of her pen into a bottle of ink. The long and tumultuous season of a houseguest, who had become less and less welcome, had come to an end. A part of her was relieved; another part, disappointed. She had tried to overlook Edwin Waite's faults, but his consumption of tobacco in all forms had tested her hospitality. Education and breeding aside, he was sloppy and inconsiderate, leaving ashes, spent chews, and spittle wherever he pleased. This was excuse enough for his dismissal. This she could write as true.

What she could never admit was that her husband was too soft when it came to their servants and far too sympathetic to their needs. On this, Bertram and Caroline would never agree.

September 15, 1872
My dearest sister,

I am quite disappointed that no spark of affection appeared between my Geneva and Edwin. On reflection, though, I don't believe that they could have cobbled together much of a marriage. They are both rather stubborn—and I don't wish unhappiness on either of them.

I must confess that his personal habits are rather slovenly. While my tolerance of tobacco is great, his personal habits were distasteful and inconsiderate. I say this to you alone, trusting that you will not convey my opinions to any of his relations, as I would not want to appear overly critical.

While my plans are dashed, my hope is not. Perhaps in time, our spirited Geneva will find a young man able to handle her strong will—and one who does not leave a trail of tobacco juice wherever he goes.

With this letter, I am enclosing a note for Edwin's aunt. If I might trouble you to convey it, I would be most appreciative. I have written to his mother and father, but I had no address for his aunt.

The weather is beginning to turn cold here, and judging by the puny size of the caterpillars this fall, I hope we shall have a mild winter.

Bertram has several trips planned, and I have told him I would like to visit Richmond sometime soon. I shall let you know if we are able. It has been far too long since I have seen you, dear sister. And perhaps, if we were to come, you might find some young men for Geneva to meet.

I am as hopeful as ever and determined not to become discouraged. Please give my regards to the rest of the family.
Your devoted sister,
Caroline

Geneva stripped all the linens from the guest room bed, dumped them over the banister onto the floor below, and then wielded a feather duster with glee. She was elated to be done with Herman, whom she referred to thereafter as "the late Herman Waite." She had eagerly volunteered to help clean out the guest room.

Simmy, on her hands and knees with rags and a bucket of hot vinegar water, rubbed tobacco stains off the floor.

"Look at this," Geneva said, pinching her nose and holding with the tips of her fingers a dirty piece of men's hosiery. She shuddered as she tossed it into a basket of trash. "I am so glad he is gone."

CHAPTER 25

1873

Baskets & Books

Geneva stood in the barnyard, remembering a time when it was full of horses. Only Dally and a few dobbins were left. The yard seemed bare and lonely, sentiments she recognized in herself. She was dressed to ride in a narrow skirt over top of her chamois breeches. Although she had been taught to ride astride in public, she never did on the farm because it was impossible to gallop that way. And Geneva loved to gallop.

"Dally," she yelled, and she clicked her tongue. The horse, already saddled, ambled toward her. Geneva grabbed the reins and tightened the cinch before she climbed the boards of the fence to mount her horse. She hiked up her skirt around her waist and tucked it under her thighs so it would not flap. *One day,* she thought, *I'll dispense with the skirt altogether.* She drew in the reins and clicked her tongue again, giving a nudge with her knees.

Dally, the chestnut mare with a white blaze on her forehead, had carried Geneva all over the farm, providing her relief during the unfortunate visit of 'the late Herman Waite' and allowing her to escape the loneliness that had deepened during Hayes' three-year absence.

It had been bitter news when she learned Hayes, after graduating from college, had accepted a position in a city more than fifty miles away. Geneva felt betrayed. He had promised to come back to Cairnaerie. Her dashed hopes for a reunion with her brother had compounded her isolation. By riding, though, she could escape.

She had often begged her father for permission to ride alone to Hyssop, but he always said no. What had once been a war to hide from had become a world of ambiguity that no one, least of all Geneva, knew how to navigate. This was Bertram Snow's assessment. Her naiveté also scared him, even though he knew he was partially responsible.

With few other options, Geneva spent more and more hours riding out across the farm's rolling hills. In truth, she didn't know where the farm ended and the wild mountains to the west began.

Ever since Hayes had left, Cairnaerie resembled a tomb. Her mother, often locked in her studio, painting, still grieved for her lost sons, and she paid less and less attention to her daughter, especially as her matchmaking attempts failed. The studio, once a neat and orderly room, was strewn with half-finished canvases and spattered paints. Caroline's grief and frustration fueled each other.

Geneva's father was busy juggling his reinvigorated law practice with the demands of a farm. After the Waite fiasco, he had been reluctant to take on another clerk, so he, too, had little time for her anymore. She missed his company—the walks they had once enjoyed—often with Blue lumbering along behind them—and the conversations they had shared on rainy afternoons in his library. Those times were gone. Blue was gone. Lightner and Clarissa were gone. Two of her brothers were gone. And, for all intents and purposes, now Hayes was gone as well.

Compounding her loneliness, Simmy and Zeph, also busy with work, had grown more and more absent in her life. In fact, it seemed that ever since the day Hayes had left for college, Zeph avoided her. An awkwardness had grown up between them. Her attempts to engage him in conversation always found him needing to be elsewhere as if he were avoiding her. She thought she had only imagined it, but whenever she took special pains to talk to her childhood friend, he seemed distant and distracted.

Geneva, though, was determined to find some kind of freedom, even if she had to create it herself. She longed to escape from the dullness that threatened to spin her into melancholy. She dreamed of the day it would be her turn for college—if that day ever came. Of late, though, she had begun to doubt because of her father's reluctance to discuss the possibility.

Even her father's library, a place she had always found solace, had begun to feel as if it were closing in. A part of her life was missing, she knew, but she hardly understood that the missing piece would never be found in a book.

"Haw." Geneva snapped the reins. Dally galloped out across the fields to the top of a hill behind the house and halted. The sun was bright and the air, warm. Geneva looked back over her shoulder—no one at Cairnaerie would miss her. Perhaps, she thought resentfully, she would ride until she was finally free of her restricted life.

Below the hill to the south, she saw a dense grove of trees that beckoned her. She had brought along a small volume of poems. Today, she thought, would be a good day to read Robert Browning.

She bridled Dally, and they turned downhill. Pressing her knees into her horse and holding the reins at the withers, they galloped toward the woods. Fresh air blowing through her hair lifted her spirits.

Reaching the edge of the woods, Geneva dismounted and wrapped the reins around a tree. She loosened the cinch on the saddle—a gift from her father for her eighteenth birthday the prior spring. She tucked her book into her sash and headed into the woods, walking without any specific destination.

When she heard humming, she went closer where she was surprised—but not displeased—to find Zeph. He was sitting on the stoop of an old church, reading.

"Zeph?"

"Geneva!" he said, startled. He jumped to his feet. "What are you doing here?"

"What are *you* doing here?"

Beside Zeph was a square basket she recognized instantly as the one that sat on the hearth in her father's library. It was filled with books.

"You're reading," she said, stating the obvious. "Aren't you supposed to be working?"

"I'm a—I'm taking a little break."

"Where did you get those books? Those are Daddy's." Her tone was accusatory, although she hadn't meant it that way.

Zeph had no idea how to answer.

He closed his book. Should he explain it was Judge Snow who often sent him off to read and study? Didn't she remember that before the war he had allowed Zeph to go to the colored school, where he had learned to read in the first place?

"Simmy is getting them for you, isn't she?" said Geneva, making an assumption he didn't challenge. "That Simmy!"

Zeph relaxed a little, but he kept his guard up.

"I'm glad you can read Daddy's books. I really am."

"You got one too, I see." He pointed to the book stuffed in her sash.

"Robert Browning." She took it out, offering it. "Do you want it?"

"You finished?"

"I can be. You take it. Go on. Take it."

Geneva handed him the book. He stepped away and leaned against a tree. She replaced him on the stoop to rifle through the basket of books.

"Dickens! I haven't seen this one before." She opened the book. "This must have come in the last shipment."

As Zeph watched her, he guarded his heart. He had missed talking to Geneva, but he knew his place. When they were children, the barrier between them had seemed flimsy, but now that he was older, he understood it was—in reality—a stone wall, a barrier never to be breached.

"What's this?" Geneva said, looking up at the building.

"The ol' Swope Chapel," he said. "Been abandoned a long time."

"Looks like it," she said as she scanned the tall windows, the sharp pitch of the roof, the faded paint.

"Do you come here a lot?"

"Whenever I can," he said. "It's a good place to read. Real quiet."

"Yes, I can see that." She smiled. "Sit down, Zeph."

For the rest of the afternoon, away from the limits of Cairnaerie proper, Geneva and Zeph talked as they hadn't talked in years.

When the sun slumped in the sky, Geneva hurried back to the house.

Early the next morning, Geneva locked herself in the belvedere with a stack of writing paper. Yesterday had been as interesting a day as she had experienced in a long time, refreshing a part of her spirit seclusion had stolen. She hadn't realized how much she missed Zeph, their conversations, and his companionship. Having lost so much of the fellowship of friends and family, she wondered if Zeph might be her friend again, someone to talk to at least.

Dear Zeph,
 I enjoyed yesterday. I would like to meet again, if you…

She tore it up and started over three times before she got it right.

Dear Zeph,
 Yesterday, after having had such an interesting conversation with you, I realized we might both benefit from more similar discussions. Given the long history of our association, I am convinced it is reasonable to suggest that we meet again soon. If you are so willing, please send me a letter in the same way I am conveying this message to you.
Your friend,
Geneva Snow

She tucked the letter into a second volume of poetry. Later, when she found the basket in the library refilled with new books, she slid it under the others.

The letter was the first of many.

CHAPTER 26

1874

Awakenings & Confusions

Geneva strolled through the library, running her fingers along the spines of a dozen leather-bound books. Casually, she glanced at the basket on the hearth. Taking out the bottom-most volume, she flipped through the pages and found Zeph's latest note. She tucked it in her pocket, wandered upstairs, and locked her bedroom door.

> *I can meet you tonight. Bring the book about Cicero. If I'm late,*
> *wait for me.*
> *Z—*

The house was dark and quiet as Geneva tiptoed down the back stairs, through the kitchen, and slipped away from Cairnaerie. She headed straight for the chapel, where she and Zeph had met secretly for more than a year. He had insisted on secrecy. "No point in inviting trouble," he'd said.

In no time at all, Geneva had been caught in the adventure—the intrigue alone made it exciting. Their discussions about books and life in general relieved the monotony of her mundane life. Best of all, she had rekindled her friendship with Zeph, filling a need in her as great as air.

The spring night was balmy. She loosened her collar as she hurried through the forest that was awash with a full spectral moon. Light spilled through the trees. It was a good night for reading. They might not need the candle Zeph had stowed in a low windowsill. Over her shoulder, in a torn clothespin bag that she had sloppily stitched back together, she carried several new books, including Cicero. When she got to the chapel, Zeph was sitting on the stoop.

"What did you bring?" he asked her, eager to see what titles she had taken from the library, which had grown substantially as Mr. Fendell, the bookseller, had continued to send books.

"Here." She handed him a volume. "Plutarch's Lives."

"Sounds riveting," he said with a hint of sarcasm.

"It's not, but Daddy says everyone should read it."

Sitting on the small stoop, Geneva and Zeph read aloud for a while and then talked long into the night as the air cooled. The moon rose high, and after what seemed like minutes, it began to descend.

Geneva yawned, stretched her back, and bumped against Zeph's arm. He started.

"Oh," she said, and she sat forward awkwardly. Suddenly Geneva was more aware of Zeph's presence than she had ever been before. She felt heat coming from his body. It unnerved her—an odd and disquieting self-consciousness. She had sensed it before and dismissed it, but tonight it pressed her, goaded her—and frightened her. *I'm tired,* she thought. *That's it. I'm just tired.*

"What time is it?" she asked in a deliberately casual tone.

"Judging by the moon, almost three."

The wind began to whip, and clouds sailed across the sky. The moonlight faded and leaves whispered on the breeze. In the growing darkness, Geneva felt strangely callow, and for the first time, she was acutely aware of their solitude. She was light-headed, alive—and almost out of control, as if pushed by some invisible force.

"I wonder if a storm's coming," she said, trying valiantly to sound composed. "Do you think it will rain?"

"You all right?" asked Zeph, hearing something odd in her voice.

"Oh, yes," she said. "I'm just tired." She sighed purposefully. It was all she could think to do as she grappled with a flood of feelings she didn't understand—feelings that threatened to undo her.

"It's getting darker," Zeph said.

"Are you going to light the candle?" she asked.

"In a minute."

Just then, the darkness captured them. She heard Zeph shift positions and close his book. She could hear him breathing. Her pulse quickened, and almost without thinking, Geneva touched his arm. He froze and then put his hand over hers. Emboldened, all her cautions fell away, and she leaned into his chest. Blindly, he wrapped her in his arms and pulled her close. Time stopped.

"No!" he said, pushing her away. She heard an unmistakable panic in his voice. He stood up and stepped away. Had there been light, he would have seen her face blush crimson and her body wilt like a discarded blossom.

"I should go," Geneva said, rising quickly and stumbling over the basket of books, spilling them. She didn't stop. She disappeared into the forest, running as fast as she could.

Zeph dropped down hard on the stoop and angrily knocked his head back against the door. *What have I done?*

The next morning Geneva woke from a dream with a start. She was covered in perspiration and shaking. Opening her eyes as wide as she could, she crossed her hands on her chest and tried to calm her thundering heart as the dream lingered.

The sound of dishes clanking in the dining room jerked her awake. *Breakfast. I'm late.* But when she stood up to dress, she collapsed back onto her bed, still groggy, confused, and exhausted from staying up most of the night. She rose up on one elbow. Dropped in the middle of the floor was the dress she had muddied when she tripped running away from the chapel. *What happened last night?* Suddenly, part of her wanted to retch. She groaned and flopped back on her bed.

"Geneva?" Her mother was on the stairs. "Geneva, are you up? Vivvy has breakfast on the table."

Geneva jumped up, balled up the muddy dress, and stuffed it under her bed before throwing herself back onto her bed and underneath her coverlet.

"Geneva?" her mother said as she appeared in the bedroom. "Why are you still in bed? Did you forget it's Sunday?"

"I need to stay home," she said, her words murbled.

"What?"

Geneva uncovered her mouth. "I need to stay home."

"Are you ill?"

"My stomach," Geneva said truthfully because in the moment her stomach was revolting.

Caroline was not in a mood to argue. "All right. I'll tell Vivvy to leave you some breakfast before she goes."

The minute her mother left, Geneva pitched back the bed covers and stared out the window. Above the mountains, clouds drifted along as if on a placid sea, but there was no calm in Geneva this morning. She heard her parents talking, their voices far away. She listened when Zeph brought the buckboard up to the house for them to drive to church. She heard the springs squeak as they climbed in. She wondered if Zeph would notice her absence—or if he remembered the night the way she did.

"Haw." Her father urged the horses forward.

Geneva rolled over and went back to sleep.

When she awoke again several hours later, the house was quiet. The dream was still as vivid as it had been when she had first awakened. Feelings wholly unfamiliar and nearly unbearable coursed through her like a fever. She started to write a letter to Zeph, but could not begin it. Instead, she took out a new journal. It was covered in red silk.

Last night, I met Zeph at the chapel and something happened I cannot—I dare not—put into words. It prompted a dream so real that at first, on waking, I wondered if I had really done this thing so unimaginable.

My dream began in a grove of trees. Zeph was dressed in a fine coat. A preacher stood beside him. The air swirled around us in colors muted as a rainbow—eddies of colorful wind. I heard happy voices murmuring, but there were no words. Zeph held out his hand to me, and I floated to him. He led me through the forest to a small church. His hand reached out for a polished knob, a door opened, and a vaporous brightness greeted us. The pastor spoke, but all I heard was a heartbeat. Zeph slipped a gold band on my finger and whispered, 'My Beloved Wife.'—and then I awoke.

What a strange and unsettling dream.... July 31, 1874

When she finished writing, she tied the journal closed with a red satin ribbon and hid it in the back of her wardrobe, determined never to think of the dream again, its meaning utterly unthinkable.

But despite Geneva's good intentions, despite her iron will, despite everything she understood as right and proper, something had been set in motion even she could not change.

CHAPTER 27

1874

Impossibilities & Entanglements

For more than a month, Geneva and Zeph avoided each other. The notes stopped. The rendezvous ended, and Geneva's heart ached.

By the time summer became fall, fewer than a dozen words had passed between them. Simmy knew something was wrong, but neither Geneva nor Zeph would talk to her about it. Geneva stayed in a mood even Caroline found hard to ignore. She moped around the house and spent lengthy hours alone in her room. Her father was concerned about her, but her mother assured him the behavior was typical for an unmarried girl almost twenty with no prospects. She had explained with a voice that was part remorse and part disappointment. Geneva was, her mother fretted scornfully, getting what her stubbornness deserved.

Geneva, as lonely as she had ever been, poured her thoughts into her journals.

I try to discipline myself. I even consented to an afternoon at a church social, where I was followed around by a collection of young men—none the least bit interesting. They pant like puppies and talk mostly about themselves, and none has a brain or an inclination to discuss interesting things. I asked and not one of them had read Cicero.... October 3, 1874.

I do not understand why I cannot rid myself of these feelings. I worry that if I fail to erase them, I am destined to spend the rest of my life suffering them—as frustrated as a man who wishes to fly. I am becoming Mr. Alonzo—perhaps I should change my name to Geneva Quixote. And if I should ever find a husband, I shall forever be burdened by the imagined—or dare I say real—emotion for Zeph. I am captured body and soul. Is there any relief for me?.... October 12, 1874

I am miserable.... October 27, 1874

———

By autumn, Geneva's state of mind was burning a hole in her as if a torch were aflame in her belly. She could not shake feelings that seemed illicit and that created such inner conflict. Gaunt and ill tempered, she ignored her family's attempts to engage her. Even Hayes, when he visited, was mystified. She might have confided in her brother, but she feared he would think her foolish—or worse, childish. And besides, she thought ruefully, Hayes had embarked on a new life and left her behind. Her longings, be they childish or otherwise, would be of scant interest to him. She was trapped in a temper she could not escape.

Sitting alone in the belvedere one afternoon, pondering her miserable life, Geneva realized the only way she would ever free herself was to talk to Zeph himself. She was convinced that she had exaggerated what had happened at the chapel. *He'll tell me how foolish I am,* she thought. *And ridiculous. I am ridiculous—of course I am.*

Talking to Zeph would be a painful remedy—every bit as gruesome as an amputation. But Geneva could stand it no longer. She needed relief—and Zeph had always been so wise and kind. Surely he would take pity on her and help her. They had discussed so many things. Certainly they could discuss her confused state of mind.

What she knew absolutely was that she was suffering hope for something that could never, ever be—and she wanted desperately to be free of it.

> *Dear Zeph,*
>   *It is of the utmost importance that I talk with you. Please meet me at the chapel tonight.*
> *Geneva*

The night air was close as Geneva threaded her way through the woods. An Indian summer had reprised the nights, hoarding some warmth. With the dew rising, her skin was damp and her undergarments clung to her body. Her corset squeezed her so, she considered stopping and dispensing with it, but she was too eager to find Zeph and solve this problem once and for all. As she walked, she steeled herself—and hoped Zeph wouldn't think her too shameful or childish.

A full moon shone as she approached the chapel, but Zeph was not there. She felt foolish and full of doubts. *What if he doesn't come?*

She waited, wandering in the woods around the chapel, trying to quell her anxiety, which grew sharper with each passing minute. The sound of her footfalls in the spent leaves hung in the air. When a deer snorted nearby, she stopped, hopeful, until she realized what the sound was. Time crawled by. Judging by the moon, it was approaching midnight. *He's not coming.* She considered leaving. But she waited.

Another hour passed. Geneva propped herself up against the chapel door and, in her distress and fatigue, dozed off.

"Geneva?" whispered Zeph, touching her arm.

She started awake.

"Zeph. What took you so long?" She rubbed her eyes.

"I wadn't sure I should come. What did you want?"

She balked at his question. Instead she asked, "Why did you come?"

"Because you wanted me...to come," he said, revealing more with his pause than he had intended.

Geneva began to cry. Everything she had held inside, all the emotion, all the pent-up feelings, began to tumble out.

"What's the matter?" Zeph said, alarmed.

Without a word, she crumpled. Everything she planned to say, her reasoned appeal, evaporated. "I can't help it," she said with a sob. "I love you."

Zeph, shocked and no longer able to deny his own feelings, embraced Geneva as if he would never let her go.

This was not what Geneva had planned. This was not it at all.

The mountains were outlined with a ribbon of first light as Geneva slipped back into her room and locked the door. Stripping off her dress, she stood in the moonlight to cool her overheated body. She was overcome with a confusing mixture of ecstasy and fear. How she wished Zeph were with her. Her breathing was shallow, and every nerve in her body was alive. Tears flowed and dripped from her soft cheeks. As dawn broke, she crawled into her bed, but she could not sleep.

———

For the rest of the fall and winter, moonlight after moonlight, whenever opportunity arose, Geneva and Zeph met deep in the woods, driven by love and a desperate need to hide it. Zeph jimmied open the chapel door to give them shelter from the cold, and Geneva became adept at slipping out of the house at night and returning without being seen.

They changed their messages to a simple code passed at the barn that would be meaningless if discovered. Writing with a piece of charcoal on the underside of a large flint rock hidden behind the barn door, they scribbled a day and a time to meet at the chapel. An erasure meant something had happened, and one or the other could not come.

No one noticed anything out of the ordinary. Rather, on the surface at least, Geneva and Zeph's relationship soured. It was the best protection for their secret. The fog of love consumed them as it sometimes does to mask what is foolish and ill-considered, but sometimes to shelter what is good and tender and perfect—something worthy that only this strange immutable fog can protect.

Even Simmy, who knew Geneva and Zeph as well as any anyone, was unaware. Occasionally she would catch Zeph coming in late or even early in the morning, but he always had a plausible explanation.

Eventually, though, Simmy grew suspicious.

CHAPTER 28

1875

Risks & Decisions

Zeph arrived back at the cabin late and tried to slip in unnoticed, but Simmy was waiting. She had been up all night, worrying, after she found a note from Geneva her brother had carelessly saved. She wanted answers.

"Where have you been?" she said, as he entered the cabin.

"Out."

"Out where?"

"Just out. It's late. You go to sleep. I'm tired." He stretched and yawned and started toward his bed.

"Were you with Geneva?"

Zeph halted. He turned to look at Simmy and started to offer an excuse, but he couldn't. He couldn't lie to Simmy. "Simmy, I..."

"Don't 'Simmy' me, Zephyr Elias. Answer me," she said angrily. "Answer me!"

Zeph had never meant to deceive his sister, but this was more than a secret, more than life itself. He was sparing her, wasn't he? Just as Geneva was sparing Hayes.

He sucked in a deep breath. "How'd you know?"

"I know you—and I know Geneva—and I found this." She threw the note at him. "You gotta stop. You gonna get yourself in trouble. If the Judge or Miss Caroline find out…." Simmy choked; fear stole her words. Cairnaerie was her home, and the prospect of being tossed out terrified her. "I don't want you getting us in trouble. You always told me, 'Don't invite trouble, Simmy.' Well that's exactly what you're doin'. Inviting the worst kind of trouble a colored man can."

Zeph propped his forearms on his thighs. "I need to tell you something."

"I ordy know," Simmy said. "You think you love her."

Zeph raised up. "I do love her. And she loves me. I'm gonna marry her, Simmy."

Simmy began to shake. She closed her eyes and put her hand to her chest as pain arced through her. She was shocked to have it all out in the open—everything she had feared laid out like a butchered hog. All the signs had been there. She had sensed something—this love—the way the air changes before a storm. But she had never considered marriage—that was unthinkable.

"You cain't," Simmy said. A choking cry escaped her throat.

"Simmy, don't."

Zeph stood up and paced.

"I love her, too, Zeph," Simmy cried. "But this is dangerous. It's crazy. You cain't do this."

"Yes, I can." His voice was resolute. "And I will."

"Who you gonna get to marry you, Zeph?" she said, challenging him, her desperation rising. She banged the table. "Who? Reverend won't do it."

"Why not? You don't know."

"I do know. He's got six little children to look after. He's not going to marry a colored boy to a white girl who's gone crazy in her head. Think about it, Zeph. Think about it." Simmy collapsed into a chair and put her head in her hands.

Zeph propped his foot on the rung of a chair and gripped the back of it. "I have thought about it," he said, more belligerently than he intended. "More'n you know."

He picked a loose piece of straw off his pants and rolled it between his fingers. He let a measure of calm return before he spoke again. A fly buzzed against the window. "One time when I was little, one of the farm hands dropped an ax on his foot—cut himself real bad. He was white—hair the color of straw. I remember leaning over Mama's shoulder while she bandaged him. I wanted to look inside him. I wanted to see if he was white all the way through—like a squash is yellow all the way. Mama told me the insides of a colored man are no different from the insides of a white man. Only difference is what's covering it up. 'All about the wrappin', Zephyr.' That's what she told me. All about the wrapping. That made an impression on me, Simmy. I never forgot it."

Simmy wiped her eyes with her apron and looked up at her brother. "You believe that?"

"Don't you?"

"I don't know. We're still different," she said.

"Well, maybe we ain't supposed to be."

Simmy softened. She came over and hugged his neck. "All I know is that if you keep going down this road, you don't know where it'll end."

Zeph crushed the straw and tossed it on the floor. He slumped against Simmy, leaning on the strength they had always given each other.

"I've spent my whole life doing for people. My whole life. Doing what anybody asked me. I want to do this for me, Simmy." He stood back and thumped his chest with his fist. "For me. More than I ever wanted anything in my life. I'll never have a day of peace if I don't."

The next afternoon Simmy cornered Geneva in her room. "You gotta stop with Zeph."

Geneva closed her wardrobe and tried to be blasé, even though her heart was suddenly thumping. "I don't know what you're talking about."

"No use pretending, Geneva, I know."

Geneva froze, and then her eyes flashed. "Who told you?"

"You know who. But I ordy figured something." Simmy was scared and angry all at once. "You cain't do this."

Geneva turned away and escaped toward the window. Simmy's vehemence unnerved her. It was not like her to be so forward. Geneva had always been the one in command. Never Simmy. As she stood at the window, anger, fear, determination all crowded her brain.

"I love Zeph. It..it..it doesn't matter...." stuttered Geneva, grasping for straws. "I don't care what color he is....and neither does my daddy."

"Oh, Geneva. You're saying your daddy'd let you do this?"

"Yes," said Geneva, posturing. She had never fully considered the question, but she did quickly—and she would not back down. "Yes, he would. He wants me to be happy. Mama's the one who would throw a fit." She dared not turn around and face her friend.

Simmy put her hands on her hips. "If you're so sure, then why don't you tell him?"

At this, Geneva flipped around. She was defiant. No one would tell her what to do, especially not Simmy. "No. I won't do that to him—I won't make him cross Mama. It's better this way. To keep it all secret."

"Geneva, you cain't marry Zeph. You cain't!"

Geneva picked up a book and threw it at Simmy. It hit her shoulder and landed with a thud. Simmy looked stunned. Then Geneva addressed her in a way she never had before: "Stop it, Simmy! I can and I will. You have no right to tell me what I can and can't do. It's not up to you. It's my life. And Zeph's life. He's a good man. And I love him. So stop it! Stop it right now!"

Simmy, pummeled, cowered near the footboard of the bed. Geneva's words, much more than the book, had hurt her. Looking down, she found a loose button and picked it up. "I know he's a good man. He's my brother. I love him, too."

Geneva, shocked at her own words and actions, softened her tone and pulled Simmy down to sit with her on the bed. She took her hand. "Nobody will ever have to know, Simmy. And why not Zeph?"

"You know why not," whispered Simmy, trying not to cry.

"But I love him. Isn't love enough? Shouldn't love be enough?"

Simmy's eyes filled with tears. As Geneva watched her, empathy replaced her anger. This was Simmy, her dearest friend. She rubbed her hand. "We'll keep it a secret, Simmy. Forever. I promise. No one will ever have to know. Mama's already resigned to having a spinster daughter."

Simmy looked up. "You mean you'd go through your whole life pretending? Just so you can marry Zeph?"

Geneva paused. "Yes." For a few minutes, neither of them spoke. "When Mama married Daddy, she gave up her life in Richmond to come here. She left it all behind, all the fine things, all her friends and her family. What's the difference? I'll be giving up one life— and getting another. The one I want."

"There's a big difference. Do you know what could happen?" Simmy said. She stopped, afraid to go further. What she knew—but didn't have the courage to voice—drove a stake into her heart. "Do you know?"

But Geneva was no longer listening.

Simmy left Geneva's room that afternoon still hoping to stop a terrible mistake. But she was up against a kind of love too genuine to move. She wanted to warn her friend, wanted to warn Zeph, but she was not one to argue endlessly. She was the kind who supported, who served—who made other people happy. She wanted to tell Geneva much more, tell her what she could expect, tell her there was more to marriage than the excitement of it all—that there was more to love than love. Simmy knew all too well. She had learned too much after a field hand had forced her into the barn once when the fields were deserted. No one heard her cries. He had thrown her down into the hay and had his way with her young body until she was bloodied and bruised. She had never told anyone, not even Geneva. She was too ashamed, too timid. And so Simmy remained silent, hiding her fears, hoping against hope.

For the next few weeks, Simmy watched. She watched Geneva and Zeph. She watched Vivvy. She watched the household staff, and she watched the Judge and Mrs. Snow. She watched—worrying every minute that this would not have a good end. Unless something changed, she feared they were all headed for heartache. She hoped and prayed that Zeph and Geneva would come to their senses.

But in the end, Simmy gave up. She became their go-between.

CHAPTER 29

1876

Dresses & Deceptions

Geneva pinned back her hair with a pair of silver combs. On her bed lay her small silk reticule, a carriage blanket, and assorted fabric samples. She was happy to have a nice day to travel to Mrs. Lowman's. Easter was approaching and with it her annual trip to the local dressmaker. Customarily, she traveled with her mother, but she had asked to go alone, with Simmy as her chaperone. Her mother had acquiesced. It had been far easier than arguing.

Caroline had given up on finding a suitable husband for Geneva. At times, the tension between mother and daughter was palpable. Geneva had also announced, quite decisively, that she was no longer interested in attending the women's seminary. This disappointed her father, but he had grown weary as well. At fifty-five, after surviving the war and the loss of two sons, he was busy maintaining his practice, once again thriving, and his farm.

Spring had come early to the valley after an icy winter that had laid waste to parts of the orchard and toppled an outbuilding. Almost overnight, winter had released its grip, and from it blossomed a spring as intoxicating as Geneva had ever known. She had watched with anticipation as the small yellow and purple crocuses pushed up through the damp February soil—like her own new dreams. Her spirit was alive with a delight that threatened to send her into showers of happy tears.

The decision had been long coming—and not casually made. After declaring their love, Geneva and Zeph had continued to meet secretly at the chapel, drawing closer and closer until neither could resist the pull of desire, impossible as it seemed. In the fog of love, the impossible had gradually become possible. On more than one occasion, they had nearly stepped beyond the limits of what was proper and decent. There was no other step to take—except to relinquish a love they could not deny. They were captured completely.

Once their decision to marry was made, Geneva was jubilant. Outwardly Simmy lent her support, but privately she feared trouble lay ahead.

Geneva tied a straw bonnet under her chin, ignoring the toque hat her mother had suggested. Looking out for the rig, she raised the window. Fresh spring air blew in. She collected her things and stepped out of her room.

"Good morning, Miss Geneva," Zeph said, and he tipped his hat. Their eyes met as he climbed down from the buckboard, but nothing passed between them that a casual observer would detect.

"Good morning, Zeph," Geneva said. "Thank you for bringing up the rig. We will be back late this afternoon."

Zeph helped Geneva step up beside Simmy, already seated, and handed Geneva the reins.

"Be careful," he said. "Keep to the middle of the road. Last week's rain washed out a gully beside the swale. Make sure you keep the wheels away from it."

"We will," Geneva said with a look both intimate and proper. She slapped the reins, and the rig jerked forward. Zeph watched them ride off, a lacy train of dust trailing.

As soon as they were out of sight of the house, Geneva turned to Simmy. "Did he talk to the Reverend?"

"Yes. Last night."

"What did he say?"

"Said he would."

Geneva squealed. "Oh, Simmy. But who will take him out to the church?"

"Says he knows it."

"How?"

"Said he went there when he was a little boy. Knows exactly where it is."

"What if he gets lost?"

Simmy, bemused, said, "Quit your worrying. He won't get lost. You ever 'member Zeph saying something was so and it wadn't?"

"You're right."

Geneva tried to relax, but she was still concerned. Something could go wrong. Someone could find out. Until it was done, she could not help but worry.

The sun, a low brightness in the sky, warmed their faces as the horse trotted at a steady pace. They passed forests flecked with red-buds that mingled among the dark green of pines and hemlocks as they navigated the switchbacks that took them down the mountain.

Geneva noticed chill bumps on Simmy's bare arms. "You're cold." She took the blanket from her knees and pushed it toward Simmy. "Put this around you."

They wound eastward through the countryside to the north fork of the Cleary River where Mrs. Lowman kept her shop. Except for the years interrupted by war, Geneva and her mother had always made this pilgrimage, a concession to the mother's fashion sense. Today's trip, though, had another purpose entirely for Geneva.

Katy Lowman met them at the door.

"Did not your mother come along with ya, Miss Snow?" Mrs. Lowman asked in a voice still flavored with her father's Scottish brogue.

"No, ma'am. Simmy came."

"Oh, I see," said Mrs. Lowman, examining Simmy, who positioned herself outside the narrow doorway at an angle to see the dressmaker work but to avoid offending her.

Geneva handed the fabric samples to the seamstress and stepped up on a wooden box in the center of the room, strewn about with bolts of fabric. Half-made garments hung along pegs on one wall, and a Singer sewing machine, its treadle well worn, was piled high with fabrics and notions. Strategically, it took up the space beneath a window where the morning light shone on its black curves.

"Mama wants a Dolly Varden—or something similar in the green silk," Geneva said. "And another one out of this blue—whatever you'd suggest. I want a simpler one from the cream."

"'Tis lovely," Mrs. Lowman said. She rubbed her hands across the light fabric. "Could I persuade you to have a little eyelet around the neckline or maybe some Battenburg? I have some from Philadelphia—came in just yesterday—very elegant." She held up a sample of the fine lace.

"It is lovely," Geneva said. "Maybe a little on the blue dress, but not for the cream one. I want something simple."

"I could do a little pipin'."

"That would be fine."

"All right, Missy, then pipin' it'll be. And a little lace on the blue dress."

She measured Geneva and made notes on a scrap of paper with a pencil stuffed in her knot of copper-colored hair.

"You're Presbyterian, aren't you, Miss Snow?" she said, drawing a string from Geneva's shoulder down to her wrist.

"Yes, ma'am."

"Have you ever visited our church? At the North Fork?"

"Yes, I have. A while ago. My father has spoken there on behalf of the Synod."

"I was married there nearly fifty years ago," she said brightly while she measured and jotted. "Turn, Miss Snow."

Geneva pirouetted. "I'm sure it was lovely."

"Oh, 'twas indeed. My Mr. Lowman cut a handsome figur'. I remember him standing at the altar looking like he come right out of the pages of a picture book. All dressed up but sweating like a pig." Mrs. Lowman laughed. She wrapped the measuring tape around Geneva's waist. "I was so nervous. My daddy had to hol' me up—wadn't hard since I was a little bitty thing. I was sixteen and not much bigger than you."

A shiver of anticipation wriggled down Geneva's back, as if a beetle had slipped down behind her collar.

Mrs. Lowman stood back, letting the measuring tape droop. "My daddy was so happy that day. I was the last of his five girls to marry, and by that time, he'd had enough of weddin's. Can you imagine? Five girls."

A small ache stirred in Geneva, and for an instant her mood dimmed.

"Five was a lot for a simple farmer like my daddy," the seamstress continued. "He had always wanted a son—never got a live one. Two little boys died shortly after being born. After I come along, he and my mother—they gave up. Always said the good Lord give 'em five sons through marriage though. He never called 'em his sons-in-law—always his sons-in-love."

"What a kind man."

"He was indeed—and a Scot through and through. Would walk fifteen miles outta his way to save a nickel. Saving was a sacred duty to my father." Mrs. Lowman patted Geneva's shoulder. "There. I'll have these made up and sent to you before Easter."

A box of dresses arrived a few weeks later. Caroline, doubting her daughter's choices, insisted Geneva try them on for her so that she could certify them. For Geneva, it was tacit approval she would fasten to her own intentions.

Caroline, arranging forsythia in the foyer, waited.

Geneva slipped out of the second dress—the stylish green Dolly Varden that her mother loved and she loathed. Simmy helped her into the last dress, the plain, cream-colored one. While Geneva squared it over her shoulders, Simmy buttoned up the side, a row of covered buttons with small, embroidered eyelets. Two lines of piping shaped the bodice and an unfussy sash encircled her waist.

When she turned around, a tiny gasp escaped from Simmy. "Oh, Geneva. It's so pretty."

The dress was exactly what Geneva had hoped for—a pale Isabelline taffeta with a narrow skirt, a plain high collar, and cuffs—and no lace. "Do you think Mama will be suspicious?"

"No. 'Course not. How could she? Especially if we do this." Simmy untied the sash and substituted a blue one. "Now, go on. Go show her. And put this on." Simmy handed her a bonnet. Geneva skated out the door in her stockings and down the stairs.

Caroline scrunched up her nose when she saw her. "That one is terribly plain, Geneva. Didn't Mrs. Lowman have any lace?"

"I didn't want any."

"Of course you didn't," she said, her tone sarcastic. She broke off a stem to shorten it and pushed it into the vase. "Well. Turn around. We can add a brooch or pearls—something to dress it up."

"Which one should I wear for Easter?" Geneva asked, hoping to appease her mother at least a little.

"The green one." Caroline turned again to her flowers. "Hang them up in your wardrobe. Don't just dump them on your bed," she said as if she were instructing a child.

From the upstairs landing, Simmy watched Geneva climb the winding stairs, holding her bonnet at her waist like a bouquet and swaying to a silent choir. They retreated to Geneva's bedroom.

"Oh, Geneva. You're so beautiful." Simmy pulled her toward the cheval mirror in the corner of the room. They stood together gazing at their image: Simmy so plain and dark, Geneva so fair. Self-consciously Simmy reached up to smooth her unruly hair. Yet each saw the other one as they always had, as the dearest of friends. No civil codes of conduct had ever impinged on their friendship and never would, at least in private. It was too longstanding, too deep, and too genuine to break—even by the step Geneva would soon take. Behind the locked door, there was no pretense, no hint of superiority or inferiority, no difference of color or class. Behind the locked door, they were sisters.

Simmy slipped her hand into her pocket and brought out a small, dark red blossom. "Squeeze this in your hand real tight. It's from the sweet bush 'round back of the smokehouse." She placed it in Geneva's palm and closed her hand around it. Geneva clenched her fist.

"Now open up. Smell it," Simmy said.

"It's like perfume."

Simmy looked down, and then hesitating, she set her eyes straight on Geneva. "Are you sure?"

"Yes, Simmy. I am sure."

You've never been anything except sure, Simmy thought. *I hope you're right*.

CHAPTER 30

1876

Omens & Eddies

Geneva awoke before dawn. A faint hint of brightness was beginning to outline the mountains. "April 27, 1876," she whispered as she lay on her bed. The long wait was finally over. It was as if years had passed since she first loved Zeph—and they had. Time had swept past them like cold breezes. What would happen today was her destiny, fate, something almost out of her hands. Yet nothing had ever been out of Geneva Snow's hands—at least not to this point in her twenty-one years.

She could hardly believe her good fortune. She took it as a good omen—and another unspoken approval. Her parents had been called away to the funeral of an acquaintance. Hayes, back for a few weeks to help his father with the spring harvest, would be in the fields all day, cutting winter wheat. Geneva again had considered telling her brother, but she decided against it, saving him the anguish. If her plan worked, no one would have to know—ever.

Throwing on a dressing gown, she escaped to the belvedere, the pinnacle of her world. She watched the sun pierce the dawn and melt over the mountains. Her joy was unspeakable. Her anticipation—nearly unbearable. As arranged, Zeph would take the farm hands out into the fields before he slipped away, ostensibly to repair a broken hame or mend a harness. Geneva would try to wait with some measure of calm.

At the designated hour, Geneva made certain Vivvy was distracted in the kitchen before she slipped unnoticed out through the library. Carrying the cream-colored dress tucked into a pillowcase and tied loosely with a ribbon, she walked quickly, holding her breath until she cleared the yard and disappeared into the woods. When she was safely out of sight of the house, she stopped and gazed up into the green cathedral where white sunlight stood like pillars. If she were to turn back, it would have to be now, but not a whit of doubt possessed her.

She wound her way through the forest and down the hill toward the woods sheltering the chapel, a place as dear to her now as any on earth—the place where love was declared, where love would be confirmed, and where the impossible would become true. She crossed through an overgrown orchard to the vague path that long ago had led worshippers to the church. When she neared the chapel, she hid in a copse of thick white pines. Unbuttoning her day dress, she let it drop to her ankles and slipped the new dress over her head. The folds of cloth fell across her shoulders and hips. She started when two hands encircled her waist. Turning, she saw Simmy, her fingers pressed to her lips. Without a word, Simmy buttoned the dress and tied the sash.

"You look beautiful," whispered Simmy, putting her cheek against Geneva's. But hidden in Simmy's heart were concerns she could not bring herself to voice.

Zeph broke into a broad smile when he saw them. Standing beside him was a robust man in a dark coat and a hand-made clerical collar. Zeph introduced him as Reverend Hawkins.

"Hello, Simmy, Miss Geneva." His deep voice was reassuring. "Why don't we go in," he said. "It's been entirely too long since this church saw a wedding."

Reverend Hawkins held open the door for the small party to enter. Muted light flowed through tall peaked windows that lined the walls like silent guests. Air and light intermingled, rising toward the bare-beamed ceiling and drifting throughout the room. High narrow windows rose behind a plain, roughhewn cross. Through moist eyes, Geneva saw eddies of colored light.

No one spoke as they walked toward the altar. They took their places while a choir of birds—the varied voices of God—heralded the sacred ceremony.

"We are gathered here in the sight of Almighty God..." Reverend Hawkins' voice echoed, filling the rafters of the church.

Geneva's spirit soared.

Simmy made a silent, desperate prayer.

CHAPTER 31

1877

Signatures & Secrets

Rain throbbed against the windows of Geneva's locked bedroom. It was hot rain, the kind that came in August, not like spring showers that refreshed or even sterile winter ones that cleansed. This was hot, heavy rain, as if dirty wash water spilled from heaven.

Over and over Geneva wrote her name—her married name—in long and elegant flourishes: Geneva Caroline Snow Elias. After more than a year married, the thrill of it all had not left her. She dipped the nib of her pen into the well and drew ink across the white linen stock, an extravagance given the scarcity of good paper. She smiled at the memories she now possessed of her husband whose body was as strong as his spirit was tender. Their times together, stolen nights in their chapel, had been the happiest Geneva had ever known, and remembering them sustained her during their separations. The secrecy of their vows added mystery and romance that an ordinary bride would never know. It was a charade of the heart that suspended her above her circumstances.

As the rain droned, her pen scratched across the paper. How she had imagined it would feel to be joined in marriage was a shadow now that she knew Zeph as her husband. She was complete—an unanticipated emotion that came as a forceful confirmation of love. He had long been her companion, her friend, always a part of her life, but to have joined him body and soul brought her a happiness surpassing even her dreams.

At Cairnaerie and throughout the community she avoided, she remained the unmarried daughter of Judge and Mrs. Snow. Scuttlebutt said she was so particular that suitors no longer pursued her. To the world she would be a spinster, but the label became her hedge of protection, a safe and respectable identity to hide the marriage she cherished.

Whenever Geneva wrote their names, she was careful to lock her door and, afterwards, to carry these letters of deep devotion and throw them into the hot coals of the smokehouse, always waiting to make sure the flames consumed every last letter. Only her journals and letters from Zeph could betray her, so she kept them in a narrow wooden box, which she hid in the deepest recesses of her tall wardrobe behind a board she had loosened.

She met Zeph at the chapel as often as she could. Weather like today's rain, however, kept them apart. Geneva could not risk returning to the house dripping wet and explaining where she had been in such a storm. Not even a dog would venture out in such a deluge. So long as the weather was foul, she could do little more than watch the farm from her bedroom or the belvedere, hoping for a glimpse of her husband.

She busied herself reading and writing, and feeding her voracious appetite for learning by studying her brother's cast-off schoolbooks. Hayes, as good as his word, had brought her his books and regularly sent her more from the city where he was carving out a career. She spent whole afternoons pressing into a book or scouring her father's ever-expanding library looking for an answer.

On pleasant days, Geneva walked or rode on the farm. When Simmy could be relieved of her chores, she joined her, the two women riding side by side and stride for stride. Geneva still rode Dally, who had first come to the farm mistakenly with a load of cattle. Simmy rode whatever mount—usually a dobbin—that was not being used in the fields.

It was not unusual for Geneva to be gone from the house all day. Often she would wait hours at the chapel for the joy of seeing Zeph alone for minutes. But when the weather closed in like today, cutting Geneva off from Zeph and the outdoors, she grew restless and irritable. Nothing, however, could keep her from dreaming, from removing herself from the mundane, from spiriting herself into the secret world where she lived with Zeph. If she had to, she could exist there for days.

One luxury Geneva never allowed herself was imagining how it would be to live openly with Zeph. Instead she willed herself to be happy, and she never thought about what might have been. She never succumbed to self-pity; Geneva had gotten what she wanted.

She laid aside her pen, rose from her desk, and went to the window where the sky was bloated and colorless. Rain was now coming down in sheets and blowing against the windows. The yellow curtains stirred. For days, a vague malaise had shadowed her. Certainly, the dreary weather was the cause of her melancholy.

When Simmy came to tell her lunch was ready, Geneva said she wasn't feeling well and would rather sleep. Shortly, her mother came in and touched the back of her hand to her daughter's forehead.

"You don't seem to be feverish. Why don't you rest?"

Geneva curled up in her bed and, listening to the drone of the rain, fell into a deep sleep.

By Sunday, the weather had cleared, and Geneva felt better. Still she begged to be excused from Sunday services, a request that had become habitual. With a fever, the weather, an ache, a pain, any number of excuses, she avoided trips to Hyssop and excused herself from events that had once been routine.

Vivvy, finished with the breakfast chores, had left for church with Briscoe, riding in a wagon so rickety she bounced around the bed like a melon. It would be after dark before she returned to Cairnaerie. Soon after, the Snows departed.

From an upstairs hall window, Geneva could see the rig sitting in the side yard, waiting for Zeph and Simmy to leave for church themselves. *I wonder,* she thought. Dressing quickly, she raced down the stairs.

Relishing the morning's solitude, she hurried to the side yard and knocked at Zeph's door. Simmy, dressed for church, answered. "What you doing here?" she said, looking askance at Geneva, who was standing in a hastily thrown-on dress and stockings with no shoes. "You begged off church again, didn't you?"

"Where's Zeph?"

"Out back."

Geneva found him washing behind the springhouse, his shirt off, a ratty huck towel slung over his shoulder. Sneaking up behind him, she grabbed his bare waist.

"Geneva!" he said, tensing and pushing her away. "What are you doing?"

She laughed. "It's all right, Zeph. Nobody's here except me."

"Where's Vivvy?"

"Gone with Briscoe."

"You sure?"

"Yes." Geneva was giddy. "I am absolutely sure."

"In that case." Zeph gathered Geneva in his arms and twirled her around as Simmy rounded the corner of the house.

"Zeph," Simmy interrupted. She had changed her clothes and now wore a faded work dress. On one hip, she carried a bushel basket. "I think it would please the good Lord right much if you'd take up with your wife for the day."

"You think so, Simmy?" Zeph said, holding Geneva and smiling.

"I do, indeed. And as for myself, I b'lieve I'll go up to the orchard and pick peaches. I 'spect that'll take me a good while."

"Take the rig, Simmy. It's all ready."

Zeph loaded several more bushel baskets and helped his sister into the seat before handing her the reins. As she headed off, Zeph embraced Geneva. They stood together for a long time in the open yard, savoring a rare taste of freedom.

"You don't think God will be mad at me, do you?" she said. "For skipping church?"

"Not the God I know."

———

A hard freeze had set in motion the engine of autumn. Overnight the countryside had changed from summer's succulent greens to the crimsons and yellows of fall. Throughout the extended Indian summer that followed, Geneva and Zeph spent long nights together in their chapel. Still, she could not escape an oppressive feeling of gloom, as if their door of opportunity were closing. She knew the coming winter would make regular rendezvous difficult.

With her journal opened in her lap, she leaned toward the window. She watched cloud shadows brush the landscape and listened to the dried lilacs rattling outside her window. The last harvests would be put up soon. Most fields had been cut and windrows left to dry in the sun. The hog slaughter would follow, on a cold day if possible. One or two large barrows would be shot, vivisected, and hung by their hind legs. They would be dipped in boiling water to loosen the hair and scruff before being scraped and butchered. Though the process was indelicate, it had always fascinated Geneva.

Lately, she had found it harder to rise each morning and continue the charade—although her resolve never wavered, and she had not a single regret. But more than a year of living a lie had worn on her, and the thought of another winter coming left her cheerless.

Geneva watched a wagon crisscross a field in the distance and two farm hands throw hay onto the back. The sights and sounds of the farm had always been like this, regular and reliable—only weather or war had been powerful enough to disrupt them. She heard a screened door slap near the kitchen and a chair squeak. Her father was home. He always came in that door, hung up his coat on a wooden peg, and rested for a few minutes on a short rush-bottomed chair. Through the window, raised a few inches, she smelled fatback frying and pictured meat sizzling in Vivvy's heavy cast iron skillet. Geneva's stomach growled, and she put her hand on her belly.

The sun was low on the horizon, and the yellow curtains faded to sepia in the disappearing daylight—along with the last glimmers of her childhood.

CHAPTER 32

1878

Fear & Expectation

In a corner of the barn loft, Simmy hid behind a pile of hay and hugged her knees. She rocked back and forth, too scared to cry, too involved to escape. She had come from Geneva's room where her worst fear was confirmed. The future had abruptly taken a sharp and dangerous turn, like a carriage running too fast and careening—and Geneva had charged her with delivering the news to Zeph.

Simmy had attended births, both human and animal, and knew more about it than Zeph and Geneva combined. She knew how to press down on the hard abdomen and peel back the opening womb to coax a baby into the world, how to turn a little one coming out face first, how to slip out the shoulder and support the head. She knew to wrap up a trembling mother and let the baby suckle as soon as it cried. She knew to wait for the afterbirth, to help it come by kneading the mother's flaccid stomach. She knew it was painful, but she had seen what happened when a careless doctor hurried. Women had bled to death right before her eyes, despite her own mother's best efforts and considerable skill. Simmy alone fully understood what lay ahead—and that Geneva and Zeph's secret union could not be hidden but for a few more months.

From the rafters an owl hooted. "Wish I could fly up there with you and leave all this trouble behind," she said. She clasped her hands together and prayed like she had never prayed before, and then she left the barn to head home. Simmy had a job to do.

"Zeph," Simmy said as she walked through the door. "You let the fire die."

Zeph, absorbed in a book and wrapped in a blanket to ward off the February cold, heard the irritation in his sister's voice. He dropped his book and jumped up.

"Sorry. I'll get some wood." He headed toward the door.

"No. Leave it. You gotta listen to me."

When he turned around, he saw her face, chiseled with tension.

"What's wrong?"

She took a deep breath and, momentarily, closed her eyes.

"Zeph, I don't know how to say this better than to just say it: Geneva's gonna have your baby."

He fell back toward the bed, as if the wind had been knocked out of him. "You sure?"

"Sure as I'm standing here," she said with a blend of anger and fear. "You two built this fire, now you gotta walk through it. You got no other choice."

With it out in the open, her job done, Simmy began to sob.

Geneva huddled in Zeph's lap. Moonlight streamed through the chapel's high windows, and cold snaked across the floor from gaps in the walls. Conflicted and frightened, she hardly noticed the frigid air.

She had not expected this. She had not even anticipated the possibility. For one so informed of natural things, it seemed absurd, but to her peril—and perhaps because of her own stubbornness— she had ignored Simmy's oblique cautions. Ignorance of a deliberate kind had brought them here. Now all her careful planning, her determination to live a shadow life, was crumbling. Zeph tried to reassure her, but he was frightened as well, an admission he kept to himself.

"What am I going to do, Zeph?"

He kissed her forehead. He had no answers tonight. All he could offer her was comfort. "I can't think but this is the Lord's will. He's mighty. The Bible says we have trials. This is a big one, but I know He looks kindly on every new life." He reached out and put his hands on her belly. "It's gonna be all right. Hey, we're gonna have us a baby—you and me," he said, trying to elicit a smile.

She brightened. "Let's run away, Zeph. We can move to the north— somewhere—we can live there. Washington. Or Philadelphia. There must be places. I'll leave a note, so they won't worry. Of course, they'll worry, but I'll tell them that I've left on my own. I'll tell them…."

Zeph listened patiently, wondering how one woman could have so many ideas.

"…. Or we could go away, and then I could write to them. We could do it, Zeph."

He reached out and took her hands. Geneva had the optimism of dreams—but no understanding of the savagery of prejudice, especially beyond the confines of Cairnaerie. She was naïve to the darker hearts of men. Zeph was quiet for a moment. In him was truth—and sadness.

"It's not so easy, Geneva. And if you left, it would break your daddy's heart."

Geneva had no reply.

The night embraced them and held them as if they were alone in the universe. It was a momentary reprieve from what was coming, from what they could not undo.

"I have to tell him, don't I?" she said.

"Yes."

But Geneva could not fathom the narrative. "How, Zeph? What can I say?"

Again, he placed his hand on Geneva's belly.

"Maybe this little one will persuade them. If your father is the kind of man I think he is, well, there's hope. There's always hope."

CHAPTER 33

1878

—◆—

Knowledge & Disgrace

Outside Geneva's bedroom window a crow cawed. It was barely mid-morning and already hot. A haze had settled across the valley with damp and stagnant air. She fanned her face and fluffed her dressing gown, thinking how she would welcome a breeze. Winter had loitered into spring like an inconsiderate guest, but it had also made it easier for Geneva to hide her condition beneath quilts and capes. Simmy had adjusted her undergarments, made excuses for her, and even devised a girdle of sorts to hold in her belly. If a trip to town came up, Geneva feigned illness, a practice she had altogether perfected. But now summer was eclipsing spring and hiding was becoming harder.

A sultry breeze floated through the window. She was relieved to be out from under heavy garments, but with the weather changing, her revelation was closing in. Still she delayed, unable to marshal enough courage.

Every day she watched for the right time and place to tell her parents, but she had lived with paralyzing worry whenever she imagined the scene. Would she confess in the parlor? Or the library? How would she begin? Should she explain she had married Zeph and now carried his child? Could they possibly be happy for her? Or should she disappear and return with some concocted story? One question remained paramount: What about the child? How could she raise their child—this new life growing in her that she cherished more each day? For Geneva, to consider a life other than her own was a strange and transforming feeling.

Her skin felt sticky. Her gown clung to her heavy belly. She stood up, pulled it off, and tossed it on the bed. Deep in thought, she rifled through her wardrobe and lifted a dress. She was turning around when, unexpectedly, her bedroom door opened.

"Geneva?" Her mother, walking in casually, stopped.

"Wait!" Geneva exclaimed, but it was too late. Fumbling, she dropped the dress, exposing her body. Futilely, she grabbed a throw and tried to cover herself. Geneva could not breathe. She opened her mouth to speak, but no sound came out.

The expression on her mother's face was a mix of shock and confusion. And then Caroline went ashen as a thousand scenarios rushed her brain—none of which made any sense. She grabbed the doorframe and closed her eyes. She knew instantly that her daughter was no innocent. No man could have taken advantage of a girl so strong and determined.

"What have you done?"

Geneva, without words, pleaded with her eyes.

Caroline stumbled out of the room, closing the door. Geneva heard her take several deep breaths before hurrying off. Far down the hall a door slammed. The sound reverberated through the house and out across the farm in a wave of accusation as if to announce Geneva's apparent sin.

Geneva groaned and collapsed onto her bed. After a few minutes, she heard a key turn in the lock, followed by soft footsteps, retreating. In a crushing flash of prescience, she understood the footsteps would never come to her room the same way again. She had lost her mother forever. Horrified, exposed, guilty, she sobbed into her bed covers. Her world had come to an abrupt and ruinous stop—unless her father could rescue her—but in the calamitous moment, even that seemed doubtful.

No one called her to supper that evening. Throughout the house there was hardly a sound as if everyone had vacated Cairnaerie and she had been left behind. The silence, broken only by the hourly striking of her father's clock, magnified her fears.

The moon rose.

Finally, she heard footsteps in the hall outside her room. A key rustled. The door latch clicked. Caroline, eerily composed and un-emotional, entered and spoke as if she were conveying the most mundane of messages: "I have explained to the servants you are ill. I will have Simmy bring your meals. Under no circumstances are you to leave this room. Do you understand?"

Unable to speak, Geneva nodded.

The next morning Caroline was alone in her studio, fretting. Deep circles framed her eyes. She had paced all night, questioning why such a circumstance—this horrible nightmare—had befallen her. How she wished she could sleep and awaken to find it all gone. But whether her eyes were open or closed, the image of Geneva's distended silhouette haunted her. No pain had ever been so unex-pected, so frightening, or so shocking. Even her parents' deaths did not compare. In the natural order of things, their passing had been foreseen—and had not carried betrayal. How could she face such unmitigated disgrace? What had she and Bertram done to deserve this—and what must she do about it?

She tried to paint. She held her brush the way one might touch a cobweb, but her hand trembled so much she could not apply a single stroke. And she could hardly look at her half-finished canvas—a landscape she had planned to give Geneva on her next birthday. She had still imagined—still hoped—it might someday grace her daughter's home, one with her own husband and family. But that dream, which had lingered stubbornly despite Geneva's declarations to the contrary, was gone—as completely as the hardened pigments on her palette. She had no desire to finish the painting now, no desire to paint at all this awful morning. But she had to force some action, something to move her forward. At least here, alone, locked in her studio, she could think.

Caroline gripped her paintbrush and tried to steady her hand. She stared at the pots of colors sitting on the table, the tubes of oil, and her palette covered with mixed colors, dried and useless. She stood up and walked to the window. In short order, summer would produce sights she would have relished—under any other circumstances—but this morning's landscape was shriveled, dull, and shrunken, the way leaves wither when stunned by a sudden freeze. Even the mountains that should be smoldering with fresh colors, looked drab and sad to her.

In a brazen and selfish prayer, she hoped Geneva's child might not live—but in a second thought that followed with terrifying speed, she realized that to wish for the death of a child was horrible. She could not voice it, even in this moment of utter desperation. Instead, she stifled a sob and threw her brush across the room.

Caroline desperately longed for Bertram's comfort, yet at the same time she was strangely glad he was driving cattle to stockyards in the northern valley. It would give her a few weeks to think and time to find a solution—if one could be found.

After a few minutes staring, she returned to her easel and se-lected a fresh brush. But it was no use. Caroline was impaled by the possibility of disgrace. The thought of someone else learning what she wished she didn't know herself overwhelmed her. Nothing else mattered—not who the father was or what would become of the child. Nothing mattered except that disgrace be avoided. With her thumb, she stroked the delicate bristles, brooding. She had no choice but to take Vivvy and Simmy into her confidence, but she would assure their silence with threats of the severest kind.

But how could she dispense with the baby—if it were born alive? Local people cared for orphans. Surely an infant left on the steps of a local church would be taken in. *Yes. That was it.* Caroline's mood lightened, and as if to signal a small victory, sunlight flooded her studio. *When the child is born, Simmy will take it to town and leave it. In a few months, Geneva will recover, and then all will be well—like it had never happened.*

Caroline sat up straighter, calmer, relieved. She would weave a story of a prolonged illness from which recovery depended on uninterrupted rest and solitude. *If we're careful and discreet, this can be arranged. Yes, of course it can.* She laid down her brush and lifted her grinder to prepare some more paints: viridian, cerulean blue, and cadmium yellow. She scraped the pigment onto her palette. *Bertram will be distressed, but I will talk to him as soon as he returns. His reputation is at stake, too.* She opened a vial of oil. Carefully, with a small blade she mixed it into the pigment. Again, she studied the view outside her studio window; it seemed to improve. An ember of sun smoldered in the sky, as she turned again to her canvas. *Perhaps sister would enjoy having this landscape.*

Caroline painted straight through supper, shooing Simmy out when the girl came to tell her the evening meal was served. She painted until the sun went down and no natural light was left to see her canvas. And then she painted for several hours more by the light of a kerosene lamp until finally she was able to sleep—assured that she could hide this awful secret.

But Caroline had not considered the determination of Geneva Snow.

———

It was after midnight when Geneva unlocked her bedroom door with a key that Simmy had brought her, and she slipped out. She could no longer endure the confinement. Already several weeks had passed—and the only saving grace was that she could finally dispense with the capes and blankets. There was no more need to hide.

Without making a sound, she closed the library doors and stood on the terrace. The night mist swarmed around her like a hot sea. The high full moon burnished parts of the yard and erased others as it sailed behind scattered clouds. A calico cat sauntered up and wove between her ankles, purring before meandering out across the moon-spackled yard. She went to a low bench near the edge of the terrace, sat down, and let the night bathe her.

How had she let this all happen? How could she have been so naïve? Now her decisions, her desires—all her plans, hopes, and dreams—were collapsing around her, and she was beginning to understand the full bolt of consequences. How could she protect Zeph? Would her mother ever accept her child in her family? She had heard her belittle mulattos, likening them to cattle roaming through Cairnaerie's fields. She prayed for the child to be born with light skin or to have her own blue eyes, but she knew her prayer was a selfish one. Geneva knew she was strong enough to refuse their inquiries, but would the child betray the father by the color of its skin and the composition of its face? How could she explain?

The possibility of being separated from her child never entered her mind. Had she known what her mother was planning, Geneva would have insisted that she and Zeph run away. But she was afflicted with the unrealistic hope the young suffer. She believed it would all work out. Somehow. More importantly, she believed her father would understand, that he might even take her side. She clung to that hope like one who is swept away in a flood and grabs onto a branch. It was the single hope she held.

She had always counted on her father's affection—and his sense of fairness. She had never heard him disparage coloreds—or anyone, for that matter. If anything, the matter of their treatment had been the one point of contention in her parents' otherwise harmonious marriage. Perhaps it was the strong nature she and her father shared, or perhaps it was her father's determination to practice his faith. Whatever the origin, Bertram Snow had conveyed to Geneva something deeply personal, something never spoken outright, but something true. And in her father, the daughter had found a perceived permission that had allowed her to love Zeph completely.

While she remained confident of her father, she worried nonetheless. Privately, Geneva and her father had often laughed over her mother's obsession with decorum—yet hadn't he often acquiesced to his wife? Could this break the bond between father and daughter? Would she still be his Little Bird?

A hawk flew through the yard and alighted on a branch where it was perfectly silhouetted against the moon—as if a great painter had commissioned it to pose. Geneva watched it preen, turning its head back and forth until it took to the air again, this time squealing. It flew away into the night.

CHAPTER 34

1878

Blame & Betrayal

The week before her father was expected back home, Geneva listened to the preparations being made for his homecoming. Ordinarily, his return was a happy occasion. This time, however, she knew any celebratory mood would be short-lived. The thought of him learning of her condition worried her until she could barely eat or sleep. While her mother's reaction had not surprised her, her father's held a measure of hope.

With her journal open on her desk, Geneva squirmed in the stiff, cane-bottomed chair to find a more comfortable position. Nothing felt right today.

Daddy will be back early next week, and I want desperately to see him—but I fear what is ahead. I hope I can talk to him before Mama does. Under other circumstances, I know he would rejoice with the news that will greet him, but I also know Mama will try to persuade him to her way of thinking. I must devise a line of reasoning to make him my advocate. Mama surely speculates on my actions, but I hope Daddy will find the good in what I have done.

I know I must walk through this fire, as Simmy tells me, but I hope we are not all consumed by it.... June 10, 1878

Geneva closed her journal, hid it in her wardrobe, and climbed on her bed to rest. She tried to be optimistic, but instead she was irritable and unsettled. The temperature had soared, and the heat made her ankles swell. She lifted her thick hair off her neck, drenched with sweat, and struggled to find a comfortable position for her ballooned and awkward body. In one of many kindnesses, Simmy had brought a pitcher of cold water from the springhouse. Geneva could barely drink a drop, though, until she had to relieve herself in the chamber pot stowed under her bed. As she tried to rest, she watched a bead of moisture wallow down the edge of the pitcher. Eventually, she fell into a fitful sleep.

—

By the next morning, it was clear Geneva's child was coming. She awoke with pain girdling her, and her bedclothes were soaked. With the efficiency of a dispassionate administrator, Caroline ordered the help away for the day, except Vivvy and Simmy. She locked all the doors and closed all the windows, making the house insufferably hot. If the secret were to be kept, a midwife was out of the question, so Geneva labored with Simmy at her side.

"Make sure she's quiet," Caroline said. She handed Simmy a piece of leather for Geneva to bite, to silence the agony. "Tell me when it's over."

Caroline tried to stay busy, but the tension in the house was as stifling as the heat. It felt like a death had occurred, and they all were waiting for the undertaker. When a new girl, hired a month earlier, knocked at the kitchen door, Caroline snapped at her and shut the door in her face. Even Vivvy, infamous for her insubordination, kowtowed to her every demand. *Miss Caroline is in a mood,* the cook thought.

Late into the night Simmy tended to Geneva, whose breathing was shallow and quick, almost frantic. What modesty she might have had otherwise disappeared as wave after wave of pain and nausea washed over her. Her back ached, her head was foggy, and her nightgown, soaked to translucent, clung to her body. Each contraction of her womb brought agony, yet she remained silent. This was her first punishment, but it would not be her last.

"When is this going to end, Simmy?" Exhausted and pressed by pain, Geneva began to cry. "I can't do this. I can't, Simmy. Help me."

"Shh." Simmy wet a cloth and wiped Geneva's face. The light from a lamp flickered. "It'll be over soon."

Near dawn, Geneva muffled a scream with her pillow. It was followed with a deep and sustained groan as she strained. Her face reddened, and she clenched the bed linens as she pushed her child into the world. Simmy, kneeling at the foot of the bed, watched the child crown and then emerge into her waiting hands. Geneva lay spent as a weak but distinct cry rang out.

"A little girl, Geneva. A girl."

The child, small and wrinkled, had a full head of dark hair—raven's hair Vivvy had always called the downy hair of an infant. Simmy tucked blankets around Geneva when she began to shake, and she wrapped the baby in a pillowcase, placing her in Geneva's arms. Later, Simmy would bundle up the soiled linens and burn them. But for now, they stared at the beautiful face of Geneva's newborn daughter.

"What are you going to call her?"

Geneva smiled. This was one decision she knew was right. "Alice Lyford."

Simmy wept—it was her mother's name: Clarissa Alice Lyford Elias.

———

Caroline stood next to Bertram's desk with her hands on her hips, waiting for his reaction. Weary from traveling, he was stunned by the news that had greeted him, and especially by the second revelation.

"Are you sure, Caroline?" he said, fixing his gaze on her.

In his eyes was a depth of sadness she had never seen before, but her anger overwhelmed her compassion and she tore into him unmercifully. "Yes, Bertram. I'm sure. It's Zeph. Vivvy confirmed it. Your precious little nigra boy has had his way with your daughter." Fury flashed in her eyes.

From deep within him came a guttural moan. *Oh, my Little Bird.* He wanted to weep, but he could not. He wanted to flee from this altered future, but he could not. Duty—the word rose up through his core like bile.

"I feared something bad would happen. I warned you," Caroline continued bitterly. She splayed her hands on his desk and challenged him. "You can't treat them like equals and expect them not to take advantage of it."

Bertram clenched his jaw. He knew he had done right by Zeph—and by Lightner and Clarissa—but had his own sense of justice betrayed him? Was Caroline right? Had he been a fool? In a single and poignant flashback, the same despair that had stalked him decades before in Baltimore threatened him now. He could almost feel his grandfather's watch against his skin. Who would save him this time?

Caroline continued her tirade. She was rarely accusatory, but this day she was more than so; she was condemnatory. "I tried to tell you, Bertram. I tried to tell you when you first sent that boy off to school. I warned you! Now look where it has gotten us." She raised her arms in a gesture of surrender. "I tried. I sincerely tried. But you would not listen to me."

All her dreams of marrying off her daughter to a man from a family of prominence were trampled—unless they could cover it all up. She pressed hard to get her husband to agree.

"We have to get rid of it. If we send it away—someone in town will take it in. Or I can send Simmy to Lynchburg or Winchester and we will never see it again. And then Geneva can make a new life. Lord knows she needs a new one! It's her only chance, Bertram. We will all be spared, if we can get rid of it."

Suddenly Bertram exploded. "It?" This was more than he could stomach. "It?" he yelled with a voice that held equal parts disappointment, disbelief, and hurt.

"Yes! It!" Caroline fired back. "And Zeph must go as well. We have to get him away from Geneva. I will not live with a reminder of this whole sordid mess slinking around my house. He's got to go—the sooner the better—and take his sorry sister with him. It's the only way we can...."

"...Stop!" Bertram banged his fist on the desk, upsetting his inkwell. Black ink flowed across the mahogany surface and dripped onto the floor. Neither of them took notice.

Bertram stood up and turned his back to Caroline, his shoulders rigid, stone-like. He stared out the window, struggling to calm himself. When he finally spoke, it was with a maddening tranquility that further inflamed his wife. "That's not the solution. Whether you like it or not, Caroline, this baby is our grandchild."

"No!" Caroline stomped and screamed like a mad woman. "I don't want it. I don't. It's not mine! You're a fool, Bertram Snow. You're a fool!"

She ran from the room. Bertram covered his face and wept.

CHAPTER 35

1878

―――――◆―――――

Plots & Plans

Geneva propped herself up on her bed. Opening her blouse, she pressed her engorged breast into the open mouth of a Mason jar. At the gentle suction, her milk let down and dripped into the jar. Leaning against the headboard, she cradled the jar, wishing it were a tiny mouth and not hard glass pulling her breast.

Only Simmy and Vivvy were allowed into her room. Both had been warned against spreading rumors or the consequences, Caroline had declared in no uncertain terms, would be severe. Whenever Vivvy brought a meal, Geneva suffered the cook's scorn. Every smidgeon of contempt Vivvy had ever had toward Geneva was heightened by a new sense of superiority. She would deliver a tray of food, set it down, and sneer, as if to say, *now who's so high and mighty?*

Vivvy's disdain, though, paled against the breach in Geneva's relationship with her father. Nothing tore at her more viciously. They had spoken once when she had defied her mother and sought him out. But their conversation had nearly undone her. To her dismay, telling him she had married Zeph did not alter her father's disposition at all. Instead it had seemed to create in him an even deeper root of bitterness. Emotions she had not anticipated made her feel guilty—yet she remained resolute. There was nothing else she could do but walk through this fire.

She had forced herself to believe she could pull together the now disparate parts of her two families and hold them together tightly, permanently, but she was learning quickly this might be a foolish dream—perhaps the most foolish dream she had ever entertained. Her actions and their stupidly unanticipated result had hit cataclysmically, breaking her family into raw, jagged shards. Geneva choked at the power of the devastation, but she refused to let it break her.

From the start, Simmy was given the role of mother to Alice Lyford—a temporary situation—while Caroline continued to press her husband for a more permanent remedy. She reminded him constantly—and cruelly—that he could never publicly acknowledge the child. She would leave him if he did and return to Richmond. She would not suffer disgrace. Caught between his wife and a justice he knew in the marrow of his bones to be right, Bertram Snow agonized. And he remained unmoved. He could not disavow this baby any more than he could have disavowed his own daughter. What he prayed for was wisdom—and a solution.

As her milk filled the jar, Geneva tried to relive Alice Lyford's birth. She had been too groggy from her labor to think with much clarity, so Simmy had thought for her: "Geneva, this baby ain't gonna do too good without your kind of feeding." It was Simmy who had suggested the plan.

And it worked perfectly. Twice a day, Geneva collected her milk in a clean jar. In the early morning and late at night, she lowered the jar from her window to the ground where a thick stand of dark purple lilacs formed a screen. Zeph or Simmy collected the jar, placing an empty one in a leather sling Zeph had made from the soft underside of a broken saddle. Simmy hid the jar in the springhouse until the baby needed to be fed. In this regard, Geneva's confinement had become an unintended blessing. Although every ounce of her body ached to hold her daughter, to have her again suckle, the best she could do was to close her eyes and imagine she was holding her baby, not a cold, glass jar.

Geneva finished her task and carefully screwed on the tin lid before stashing it underneath her bed. As soon as it grew dark, she would open her window and lower it to the ground. As she stood by the window to capture a little breeze, she heard a key rattle in the lock. Turning around, she saw Simmy.

"Brought your dinner."

"How is she?" Geneva asked.

"She's growing good. Your milk, it lays on her belly like a rabbit to a child's cheek."

"Is she good for you?"

"Good and sweet as she can be. She's smiling some. Zeph can make her giggle, but if he gits her goin', she's like to throw up all over him."

Geneva teared up. She was learning to endure separation—but it tore at her as deeply as anything ever had. Every bone and muscle, every limb and organ longed for her child. "I would give anything to hold her. And I wish you could stay with me longer."

"I wish a lot, too, Geneva, but wishes don't do my chores. And I gotta take care of your little girl. Remember? I'll come back later." Simmy stood to leave, looking with some concern at Geneva's pale face and hollow eyes. "Are you feeling all right?"

"Yes, I'm fine. I'm just hungry all the time."

Simmy smiled. "That's from giving away all your milk. I'll bring you something later."

"Did I smell cherry pie?"

"Sure did. Vivvy baked some this morning."

"I'd love some."

"I'll see what I can do. You need you some sunshine, too. How long is your mama gonna keep you locked up here?"

"I don't know," Geneva said, and she thought dismally: *Until I give in.* "Have you seen Daddy?"

"He's not around much. He'll be here for a day or two then packs up and goes off. I overheard him tell your mama he had a meeting with somebody—and she has to go with him. She said Lydia was coming. Who's Lydia?"

"Lydia Bauer. An old friend of my mother's. Did he say where they're going?"

"No." Simmy took Geneva's hand and patted it. "I'll find out. All you need to know right now is your girl's healthy. Me and Zeph are taking good care of her. Loving on her jes like you'd do." Simmy picked up the tray. "I better get these dishes back to the kitchen before Vivvy realizes I been up here so long. You sure you're all right?"

"I'm fine. Why?"

Simmy paused. Her face grew serious.

"The Reverend was visitin' the other day, and I heard your mama tell him you're sick."

"Oh, Mama! I'm fine, Simmy. Really, I am. I guess in my case a lie is easier than the truth."

———

Before long, Geneva's regular absence at church was accepted. How sad, the congregants agreed, that the Snow's only daughter had been so stricken.

CHAPTER 36

1878

Respite & Renewal

The opportunity was too good to pass up, but Geneva still had qualms. "You've lost your mind," Geneva said as she and Simmy huddled, sitting cross-legged on her bed. It's too dangerous."

"It'll work. I'll be your lookout."

"If Vivvy catches you up here…"

"…I can take care of Vivvy. I'll be careful. You want to see Alice Lyford, don't you?"

"Of course I do." Geneva leaned back on her arms. "More than anything."

"If I'm willing to do this, you surely have to be. Besides, Zeph wants to see you awful bad."

Geneva bit her lip, torn between what she wanted desperately and the very real possibility of making the whole situation worse.

The Snows, Simmy had learned eavesdropping, would be traveling soon. And Hayes, who had begun visiting Cairnaerie more regularly to help his aging father, was in the southern part of the state surveying land holdings for him.

"I can't believe it's me talking you into a scheme," Simmy said. "Always been you havin' the crazy ideas."

"I know." Geneva smiled, swallowing her doubts. "I've changed, Simmy. We both have." She flopped backward and stared up at the ceiling. Holding her baby and being with her husband was worth any risk. She pushed herself back up and looked squarely at Simmy: "You really think we can do it?"

"It was my plan, remember. So we agree?"

"Yes, we agree."

———

The trip would take only a week, Bertram had told Caroline, and she had to go. In the back of his mind lingered a secret fear that she would follow through on her threat to return to Richmond if he didn't soon find a suitable resolution to Geneva's problem. And this trip for the meeting he had arranged was the only way forward that he could see—at least for the time being.

Out of her keen sense of propriety, Caroline promptly asked her friend Lydia to stay while she and Bertram were away. Leaving an ailing daughter unattended would reflect poorly on her, she had argued—demanding the invitation was a condition of her going. "There is no point in inciting speculation. What would people think? If you insist I go, then I insist Lydia come."

Prior to Lydia's arrival, Caroline worked in a distracted state, attending to the details of hosting Lydia and preparing to travel. She snipped at the staff, sending a nervous unease rippling through Cairnaerie. She ordered Simmy to polish all the silver, shine the brass hardware throughout the house, and clean all the fixtures. Standing on a step stool in the front foyer, Simmy spent an entire afternoon with a bucket of vinegar water and rags cleaning one by one the crystals of the foyer's chandelier and changing out the burnt candles. A large canvas tarp spread out underneath her prevented scratches and drips of vinegar from marring the floor.

The guest room rugs were taken out and beaten, the curtains pulled down and aired, and all the bed linens were washed and hung to dry in the open air. By the end of the week, every window was washed, every tabletop dusted, every floor swept clean, and fresh flowers festooned the entry hall, the parlor, and the dining room.

The busyness was a blessed distraction to Caroline, who privately looked forward to the trip. She hoped to find some sort of respite—as much of one as could be found—and to repair her marriage, which had been shaken by Geneva's revelation. She and Bertram had reached a détente, agreeing on a temporary solution to satisfy both their ends—if it could be arranged. And that was yet to be determined. Only the trip to Richmond would tell.

Geneva listened to the preparations and saw glimpses of the flurried activity from the belvedere. Defying her sequestration, she sneaked there regularly where she could sit for hours, unnoticed, and watch the landscape respire beneath her. She had grown deliriously tired of her bedroom, cut off and isolated as if she were invisible.

Her mother saw her rarely. Torn between love and duty, her husband and daughter, Caroline Snow eventually chose the easier road. As her mother withdrew, Geneva slipped into another world, a ghost in her own home.

———

On Thursday morning Geneva awoke well before dawn after a night of fitful sleep. She lay tired and wakeful until Simmy tapped at her door.

"Are you hungry?" Simmy said, bringing her a breakfast tray.

"I couldn't begin to eat. I'm a bundle of nerves."

Simmy set down the tray and pushed open the curtains. "You think you're nervous. How do you think I feel? Lord, Geneva, I never been so scared to do something in my life. I can't believe this was my idea. I musta been moonstruck or somethin'. I never once laid my head down in this house—never, ever thought I would. Feels like something's out of order."

"Everything is out of order, Simmy, and I've done it," said Geneva, downcast.

"No, Geneva, that ain't what I meant. And you cain't feel sorry for yourself. You got another life to think about now," Simmy said, trying to encourage without scolding.

"I know, but if…"

"…Hush," Simmy said. "You hush. You cain't change the past. It's gone for good. All you got is the future—and there's a sweet little baby girl out there who needs you—and you got a husband. He needs you, too."

Geneva stood up and put her arms around Simmy. "I love you, Simmy. What would I do without you?"

Simmy pushed her away and grinned. "You'd starve."

They laughed, and for a split second they were girlhood friends again, planning one more adventure.

"Have you told Mama about my 'illness'?" Geneva said.

"No, not yet. I wanted to wait till she was so distracted she'd say yes to anything."

"What about Vivvy?"

"Vivvy won't know. Besides, she'll do jes what I tell her to do, so long as I promise to clean out the cistern for her next time."

"Oh, Simmy."

"Hush," she said again, raising her hand in protest. "I'll git Zeph to help me. Listen, you jes think about your little family. I'll have everything you need waiting for ya. Zeph'll show you what to do."

"What if she cries?"

Simmy threw up her arms. "Lord have mercy, Geneva! That's what the good Lord gave ya bosoms for—and I'll come if you need me. Jes get Zeph to throw a little stone up at the window. I kinda doubt I'll be doing too much sleepin'. Where's the key?"

"Here." Geneva handed the key to Simmy. "If you get locked in from the outside and you need out, you can push the other key out of the lock."

"I'm jes fine to stay locked in," Simmy declared. "Don't think I'll be roaming around the house. Soon as they're gone tomorrow and it's good and dark, I'll come."

Late that afternoon, Simmy told Caroline that Geneva wasn't feeling well. Caroline was oddly relieved, as if her invented excuse about Geneva's confinement were the truth. Lydia was a good friend, but even she would not be told the real story. All she needed to know was what the community knew: The Snow's spinster daughter was ill and confined with a condition that was likely contagious and required bedrest for recovery—if recovery were possible. It was a prevarication that Simmy's news made partially true and assuaged Caroline's conscience.

When Lydia arrived the next day shortly after noon, the weather was hot and breezy, though not nearly as humid as late August could be. She arrived rather disheveled. The train had been crowded and hot, and the buckboard was not the fancy landau she had anticipated. Still she was genial and complemented the well-prepared house and grounds.

"Oh, sweet Lydia," Caroline said, embracing her friend. "You remember Bertram?"

"Of course, Judge, it is a pleasure to see you again."

"It's nice to see you, Lydia," he said politely, though his demeanor was somber, which Lydia attributed to the daughter's illness.

"Let's have some refreshment," Caroline said. "I'm sure you're tired after traveling."

Geneva listened from the belvedere. With all the windows opened, voices floated up on the summer air as if invisible guests surrounded her. Lying on her back, her hands cushioning her head, she shut her eyes to picture the scene—her parents chatting with Lydia in the parlor with its tall walls covered in the elegant blue and yellow wallpaper that her mother had ordered from England, white-painted woodwork and matching lambrequins above long white draperies and glass curtains that would sway on the sultry breeze. Her father would be sitting in one of the carved rosewood chairs flanking the fireplace. Her mother would share the settee with Lydia in the room decorated with brass sconces, Wedgwood vases, and her mother's copious landscapes.

"Simmy, put the tea here," Caroline said, patting a low marble table adorned with a small vase of forget-me-nots.

"How can anyone survive summer without mint tea?" Lydia said blithely. She rearranged an errant piece of hair that had plastered itself to the side of her face.

"How was your trip?" Caroline said.

"Long, but you're so kind to invite me. I won't complain about the trip. Your home is beautiful, Caroline. I couldn't help but notice the magnificent floor in your entry hall."

"Thank you. It was Bertram's design," she said. "When we built the house, he engaged a craftsman from back East, a furniture maker actually. It is ash and walnut, all milled here on the farm."

"I look forward to seeing the rest of your home. Now tell me, Caroline, how is your daughter? Your letter said she hadn't been well."

"No, she's not well at all," Bertram said. His words were so abrupt that Lydia took them as confirmation of the girl's grave condition.

Bertram had agreed to the ruse reluctantly, only so Caroline might save face. But while he agreed to this temporary plan, he did not enjoy it.

"I'm so sorry," Lydia said. "Is there anything I can do to help her while I'm here?"

"No, not a thing," Caroline said smoothly, evoking a precarious balance between necessity and truth. "She is confined and I am afraid, contagious. Simmy takes good care of her. All you need to do is rest and enjoy yourself, Lydia. Vivvy will get you anything you want. All you need do is ask."

An uncomfortable silence fell, which Geneva heard Simmy redeem masterfully. "Excuse me, Judge, but Dewitt needs to know whether you want to groom the horses yourself or whether you want him to do it."

"Thank you, Simmy. Tell him I'll be right there. If you ladies will excuse me."

Even from the belvedere, Geneva could hear the tension in her father's voice. She sat up and hugged her legs to her chest as the women talked. Tomorrow her mother and father would be on their way to Richmond, and she would be with Zeph and Alice Lyford. Until today she had not allowed herself the luxury of imagining it. Now, she could barely contain her excitement. Simmy would take her place in the house and in her bed; Geneva would take hers. Her body tingled as she thought of Zeph's touch, and she folded her arms pretending to rock her daughter.

As the afternoon wore on, the air rushing up through the house cooled down. Quietly, Geneva climbed down from the belvedere, making sure she timed her trip across the back hall so she was not seen. She stole back into her bedroom and re-locked the door. Loosening her dress, she lay down across her bed. A deep sigh escaped from her throat. Her arms and legs relaxed as a breeze caressed her body. She drifted off to sleep.

———

Geneva, hardly breathing, crept into the night. The carriage was gone from the shed, and Lydia had settled into her room for the night. The house was quiet. A flake of moon, caught up in web-like clouds, drifted above Cairnaerie. In the warm, still air, night creatures sang slow songs. She crossed the flagstone terrace outside the library and headed for the line of buildings that buffered the backyard—the springhouse, the carriage shed, the smokehouse—and rounded them to reach the cabin where Zeph and Simmy lived, where Clarissa had birthed them both, where her husband and daughter waited.

Zeph was standing in the threshold, his muscular frame silhouetted against the pale light. When he saw her, he smiled. He took her hand and led her inside, closing the door. "She's peaceful as a lamb," Zeph whispered.

The cabin was unadorned and utilitarian with a plank floor, bare wood walls, a simple pot-bellied stove at the center, and a loft accessed by a small staircase. A single oil lamp cast smoky light, and even though the room was humble, it invited Geneva as if she were coming home. It was obvious that after cleaning Cairnaerie, Simmy had washed and readied every inch of her own home.

Alice Lyford slept peacefully in the cradle Zeph had carved from the heart of a white oak tree. Masterfully worked, its runners rocked it like a sailboat on a placid sea. It was lined with a tasseled blanket—Simmy's gift to her niece. For the months before the birth, Zeph had slipped away after his evening chores to carve the cradle while Simmy worked on the blanket, making tiny, perfect loops in the soft creamy wool. Geneva ran her hand along the finely worked edge of the cradle. She could not speak. Her child was more beautiful than she could have ever imagined—so changed from the wrinkled newborn she had held. She touched the sleeping infant's cheek and tiny closed fists. If she understood anything at that moment, she understood love.

A roiling mixture of pride and desire stirred in Zeph as he stood with his wife and daughter. He ached for Geneva. Had he been another kind of man, he might have rebelled against the circumstances that kept them apart, but he was a man who didn't invite trouble. He would be father to this child and husband to this woman regardless of the circumstances he had to endure.

Zeph latched the door before blowing out the light. In the moonlight, he wrapped Geneva in his arms.

CHAPTER 37

1878

Legalities & Solutions

The train carrying Anderson Goodwin from Baltimore lumbered into Richmond shortly after the clock in the station's cupola struck noon. As it slowed down in front of the station house, the conductor jumped through billows of steam onto the platform, and when the train rolled to a full stop, men and women attired for traveling departed.

Anderson took his valise in his hand and stepped off the Pullman. He set his bag on a bench at the side of the building, pulled back his shoulders, and stretched. He asked a porter to direct him to the Willis Hotel.

"Right down this street here, Mister. You jes look for the green awning," said the man, directing him east.

In the shade of a towering chestnut tree, Bertram and Caroline waited on a secluded terrace at the small hotel a few blocks from the station. They had arrived in Richmond the prior day after a long coach ride across the valley and an overnight stop before catching the train. The isolation of traveling had, at last, given them an opportunity to forge some semblance of peace. But both tired, emotionally and physically, they talked little.

As they waited on the terrace, the city around them bustled with a disharmony of sounds to which neither was accustomed. Bertram's expression was grave. He didn't know whether it was Geneva's act or Zeph's betrayal that pained him more and filled him with self-doubt. Where had he failed? Had Caroline been right all along when she had warned him he was too generous with Zeph and too permissive with Geneva?

A door opened nearby and a waiter, dressed in a starched white coat and black pants, stepped onto the private terrace. He carried a tray filled with glasses, a tall pitcher, and a plate of tea cookies and finger sandwiches.

"Thank you," Caroline said to the man as he set the tray on a wrought-iron table and then disappeared with a nod.

Bertram was haunted by the one conversation he had had with his daughter. Defying her mother, she had slipped into his library when he was alone and immediately—without so much as an apology for her deception—mounted a spirited defense. Facing her was a horrible, awkward, and unnerving moment. Bertram had not known what to say, so he had listened....

"He's a good man. He's as good a man as any," Geneva had shouted at him defiantly, emotion rising in her voice. *"A man's a man. That's what the Bible says. Doesn't it, Daddy? Doesn't it? Doesn't it say God is no respecter of persons? You taught me that. If Zeph is less than any other man—colored or white—then the Bible is wrong. I don't care what anyone thinks. I chose to marry a good and decent man. You know that—Zeph is a good and decent man..."*

Bertram had listened stoically to his daughter's tirade. Her words had impaled him. There was little point in arguing with her because she was right. *Dear God,* he had thought, *she is right.* It was society that had it so wrong. But how could he defy all of society? He was a man sworn to uphold laws—not to flagrantly violate them.

"...*Zeph is my husband—and we have a daughter. You cannot expect me to pretend they don't exist.*" Her words had exploded in his head, his own blind denial crashing into their verity. They broke his heart.

Geneva had dropped into a chair. She brushed away tears. This beloved daughter, this iron-willed child who had always spoken her mind freely and who had now chosen her own destiny, could not go without a fight. Bertram would have expected nothing less. But she would not win this battle—they both knew it—but she would wage it nonetheless.

As she had spoken to him, he realized that her resolve not to break into sobs must have required all her strength; to be silent had required every ounce of his own. He had watched her—this girl who had grown into a woman, his cherished Little Bird—now fighting for a life he could not allow.

"*I have a daughter who needs me,*" she had continued. "*I want to be with her and raise her. I will do anything to be with her. I will do anything to keep from hurting you and Mama more, but I cannot stay locked up in my room forever! Can I, Daddy? Can I? I will not leave them. I will not be separated from my husband and my daughter any longer.*"

Desperately, he had wanted to embrace her, comfort her as he had done so often before. But he could not—not this time. She had spun out of his grasp. What was clear, the more he listened, was that he had lost her. She had escaped beyond the point where he could reach her, shelter her, and spare her pain. There was no going after her. She must come back to him.

Her plea had ended abruptly. It was futile. She was up against an impenetrable wall built by convention and society, a wall as cruel as it was unassailable. She had little to bargain with, no collateral at all—except for some fragment of love between father and daughter.

Then her voice had softened, and she retreated from her combative tone. *"Daddy, I beg you, do not separate us. Do not deny me my husband and child."*

Recalling the conversation was wrenching for Bertram as he sat with Caroline awaiting the arrival of Anderson Goodwin. Geneva's unrepentant and bitter words worried him. He would do anything for his daughter, but some things were beyond even his abilities. All her determination—or his—could not change the outcome because what she wanted was impossible.

Something, though, had to be done. He could not risk her life or her future—it was his duty as a father. Neither could he entrust it to her. Until Geneva came to her senses, he would have to act on her behalf. She had given him no other choice—no other choice at all.

Now he and Caroline waited in a strange and cacophonous city far from Cairnaerie, but their pain was still close. Caroline, composed and elegant as ever, clasped her hands tightly in her lap. Bertram was pinning his hope on the young attorney from Baltimore, who was an acquaintance and a second cousin to Caroline. They both knew him to be open-minded and excruciatingly discreet.

"I expect him shortly," Bertram said, pulling his watch from his pocket. He pondered the face of the silver watch. It seemed to give him strength. He thought of his father, his uncle, and of Ezekial Coker. *I have survived tough times before,* he thought.

The door opened again, and this time a strikingly handsome young man stepped onto the terrace. He carried himself confidently.

"Anderson," Bertram greeted him. "It's good to see you. I can't thank you enough for coming."

"Happy to," he said, setting his valise down beside the table and embracing his cousin. "Caroline, you look as lovely as ever."

"I know you're tired after your trip," she said. "May we offer you some refreshment?"

"I would welcome it. Thank you."

After the requisite pleasantries, Caroline excused herself. She would take a rest, she told the men, but she was too anxious to rest. She had given up her fight to have the child sent away—on that point Bertram had not wavered—and she had finally acquiesced as they crossed the mountains toward Richmond. All she hoped for now was a temporary patch to give Geneva time to change her foolish mind. From her room, she watched as the two men talked for most of the afternoon. Although Bertram was a man of great strength, she saw him at one point turn his face away to wipe away tears. It stirred her deeply and caused her to whisper a prayer of thanks for Anderson Goodwin.

"Have you considered sending her to a school in the North?" Anderson asked Bertram as he lifted a glass. "I could arrange a teaching position. Certainly, from what you have told me, she would be qualified. More than so."

"She won't go," Bertram said flatly. "Geneva is headstrong, Anderson, and…." He paused. "Short of physically tying her up and taking her, she would never go."

"She has given you no choice then."

"None at all."

"Does she understand all the implications? For herself? For the colored boy?" Anderson said. "And for the child? A girl, I understand?"

"Yes, a girl. And no, she doesn't understand. She's completely irrational right now. She has threatened to openly claim the child. It will destroy her life, but she refuses to believe me. I have no choice but to protect her."

"Save her from herself?"

"Exactly. You understand."

Anderson set down his glass and perused the plate of small tea cookies and sandwiches. He selected one and held it between his thumb and forefinger. "Most women would be destroyed by the arrangement you propose," he said.

Bertram made no immediate reply. He found the young attorney's understanding of the situation reassuring, but his assessment was less so. Still, he knew Anderson would be thorough—and faithful in the long run. Had he not been willing to help, Bertram would have had no other good alternative.

"My Geneva is not like most," Bertram said with a tired smile.

By five o'clock, the papers were signed. Somewhere across the city, a carillon toned five times.

"I have a train to catch," Anderson said. He slipped the documents into his valise and stood.

"I am in your debt, Anderson," Bertram said.

"I am glad I can help. Tell Caroline goodbye for me. I will write to you soon."

The two men shook hands and Anderson departed.

Bertram was noticeably brighter when he returned to the room to join Caroline. Now they could move forward—at least for the present. The despair that had threatened to sink them both had lifted somewhat after his conversation with Anderson, and though Bertram was one not naturally given to emotion, upon seeing his wife he took her in his arms and held her tightly for several minutes.

CHAPTER 38

1878

Freedom & Frustration

Deep into evening, the milky light from Zeph's lantern cut the darkness as sharply as a sound while he hid behind a line of cedars along the pasture. When he heard footsteps, he blew out the light and watched Geneva's father go into the barn. Steeling himself, Zeph waited, searching for the right tone of voice, the right words—he had to find the right words. When he was ready, he re-lit the lantern and followed. Zeph opened the door, ready to walk through the fire.

The older man was sitting alone in the darkness. He was hunched over and his shoulders slumped.

"Judge, it's me, Zeph. Could I speak to you?"

Bertram raised his head slowly, and when the lantern's light hit his face, it reflected an anger that hit Zeph so hard it felt as if he had been punched. But that look was only a pale augur of the words that followed.

"I have given you everything. A place to live, a job, your freedom—and you repay me by taking my daughter." Bertram stood up and bellowed, his hands knotted into fists, overwhelmed by the betrayal of two people he loved. "I should have you arrested. Another father would have thrown you out—or strung you up with his own hands."

Zeph did not try to deflect the blows. Instead, he let them fall. He had never seen this kind of rage come out of Bertram Snow. It shocked him, but he listened with the same respect he had always shown this upright man.

"Why did you do this? Why?" the Judge demanded. Bertram was fighting the toughest battle of his life. He was a man of reason and fairness—and he was caught between them like an innocent man facing the gallows. "As long as you stay at Cairnaerie—every time I lay eyes on you—I will know that you have taken the most precious thing in my life. And your child will be a constant reminder. Always. How do you expect me to live with that?"

Zeph was silent. He had no defense. He knew he had deceived this man who had shown him so much kindness. He had let himself be caught up in honest love and persuaded—perhaps foolishly— that Geneva's secret plan could work. Now all their faulty wisdom, the carelessness of their decision, their own ignorance—all the consequences had come home to roost.

"If she publicly claims the child or you—as she threatens to do— her life is over. Your life is over. They'll run you out of town or worse."

The flame flickered, and Bertram fell silent. He bowed his head. Zeph waited.

Finally, with his silver hair falling across his deeply etched brow, the Judge looked at Zeph. In his eyes shone a kind of agony that only a father could understand, a blend of responsibility and deter- mination and heart-wrenching devotion. "I have no choice. Geneva has given me no choice. Close the door."

Just before dawn Zeph Elias and Bertram Snow emerged from the barn, each drained. Zeph and Simmy would raise the child, and when Geneva came to her senses, she could resume her life. Until then, she would remain sequestered at Cairnaerie.

The full measure of what transpired during the long night, no one except Bertram and Zeph ever knew. For the rest of their lives, neither would ever talk about it to another living soul. They had made a pact, an understanding, a kind of necessary truce. What Zeph learned, what Bertram realized, and what they forged together could not change the past, but it could mold the future—the way light is bent in a prism.

The next morning Zeph stood in the center of the farthest field, a lone shadow in acres of pale wheat. The sun beat down on his up-turned face. His hand gripped a sickle and sweat rolled down his face and arms. With strength like ten men, he struck at the wheat, cutting wide swaths and unleashing from the depths of his broken soul a cry of bitter frustration.

"I am a free man," he bellowed with each furious pass. But Zeph wasn't free anymore. Geneva's threat to expose their marriage and claim their child—as noble and as right as it might have been—had imprisoned them all. And it was a prison stronger than cells and bars.

He swung and cut and raged against the weak wheat, against the society that denied him his wife. He shouted. He unleashed all the pent-up rage he had held in for so long. Freedom was not enough. He wanted more. But more was impossible—as impossible as darkening the white sun that seared his flesh. He unleashed a lifetime of anger—anger suffered secretly, anger he would never let Geneva see. He vented his frustration in the sight of God, and then he vowed: For the sake of his wife and his daughter, he would remain a man of calm—and duty.

———

The forest was still. No breezes blew other than the suffocating hot breath of the dying summer. Even the cool of the forest was hot tonight. Zeph sat back against the chapel door, waiting for Geneva. Sweat plastered his shirt to his chest. He shifted to get comfortable and rubbed his back against the door. The task he faced was hard. Looking up into the heavens, to the black sky swollen with humidity, he imagined Simmy slipping his note to Geneva.

When he heard her footsteps, coming light and fast, he stood up. In one motion, she was in his arms. He held her, steadying himself, steeling himself, preparing to explain the arrangement that would shape their future. Her father had made him the messenger, a punishment perhaps—or perhaps a concession to the new understanding her father had gained of Zeph's devotion.

He opened the door of the chapel—their sanctuary—and went in, half carrying her. Ignoring his own disappointment, Zeph knew he had to speak with tenderness and reason. Long ago he had learned to make the best of his circumstances. His father had taught him that. Now he must live out that understanding.

He pulled up windows to ventilate the hot room and lit a lantern as she spread out an old tattered quilt. Strewn around the dim room was evidence of long nights, of a shared life; books, candles, clothing, bedding, and several journals. In the twilight, they embraced where they had first known each other, where a child was conceived. He held her close, and with all the tenderness he owned, he began: "I talked to your daddy last night, Geneva..."

While Zeph talked, Geneva was silent, reading his eyes as accurately as she would have read a book and listening to him explain the arrangement. Zeph's words were tender, conciliatory.

An hour passed and she remained stoic. Then she erupted. Now it was Zeph who was quiet. He let her vent.

"I cannot be locked up at Cairnaerie. I will not!" she shouted with venom that alarmed Zeph at first. But he knew it came from disappointment, brewed with the same desire and fortitude that had brought them together. "I will not be imprisoned in Cairnaerie."

"What else is there, Geneva?" he said quietly after her tantrum was spent. "I can't take you and Alice Lyford anywhere—and be sure you'll be safe."

"What about going north? We could…"

"Listen, Geneva. Listen to me." He cut her off and cradled her face with his hands. "Listen. There's no better place for us anywhere than here. It's safe. Think about it. If we stay here, we'll always be close—and safe."

"Close is not enough." Geneva was crying. She buried her face in his chest. "Daddy expects me to live like I'm a ghost—I can't. Alice Lyford won't know me."

"Yes, she will. We'll make sure."

"It's not fair, Zeph. It's not right."

"I know that." He wrapped his arms around her and held her still. "Sometimes what's right idn't what's wise. And we've got to do what's wise."

Geneva's body slackened against him. Zeph had said that to her once before—and once again she realized he was right. For the first time in her life, she had lost a battle and this time she would not get her way. Zeph held her close as her defeated body melted against his chest.

"I need to be wise, don't I? It's hard." Her voice quivered.

"We both need to be wise."

"For Alice Lyford," she said.

"For all of us, Geneva."

It was the giving up Geneva found so difficult—the moment she had to let go of her hopes and unselfishly consider her husband

and daughter. Maybe her father was right, after all—or maybe he was wise.

Reality was more painful than Geneva had ever imagined it could be. She had not counted this cost—now it had been counted for her. It evoked the same sense of loss she remembered when Thomas and Grayson died, when Hayes first left. This time, though, it was herself she was losing.

Geneva surrendered. She lay back and Zeph leaned over her, kissing her deeply. Taking her in his arms, he comforted her as best he knew how.

Geneva crept back into her bedroom before daylight, exhausted and heartsick. How could she possibly live this way? She had always been a fighter, but how could she fight this situation of her own making?

Despite Zeph's persuasive words, by the next morning, she awoke with a dull headache—and with her anger and courage fully reignited.

Surely her father's arrangement was temporary. Maybe only a stopgap—until she could devise a better plan. She knew she had to talk to her father again. She was certain she could persuade him to find another way.

—

The house was quiet. Geneva slipped down the stairs. Her mother was traveling to town and had taken Vivvy and Simmy along, so she knew her father would be alone in the library.

The door was ajar. He was sitting at his desk, working. She had always been so close to him that she was optimistic—for a moment at least. How could her adoring father imprison her? She watched him, all the love she had shared with him bubbling up inside her. He would understand—of course he would understand. She was his Little Bird.

She tapped on the door. But when he looked up and saw her, every bit of her hopefulness vanished the way a soap bubble disappears. The look on his face portrayed the hurt and betrayal she had caused. It staggered her, but she had to continue. She had to plead her case one more time.

He said nothing as she entered the library. She wanted to run to him, to grab his neck, to have him lift her up and take away all the pain and conflict, to twirl her around—his Little Bird. She wanted the distance between them to be gone, but instead it loomed like a chasm.

"Daddy, I want to talk to you."

She saw him purse his lips, a gesture she recognized as one of discomfort.

"There is nothing to discuss," he said coldly. "I trust Zeph explained the arrangement?"

"Yes. He told me," she said with deliberate calm. "I don't think I can do this."

Her father was silent. He hadn't expected her to argue—although why hadn't he? This was his Geneva. For one fleeting moment, he hoped she had come to her senses, but she quickly dashed that hope.

"I can't live here so closed away. I think it's cruel of you."

"Cruel?" His eyes narrowed. "You think I'm cruel?"

His reaction shocked her. Her hope plummeted as the edge of his voice rose. "Cruel? You think I'm cruel? You don't know what you've done..."

"Yes, I do," she interrupted. "I married the man I love."

"Love!" He had not intended to engage her, but he could not let this pass. "What do you know about love?"

"I know what's in my heart," she said.

He stopped and stared at her. In his eyes was a misery that caused her to falter. She took a step back. The longcase clock ticked. The room filled with a silence that felt mocking and accusatory. Geneva began to drown in it.

"Do you know what's in my heart, Geneva?" he said quietly. "Do you?"

With this, she was undone because she couldn't answer his question. She had counted on his love for her, but was it still there?

He continued with an unsettling calm: "You have put us all in an impossible situation. You are naïve if you think you can live openly with Zeph."

"But..."

"No, Geneva, there is nothing you can say to change my mind. You have made your intentions abundantly clear. I cannot trust you to be reasonable and sensible. You cannot acknowledge this marriage or this child. You don't understand the ramifications. I must think for you. I have considered this carefully. There is no other way—unless, of course, you want me to send Zeph and the child away."

"No!" Geneva yelled. "No, you can't do that. You wouldn't."

She flew into a panic, but her father remained calm.

"Until you give up this impossible idea and continue to demand your way, you leave me no choice."

Geneva fled from the room.

Unforgiveness swallowed father and daughter. Neither would move an inch. Theirs was a feud that neither knew how to end, a fight riven with pride and resolution—and with a wholly ironic intent to do what was best for another, however ill-conceived. Both believed they had all of heaven's righteousness on their side. Geneva knew she did. Bertram was torn, but his doubts did not sway his understanding of the reckless path his daughter had taken. Unless she relented, she was better off cloistered. This he knew with certainty.

Thus, the stalemate began. It was never Bertram's intent to lock his daughter away forever. Daily he prayed she would come to her senses, but as weeks stretched into months, he began to lose hope.

———

Geneva stood in the window of the belvedere looking out, but tears obscured her vision. She gazed blindly into the last blazing remnants of the setting sun. *Can I bear this? Can I live like this? Will Daddy ever give in?* The sun dipped, and as if a candle had been snuffed out, darkness fell. She stood utterly alone. She might as well have been inside a coffin.

For the first time, she wondered if love could survive.

1928

CHAPTER 39

1928

———◆———

Trust & Tribune

Zeph bent down, pressing into the churn, the paddle cutting through the thickening milk. Geneva sat nearby on a bench beside the smokehouse door.

"I appreciate your helping me, Zeph. My hands get so stiff from turning, I can hardly move the paddles anymore."

"Glad I can help," he said in a way that conveyed more than casual sincerity.

Geneva pulled her sweater across her shoulders and wrapped her hands around her cup of tea to soothe her aching fingers as she watched him work—his old hands still strong.

Zeph cranked the churn with complete commitment. This was the way he approached every job. He absorbed work—and he drew strength from being needed. Geneva had never failed to need him and he had never failed to respond.

"I believe the old churns were easier," she said.

"I kinda think I agree with you. These new ones don't give you much butter and turning gets awful hard t'ward the end. The wood ones, you could put your shoulder into 'em—this crank here does get right hard in your hand."

"When it's ready, I'll make it up and you can take some home," she said.

Zeph kept working until he could see hard white streaks of butter coagulating inside the glass churn. The wind was stirring, and clouds passed overhead. He glanced up. "Looks like we might get us some rain," he said. "Smells like it." He closed his eyes and breathed deeply. "Smell them pines, Geneva. Nothin's sweeter than wind rustling through the pines."

The crank slowed and Zeph tipped the churn to examine its contents. "I believe this is 'bout ready," he said. "You get a crock, and I'll pour this buttermilk off for ya."

Geneva stepped into the house while Zeph unscrewed the top of the churn and jiggled the paddles to loosen the butter. "Bring a tray to put these paddles on," he called after her.

She helped him pour the buttermilk into a crock that she covered with cheesecloth and secured with a piece of twine. Zeph carried the paddles into the kitchen where she scraped them clean. While she was kneading the liquid out of the butter, he carried the crock of buttermilk to the springhouse to cool.

"Door on the springhouse's still sticking," Zeph said when he returned. "Don't think that paraffin I rubbed on it helped much. Next time I come up, I'll bring my rasp and take a little off." He picked up a broom and swept leaves off the terrace as Geneva salted the butter, pressed it into a mold, and turned out several portions. She covered each with clean cloths and set aside two butters for Zeph to take home.

"You will stay for supper, won't you?" she asked.

"Depends on what you're cooking."

She smiled at him. "Is that a yes?"

"That'd be right nice. Joly's gone off with Thatcher."

"He sounds like such a fine young man."

"He is, Geneva. Thatcher Oden's a good man. He'll be good to Joly."

Zeph walked into the parlor, and Geneva followed, sitting down next to him and leaning her head against his shoulder. He put his arm around her and pulled her close. "This is nice," he said. The smell of ham and beans drifted through the room. He sniffed. "Oh, I'm staying."

"What did you think of Professor Klare? Did you ask around about him?" she said.

"Briscoe thinks he's all right. He takes a room over at Miss Armenia Grubb's place. Says he treats her right nice."

"Why Briscoe?"

"He does a little cleaning up for Miss Armenia. Cuts her grass, totes groceries for her. Jes like he used to do for Vivvy."

"Do they still have old Mr. Crockett lying out on the porch?"

"Sure do. They got his bed laid out right on the front porch and Briscoe jes sits there and sings to him."

"He's a devoted soul. How old is Briscoe now?"

"Well up over ninety. Got to be. Still right spry, though."

"Remember how he'd tease Vivvy?" she said.

Zeph chuckled. "Only one I ever saw could make her smile, but you had to be on the right side of her to see it. She hated you to see her smile. She could be sour as a persimmon. Briscoe was good to her."

"Briscoe was good to everybody," Geneva said. "He used to bring me gold."

"I remember that."

"Fool's gold. He'd find it everywhere. He'd wink at me when Vivvy wasn't looking and slip a rock out of his pocket and give it to me. As a child, I loved it. I'd hide them from Vivvy. I expect there are still some of those rocks around here."

"He's a good soul."

It began to rain. Geneva got up and pulled down the parlor windows.

"So your mind's made up?" Zeph said.

"I think so. Yes."

"When you gonna ask him?"

"I don't know." Geneva sat back down and tucked her hands in the crook of Zeph's arm. "I need to tell him everything first."

"I don't see how you cain't. You take your time."

"I wish I could, but we're running out of time."

Zeph closed his eyes and leaned back, a half smile on his face.

"What are you smiling about?"

"Briscoe told me Mr. Klare's got him a right fine car."

"Is that why you like him? Because he has a car?"

Zeph grinned at her. "You think he'd give me a ride sometime?"

"You'll have to ask him."

"Someday, Geneva, I'm gonna have me a motor car." He shoved his arms out like he was steering. "Can't you see me?"

"You always did want a car—ever since you saw your first Model T."

"That's right. But I haven't bought one yet 'cause I don't want to make Claudine jealous."

Geneva laughed and slapped him playfully. "I didn't know horses could be jealous."

"Oh, sure they can. Claudine, she's like to quit carrying me if she thought I'd replace her."

"That's the poorest excuse I have ever heard." She patted Zeph's round belly. "Claudine might appreciate it."

He laughed. The room brightened, but the rain continued.

"Looky there. Got us a sun shower."

"I'll set the table," she said. She started to rise, but he stopped her.

"Sit. Just a minute more. Then I'll help you."

She saw a little muscle in his check twitch the way it did when he had something on his mind.

"Geneva, you know I trust you, but you don't know much about this fellow. He could be all right like Briscoe says—might be as fine as they come, but you got to be careful." He narrowed his eyes at her. "I'm thinking you know more than you're letting on."

"You know me too well, Zephyr Elias."

She stood up and disappeared into the library. He heard a desk drawer open and close. When she returned, she was carrying a newspaper clipping. She unfolded it and handed it to Zeph.

"Chicago Tribune?" He squinted. "I believe you're going to have to read the rest to me. I can see fine a ways off, but my up close done got up and gone." He laughed.

"Zeph, you have got to get some spectacles," she said, scolding but smiling. She took the clipping from him as she lifted her own pince-nez and slipped them onto the bridge of her nose to read. "The board of trustees at St. Ballard College dismissed three faculty members on Monday, the college announced this week. Wilbert F. Lacey, professor of linguistics, Angus W. Reeke, assistant professor of political science, and John H. Klare, associate professor of history, were terminated ...."

She finished reading, rubbed her eyes. "Now do you understand?"

"I do," Zeph said, "but I never woulda figured Mr. Klare to be a rabble rouser."

"Our kind of rabble rouser."

"I believe I like him."

Geneva faced him with determination that was all too familiar.

"I'm going to tell him everything. I must," she said. "If I am going to ask for his help, he deserves to know."

CHAPTER 40

1928

Names & Disclosures

"I love hummingbirds," Geneva said as she pushed the draperies aside and peered out the window. "Did you know they cannot walk like other birds? They can only fly."

"I did not," John said. "Interesting." Sitting next to Helen in the parlor of Cairnaerie, he wondered why Miss Snow was talking about birds. His newest invitation, arriving unexpectedly and marked 'urgent,' seemed incongruous with hummingbirds.

"I love watching them. Some are so small you might think they are large insects."

While John and Helen waited, Helen took in the room: crocheted doilies covering the worn-out arms of several chairs; small china bowls scattered about, holding assortments of hairpins, buttons, cedar pencils, pen nibs, feathers, and rocks. A large translucent flint rock sat on the hearth next to a dented ashcan. An iron poker, a whisk broom, and a shovel were propped up behind it. Thick stacks of newspapers and piles of yellow and black-bound *National Geographic* magazines, tied with twine, filled the room's corners. A book about birds lay open on a nearby table. Books, in fact, were shelved and stacked everywhere. The room's contents reminded her of her library's attic.

Escaping her reverie, Miss Snow left the window.

"You have been kind to come—and you have been so patient. I do appreciate it." She paused, seeming to steel herself. "Before I go any further, I want you to know my story."

John and Helen exchanged glances.

"Before today, I have never told anyone—and I do so with trepidation. I only ask that you listen to everything I have to say before you make any judgments."

"Of course," Helen said, speaking for them both as John leaned forward and planted his elbows on his knees.

The longcase clock ticked as Miss Snow moved toward a large breakfront where a faded purple tassel hung from a key. She opened the door, lifted out a magazine, and handed it to John. He recognized it immediately, the obscure academic journal, *Southern Historical Society Review*. An article he had penned was marked with a crow's feather. He looked up, puzzled. "Is this how you found me?"

"It is indeed. When I learned that you had come to Haverston, I believed providence had shined on me."

John passed the magazine to Helen.

"You wrote about Mr. Lincoln's emancipation. I believe you said, 'Social liberties will not come until society deems it appropriate.' I hope I'm quoting you correctly."

"Yes, you are," said John, not a little dumbfounded. "I'm flattered."

"You are wise beyond your years."

"Thank you," he said, "but I'm still confused."

"I'm sure you are. Let me explain." She sat down across from them and put her hands together. "During my lifetime, I have always hoped the breach between the North and the South would heal, but I have realized there is still a breach—a separation that remains between the races. When I read your work, I believed you understood this—and hoped you would be sympathetic to my situation."

"Your situation?" John asked.

"Yes. It is … unusual. I am in the last years of my life, and there is something I must do that I cannot do alone. I need your help." Her demeanor was anxiety and purpose allied.

Miss Snow stood and returned to the breakfront. This time she took out a red book with a red satin ribbon. Untied, the book fell open as if divined. Inside was a document, which she handed to John.

"I have asked for your indulgence and you have been quite gracious in granting me that. Now I must ask for your forgiveness. I have not been completely forthright with you." Her voice was gathering strength.

Helen stole a quick glance at John, who looked concerned.

"I am not who you think I am. My name was Miss Geneva Snow—that you know—but since April 27, 1876, I have been Mrs. Zephyr Elias."

"Oh," John said. Not making the connection, his face was blank.

Helen, though, understood instantly. "John." She squeezed his arm. "Mr. Elias is her husband."

"Mr. Elias?" said John, befuddled. "I don't understand."

Helen stared into his eyes, trying to speak telepathically. "Mr. Zeph Elias."

Suddenly it all fell into place for John, and an awkward silence swarmed as all the legal and societal proscriptions of such a union blew through his head like confetti.

"You have it there," said Miss Snow, pointing to the paper.

John unfolded the document and stared at the handwritten marriage license of Geneva Snow and Zeph Elias. Dumbfounded, he started to speak but then reconsidered.

"So Joly is your granddaughter?" Helen said, giving John a moment to collect his thoughts.

"Yes. And she is the reason I've asked you here."

"But you said you've lived here alone," John said, still trying to absorb this disclosure. "I'm confused."

"I know you are," she said. Her voice trembled. "I have more to explain, but I am sure you can understand my caution—my need for secrecy." She stood with her hand to her mouth, gaging the reaction of the man she was entrusting. Had she misjudged John Klare? "I hope you will forgive my deception."

John's own past came back to him like the taste of bad fish. He swallowed hard. He had tried to follow the straight and narrow since his dismissal from St. Ballard.

"Nothing to forgive," he said finally—and honestly. "But I still don't understand. Why me? I'm just a history professor—and a junior one to boot."

"I needed someone sympathetic to my situation. And I believe you are. I have spent nearly fifty years confined because white girls couldn't marry colored boys. Whatever odds Zeph and I faced, we have somehow mercifully beaten them. Do you understand how remarkable that is?" She paused and addressed John directly. "I have a proposition for you."

"A proposition?" Wary, but wholly intrigued, John waited.

"For almost seventy years, I have kept journals—since I was a child. I will share them with you if you will help me. And I will pay you handsomely for your trouble. I am a woman of considerable means. All I want you to do is help me go to Joly's wedding."

"A wedding? That's all?" he said, and he almost laughed. "I'm afraid I still don't understand. Anyone can take you to a wedding."

"No. Not anyone, I am afraid," she said. "I have been gone too long. I cannot explain my life, so I need a plan—a ruse you might say. And I suppose I need an automobile. I am far past the age of riding a horse or managing a carriage, even if one here were useable."

"But why me?" John asked again.

Geneva touched his sleeve and spoke to him quietly. "You are a man of principle. I know what you did at St. Ballard."

John tensed—the expression on his face clearly told Helen: 'Don't ask.'

Geneva slumped against the front door after her guests left Cairnaerie. Her head ached and her chest tightened. The stress of the afternoon and her age were catching up to her, yet she was optimistic—more so than she had been for a long time. *The task is engaged,* she thought, returning to the library. *Another step taken.*

She moved a chair near to the window and opened the red silk book, tilting it to let the afternoon sun illumine the text.

It was not quite dawn when she came into the world. Simmy laid her on my stomach while attending to my needs. I examined this tiny girl through tears of joy and pain. My labor had been long and difficult, and I felt more wrenching pain as Simmy finished her duties.

All day I held my daughter, letting her suckle and sleep. With fascination, I noticed the contrast of her smooth skin, the color of a brown egg, against my breasts. Before supper, Mama came to my room. Her eyes, red and swollen, were downcast, and she avoided my gaze. In a voice burdened with despair and collected courage, she told me Vivvy would come and I was to give my baby to her—the woman I despised. I was at that moment broken. I knew the hurt I had caused was so egregious that I had no choice but to comply.

That evening Vivvy took Alice Lyford away from me and gave her to Simmy and Zeph to care for, a small consolation. It will be whispered, I suppose, that my daughter is a product of incest—a sin so much easier to forgive than the one I have committed.

A day or so later—my memory is foggy as if my days and nights ran on in one continuous cloud—Mama returned with a different mission. Just as the moon came through the bedroom window, she was there again, carrying several lengths of muslin. With the clinical efficiency of a nurse, she told me to take off my nightgown, and as I stood naked, she bound my breasts so tightly I could barely breathe. In the darkness, she worked silently as I endured the pain and shame. "It will keep your milk from coming in." She said nothing more and then slipped out of the room, and in large measure out of my life.

I cannot explain what happened next, but I arose from my bed and walked to the window. The air, still and balmy, drenched my aching body in a soothing lotion. From out of the night, tree frogs sang to me a comforting song as sweet as any my ears had ever heard. Through the trees I looked toward the small house where Zeph, Simmy, and my daughter were together, and I heard a small cry that made my heart jump. In the moonlight, I un-bound my aching breasts and felt a surge of life. Slipping on a nightgown, I went barefoot into the night.

When Zeph opened the door, the hungry cry summoning me thundered in my ears. Without a word, Simmy held Alice Lyford out to me while I untied my gown. Her cries ceased instantly and the sense of relief made me weak in the knees....

Geneva closed the journal and wrapped the satin ribbon around her hand. She tilted her head back, shut her eyes, and relived it all.

CHAPTER 41

1928

Revelation & Rectitude

As soon as they were back on the road to Hyssop and Helen turned to face John, he knew what was coming. "What happened in Indiana?"

John shoved his car into gear and headed down the mountain without answering. *How do I explain this?* He had no way of knowing where Helen stood on the colored question—although she had not flinched at Miss Snow's revelation. That encouraged him.

The landscape blurred as he navigated the mountain's switchbacks. Halfway down, he pulled into a small clearing and cut the engine. He rolled down his windows and then slung his arm over the seat like a gambler throwing dice.

"I'll tell you—but you have to understand this. When I came to Haverston, I vowed to stay out of trouble. I can't afford to lose another job. And I don't intend to."

She raised both her hands, palms out. "Understood."

John blew out a deep breath. "Do you know what eugenics is?"
She frowned. "Yes."

"When I was hired at St. Ballard, I was one of three new faculty members. We were new, all fresh out of graduate school. We became great friends. One of the fellows was Theodore Benwick—one of the best teachers I'd ever met. Benny Benwick. Great guy. His students loved him. Unfortunately, someone discovered he was colored. He looked completely white to all of us. *He* thought he was white."

"And he wasn't? That's hard to believe. How?"

"Apparently, an overzealous official had taken it upon himself to examine all employees on the state's academic rolls. He informed the college that they had several colored employees. Benny was the faculty member. The other two were maintenance men."

"Eugenics?"

"Correct. The man had determined—without asking Benny, mind you, and with no evidence other than his own 'research'— that Benny apparently had a drop of colored blood. One drop. He classified him as 'colored'—and the board of trustees fired him."

"How ridiculous! And unfair."

"It sure is. But eugenicists have science behind them," John said, making science sound villainous. "It's a huge movement in academia."

"How do you know so much about it?"

"You learn a lot when it's your friends," he said wryly. "We practically got run out of town on a rail."

"But why all three of you? You're not...."

"No." John cleared his throat. "We got in trouble for defending him. The trustees had voted unanimously to fire him, and we challenged them. Rather publicly, I'm afraid—bad judgment on our part."

"They didn't like being challenged?"

"That's putting it mildly. They especially didn't like it when we got the newspapers and our students involved. That really incensed them. The president called us 'rabble rousers.' We were fired on the spot."

"No appeal?"

"None. On the word of one nameless state official, Benny was out—and so were we. But I will tell you this: I'm not sorry I got involved. I've never been sorry. It was patently unfair."

"You're a crusader," Helen said, trying to lighten the mood.

"Not anymore. I can't risk losing another job." He threw his head back and rapped his knuckles on the steering wheel. "But here I am. I can't believe I've gotten pulled in again. At least this time, I know not to call the newspaper. Amazing how mistakes can follow you."

"It depends on how you define mistakes, John."

Relieved by Helen's reaction, John relaxed. And a new resolve began percolating in him. They fell silent. Even the fields, usually windblown, were still. John's stomach growled.

Helen laughed. "Are you hungry?"

"Apparently, I am."

He started his car, startling a dozen buzzards scavenging nearby, and headed down the mountain. At the bottom, he drove along the Cleary, its banks flush with summer foliage. Late afternoon sun sparkled on the water. It was the kind of afternoon that made John glad he had bought a car. Kate was right about his wanderlust.

When they arrived back in Hyssop and pulled along the curb in front of McClanahan's, the restaurant's shade was pulled down with a 'closed' sign on it.

"Looks like we're out of luck," John said.

"I could fix us a little supper in my apartment."

"Sure," he said, thinking of his hunger rather than propriety. He quickly reconsidered. Helen was a single woman, and they had no chaperone. "But I don't want to...."

"... to set tongues wagging?" she interrupted with a smile that was half-dare and half-determination. She leaned toward him.

"Listen, John Klare. If you can challenge the eugenicists, I can make you a little supper."

Eight white frame apartments lined up along Baxter Street. Each had black shutters, a picture window, and a set of small brick steps leading to a front door. They were linked to the street's sidewalk by brick walkways and all together resembled a giant comb with an elm tree planted in between each of the teeth.

John escorted Helen to her door, Number 5, before parking several blocks away—a discreet distance. There was no need to inflame the gossip mill, which grew proportionately as the size of a town decreased.

By the time he got back and tapped at her door, Helen had pulled down all the window shades, leaving an inch or so at the bottom for ventilation. "Make yourself comfortable," she said, inviting him in. "I've put some stew on. It'll be ready in a minute."

Helen's apartment was warm and inviting. A crocheted Afghan was folded across the arm of a small, camelback sofa; a colorful Tiffany lamp glowed beside an upholstered chair and ottoman. Somehow he had expected it to be more bookish—more 'library-ish.' A bric-a-brac filled with shells caught his eye.

"Seashells?" he asked.

"I collect them. My family vacationed at the beach every summer. Cape Cod," she said, coming in from the kitchen, drying her hands on her apron. She picked up two particularly ornate shells. "This one's my favorite—a reticulated helmet. And this one is from Australia. My uncle brought it to me."

"They're beautiful. I've never been to the beach."

"Well, I've never seen the Mississippi," she said

"I guess we're even."

She smiled, replacing the shells. "Why don't you come in the kitchen?"

John sat down at a small table where Helen had set out two plates. She adjusted the gas beneath a heavy pot and lifted a percolator off the stove where it was bubbling.

"Coffee? Or would you prefer tea?" she said jokingly.

"Coffee. Please." He laughed. "Thank you."

She poured two cups.

"What about Miss Snow's request?" she asked. "Going to a wedding shouldn't be so difficult. Nobody knows her anymore."

John leaned back and stretched his legs. "It shouldn't. You're right. It's the appearance. A white woman showing up at a colored wedding would raise eyebrows. They don't mix—especially socially."

"And people talk."

"Yes, they certainly do." The line between coloreds and whites was formidable. John saw it at the newly constructed movie theater where 'coloreds' were relegated to the balcony and had separate bathrooms. He saw it in the patronizing smiles whites gave Negroes—an acknowledgement of their presence but not their humanity. In Hyssop, though, he had noticed there was little open animosity. Instead, there was a comfortable acceptance of the status quo: Negroes were welcome to participate in society, but at their own places, separate and apart. And the union of Zeph and Geneva Elias was anything but separate and apart. Plus, John knew the law. "Do you realize their marriage is illegal?" He sat forward and blew on his hot coffee.

"What do you mean?" she said. She stirred the stew and tapped the spoon on the edge of the pot before sitting down at the table.

"Do you remember the date on the marriage certificate?"

"1876."

"Right. That's three years before the General Assembly voided all interracial marriages. In 1924, they criminalized them."

"So you're saying they could be arrested?"

"If they were found out, yes," John said. "Not likely, though. They've actually done a good job keeping everything secret."

"How could anyone know?"

"Someone must know." John furrowed his brow. "What about Joly? I assume she knows. Wouldn't she have to?"

"I guess so," Helen said. "But Miss Geneva didn't say. What if she doesn't?"

Steam and a flavorsome aroma rose from the stew. The room was getting stuffy.

"Would you mind if I opened the window?" John said.

"Sure. Go ahead."

He stood up and raised the sash but made sure the curtains stayed closed. Cool night air drifted in.

"What about her journals?" Helen asked.

"Those were a surprise," John said, leaning against the sill. "She didn't mention those before. Can you imagine the history in them? And in the house—I'd love to explore it." He stepped away from the window. Cairnaerie was not the North Pole or China, but it *was* the unknown.

John was beginning to feel protective of Miss Snow, this hot-house woman so vigorous and determined. Like in Indiana, a kind of righteous indignation was stirring in him. Maybe Helen was right. Maybe he was a crusader, after all. The thought made him smile. "Helen, if we don't help her, who else will? At the very least, I think I'm trustworthy. If anyone is ripe for exploitation, she is, living alone all these years."

Helen was quiet for a moment as she wrapped her hand in a tea towel and set two bowls on the table. "What if Joly doesn't know?" she said. The question hung in the air.

They ate Helen's dinner in silence. Outside, crickets chirped in the darkness, and in the distance a dog barked.

Helping Miss Snow might be as simple as giving her a ride to the wedding, John thought, but someone was bound to ask questions. He tried to picture the conversation, mulling it all over in his mind, poking at it like one might examine a misshapen vegetable. He needed a plan.

Late in the night—much later than either had anticipated—John slipped out of Helen's apartment. It had been a pleasant evening, and he was beginning to see Helen in a new light.

A very new light.

CHAPTER 42

1928

Rabbits & Woods

Tobias opened his back door and threw the half-eaten carcass of an opossum in Buster's direction. It tumbled through the air like a hammer throw and splatted on the ground next to the hound. Buster stirred. Tobias surveyed the yard and left the door open after he pulled a log out of the wood box. Presently, he heard footsteps coming around the side of the building and stomping on the small, crooked stoop.

"Come on in, Cletus," he said as he crouched in front of the stove with a poker in his hand. He stabbed at a burning log and pushed it to the back of the firebox.

"Brung ya a rabbit," Cletus said. He proudly held up his quarry.

"Who-wee. That's a biggun," Tobias said, looking up at the fat, ginger-colored rabbit that Cletus held by its hind legs. "Where'd you get him?"

"Same ol' place."

"They're gonna catch you one of these days, Cletus."

"Naw. I'm too fast."

"You gonna skin him?"

"Yep. Give me your knife."

"Over there," Tobias said. He gestured toward a large buck knife hanging from a nail by the window.

Cletus lifted the knife and ran his finger along the blade. "This is a right fine frog picker you got here, Tobias."

They put the rabbit on a spit over a fire they built in the backyard, and when it was cooked they shared the bounty. Tobias kicked off his boots and opened a Mason jar they passed back and forth until both were warm and satisfied.

"You know that nigra Zeph?" Tobias asked.

"Yep."

"You seen his girl?"

"Course I have. I ain't blind. She's mighty fine," Cletus said.

"You know where they live?"

"Nope."

"Well, how come you don't?" Tobias picked his teeth with a bone. "You take mail out that way, don't ya?"

"I jes go as far as Blast Holler. He's on out t'ward the Soot Woods."

"Where's that?"

"Someplace you don't wanna go to." Cletus said this with an air of authority.

"Why not?"

"'Cause it's haunted, that's why."

Tobias sat up straight and narrowed his eyes into black slits.

"Haunted? Ain't no such thing."

"You ain't been here long enough or you'd know. Everybody knows about it."

"Knows what?"

"Knows better than to fool around them Soot Woods—it's haunted, I tell ya. Everybody and his brother knows." Cletus puffed out his chest. "Everybody."

Tobias was unconvinced. "You're an idiot, Cletus. Ain't true—no such thing." But still, the subject of a haunted wood struck Tobias like the shingles. "You sure nobody goes in there?"

"Sure as I'm sittin' here. Nobody. Well, maybe some niggers livin' back there, but nobody I know." Cletus poked their dwindling fire with a stick. "Don't you go getting any ideas. You ain't getting me to go in there. No, sirree."

"Suit yourself," Tobias said. He would ponder those woods for the rest of the night. To him, isolation meant opportunity.

CHAPTER 43

1928

――――――◆――――――

Hats & Corners

A heavy rain at sunrise had boosted the humidity, making the air thick and close. Zeph mopped his face. He would soon head to town to pick up a bag of penny nails for Thatcher and gather the mail.

"You need anything from the mercantile while I'm out?" he asked Joly, who was sitting at the table sewing.

"Don't think so, Grandpa." She pushed a needle through the cloth with a thimble.

"I'm going to go out by the mill, too—take Thatcher the nails. Anything you want me to tell him?"

Joly smiled at him. "You jes tell him that I'm waitin' on him to come visit me."

"Maybe I'll jes bring him back with me."

"That'd be fine with me," Joly said, pulling the thread tight before cutting it with her teeth. "There. Good as new." She shook out a heavy cotton shirt, set it aside, and picked up another garment to mend.

Zeph dug through a small cabinet. "You seen my hat?"

"Which one?" Joly said. Without looking up, she motioned toward a homemade coat tree littered with more than a dozen men's hats. "Ya got plenty. That's for sure."

"Hat makes the man," he said, choosing an old top hat he had found at a flea market. He set it square on his head. "This one look about right?"

When Joly looked up and saw him, she laughed out loud. "Don't you dare wear that, Grandpa. You look like an undertaker."

"If you say so." He winked at her, picked up a tan flat cap instead and squared it on his head. "Oh, and I'll prob'ly go on up to see Miss Geneva, too."

"Take my umbrella, if you want. Maybe you can shake some more rain out of the sky."

When Zeph pulled his rig up to the post office, Cletus was coming out, carrying a sack of mail for Blast Hollow where a few dozen families lived.

"Mornin', Mr. Jurden," Zeph said.

"Mornin', Zeph. How you like all this hot?"

"Coming on awful early. We need us some rain. My garden's lookin' kinda parched."

Zeph climbed down out of his rig and tied up Claudine. Brushing flies off her face, he patted her neck, making a soothing, clicking sound. The horse was long in the tooth but solid as rock and faithful as daybreak. Zeph and his horse were a good team. "Be right back, Claudine," he said to the mare.

Miss Perfader walked by on her way to open the bank, and Zeph doffed his hat. As he stepped into the post office, he immediately put up his guard—a gut feeling, probably unwarranted—but he was increasingly wary of this new public servant.

"Mornin', Zeph," Tobias said from behind the counter. "We gonna get some rain?"

"Well, I don't know, Mr. Jebson. It's right dark over to the west, though. I jes got some cabbage planted, and a little rain would get it going right good."

"You quite a talented feller," Tobias said.

"I don't know about talent, but I love them fresh things, love to eat 'em. You got 'ny mail for me today?"

"Here you go, Zeph." He handed him a stack of mail, several magazines and circulars, and one newspaper. "You get the prize today," he said slyly.

"The prize?"

"Prize for the most mail."

Zeph, uneasy, slid the mail into his satchel. "That's a bundle, I guess. Thank ya, Mr. Jebson." He was trying to avoid more conversation and stepped aside.

But Tobias crossed his arms and stood back like a cat with a pawed mouse. "Why'd you get so much mail, boy? I never could figure why any nigra gets so much. Newspapers from all over— Washington and all them other damn places." Tobias was fishing. "You must be a right smart nigra. Smartest one I ever seen. You read all this stuff?"

The hair on Zeph's neck stood up, but before he was forced to answer, the door opened. Cletus stepped back in.

"What you want, Cletus?" Tobias said, irritated at the interruption.

"Forgot my hat," he said, leaning down and picking up a dirty cap off the chair.

In that instant, Zeph took his leave. "I'll be seeing you, gentlemen." And he was out the door.

"Hell, Cletus. You show up at the damnedest times."

CHAPTER 44

1928

Gardens & Guests

G eneva crouched down in the corner of the garden. She was wearing an apron over a faded dress and a straw hat shaped like a coal scuttle as she pulled weeds from dirt that was as fine as cocoa. Tamping down each eruption, she periodically stopped and stretched out her knotted fingers. She smoothed out the rich, black soil so her flowers—Simmy's flowers—would flourish. She nourished the beds from a small compost heap outside the kitchen door, the same one where Vivvy had dumped potato peels, eggshells, and vegetable scraps decades ago.

She sat back on her ankles, pushed back her hat, and wiped her brow. For so many years she had worked here with Simmy kneeling beside her. Often they would go all morning without speaking a single word, so strong was their bond and so pure their understanding of each other. She missed her dearest friend every bit as much today as the day Simmy left them. Here in the garden, she still sensed her presence.

Without the schedule of society to arrange the hours of her days, Geneva had relied on the seasons. Her appointments were visits with the first blossoms that braved the chill of late winter—or summer concerts of tree frogs—or exhibitions of the showy tasseling of corn—or meetings with fall's rubicund face. These ordered her life, day after day, year after year. Each sound, each fragrance, charmed her as completely now as they had when she was a child. Without the world's distractions, she depended on their faithfulness. Unlike the lessons of domesticity that she had neglected, the lessons of the natural world, she had absorbed eagerly. Simmy had taught her much. The rest she had learned from reading. Zeph still made regular trips to the mercantile, bringing her seeds and seedlings, which she planted with an untarnished hope.

She took a sip of tea from her glass nestled in a bed of moss. High in the trees, a choir of cicadas rose and fell in rhythmic crescendos. Scents of lavender and mint perfumed the air with honeysuckle and polyanthus, which in good years followed one another.

For the second time in her life, Geneva Snow was risking everything. By revealing herself to John and Helen, she could become a historical oddity—one of her own making—but an oddity nonetheless: an old woman living alone, removed from the parade of life. If newspapers were to get hold of her story, she could become like a trapped animal, assailed by gawkers and pointed fingers.

But what unsettled Geneva most was the tenor of the community—the stubborn intolerance for any mixing of the races that still lingered. She had watched it from afar through the lens of the current news she devoured. It was a bitter disappointment to her, a lacerating blow to a long-held hope for acceptance of her marriage.

She should have feared her revelation would chill any smidgen of friendship with John Klare, but her optimism was leavened with naiveté, as it had always been. She did not grasp the immensity of the risk to John—or Joly—or Zeph. She only knew she had to do everything in her power to fulfill Joly's request.

Geneva pulled up the last of the weeds and stood up with the aid of a mattock. From inside the house, the clock struck ten. She gathered the weeds on an advertising circular and shook the loose dirt onto her garden before she went inside to prepare for her guests.

As John and Helen approached the house, they both noticed something was different, like clean air on the cusp of a new spring. Windows on the second story were unshuttered and some were raised.

Geneva greeted them warmly. An amiable familiarity was developing between Geneva and the couple. Helen felt it acutely; perhaps it came from knowing her secret. Whatever the reason, though, it was indisputable.

In the dining room, an assortment of foods awaited them—tiny beaten biscuits filled with ham, cucumber sandwiches, bread and butter pickles, and a plate of orange blossoms—all arranged on silver trays.

"I hope you all don't mind a cold meal," said Geneva. "Growing up, our noon dinner was a feast. Everyone working on the farm had to be fed. But I have always loved anything between slices of bread, and it is so much easier than cooking—an art I never mastered. I do what I must and that is about it. I do bake, though. There's something quite satisfying about kneading bread and waiting for it to rise."

"It all looks delicious," Helen said, acknowledging the effort their hostess had made. Covered in a cutwork cloth, the dining table was set with fine blue willow china, sterling silver flatware, and pressed glass goblets full of sweet tea.

"I have learned that nutrition is not a matter of culinary skill but of planning," Geneva said, as John seated her and then Helen.

"I've never heard it put that way, but that makes good sense," Helen said as she unfolded a crisp linen napkin.

"Toward the end of the war when our currency was nearly worthless, the price of flour was almost one hundred dollars a bushel. Can you imagine! I remember Vivvy complaining because she had to grind wheat herself."

"Vivvy?" John asked.

"Our cook. She made the best bread you ever tasted. For us, wheat bread was a delicious treat. Most of the time we ate cornbread."

"Your memory is remarkable," John said.

"Not my memory—my journals. I wrote everything down."

"How many do you have?" John asked, and he took another cucumber sandwich, which he found surprisingly good.

"I don't know. Fifty? Sixty? I've never counted them. I should do that. Every entry is dated and each book filled—I made sure of that. Daddy taught us to be thrifty. Empty pages were wasteful and writing paper was not always easy to get, especially after the war."

Helen set down her fork and wiped her hands on her starched napkin. "Why did you begin keeping journals?" she asked. "I started a few myself, but I never stuck with it."

"I'm sure it was my father. His influence. He surrounded me with books—and taught me to read. I would sit in his lap, and he would go over each new word. He gave me my first journal and showed me how to make them—how to cut and fold each signature—how to sew the bindings on. We would cover them with fabric—he always let me choose the color."

"You must have loved that," Helen said.

"Oh, I did. In the beginning, it was all to please Daddy. I worked hard to finish a book so that he and I could make another. And he insisted I date every entry—on that he was quite firm. He was an orderly, precise man. Now I am especially glad. Later, my journals became my escape. I could write things that I could never say out loud. Young girls were not always allowed to speak their minds—although I often did, much to the consternation of my mother. After Alice Lyford was born—Joly's mother—it seemed even more important. My journals became like old friends to confide in." She laughed. "They never argued with me."

"But you had family here?" John said.

"Yes. I did. But I was so determined to have my way, I alienated them all, I'm sorry to say. I was quite stubborn."

"You never left the house? Never went into town?" asked Helen, incredulous.

"Only to go to the chapel."

"The chapel?" John asked.

"Yes—where we were married. Zeph and Simmy took Alice Lyford and moved there after she was born. I was forbidden to leave Cairnaerie. It was an arrangement my father insisted on—until I gave up my marriage, which, of course, I never did."

Hard as she tried, Helen could not hide her misgivings. It seemed preposterous for a woman to be shut away in a house and forgotten for a lifetime. Listening to her, Helen struggled with her own indignation. "You agreed to your father's arrangement, even though it meant giving up all chance of a normal life?"

"I know it must be hard to understand," Geneva said kindly. "You are a modern woman, my dear, and I am a Southern woman. Until I betrayed his trust, my father was like a god to me. I've often thought of how Southern girls say, 'Daddy.' It sounds so like 'deity.' "

"Couldn't you have run away?" she asked.

"I wanted to. I asked Zeph to take us away, but there was nowhere for us to go. In some places, Zeph would have been lynched for marrying me. And then where would I have been? A white woman with a colored child? No. At least by staying here my family was protected. I had two choices: what I wanted—Zeph and Alice

Lyford—or the life my father expected of me, and that would have meant disavowing my husband and child."

"What did their friends say—your parents' friends?" John asked. "They must have wondered."

"My parents said I was ill. I'm sure their friends were interested—but polite. I'm sure they offered sympathy but gradually forgot about me. Particularly after my father died. My mother became quite reclusive, so I'm sure she was forgotten as well."

"You're not bitter?" John said.

"No, I'm not. I never was really. Of course, I wish I had lived in a different time when Zeph and I might have lived openly, but it was not meant to be." She paused and looked toward the window.

"You never felt trapped?" Helen asked.

"No, not really. Not for long anyway." Geneva smiled. "Even though it was difficult, especially at first, my father had given me what I wanted. He was a brave man, but he was not a crusader. He could not change the world, so he created one—whether intentional or not. Cairnaerie became my whole world. Other than my family, you are the only two people who have set foot in this house in decades."

"Miss Snow...Mrs. Elias," Helen said. "I'm curious."

"Yes? But, please, just call me Miss Geneva. It will be easier." She said this with the same munificence that had disarmed John at their first meeting. "After all, you know my secret."

Helen smiled. "Miss Geneva, then. When your parents were gone, why didn't Zeph and Alice Lyford move into Cairnaerie with you?"

"That was Zeph's choice. I begged him to, but he thought it best to stay as we were. It would be safer, he said. If I were ever discovered, I would be a woman living alone in a forgotten house—no threat to anyone."

"I see," Helen said to be polite, but she did not understand at all. She wondered why men were always so cautious when it came to women.

"By living close by in the chapel, Zeph could help me but not draw attention to Cairnaerie. Daddy set up a trust, and payments went directly to Zeph. For all these years, he has brought me food, books, mail, seeds—anything I needed. He has been my connection to the world. If anyone were trapped, I suppose it was Zeph."

"It must have been hard at times," John said.

"Of course. There were many difficult days..." Her voice trailed off. From the ledge of an open window a full-throated bird sang. "...But what family does not have hard times? Hardship makes you strong. Yes, it was difficult at times—but I have never been lonely. I have always had Zeph. And I have not been deprived of the world. Not really. I have kept up." For the first time in the afternoon, her voice became strident. "But the world has not changed as I had hoped. I'm afraid Zeph and I are still unwelcome."

Her words hung in the air.

CHAPTER 45

1928

Hauntings & Malevolence

With pleasure in the offing, Tobias crept through the Soot Woods, the dense hardwood forest that ran across the mountaintop and constituted the southern border of the Cairnaerie estate. Long burdened by superstition, the woods were dark and foreboding, rising like a wall. For decades, with fear and false notions, it had protected the Snow's privacy and increased the mystery on which abandonment lay. Its legend had been a fortuitous blessing to Bertram Snow's arrangement, helping to preserve the sanctity of Cairnaerie. It was a wilderness left to ghosts, a sylvan armament—as secure as a powder arsenal—that had guarded the Snow family from the ravages of the Civil War and later hid the errant daughter. A hundred years before, local legend said, a family had been brutally murdered by Cherokee, and their spirits haunted the woods. The oft-told tale warded off all but the most daring. Over the years, Zeph had deflected a few brazen boys, reinforcing the myth and keeping strangers out.

Greed and lust, however, proved stronger than fear.

Crouching in the underbrush, Tobias watched Joly move around the chapel's yard. Bolstered by moonshine, he had come to feed a temptation he could not resist. He slipped down into a crook of roots at the foot of an ancient black jack oak and took another swig from the jar. He grimaced as the hot liquid burned his throat and wiped his sleeve across his mouth. Nothing would keep him from something he wanted—certainly no ghost tales. He had come before to watch, biding his time, awaiting opportunity. Tonight, he would take his black beauty.

He craned his neck to see around the tree. This was all too sweet, too opportune, this chance prospect for pleasure. His head was heavy and muddled, and his excitement grew as he watched her. Whatever courage he had ever found came from the clear burning liquid he made and consumed. He took another swig and stretched out on his belly to wait, like an animal stalking its prey. He lay motionless in the leaves until he heard a voice at the door: "I'll see you after a while, Grandpa."

Quickly Joly took the path leading north. Slung over her shoulder, she carried the satchel filled with books and mail and a fresh loaf of bread. She moved swiftly up the path, unaware of the ugly presence stalking her. She had walked this path a thousand times. To the west, the sky was a wall of luminous fire. To the east, evening was descending.

Tobias trekked parallel to her, hidden, waiting for darkness to fall. Without the glare of daylight, he would have his black beauty. His body shook at the prospect.

Just as the last redness began to disappear from the western sky, Tobias closed in. He crept from the shadows, but suddenly he halted. Ahead loomed Cairnaerie—distracting the predator from his prey. After he watched Joly approach the house and disappear inside, he slipped to the nearest window and peeked in.

"Well ain't that cozy," he whispered in the half-light.

What he saw made Tobias a happy man.

CHAPTER 46

1928

Epistle & Entrée

"Slow down," Helen said. She stepped fast to keep up with John. "What's your hurry?"

"Oh, sorry," he said, shortening his stride as they walked behind McKuin Hall. "I've got something to show you."

It was late afternoon, and the sun glinted off the river below them. July, hot and merciless at noon, had mellowed. Still, John was perspiring. He pulled a handkerchief from his pocket and wiped his brow.

When they reached the overlook, John handed Helen a letter. He was smiling broadly.

"From Miss Snow?" she asked.

"No. Read it."

"You're not tricking me again, are you?"

"No. This is encouraging news."

She slipped the letter from the envelope.

Dear John,

I hope this letter finds you well and that your first year at Haverston has been a success.

I am writing to ask for your help. The state has commissioned a new history of the commonwealth. Our university has been assigned several topics and one requires me to send students out to conduct research. I have asked Mr. Jacob Lassiten, one of our recent graduates, to document the history of Negro churches. I am sending him to you in hopes you can give him some direction. He is a young man of considerable intelligence but less understanding of life. Given your experience, John, you are a perfect mentor for him. You'll know what I mean when you meet him.

He will arrive in early August, and I have instructed him to look you up. I would appreciate any assistance you could offer, and I suspect, John, he may need substantial guidance. Mr. Lassiten is not your kind of fellow, so I do caution you to be careful.

I have corresponded with Dean Rollins, suggesting you would be an excellent counselor. You may call on the dean for assistance—it is my understanding he supports the project, as your college also has its own part in this new history.

I hope this letter finds you hale and hearty.

With kindest regards,

Smalley

"Who's Smalley?" asked Helen, handing the letter back to John.

"My former professor. What do you think?"

"I think it sounds like an interesting project—but judging by your mood, I'm guessing there's more," Helen said.

John grinned. "Miss Geneva."

"Wait! You've lost me."

"Think about it, Helen. She wants to go to the wedding. But she can't go as Mrs. Elias."

"Obviously," Helen said.

"She'll need a new identity, right?"

"Right. That part's easy— give her a different name."

"Agreed. But how does she get there?" John posited. "I mean— she can't just show up."

"Hmmm…good question. Most people don't invite strangers to weddings," Helen said. "And she's definitely a stranger."

"And they don't cross the color line without good reason."

Helen tilted her head quizzically. "What are you getting at? I'm still not following you."

"A good plan is one that won't raise suspicions. Right?"

"Right."

"That's tough in a small town like this. Doing this research, I'll have a chance to meet Zeph's community. Official business. And then Zeph and Joly can invite me to the wedding. It will all be on the up and up."

"And you'll take your dear Aunt Geneva, of course."

"Exactly."

"John, that's brilliant. And you'll take me."

"Of course." John smiled. "The best part of all this is I'm protected. Rollins and Smalley are friends—and this research is as legitimate as it gets. No more St. Ballard."

CHAPTER 47

1928

Churches & Congregants

John pulled his Ajax up beside Nicodemus Baptist Church. It stood in a clearing high above the north bank of the Cleary River and was painted so white it glowed in the midday sun. Reflected light bore deep into the surrounding forest that shielded the church when prevailing winds rolled off the western mountains. Devoid of shutters and other ornamentation, the church, ringed by a tidy lawn, had two stone steps, a deeply pitched tin roof painted green, and a steeple that challenged the tall oaks, whose roots snaked deep through the earth to drink from the river below.

Finding the door unlocked, John stepped into the empty sanctuary. Twelve rows of benches, each with straight flat seats and backs, filled the church. Slipping into the back row, he realized the benches were as uncomfortable as they appeared. *Nobody falls asleep in this church*, he thought. Windows fitted with swirling shades of green glass flanked the sanctuary and sunlight fluttered through them like leafy shadow puppets. On the back wall, a stained-glass window—the single extravagance—shone in the backlight of the afternoon sun: an angel in heavenly regalia holding a dark child.

"Professor Klare?" John rose to see a tall, lean man coming through the door. "I'm Pastor Banks."

"It's a pleasure to meet you," said John.

"Sorry I'm running a little late. We had a death in our congregation. I was with the family."

John was impressed by the man's dignity and openness.

"Now, how can I help you?"

"A student from the university is coming to research churches in the area, and I thought Nicodemus would be a good place to start. It's all part of a state history project. I thought I'd go ahead and make some contacts for him."

"That sounds right interesting. There's a lot of history in this church—nearly a hundred years of it. Nice somebody's studying it."

"I noticed your sign. 1829," John said. "The building's not that old."

"You're right. This building went up right around the turn of the century. But the building idn't the church, you see. The church is the people. And next year we'll celebrate our centennial. We're making big plans. You'll have to come."

"I'd like to," John said, and he meant it. "I was hoping you could introduce us to your members. Pave the way a little."

"Be glad to. You oughta talk to some of our older members—Miss Gladiolus Tinker, Zeph Elias, and any of the Robinsons, especially Briscoe. They go way back—long before me. And I'd talk to the Odens or Pea Rudolph and his kin. They can give you about as much information as anybody."

John slipped a card from his pocket and jotted down the names.

"How do I locate them?" he said.

"I'll get you their addresses, but most of these folks live down by the river in Skunktown. South of town. These folks'll know a lot more than me. I've only been here for twenty years—I'm a newcomer," he said, laughing. "So I 'spect you might want to start with them.

We have some records here—weddin's, deaths, baptisms—but they don't go back too far. Let me show you where they are."

He led John to the back of the sanctuary to a small room lined floor to ceiling with shelves, every one filled to overflowing.

"If you'll look up there on the top shelf there—see those boxes? They'll tell you all about the official life of the church. Most everything else you'll have to track down. I've got a ladder hangin' out back. I'll bring it around and leave it in here for you."

"Thanks. Will people talk to me?" John asked.

"Oh my yes. Some'll like to talk your ears off." He chuckled. "Miss Gladiolus—now there's a storyteller. All by herself she could pro'bly tell you everything that's happened since she joined Nicodemus as a child. If you don't talk to anybody else, you got to talk to her. And if you get by to see her, make sure you give yourself the best part of an afternoon. Some of those folks'll be easy to find. Miss Gladiolus lives in a little house painted bright yellow with pink, green, and purple trim. Kinda looks like a gingerbread house."

"I know the one."

"I thought you might," the Reverend said, laughing. "I don't know when you want to get started, but I'll say something from the pulpit Sunday—let them know you'll be calling. And I'll leave that ladder up here in the back."

CHAPTER 48

1928

Satins & Veils

D ust swirled through daggers of light pouring through small windows tucked under the eaves as Joly pulled a heavy trunk from beneath the rafters and dragged it across the floor to the center of Cairnaerie's expansive attic. Strewn throughout the space were cane-bottomed chairs needing repair, head boards, stools, wooden crates filled with books, empty picture frames, and sundry household goods. Cobwebs clung to hand-hewn beams and connected odd pieces of furniture with a gossamer lace.

"Whoo! Sure is hot up here," said Joly, fanning her face. "I hope it's in here."

As Joly knelt in front of the trunk and fumbled with the lock, Geneva stood back watching, holding a small hand-colored daguerreotype encased in a tooled leather frame. It was a wedding photograph of her mother that had always graced her father's desk.

"Are you sure this is the right key?" Joly asked.

"I thought so."

"Well, I'm having a little trouble—oh, there. Now I've got it." The round lock plate fell away from the trunk, and Joly smiled up at Geneva.

Together they brushed dust off the rounded top, lifted it, and propped it against a table for support. What they found first were random pieces of lace and quilt squares sprinkled with dry sprigs of pennyroyal and rosemary, and a small silk bag still redolent of cloves, nutmeg, and bay that had been tucked away decades ago to keep out moths.

"This comes out," Geneva said, pointing to a removable tray.

Joly lifted it out and set it off to the side. Underneath, a blue cloth was sprinkled with more herbs. Carefully, she pulled it back, and for the first time, they saw Caroline Snow's wedding dress.

"Oh...It's beautiful," Joly said. The aged trunk, stowed in the dry attic for more than ninety years, had done its duty well. The dress appeared almost new.

Carefully, they took the dress from the trunk. As they unfolded it, more bundles of herbs fell from the creases. The satin brocade was still soft and had yellowed little beneath the protective blue cloth. The neckline and bodice were outlined in a fine Honiton lace, as were the cuffs of the then-stylish gigot sleeves. Tiny covered buttons with parallel loops lined the back.

"Try it on," Geneva urged excitedly.

Joly slipped out of her day dress, and Geneva helped her lift the gown over her head.

"It fits you perfectly," Geneva said, holding the back closed. "Go look." She pointed to the cheval mirror that once stood in her childhood bedroom, the one she and Simmy had gazed in as girls. As she watched her granddaughter turning in the dress Geneva's mother had worn on her wedding day, she imagined Clarissa packing the dress away, storing it for a daughter some-day. A vague, unwelcome regret washed over her, but she dismissed it—as she had always dismissed those things she could not change.

Standing in the dim attic light, Joly was suddenly reflective. She ran her hands down across the fabric. "I wish I could have known my mother," she said. "Especially now." Almost weeping, she laughed instead. "But Grandpa has talked about her so much, I guess I do know her in a way."

Tears stung Geneva's eyes as a potent mixture of joy and sadness and a trace of regret welled up inside her. "She would be so happy for you. You are so much like her. Sometimes when I look at you, I think I'm seeing your dear mother."

"Are you sure you want me to take this?"

"Of course. Who else is going to wear it?" Geneva patted the puffy sleeves. "You may need to remake it a bit so it is more fashionable."

"I'll see. It's so beautiful jes the way it is."

Joly and Geneva had pulled chairs out onto the terrace where a mild breeze and abundant shade trees mitigated the hot afternoon that had settled in around them. Geneva cooled her face with a paper fan, a picture of Jesus with small children printed on it.

Inside the house, Caroline Snow's wedding dress lay on the dining room table. Wrapped in an old sheet, it was ready for Joly to carry home.

"I used to love the summer heat," Geneva said. "It bothers me now."

"You want me to get us some sweet tea?"

"Oh yes, that would be delightful. Thank you."

"From the springhouse?"

"Yes, but you have to push hard on the door. It sticks this time of year."

"Be right back."

Once more, as Geneva had done a thousand times, she restrained her enormous desire to reveal herself to her granddaughter.

Her longing begged for satisfaction, yet she resisted. Once again, the time did not seem right. She could not burden Joly before her wedding.

How she wished Alice Lyford had survived Joly's birth—and that Joly's father had stayed. But after the conflicting day of birth and death, he had disappeared. Zeph had said that Fulton Jennings had gone looking for work, but Geneva always suspected he had met with a different fate. He had not been the kind of man to desert his newborn daughter, but he had disappeared nonetheless, and once again Zeph and Simmy had found themselves caring for an infant.

Simmy had named the child after the hope she held for her great niece—joy—and for the child's late mother—Lyford. As Joly grew, Zeph and Simmy had told her what they could—that her grandfather and Simmy had once worked for Geneva's father and that Judge Snow had asked them to look after Geneva when he was gone. This truth was easy to explain. Joly understood their affection for this reclusive woman because it was returned in kind. Miss Geneva was their family secret and knowing her warranted a kindness for privacy that love obligated.

And Zeph and Geneva wanted to protect Joly. They had intended to wait until she was old enough to understand and accept her heritage, but the right time had eluded them. It could always wait a little longer, it seemed, to protect something precious, something bought with sacrifice. Time and opportunity had never coincided, and thus the secret remained unspoken—a procrastination of the most dangerous kind.

Joly walked back out onto the terrace carrying two glasses of cold sweet tea. "I need to get Grandpa to fix that door for you," she said. "I could hardly get it open."

"He knows about it, dear. It always swells up in the summer. He's going to bring his rasp up and work on it."

In the heat of the afternoon and in the company of her beloved Joly, Geneva tried to set aside her worries. But never in the five decades of her confinement had circumstances unsettled her quite like this. She needed to tell Joly the truth. She needed to trust John Klare. And she wanted desperately to go to the wedding. Most of all, she was determined to piece together the family she had broken so long ago.

CHAPTER 49

1928

Past & Present

July had unfolded with warm evenings and sultry nights, and to-night lightening bugs flashed syncopated lights in and out of the hollies and boxwoods that flanked the terrace. Geneva stood back to survey the scene. She pulled a corner of the tablecloth taut and straightened a silver pickle fork beside a small cut glass dish. Shortly she would fill it with some of Joly's bread and butter pickles.

She was excited about the visit, arranged as soon as John's letter had arrived with the news that he had found a way for her to go to the wedding. Geneva was beside herself to learn more. She had been able to tell Joly that she *might* come, but until she knew all the details, she had cautioned that everything was still tentative.

She looked forward to seeing John and Helen and hoped to re-create the same kind of cordial visit she remembered from the sweetest days of her childhood—before war and decisions had torn her family apart. She wanted to make it a perfect evening.

Joly had helped her prepare the meal: country ham, string beans cooked with fatback, spoon bread, beaten biscuits, apple-sauce, baked cottage cheese, and mint tea. A blackberry cobbler would top off their meal. It was one of the few recipes Geneva had mastered, a nod to her own fondness. As soon as the berries ripened, she picked clean the bushes that covered a back fence, always watching for snakes and always suffering scratches from the thorns.

Satisfied that everything was ready for her guests, she went upstairs to freshen.

"I remember Alice Lyford helping Zeph with the chickens," said Geneva, balancing a fork in her hand. Her mood was convivial and their conversation easy, almost taking on the flavor of longtime friends.

John and Helen listened with rapt attention.

"There used to be a coop on the other side of the house. It blew down in a thunderstorm years ago. Some mornings he would bring Alice Lyford with him to gather the eggs. I would watch from the belvedere. He would let her carry the basket and then stand her up on the fence with her little brown toes sticking through the pickets. When the chickens pecked, she would grab her daddy around the neck and jump up into his arms."

"Did Alice Lyford know you were her mother?" Helen asked.

Geneva ran her thumb along the back of one of her hands as if to erase the marks time had made. "No. We didn't know how to tell her. When my parents were alive, we feared it was too much of a burden for a child. It was easier to maintain things as they were. After she married Fulton and moved to Sulphur Hill—by then it was too late. We always meant to tell her, but then she left us. We waited too long."

"That must have been hard," Helen said, finding it difficult to understand.

"Yes, it was. But a mother will sacrifice anything for her children, even letting them go—especially letting them go." Geneva fingered a silver bracelet on her wrist. "Mothers earn a special self-lessness when they bear children. Your own life becomes secondary. I know I was changed forever the first time I held Alice Lyford. If anything, mothers have to fight to keep their own lives." Geneva paused and stared into the night. "I've often thought that if God had not put such strong feelings in mothers, the human race would not have survived. I would have given my life for Alice Lyford."

"I think you did," Helen said.

"I suppose so." Geneva smiled at her with an expression of gratitude.

"Do you have regrets?" asked John, his question genuine but gentle.

"I regret hurting my father. But he came to understand. I know he did."

"Did the two of you ever talk?" Helen asked.

"Only twice—the first summer—then never again. We were both waiting for the other one to give in, I suppose. I used to be so quick to anger. When I was a child, my spunk amused my parents, but my quick temper was always a concern to them—my father especially. He was such a gentle man. It took me a long time to understand, but I have learned that soft words are better. They do—as the Bible tells us—turn away wrath. I learned the lesson too late, I'm afraid. I know it must seem preposterous to you, but for all of us—Daddy and Mama, Zeph and Simmy, too—playing our parts perfectly was how we survived. If you can imagine a feather sitting on a fencepost, that's how it seemed—the slightest breeze and everything would have fallen apart. Everything."

"Do you wish it had been different?" Helen asked softly.

"Oh, of course. I wish we had lived in a different time. But that would have been like wishing to fly—like the hummingbirds. We don't live in a perfect world. We are driven by our passions. Why should we not love the same way? I did not choose to love Zeph, but I did. And I believe with all my heart that God blessed us."

"Do you ever wish…." Helen began delicately, "…that you had fallen in love with someone else?"

"For my parents, yes, but not for me." She smiled. "Never for me."

"When did your parents know about your marriage?" John asked.

"Oh, as soon as Alice Lyford was born. Vivvy told them—certainly she had eavesdropped. She was always my nemesis. I am sure it delighted her to tell them."

"Most fathers would have punished Zeph," John said with equal delicacy.

"Yes. But Daddy was not like other men. He was a man of laws— but he was forgiving, perhaps the most forgiving man I have ever known."

"So he forgave you?" Helen said.

"Yes."

"And nothing changed?" said John.

"I changed." And she smiled in a complete way, as if forgiveness were the single measure of her life.

Their conversation lulled. The night sounds were close. Night bugs darted near the light of a kerosene lamp and stirred the thick summer air. Tree frogs peeped in the darkness and from somewhere in the yard, an owl trilled.

"Listen," she said. "Hear that? Those are my friends. They have kept me company so many nights." A luna moth glided past them, hovered briefly in the light, and then disappeared. "I guess it is my Presbyterian upbringing, but I believe true love is predestined. Theologians may disagree, but I know I was destined to love Zeph Elias."

"And be Joly's grandmother," Helen said.

"Yes."

"Does Joly know?" John asked cautiously.

"No," said Geneva, shaking her head. "I have wanted to tell her so many times. Sometimes it has taken all my will to bridle my tongue, but I have for her protection."

"Will you?" he asked.

"Yes. At the right time. I love her so dearly. And I want to give Joly any gift of understanding I can. My greatest fear is that after I am gone, she and her children and grandchildren will come to know their heritage but not understand it. When your life is over, you cannot change someone's opinion of you. I do not want anyone to think ill of me—and especially my father. That would be a terrible injustice."

"I'm sure Joly will understand," Helen said.

"I hope so. When I was a young girl, my mother's aunt died without mentioning Mama in her will, even though she had faithfully tended to her. She brought her to Cairnaerie to live out her final months. I barely remember her—I was a young child—but I remember my mother's hurt. She did not expect an inheritance, but goodness, to be ignored." Geneva looked at her father's portrait. She seemed resolute. "I will not make that mistake. Some day she will know. She will need to know. Joly will have a legacy."

Geneva stood at the door until John and Helen crossed the hill and disappeared into the dark. A full moon poised in the sky gilded the landscape. She looked northwest toward the family cemetery and imagined it bathed in the same gold. At night, the separation between the living and the dead always seemed tenuous, almost as if their berths were made fluid and the quick and the dead could gather together.

Closing the door, she went to the library. John's plan sounded reasonable, and it excited her even though the thought of leaving Cairnaerie still stirred in her considerable anxiety. She listened as bobwhites whispered in the twilight and bullfrogs plunked and moaned like slow, flatulent banjo players. Tonight, these faithful sounds made her feel less lonely.

She selected a journal and opened it to the first day of 1900.

I awoke this morning to hear a great commotion in the house below me. Without being told, I knew my father was dead. When his clock failed to chime—I knew. He laid down his head on the eve of the new century and died before it could dawn. He was eighty-two years old. We have lived apart for more than twenty years—why did I think there would always be time to reconcile? Now my chance is gone forever. I can hardly bear the bitter sadness this thought evokes. I am beset with grief that aches in my every bone. Why did I not try harder? We died to each other so long ago, a silence of shame, embarrassment—and necessity. Yet I remember the affection he had for me as a girl. It sustains me—I have nothing else to hold on to. Nothing. And if I do not dwell on that, I should be the next one into the grave.... January 1, 1900

I could not attend Daddy's funeral today. How could Mama explain my presence after all these years of absence? Better I remain forgotten. Instead, I braved the frigid belvedere to watch. The brown earth framed the black-garbed mourners, who followed the hearse toward the cemetery. I observed them with a strange detachment—and with a paradoxical longing for my hidden family. They followed at the rear at the respectable distance. Which family would I have walked beside had I been there? I am torn considering it.

Once they all disappeared across the hill and I was alone, I left the belvedere and ventured into the empty house. It was as absent of sound as I have ever known it to be. No one had thought to wind Daddy's clock. And the privation of that repetitive sound was a shroud for my grief. His overcoat lay folded across the back of a chair in his bedroom. I thought how cold he would be without his overcoat, and then I wept as I stroked the wool and smelled for the first time in years the aroma of the father I so adored, the father I had so wounded. And a strange thing happened. I do not know whether I truly saw a vision or if in my grief I imagined what I longed for, but near the window there was a shadow. I'm sure of it. And I heard—with my heart or my ears, I do not know—my father's voice, speaking tenderly: 'Geneva, my Little Bird, I will love you always.'…. January 2, 1900

Her father's clock tonged eleven times. Geneva looked up from reading and listened. *Why didn't he wind the clock that Sunday? Did he know? Will I know when my time is coming?*

She closed her journal and rubbed her eyes. As she moved through the hall toward the staircase, an odd sensation overtook her—she looked toward the dining room windows, but no one was there. She shook off the strange feeling before climbing the stairs.

CHAPTER 50

1928

Commitment & Conflict

Giant crankshafts squealed, and the smell of coal and sulfur filled the air as the Roanoke steamed into the station and rolled to a stop. The day was summer hot, the kind that made people walk slowly, shade their eyes, and push up their sleeves—the kind of hot day that left the sky hazy, the color of milk when the cream rises.

Departing the train alongside other assorted travelers, a short, blocky man dressed in a black suit, black hat, and black boots stepped off. Attired better than the ordinary traveler, he seemed impervious to the midsummer heat. He did not shed his coat as others around did. He wore an air of importance and carried a leather suitcase with fine brass fittings and a small gold monogram on one side—an 'L.' Under his arm, he had tucked a small valise. He set his bags next to an empty flatbed and angled his homburg to shield his face from the sun. From his vest pocket, he lifted a pipe. Striking a match against the rough edge of the wagon, he cupped the flame and drew it down. Tossing the match to the ground, he stood with the pipe clenched in his teeth and watched the train.

Tobias Jebson, who had come to pick up the mail, spotted him and walked toward the station manager who was busy pulling cargo out of an open boxcar. "Who's that?" Tobias asked.

"Who's who?" the station manager said from inside the car, his voice muffled.

"Man over there by the wagon."

The station manager twisted around, squinted, and then went back to removing cargo. "Never seen him before."

Tobias lifted a bag near the door.

"Hold your horses, Tobias. I'm gonna get to your mail. What's your hurry?"

"No hurry. Jes trying to give you a little aa-ssistance," he said, keeping his eye on the stranger. "Looks like a right fancy gentleman."

"Mind your own business. He's prob'ly jes passing through and got off for a smoke. Prob'ly going on to Lufton. He'll git back on in a minute."

At the front of the train, the fireman shoveled more coal into the firebox. Steam billowed from the smokestack and thick smoke choked the air. Tobias watched the man swat some fly ash. Without taking his eyes off him, the postman slipped to the side of the station house where he deposited his mail sack.

The door of the boxcar shut, and the conductor, hanging one-handed off the steps of the Pullman, yelled, "All aboard."

The whistle blew. The man stood still. The postman did, too.

Like a great iron whale clearing its blowhole, the train exhaled. Smoke and soot barreled into the sky. Huge drive rods groaned as they shoved the wheels forward. Another shrill whistle pierced the air. The Roanoke lurched ahead, each stroke faster than the last, and cars rumbled one by one past the station.

Tobias picked up his mail sack, threw it over his shoulder. He walked in the direction of the stranger, approaching with calculated nonchalance, and dropped his mailbag. "Good afternoon," Tobias said casually, folding his arms across his chest and gazing out into the horizon. The stranger ignored him. After a few minutes, Tobias picked up the mailbag, fumbled with it, and acted like he was preparing to leave.

"Excuse me," the stranger said.

"Yes, sir?" Tobias stood up straight. "Can I hep ya?"

"I'm looking for McKuin Hall at Haverston. Could you direct me?"

"Well, certainly I can, sir. I'd be glad to offer you a little Southern hos-pie-tality," said the smarmy Tobias, his red tongue gliding back and forth across his lips. "I, myself, am from Alabama and in Alabama we do more'n give directions. I'm going that way myself, so I'd be more'n happy to ess-cort you."

"I would be obliged," said the man, and he picked up his suitcase.

"Let me introduce myself. My name is Tobias Jebson. I'm the postmaster of the Hyssop Post Office. You prob'ly noticed my mailbag here."

"I see."

"You jes follow me down this away. See them buildin's down the street there? That's the college. Haverston."

They walked together along Fisher Street, Tobias stepping crablike to devote his full attention to the stranger. An entrepreneur of sorts, he was always on the lookout for customers. Those with conspicuously deep pockets were his favorite kind.

"And what brings you to Hyssop?" Tobias inquired.

"Business," answered the stranger, who was as tight-lipped as Tobias was tongue-wagging.

"Hmm. Business. I 'spect that's college business. You a per-fessor? You kinda look like you might be."

The stranger ignored him.

"Oh! I know." Tobias switched his bag to his other shoulder. "Did I hear they's getting a new president here? I b'lieve I did. I bet you're him. I bet you're that new college president. Well, lawsy. Wait till I tell my friends I had the rare privilege of es-corting the new president."

Annoyed, the stranger stopped and turned to this bootlicking guide. "I am not a professor and not the president. Could you simply direct me to McKuin—or shall I have to find someone else?"

"Oh, no. No. You'll have to 'scuse my mistake, sir. I do apologize." He bowed his head repentantly. "But I mus' say you carry yourself like you could be a president. We don't get too many gentlemen dressed up like you—all fine and fancy. You a right smart dresser, mister."

"Thank you," said the stranger, who was not immune to flattery.

"What building you say again?"

"McKuin."

"Well. I b'lieve I steered you right. Here 'tis."

"Thank you," said the man, eager to dispense with him.

"You're welcome. Name's Jebson. Tobias Jebson at your service." He doffed his hat. "If you need 'nything while you're visiting you jes look me up. Hyssop Post Office. Straight down the road there as you're heading outta town. Now you remember my name. Tobias Jebson. Kinda like Thomas Jefferson. Some say I even favor him. Look here." Tobias turned sideways and raised his chin regally. "See this profile? I got the same profile as Mr. Jefferson."

The stranger scoffed. Tobias pivoted back around.

"I'm right well connected around here. So, if you need anything you cain't get at a regular store, you jes look me up." Tobias made a little gesture like he was sipping from a glass, and then winked cunningly. "You know what I mean. If you need anything special."

Without a word, the stranger headed down the brick walk. Tobias meandered along until he saw the stranger go through the door. He then doubled back to a spot with a good view—and he waited.

———

"You must be Jacob Lassiten," John said. He stood to greet the man who had walked into his office wearing a peevish expression. "Let me welcome you to Haverston."

"How do you do," Lassiten said, and he offered a doughy handshake.

Belying his diminutive height, Lassiten carried himself in an imperial way, although he was no older than twenty. His skin was olive, and his hair, dark and coarse, was plastered straight back with abundant oil above a flat, frying pan face. A large mole above his right eye mingled with generous eyebrows, giving him a doggish look—not unlike his landlady's bulldog, Chuck. The resemblance tempted John to smile.

"Please. Make yourself comfortable," said John, gesturing toward a chair.

Lassiten left his suitcase by the door but kept the smaller valise in his lap. He adjusted the buttons of his coat, but kept it on.

"I like warm weather," John said casually as he shed his own coat before sitting back down. "But today's a little hot even for my taste. How is Professor Smalley?"

"Fine I suppose," Lassiten said tersely. He fiddled with a gold cufflink.

The man's ill humor puzzled John. "Tell me about yourself, Jacob. Where is your home?"

"Tidewater. My family has been there since the late 1700s." He said this with an obvious sense of conceit. "I am completing my studies and will enter law school this fall—as soon as I finish here, in fact. This is my last hurdle."

"Professor Smalley tells me you'll be studying our churches."

"Your churches? I hardly think so, Professor Klare. I've been assigned the nigger churches."

The statement, spoken with a snarl in his voice, took John aback.

"Personally," Lassiten continued derisively, "this is a waste of my time."

"I'm sorry to hear that," said John, concerned by this disclosure.

"Smalley made the assignments." Lassiten, clearly vexed, slumped back dramatically. "He's an influential faculty member—you know how it is—you have to please them. I am at the mercy of the academy. If I want to get in law school, I suppose I am required to do this." Assuming he was in like-minded company, he let out a long tetchy sigh.

John's mind raced. The room became awkwardly quiet. Since leaving St. Ballard, his challenge had been to hold his tongue. He cleared his throat and picked up a pencil, twirling it through his fingers. "Then do I gather this is not the assignment you would have chosen?" he said tactfully. He laid the pencil down.

"Of course not! Who would?" Lassiten reached into his valise and pulled out a brochure, which he tossed across John's desk with a flip of his wrist. "It's all right there. I'm sure you're familiar with it—the science of eugenics. All academics are," he said, using academics as a synonym for 'the intelligent.'

As John picked up the brochure, a chill ran down his spine. *The Anglo-Saxon Club of America.* He was all too familiar with it. He wondered if he had moved too fast in assuring Miss Geneva of a plan.

"We have a strong chapter at the university—nearly thirty members," continued Lassiten, brightening to a subject he obviously liked better than the one he had drawn. "I'm vice president. I don't believe you have one here, do you?"

"No," John said, opening the brochure with a sick feeling in the pit of his stomach.

"I'd be happy to help you start one." He grinned, baring his teeth, clearly proud of this association—and stupidly unaware of John's discomfort.

You do look like Chuck, John thought, ignoring his offer. "You subscribe to this?" he said.

"Of course. Who argues with science?" said Lassiten. "It's modern, progressive thinking. The science is clear as a bell. And it's our civic responsibility. We simply can't allow those of lesser mental capabilities—coloreds and such—to propagate like rabbits, can we? Why, we'd be overrun. We've got to protect future generations. It's our duty as the intelligent class. Certainly you agree."

Lassiten's confidence was ballooning with the arrogance peculiar to collegians that John had always despised. He cringed. "And how do you know all this?"

"Common knowledge," he said, pointing to the brochure, "and science, as I said. But all you have to do is look around. If mankind is to survive, we have to rid ourselves of the weak and the stupid— and especially the immoral."

Lassiten paused and for the first time began to sense John's disquiet. He shifted in his chair.

"Well, it appears you still have a job to do." John cleared his throat again and began to doodle on his ink blotter. Had the request not come from Smalley, he would have kicked this buffoon out of his office. But what choice did he have other than to move ahead?

"I've taken the liberty of contacting Nicodemus Baptist for you," John said. "The pastor has agreed to meet with us tomorrow morning." He lifted some papers and tamped them on his desk. He checked his watch. As hard as he was trying to be courteous, his perturbation was evident. "Do you think you could manage to join me?"

"Do I have a choice?" Lassiten said brusquely, stuffing brochures back into his valise.

"No. Apparently you don't," John said. He stood up, unable to continue the conversation—and barely able to maintain his civility. "I have work to do, Mr. Lassiten. I trust you've made arrangements for your accommodations."

"Yes."

"Then be here promptly at ten o'clock tomorrow. Good day."

John leaned forward and leafed through the stack of papers on his desk. Lassiten, chagrinned at being dismissed, turned on his heels, picked up his suitcase, and disappeared down the corridor. When he was gone, John slumped back down into his chair. *What in the world were you thinking, Smalley?*

The next morning Reverend Banks was cordial, even though Lassiten brushed off his outstretched hand and purposefully let John be the interlocutor—as if speaking in the man's presence were beneath him. He stood aside listening with only necessary interest. In an odd way, John pitied this educated man whose upbringing and intellect had taught him so little.

Reverend Banks walked them through the sanctuary. "The church was founded in 1780 by George Lilly," he said. "Founded Baptist churches all over Virginia, and then in 1785, he went off to Jamaica to work as a missionary. When he left, Reverend Jedediah Wynter led this congregation and a few more down the Valley. They tell me he came every three or four weeks. Members filled in when he wadn't here. You ask Miss Gladiolus about Reverend Jedediah. She's told me on more than one occasion that he preached like nobody's business. She can still quote parts of his sermons word for word. He made quite an impression on her."

Unengaged in the conversation, Lassiten took notes.

"You should be able to talk to anybody in the congregation. I'm sure they'll be right interested in helping you any way they can."

"Hmmmh," Lassiten grunted without looking up from his notebook.

"I 'preciate what y'all are doing," said the Reverend.

"I appreciate your help," said John, deliberately avoiding the word "we."

"Now I'll leave you two alone, so you can get to work. I got some to do myself. There's a table back at the far end of the sanctuary. You're welcome to use it. If you'll jes pull the door shut when you leave, I'd be much obliged."

"Thank you, Reverend," John said, extending his hand to the clergyman.

It took most of the afternoon to sort through the collection of books and papers in the church after John scaled the ladder and handed the dusty boxes down to Lassiten, who refused to climb, claiming he suffered from severe acrophobia. They found a hodge-podge of Bible lessons, a slew of family baptismal records, a cemetery map, and dozens of Sunday school rolls. A few documents proved helpful, but John quickly realized the best information would come from individual members. Judging by how rude and unpleasant Lassiten had been with Reverend Banks, he dreaded the thought visiting homes with him. As John closed the church door and walked to his automobile, he wondered if one wedding were worth all this trouble.

CHAPTER 51

1928

Men & Moonshine

Jacob Lassiten stood in the yard of Miss Ida Aker's boarding-house, drawing on an ostentatious calabash carved like the fig-urehead on a ship's prow. He was eager to finish his work and leave town. Finding the dinner conversation as distasteful as the food, he had escaped for a smoke. Although Miss Ida tried mightily to please her guests, her finest fare did not meet Lassiten's approval, and he had said as much by picking at his food, eating what he required for sustenance, and leaving the rest to be scraped into the trough for the two sows Miss Ida kept in a sty at the back of her yard. Smoke coiled up around his sour face as he stared down the setting sun.

When he turned to go back inside, he noticed a familiar fig-ure coming toward him. Approaching in the waning light, the man wore the same dirty shirt as before but had added a coonskin cap, which, when silhouetted against the sunset, looked like a woman's hairpiece. Mildly amused, Lassiten waited.

"Well, if it ain't the stranger. I swanny," said Tobias as if their reunion were pure happenstance. "Never 'spected to see you again so soon. You 'member me, don't you?"

"Oh, how could I forget?" Lassiten said condescendingly. "You're my escort. T.J, isn't it?"

"You got that right. Tobias Jebson," he said, circling Lassiten like a dog. "Miss Ida, she got her a fine place here. You ought to be right comfortable."

"It's adequate."

"Listen, Mister," Tobias said as he leaned in toward Lassiten. "She taking *real* good care of you? If you know what I mean." Once again he made his little sipping gesture.

Lassiten sucked on his pipe and blew a smoke ring toward Tobias. "I believe that's illegal," he said.

"Well, now." Tobias lowered his face and arched one brow. "I'm a law-abiding citizen, you understand, but ever once in a while I need me a little li-bation—jes a little, you know. Jes enough to keep my system well-tuned, if you know what I mean."

"No, Mr. Jebson, I don't. What do you mean?"

Tobias tugged on Lassiten's sleeve and pulled him into Miss Ida's side yard behind a linden tree. Lassiten continued to smoke, upholding his bloated superiority while Tobias tuned up like a fine fiddle.

"Now we're both men here," Tobias said. "And I can see you're a man of considerable experience. You're like me—we ain't locals—me being from Alabama and you from, ah…Where you from?"

Lassiten was silent.

Tobias changed his tactics. "Well. Lemme let you in on a little secret—being as we're experienced men. I'm an entre-pre-noor. You know what that is?"

"A bootlegger," Lassiten said flatly—and louder than Tobias liked. He was enjoying his coup of this toady little man, but while he was ambitious, he was not especially virtuous. Lassiten found Tobias' proposal tempting. It had been a dry summer.

Tobias scrunched up his face. His red tongue flagged. "I like to call myself an entre-pre-noor."

"So long as I don't call myself a revenuer, right?" Lassiten heckled.

Tobias snorted a nervous little cackle. "I like ya, Mister. I do. You got you a good sense a humor. But now if we gonna do business, don't you think I ought to call you something besides Mister?"

"How about 'Mister Lassiten'?"

"Suit yourself. Well, Mr. Lassiten, let me tell you what I can do for you."

It was nearly midnight when Tobias tapped on the glass. Lassiten lifted the window and without a word took a small parcel. Tobias, smiling, strode back down the road with coins jingling in his pocket and melted into the darkness.

Lassiten pulled up a chair to a small table, opened the jar and took a swig. It wasn't long until the room was still, and the aspiring barrister lay spread eagle across the bed, snoring. Moonlight glistened on the empty jar.

CHAPTER 52

1928

Gladiolus & Nicodemus

Miss Gladiolus Tinker told them she was four feet eight inches tall and eighty-seven years old, weighed about as much as a small prize pig, and loved to eat turnips and carrots cooked in a brown sugar glaze. She also liked black coffee with a pinch of chicory and spoon bread for breakfast, and she chewed on apple peels to keep her teeth clean. Then she smiled broadly and invited her guests to come in.

All this John and Lassiten learned before they got across the front porch of her flamboyant house, which lived up to its reputation in every respect. It did—as Reverend Banks had suggested—look like a gingerbread house. Hands down, it was the brightest in Skunktown and served as a kind of landmark for travelers. Go past the gingerbread house, people would say, and then turn this way or that.

The house was small but tidy and smelled of salt pork and yeast bread. From the porch, she led them into her parlor, which doubled as her dining room, part of the kitchen, and a bedroom for two great nephews. She hauled a surly yellow cat off the sofa, shooed him out of the room, and invited her guests to sit down.

"I'm a fastivious housekeeper," she told them as she picked several cat hairs off the sofa and stuffed them into her apron pocket. "You fine gentlemens, you sit yourselves down."

"Thank you, Miss Tinker," John said.

"You jes call me Miss Gladiolus. Ev'body call me that. I'm so pleased to have you two gentlemens come pay me a visit."

Lassiten was unusually quiet—a surprising but not altogether unpleasant reversal of his earlier bellicosity. Not more than a handful of words had passed between them on their way to the house. He walked stiffly, sat rigidly, and spoke softly, his words, scarcely audible.

He stepped past a rocker offered him by his hostess and positioned himself gingerly in a straight chair. "No, thank you," he said with unusual civility. "This will be fine." He kept his head still and winced at every noise.

Reverend Banks had been right. Miss Gladiolus began talking the minute she saw them come up her front walk and did not stop except to take a sip of tea or breathe—at which time John would deftly drop another question into the conversation.

"Tell us about Mr. Jedediah Wynter. Reverend Banks said you knew him."

"Oh my, that Reverend Jedediah. All he ever preached was hellfire and damnation. But I don't b'lieve anybody can get enough of that kinda preachin'. Woulda scared the fuzzy off a wooly worm. Now, I don't usually go around saying bad words, you understand—like hellfire and damnation. But he said 'em and I'm jes quotin'—been quoting preachers all my life." She winked at John and flashed him a grin.

"Law, that Mr. Jedediah! He'd git going 'bout ten o'clock in the morning and go on all day. I was jes a little bitty thing when he come here to Nicodemus. Most every Sunday, I came along with my mama—she wadn't my real mama, but she might as well a been. She raised me right along with her eight natural chil'ren. Never did treat me any different. Jes like one a her own. Oh, I seen it all at Nicodemus—weddin's, dyin's, baptisin's. Honey, I even saw the Holy Ghost one time." Her eyes got wide as duck eggs, and she raised her hand like she was swearing allegiance. "I was on my way back from the funeral of a godly man who'd passed. I b'lieve maybe it was Pea Rudolph's Uncle Ossa. Well, whoever it was, I was in charge of all the food for after the funeral, so I was up in the back of the sanctuary checking the tables when I saw this light up at the pulpit—jes as bright as the sun. An' I jes fell right down on my knees, right there beside Aggie Spurlock's deviled eggs, and started weepin'. I never seed anything like it in my life since."

Lassiten, listing with half-closed eyes, struggled to take notes.

"I was a changed woman after that. Yessiree. You know—to this day I never tol' a single lie since my encounter with the Holy Ghost. I been tempted plenty, but I never have slipped. Not even one little white lie. If somebody asks me how I like her dress, I jes tell it to her straight out. If it's an ugly dress, I jes say it's an ugly dress. Rather have the whole world mad at me than the Holy Ghost."

She paused to breathe. John jumped in.

"Miss Gladiolus, could you tell us about the church, about the history or anything you remember?"

"Of course. But honey," she chortled. "I'm eighty-seven years old, and I got me eighty-seven years of memories. You gotta have good ears and a long-suffering backside if you want my stories."

"I'm all ears," John said, settling back in his chair, thoroughly enjoying this visit. He glanced over at Lassiten, who looked rather frangible; John thought hopefully that he might have a tolerable side after all.

After three hours, two pitchers of sassafras tea, and a plate of chitlins that made Lassiten turn green, the two men took their leave of Miss Gladiolus.

"You two come back anytime. Next time I'll have my summer sausage all made up, and I'll fry some up for you."

Lassiten's lips formed a taut line.

"Thank you for your hospitality," John said. "Reverend Banks was right. You are a wealth of information."

"He said that?" She looked exceedingly pleased.

"Yes, he did. And he was right."

"Well, if I think of anymore good church stories, I'll tell him, and you can come back for another visit."

"I would like that," John said—and he meant it.

By the next day, unfortunately, Lassiten had regained his equilibrium—and his pomposity. Even so, thanks to John's geniality, they had managed visits to a handful of other congregants. None, though, was as entertaining as Miss Gladiolus.

Driving away from Skunktown after one of the last visits, John pondered Lassiten's rudeness. He had seen professors use it on undergraduates and staff—a kind of intellectual bullying meant to demean those they deemed inferior. He hated it. It went against everything John Klare believed.

CHAPTER 53

1928

Dignity & Demeaning

Helen waited for Zeph at the library's basement door—a small awning-covered entrance used mostly for hauling coal in and clinkers out of the building's furnace. She would not tell Geneva that after all these years Zeph could not use the library's front entrance—even in the donnish realm of a modern college—and that he was allowed entry only through the back door and usually when he was pushing a broom or carrying a toolbox.

But today Zeph Elias had a special dispensation. Summoning all her professionalism, Helen had asked the head librarian to use the basement room for the interview—as a favor to Assistant Professor John Klare. Interviewing Zeph in Swope was out of the question—given Lassiten's ilk—and no public establishment would host such a meeting. The head librarian, one rung on a tall administrative ladder, had agreed—begrudgingly—after Dean Rollins approved the request.

Trying to bring some measure of cordiality to an uncomfortable situation, Helen smiled generously when Zeph came down the walk, as though welcoming a colored man into the vaunted library were a most ordinary thing. He looked dignified in a freshly starched white shirt, a narrow black tie, and a stylish tan fedora he had bought for the occasion.

Zeph took off his hat and stooped to clear the low threshold.

"I'm glad you came," Helen said, escorting him through a labyrinth of halls. "I have two gentlemen eager to talk to you. They think you know a lot of history."

"That so? I don't know about history, but I sure lived through a lot."

"It'll be in a book when they're all finished. It'll probably have your name in it"

"You reckon?"

"I would not be surprised at all."

Zeph carried his hat on top of a package wrapped in faded purple brocade, as he and Helen walked down a short flight of steps into a dingy storage room, a dank space smelling of coal and mildew. The room had one small, rectangular table and several mismatched chairs, and it was lined with random boxes. Light from a high narrow window and two oil lamps, which Helen had scrounged, cast smoky shadows.

John and Lassiten were waiting at the table, the tension between them unmistakable. Their time together had done nothing except sharpen their differences. The few words they had exchanged were terse and to the point.

Both men stood when Helen and Zeph entered the room. John greeted them warmly. Lassiten, true to form, refused Zeph's outstretched hand. John thought Zeph's devotion to Miss Geneva must be enormous to tolerate this, yet he realized that the older man was probably accustomed to such slights.

"Make yourself comfortable, Zeph." John offered him a chair at the end of the table—and Helen, the one next to himself.

Lassiten was far more engaging—to the point of fawning—when John introduced Helen. The arrogant student eyed her salaciously, and John, an unexpected surge of jealously rising, leaned to blunt his view of her.

Zeph untied his package, a large cloth-bound Bible held together with bailing twine.

"I thought I'd bring this to you, Mr. Klare." He pushed it toward John before sitting back rigidly with his fingertips on the edge of the table.

"Your Bible?" John opened it to a family tree. He saw no mention of Geneva Snow.

"Yessir. This is the one my mama kept before me. I'm 'fraid it's kinda worn, but it's got some church history. Back in the back there."

"Thank you." John leafed through it. "What can you tell us about your church? How long have you been a member?"

"Since I was a boy. My mama and daddy took me and my sister every Sunday and Wednesday from the time I can remember till they passed. Then we jes kept going. I'd tote my sister when she was real little. Till she got big enough to walk herself. The church used to be on the other side of the river, so it used to be a whole lot closer, but it got washed away in the big flood."

"Flood?" Lassiten asked without looking up.

"In '96, September 29. I believe it was a Tuesday. Rained all day and by evening seemed to stop, but commenced again a little while after dark. People living in town could hear it rushin'. The wind got all the gaslights—then all folks could do was listen. We lost one family, the Grover Harpines. All four of 'em drowned. They lived down near the stone railroad bridge. When it washed out, their house washed out, too. Never did find the little boy, but the rest, they found 'em down the river near the county line."

"And the church?" John said.

"Used to be on the west side of the river, down below Finley's Bottom—big bend in the river. It must've been some wall of water 'cause next morning the church was on the other side of the river and everything in the bottom was gone."

"Are you saying the flood rerouted the river?" John asked.

"Sure did. Never went back the way it was."

John looked at Helen, who mouthed *erosion*. He gave her a faint nod.

"You rebuilt?" John said.

"Yessir. Across the river—on the east side. Where it's sitting now. My Uncle Pap and me laid some of the foundation."

"You had family—your uncle?" John asked.

"No sir, me and Simmy was orphaned like I tol' you, but Uncle Pap and the rest of the church folk—they looked after us. He wadn't our real uncle, but he helped us. Uncle Pap was a deacon in the church long as I can remember..."

Lassiten interrupted. "What was his full name? Uncle Papoose?" He patted his mouth and made a little 'woo woo' sound, trying to be amusing.

Helen rolled her eyes and glanced at John as if to say, 'Who is this guy?' She was quickly beginning to understand John's assessment of Lassiten.

"Don't know his full name, never did. We jes always called him Uncle Pap. Mighta been a Rudolph. You'd have to ask somebody else."

John redirected. "So the present church was built in about '96 or '97."

"No, sir. In '99. We met down near the washed-out bridge for a while—till we could get another building up."

"How many are in your congregation?" John asked.

"Well, let's see. About a dozen families. Oh, pro'bly fifty or sixty folks, maybe more."

"There was only one nigger church?" Lassiten asked.

"Yessir, 'round here. Now down by Lucksville there was more, but 'round here, jes Nicodemus."

"Thank God," Lassiten murmured.

"About twelve families?" said John, trying to ignore the student's rudeness.

"Yessir. That's about right. Maybe even fifteen, but no more, I'd say."

"Are all the families from the area?" John asked.

"No. Some came from down 'round Lynchburg. The rest—born right here."

"How many of you were slaves?" Lassiten said.

"I don't rightly know. Don't know much about my pa, either, 'cept he came up here from eastern Virginia."

"As a slave?" Lassiten said.

"Yessir."

"Most of you were slaves or descendants of slaves? Is that right?" Lassiten said.

"I s'pose. That was a long time ago."

"You don't know much, do you, boy?"

"I'm a pretty simple man," Zeph said with respect that was undeserved.

"His name is *Mr.* Elias." Helen, unable to contain her disgust any longer, fumed.

"Well, 'boy' sounds fine to me." The corner of Lassiten's mouth turned up in a mocking smile.

Helen glowered.

Facing Zeph, John saw a smile behind the old man's eyes. *He doesn't suffer fools,* he thought. Soon they would be done with Lassiten. He would board the train and get out of their lives, and John could get back to more important business.

"Do you remember the pastors of your church?" John asked, reclaiming the conversation again.

"Yessir. There was a Reverend Wirt—claimed he was the great, great nephew of Mr. George Lilly. He came through and preached right regular when I was a boy. Then there was Mr. Jedediah Wynter."

"We've heard about Reverend Jedediah," John said.

"You musta talked to Miss Gladiolus," Zeph said, and he laughed. "I remember the reverend right well. He'd go on all the way till lunch time, then some Sundays he'd start up again after we'd gotten us a bite to eat and preach till dark."

"What did he find to say for so long?" John asked, genuinely curious. He couldn't even imagine lecturing that long.

Zeph smiled. "I remember him, but I don't remember much of what he said because Simmy and me had to walk most of the time. We'd slip in at the side door and, more often than not, we'd fall asleep leaning up against each other."

"Every Sunday?" Helen asked.

"No, ma'am. Reverend Wynter was a circuit preacher and he'd get to us 'bout every month or six weeks. I guess that's why he could go on for so long—had to make up for the Sundays he'd missed."

Zeph seemed to relax, while Lassiten wrote.

Helen and John exchanged smiles. He winked at her. He was glad to have her with him today.

"Is there a cemetery?" Lassiten asked without looking up.

"Yessir. Two of them. One's down on the low side of the river— up a little ways from where the first church was." Zeph paused. John saw his eyes twinkle. "Adam and Eve's buried there."

They all looked at Zeph, who was grinning. Lassiten scoffed.

"Yessir. When I was a boy, my Uncle Pap took me down to see 'em: Adam and Eve."

Lassiten opened his mouth to dispute Zeph.

"Yessir. Adam Wysor buried there right close to Eve Turnipseed. Yessir."

John laughed out loud. Inwardly, Helen gave a cheer. Lassiten, stone-faced, began turning scarlet.

"It's true," Zeph said. "I can take ya and show you."

"That would be something to see," Helen said. "Is it still used? The cemetery?"

"No, ma'am. Now we bury our folks up on the other side of the new church. We had some trouble with boys kicking over the stones. Couldn't keep it up. Made the new one sometime in the nineties, I think. You oughta go ask Miss Delphenia. She'd know. All her people are buried up there."

"Miss Delphenia?" asked Lassiten.

"Yessir, Miss Delphenia Jackson."

"Jackson?" He looked through his notes, not recalling a Jackson. "Not listed."

"Yessir. Jackson. Miss Delphenia was an orphan, and somebody gave her the name. Not sure who her real family was."

"But you said her people were buried there." Lassiten looked annoyed.

"Yessir. They took her in when she was a baby. You'd never know the difference. They was as much her people as if they'd birthed her."

"You take care of your own," Lassiten said, smirking.

"Yessir, I guess we do."

As the interview wound down, Helen checked the clock and relaxed—plenty of time before she had to be back at her desk. Lassiten continued making notes, and John leafed through the open Bible. She noticed Zeph looking intently at Lassiten.

Lassiten looked up. "What are you gawping at?" he said sharply.

"You know, Mr. Lassiten, you remind me of somebody," Zeph said. "A fellow I used to know a long time ago. Cain't remember his name, but you're a spittin' image."

Color drained from Lassiten's face. Abruptly he closed his note-book, pushed back his chair, and stood up.

"We're finished here," he said, and he hurried out of the room. The sound of his boots echoed down the hall until the outside door opened and closed.

Puzzled, John and Helen looked at each other and then at Zeph.

"Did I say something wrong?" Zeph said.

CHAPTER 54

1928

Indignation & Indigestion

Lassiten squinted at the mirror, trying to adjust his collar, cursing as he fumbled with a stubborn stay. His stomach rumbled. Sounds of clanking dishes and silverware drifted from the kitchen where Miss Ida was preparing breakfast for her boarders. Finally, after numerous attempts, the stay disappeared into the slit beneath the collar of his shirt. He patted it down and stared at his reflection. Raising his hands to his face, he pushed up his cheekbones, ran a finger down the bridge of his nose, and tilted his head from side to side. Opening the curtain for more light, he examined his full face, his hands, and his neck. In the privacy of the room, the expression on Lassiten's face was anxious.

When the dinner bell rang, he exhaled and spoke his name out loud: "Jacob Bascom Lassiten." And with a sly smile, he added "esquire." He stood as tall as his boxy frame allowed, assumed his regal demeanor, and then went to breakfast.

With his field research completed, Lassiten commandeered a table near the library's east windows to write. He refilled his Waterman with ink and shuffled his notes. He still did not see why Smalley and the great commonwealth deemed this topic important. But loathsome as it was, once his task was finished, his spot in the law class of 1931 was almost guaranteed. In spite of his indignation, he was determined.

He belched. His stomach was bothering him again. Reaching into his pocket, he drew out a small tablet and chewed it.

At the far end of the room, he spotted a familiar figure. Helen, unaware of his presence, moved a cart along the stacks as she re-shelved books.

"Good afternoon, Miss Van Soren," he said amiably when she came near.

"Good afternoon." Helen spoke coldly and quickly shelved a book.

"You're looking lovely today."

Ignoring him, she pushed her cart away from his table.

Lassiten's lip curled. "Come over here," he said.

She kept moving.

"Miss Van Soren," he said, this time louder. "Come over here."

"Shh," she turned and scolded. "I'm busy. People are trying to work."

"Well, I need some assistance."

"I'll get someone to help you," she said, and she continued moving away from his table.

Lassiten jumped up and followed her. "But I want *your* help."

"I'm busy," she said.

Lassiten didn't like being rebuffed. He grabbed her arm, digging his fingers in, and snarled close to her face: "Busy with Mr. Klare and all his little niggers? I bet you don't refuse your Mr. Klare."

Incensed, Helen jerked away and slapped him. Other patrons looked up. So did the head librarian.

"Leave me alone," she said. "Or get out."

"You're tossing me out?" He threw up his hands in mock horror. "Oh my, oh my!" He moved in close again and whispered darkly. "You and your Mr. Klare better be nicer to me. If you know what's good for you."

Lassiten's threat stunned Helen, but she would not be cowed: "Go—or I *will* have you thrown out." The entire room was watching them now. The head librarian stood up and came around her desk.

Helen was furious. "Get out," she ordered.

Lassiten's nostrils flared. He backed down. Collecting his papers, he marched out.

———

Sitting alone in McClanahan's, Lassiten chewed on a cold roast beef sandwich as he stewed over Helen's rebuff. It had undoubtedly triggered his indigestion. He loosened his vest to relieve the pain in his stomach.

The eatery was crowded and noisy. Overhead, a ceiling fan waggled and thumped. His assignment was noxious enough, but to be reproached by John and Helen exceeded his tolerance. *How dare those nigger lovers treat me like that.* He could not wait to finish his work and leave town. Only the promise of law school kept him in Hyssop. Nothing would interfere with his plans—especially not John Klare and Helen Van Soren.

He poked the dry sandwich with his finger and tried to ignore his interminable indigestion. He belched, which made it worse and left a metallic taste in his mouth. *I will starve before I get back to civilization,* he thought. Leaving his sandwich half eaten, he paid for his meal without leaving a tip. As he headed back to the boarding-house, he considered making another trip to the post office. The cola had done nothing to slake his thirst. The thought lifted his sagging spirits. Perhaps it was worth suffering the likes of Tobias Jebson.

He turned south.

Late in the evening Lassiten met Tobias near the linden tree.

"How much longer you gonna be in town?" Tobias asked. He was more than happy to accommodate his customer.

"A week. Maybe less." Lassiten thought dismally how this wretched assignment had reduced him to bartering with the likes of a repugnant but convenient ally. He blamed Smalley and John Klare.

"I'll tell you what," Tobias said in a whisper as seductive as his product. "How about I put you down on my regular de-livery route long as you're here."

"How much?"

"Oh, I'm a reasonable man. I b'lieve we can work us out an a-rrangement—something mutually a-greeable."

He proposed a plan and Lassiten agreed. To sweeten the deal, Tobias threw in an invitation for poker.

"I'll take it under advisement," Lassiten said pompously. "What time?"

"Eight. Eight o'clock sharp. And you do that, you take it—what you said."

"Advisement." Lassiten smirked and started to leave, but then he stopped. Turning back to Tobias he asked, "Do you know everyone around here?"

"I might."

"Do you know anything about John Klare?"

"No, cain't say I do—but I got my ways of finding out."

"Do that for me, and I'll throw in a bonus."

"I like you, Mister. I like your style." He threw Lassiten a casual salute. "It's a pleasure doin' business with you, Mr. Lassiten."

CHAPTER 55

1928

Courage & Confession

Geneva awoke early, the cool sound of mourning doves belying the coming heat. The air was heavy, and she felt unusually tired. Perhaps it was the humidity or the strain of having visitors to which she was so unaccustomed. Or perhaps it was her age. With so few landmarks in her life, the years had crept up on her as unexpectedly as a crocus bloom. Now here she was—suddenly old—bound by an eternal clock and compelled to satisfy overwhelming desire to tie together the past and the future. She sat on the edge of her bed and thought, pulling words together, her fingers moving unconsciously as if she were drawing ink across paper.

Geneva understood all the legalities—and she had set those in motion. But the milieu into which she would have to venture for the wedding was another matter entirely. She was no longer so practiced in the nuances of human interaction, the casual manner between men and women. She had been absent too long. John and Helen's visits had helped, but the thought of being in a crowd of people struck a disharmonious chord—a dread like an unwelcome stranger. She had been cloistered by a father protective of his daughter, and it had spared her much of the bruising and shaping one earns from the ordinary buffeting of life. Cairnaerie's protection had also denied her the toughening, the inoculation one gets in an imperfect world. In that sense, she was still childlike in her hopes and dreams, still moored tightly to the self-confidence of her youth. She had never let go of her idealism, the belief in dreams that had spurred her to marry Zeph. Nothing in her hidden life had pressed hard enough on her to change her. Certainly, she had been tried and tested from the moment she had slipped from her father's protective grasp, when she had stepped beyond the accepted boundaries of the community. But it was a different kind of testing. And now, on the verge of venturing away from Cairnaerie, she was vulnerable—though only partially aware of her disadvantage.

To her great delight and relief, she had found John and Helen easy to talk with, their openness and generosity sufficient to sustain her courage and override many of her worries. Yet imagining herself conversing with others left her unsure. But she was determined to keep her fear at bay. She would not let it interfere with what she must do.

All summer she had suffered a recurring nightmare. Night after night, she found herself alone on a platform, showered with hard light and pummeled with questions. *Who are you? Where have you been hiding? Does your father know you're here?* Sudden, concussive volleys of sound, vicious tearing voices, and flashes of light would assail her from all directions, and just as the voices would rise to a deafening crescendo, she would awaken with her heart pounding and perspiration soaking her hair and nightgown. On the nights Zeph stayed with her, he would hold her when she awoke in a panic, cooing his own special brand of calm. But even her husband's comfort had not relieved her of the nightmare dogging her. It had been unrelenting, draining her, ripping away at her resolve until one particularly long and restless night—she had finally dismissed it, relegating it to stand with all her other fears and joys, triumphs and disappointments. She dispatched it to her journal.

> *...And then I awaken. I have suffered this dream for months, and unlike others that lift me beyond my own understanding and give me courage, this one has not. It has frightened and unsettled me, stirring doubt and emotions contrary to what I know is the right path for my family.*
>
> *I have been alone so long that I cannot remember how it feels to be with people. This is reasonable, considering my long absence from society. I have tried to remember going to church with Mama and Daddy and the boys, of traveling to town with Mama and Simmy, even of large Sunday gatherings here at Cairnaerie—but it is so long ago, it seems to be someone else's life, not mine. But it was my life. The truth is I am not who I was. Of course, I am not. I am even stronger than when I first married Zeph. Certainly I am wiser. I have survived the severest of restrictions and have discovered in them freedom. My life has been one of redemption, not deprivation. Perhaps my concern for Joly and Zeph is more than enough reason to go forward. I will find the courage.... September 20, 1928*

And that night she had slept soundly. It had always been like this. The act of writing cleared her head, coalesced her thoughts, and established her paths. This morning she hoped the same would finally be true—one more time because time was running short.

Geneva rose and stood for a moment at her window, watching columns of burning dew rise from the deep cuts in the mountains. Just beyond the window, hummingbirds hovered, foraging for the last drops of nectar in the faded blossoms. She wondered if Joly had found a veil. She would look for her mother's this afternoon, but for the morning, she would be busy with one long-overdue task. She dressed and went downstairs to the library.

As she sat down at her father's desk, his clock struck seven. She filled his fountain pen with new ink, thick with promise, and took stationery from his drawer.

Geneva had rehearsed the letter for years. Countless times she had put words to paper before tearing them up; her letters had seemed weak, wrong, too much like an abject apology that crushes the confessor. It had been easier to delay—to hope truth might work itself out like a splinter and be healed. But this morning—this new morning—her words flowed.

My Dearest Joly,

This letter will come to you as a surprise, although my fondest hope is that it will bring you joy and a bold resolve to live your life with your Mr. Oden to the fullest, to love him with abandon, and to discover how good lives are made when a man and a woman, joined in God-given love, are determined to overcome all obstacles.

I have wanted to tell you about my life more times than I can count, but I restrained myself for fear that my own desire might jeopardize your happiness, indeed your life. Once, a long time ago, my father tried to protect me in a similar way—and certainly with a similar love. I hope you understand that everything I have done in my life has been for love, but sometimes there were unintended consequences. Often those we care for most dearly are the ones we hurt most deeply. I wanted your life to be happy, and I did not want my desires to complicate it. You must understand, my silence thus far has been because of a love greater than my own. Please remember this as you read further.

You see, Joly, I am your grandmother. Your grandfather and I were married on April 27, 1876, in Swope Chapel, your home. When I became Mrs. Zephyr Elias, as you can surely imagine, our marriage was not welcomed by society—so we kept it secret. When your mother was born and our secret was undone, my father, your great-grandfather, hid me away. He closed Cairnaerie to the world so your grandfather and I could live as nearly as possible as husband and wife. It was not his intention at first. It was only to buy time, I'm certain. I am equally certain he did not intend for the arrangement to become permanent, but as time passed it did and, in a kind of sweet irony, it sheltered our secret life.

My situation was not unknown. Young girls sometimes found themselves with child, caught in circumstances the community deemed unacceptable. Sometimes their little babies were given away to colored families or sometimes they were left with itinerant farmers to be carried away to distant places. Then a young woman could move again into society as if she were no different from any of her friends. If the family had been sufficiently discreet, she could marry, have other children, and live as though her lost child were merely a bad dream to be forgotten in the morning mist.

But our daughter, your beautiful mother, Alice Lyford, would not suffer that fate. She was a child we loved with our whole hearts. So we hid.

Our marriage was something I believe my father respected but found hard to accept. He was a man whose responsibility to his family, though, was second only to his devotion to God. His virtue and his love for me were sorely tested, yet neither was broken. He could never abandon my child or me to strangers—or to society's cruel condemnation.

I know my parents wanted the best for me, but what I wanted was my husband and child—your grandfather and your mother. I would not listen to reason, and I threatened to expose every-thing, which would have destroyed my mother. I was young and naïve and perhaps foolish, but I also loved your grandfather with all my heart—and I eventually prevailed, although it came at a terrible cost to us all.

My father was a man of sterling character, but his most noble trait was his ability to forgive. I remember as a child, he would read to us from the Bible each morning when we gathered for breakfast. It was a tedious ritual for us as children, yet for my father it held great meaning. His faith was the fount of his life. His favorite passages were those of forgiveness and redemption—the prodigal son, the woman caught in adultery. He would read the words with a sense of awe, like a child seeing a first rainbow. He never failed to be stirred by the Holy words. I believe it was my father's deep commitment to God that led him to devise the arrangement.

You see, I was not hidden from the world as much as the world was hidden from me—the world my father knew would harm me, the world that said I could not have your grandfather as my husband and that said your mother was unworthy. He could not bring himself to send us away, and I refused be parted from them. He chose to keep our family together in the only way he could….

Geneva laid down her pen. Finally, her words spoke. Joly would understand. But one question still loomed: *When?* Time and oppor-tunities were disappearing with each passing day.

The clock struck nine. She looked around the library where she had spent so many pleasant hours with her father. The room was still, the shelves, full of books, the rolls of surveys, the stacks of land plats tied and lined up neatly. Shelf after shelf, row after row, book after book—their owner, long gone. On one high shelf was a small bust of Plato, a gift from another lawyer. Near it was a scale with two flat brass pans and a brass standish. There was a small portrait of Caroline Snow as a young woman. And there was a glass cloche holding a silver watch—the one item her father had shown her often but had never allowed her to play with.

Geneva's journals lined an entire shelf. Above them were her father's journals—it had taken her years to find the courage to open them. Even though her father had been gone from Cairnaerie for nearly thirty years and from Geneva's life even longer, she still sensed his presence—and today, strangely, she sensed it more than ever. She could almost hear the voices of her childhood seeping from the silence around her.

She got up to fix a cup of tea and returned with her hands wrapped around the china cup. She pressed it against her cheek as she remembered her earliest lessons with her father. He had taught her to write her name with his best writing instrument, a fine pen given him by a well-traveled lawyer when he became engaged to Caroline. She could almost feel the warmth of his hand guiding hers as they dipped the nib of his pen into the ink and then drew it across the paper. She could still see the tentative black lines, often linked together with drips of India ink, crooking across the paper. Was his patience as perfect as her memory testified? He inspired her, drawing her to learn as naturally as leaves are drawn to the sun. Beyond the open doors, sunlight played on the terrace stones. She knew why her father had so loved this room.

She re-examined the letter. These words had taken her a lifetime to write. Carefully, she blotted each page and slipped the letter into an envelope. Across the front, she wrote Joly's name. For safekeeping, she dropped it into a silver pitcher on the dining room sideboard. It would wait there, ready until the time was right.

For Geneva, it would have been easier never to tell, to preserve her friendship with Joly in its present, perfect state, but she could not. She wanted her to hear the truth in her words. Joly deserved to know.

And Joly would need to know

CHAPTER 56

1928

Cufflinks & Collusion

It was getting dark—nearing eight o'clock—when Tobias moved the curtain aside to peek out; his black buggy eyes were surrounded by a white anticipation. Seeing no one, he pulled the curtain back over the window and lit a lamp. Sooty smoke rolled up out of the globe and dissipated into the room. Shadows danced along the dirty beadboard walls.

After shaking the door latch, he kicked aside a throw rug, squatted, and lifted two heavy planks out of the floor. Lying flat on his belly, he stuck his arm down through the joists and brought up one, then a second and third Mason jar. Each was filled with a clear liquid. He replaced the planks, grabbing the dusty rug and spreading it out. He put the jars in the bottom of a dry sink next to a row of dirty shot glasses. From the drawer, he took out a deck of cards and fanned the edges.

At eight o'clock sharp, Tobias heard Buster bark, followed by a quiet, furtive tapping. He opened his door enough for two small men to slip into the room.

"We might have us a fourth tonight, boys," Tobias said, his oily voice seeping through his thin lips.

"Who?" they said in unison like two diminutive owls.

"Mr. Jacob Lassiten. Soon-to-be Esquire." Before he could elaborate, another knock came, a bold knock. He raised his eyes and distorted his face in a wry, 'wait-till-you-see-this-fellow' smile.

"Mr. Lassiten. It's a pleasure to have you join us for a little game tonight," Tobias said, bending in a kind of Southerner's kowtow. "This here is Tuck Monroe and that's Cletus Jurden."

"Gentlemen," Lassiten said with a measure of irony.

"Pleased to meet ya," Cletus and Tuck chorused meekly.

Tobias latched the door and shook it again. Lassiten removed his coat and hat, which Tobias hung reverently on pegs as the other two men stood gawping.

"Y'all have a seat," Tobias said. "May I offer you fine gentlemen a little li-bation?"

"Ain't that why we're here?" Cletus said, laughing.

"It's why I'm here," Tuck said.

Lassiten said nothing.

As they assembled around a table, Tobias ceremoniously opened the washstand like a first-rate prestidigitator to reveal his contraband. He poured a round.

The locals watched Lassiten puff out his chest and down his drink in a single swig. He coughed and gulped air. Heat spread across his chest like a mustard pad and his arms tingled.

"The best white lightening this side of the Mississippi," Cletus declared, setting down his glass, ready for another pour.

Tobias cut the cards and dealt the first hand.

"You a right fine shuffler," said Cletus.

"Shut your mouth and bet," said Tobias.

As the evening progressed, Lassiten was relieved of his watch, and then two silver collar pins, two gold cuff links, and nearly twenty dollars.

Sometime well after midnight, with the necessary aid of Cletus and Tuck, Lassiten staggered back to Miss Ida's.

———

A week later, Lassiten paced the wooden platform along the edge of the railroad tracks. The train was late, the day was hot, and his stomach was bothering him again. Impatiently, he looked down the tracks for the train and started to check the time before remembering his watch was gone.

Smugly, though, he realized he had succeeded—even if he had failed at poker. In his valise, which he held tightly under his arm, was his research. His lifelong dream of adding esquire to the end of his name was within his reach. He could taste it. Soon he would be buying watches and gold cufflinks at his pleasure. He pulled down the sleeves of his coat to hide his naked cuffs that flapped open, and then he took out a handkerchief to mop his face.

Rounding the corner at Fisher Street, Tobias Jebson headed toward the station. When he heard dogs begin to bark, he picked up his pace. Momentarily, the train whistle blew, and shortly thereafter the Roanoke rumbled into the station.

Picking Lassiten out of the crowd, Tobias sidled up next to him, and with the stealth and cunning of a first-class pickpocket, he slipped a small tin flask into his hand.

"A free sample for you, sir," he said, hoping to blunt any ill feelings about their recent game. "I take good care of my customers. It's been a pleasure doing business with you, Mr. Lassiten—Esquire. Glad to do business with you anytime."

"I'll bet you would," Lassiten said with a sneer as he tucked the flask inside his coat and boarded the train.

"You remember me now," Tobias shouted over the noise of the idling engine. "You make sure you remember me."

"Oh, don't worry, Mr. Jebson, I'll remember you. You can be assured of that. You will *all* remember me."

And Lassiten was gone.

CHAPTER 57

1928

Family & Faithfulness

You want more grits, Grandpa?" said Joly, sitting across the kitchen table from her grandfather.

"Sure would. Any more ham?"

"Maybe one more serving."

Joly's chair screeched against the floor as she stood up to refill his plate. It was cool for a September morning, but heat radiating from the stove took off the edge. She held her hands near the stove to warm them.

"You think we'll get to church before it rains?" her grandfather said.

"Why do you think it's gonna rain? The sky's jes as clear as a bell," she said. "Looks to me like it's gonna be a pretty day."

"Oh, rain's coming. I'm feelin' it in my bones. And my bones, they're right reliable."

"We'll see," she said. She set his refilled plate down in front of him and hugged his shoulders.

Joly sat back down at the table, thoughtful. She was anxious about leaving her grandfather alone after she was married. He had steadfastly declined to move away from the chapel—even though

Thatcher was adamant that he was welcome to live with them. Most men would not want an old man tagging along with a new bride, but Thatcher was different. He and Zeph had often worked together, many times with other members of the large Oden family. Joly could still picture Thatcher, standing with one foot on a wagon wheel and using all his powers of persuasion, which were considerable: "Two for one," Thatcher had said. "Along with my bride, I'll be getting a good carpenter. I could use your help, Zeph—and you, Joly, and me—we can all look after each other."

"I appreciate the offer," her grandfather had said, "but I'm not much interested in moving. I got me a good garden, a few chickens, a good spot to rest in. All a man needs. No, sir, I cain't see me moving."

Thatcher had tried again, using an argument Zeph might not be able to resist: "Joly's gonna miss you. She'll miss you something awful."

"She'll be fine. And she'll come see me. She won't go and forget me. No need me moving."

Thatcher's concern for her grandfather was one of many reasons Joly adored her husband-to-be. His easy manner had won her long ago, but his generosity toward her grandfather had made her grateful to him as well.

Thatcher was older than Joly, but his age had made him mellow and kind, rather than set in his ways. He was the last of his family to marry, and already he had a good business, a small sawmill and woodshop between Hyssop and Skunktown that he ran with his brothers. Craftsman throughout the valley knew the Oden brothers to be honest and skilled—so much so that their craft outweighed their color. Even the most bigoted overlooked it to own their work.

He had grown up in a tenant house with eleven siblings and aunts and uncles coming and going like home was a hotel. He knew how to share, how to get along—and how to work hard. On any Sunday, almost a third of Nicodemus Baptist Church was populated with Odens and their kin.

Joly moved her food around on her plate. She did not want to bring up the subject with him again, but she knew she had to.

"Grandpa," she said. "Miss Geneva has been after me to tell you she'd be happy to have you at Cairnaerie. She mentioned it again the other day. She said she could open up some other parts of the house and you could stay there."

"Well, that's awful nice," Zeph said. An impish sparkle shone in his eyes and little crinkles formed around them. "But you gotta understand, honey. I've lived here at my chapel so long I can't think about living anyplace else."

"She wants you to come, Grandpa," Joly said carefully. "She needs somebody to look after her. And so do you."

"I know that, Joly. But we'll be all right. And I know the path to Cairnaerie better'n a pig knows his way to the trough."

"But you'll both be by yourself. Couldn't you even think about it?"

He smiled, touched by her concern, and reached across the table to hold her hand. "Honey, I'll be fine. Sometimes being alone's not so bad."

CHAPTER 58

1928

Solo & Sisterhood

Quit worrying," Helen said as she took John's starter key from his hand. She shoved a box across the seat and then climbed into the Ajax. John closed the door.

"Don't forget to push the spark lever forward. And give it plenty of gas," he said.

"Yes, professor."

"Is the gas turned on?"

"Yes, it is. I know how to do this. You're a good teacher."

John stepped back and stuffed his hands in his pockets. He watched her concentrate, push the clutch halfway to neutral, adjust the spark lever, and spin the engine to get it started. The Ajax rumbled awake. As instructed, she revved the engine and looked at John, smiling as if to say, 'See!'

John nodded. He had spent an entire afternoon teaching Helen to drive. Still, he was apprehensive. The road to Cairnaerie was much rougher than the asphalt roads around town. He had to admit to himself, though, his car was the least of his worries. *What if she has a flat? Or catches a wheel in a ditch?*

"Are you sure you don't want me to come with you? I'd be glad to. I'm finished for the week."

"Quite sure. I'll be fine, John," she said with confidence that was—in part at least—for show. She knew this was a big step for John; for her as well.

"You remember how to get there?" he asked.

"Yes. And I have your directions."

"The windshield wipers are on the right," he yelled over the rumbling engine.

"I don't think I'll need them." She pointed toward a cloudless sky.

Slowly, Helen engaged the clutch. The Ajax jerked forward as she turned John's automobile onto the street. With nervous excitement curdling in her stomach, she followed Main Street out of Hyssop and turned west. The bright sky mirrored the thrill of her solo venture.

Over the summer, Helen had grown fond of Geneva Snow, so she had jumped at the chance to visit her by herself. But it had taken significant persuasion to convince John to loan her his car. She smiled thinking of their afternoon of lessons. *I am a modern woman,* she thought with satisfaction.

Helen reached the gate without incident. Feeling victorious, she parked in a small clearing off the road and set the brake before heading onto the footpath toward Cairnaerie. When she was beyond the swale and could see the house, she saw Geneva waiting in the swing. She waved.

The house looked fresh and alive. A few weeks before, Zeph and John had taken a sickle and ax to the overgrown yard and created for the first time in years the semblance of a lawn. In the process, they had also found an old, long forgotten Concord grapevine in the side yard. Although it had been untrimmed for years, to Geneva's delight it still yielded a few bunches of grapes. The same day, Helen and Joly had helped by washing away decades of dust and dirt. Cairnaerie was being revived by what had become a collection of friends—a secret society—congregating around the reclusive owner. At first, all the activity was unsettling to one unaccustomed to anything more than the arrival and departure of Canada geese each summer. But Geneva adapted and was grateful for their help. It was as a kind of confirmation that the time had come for her to leave Cairnaerie.

"I am so glad to see you," Geneva said, holding the door open for Helen. "I have looked forward to your visit all week."

"I've brought you something." Helen handed her the box.

"Oh, my," she said like a delighted child. "Joly brought me a present, too."

Geneva opened the box and lifted out a birdhouse painted bright red with tiny white flowers along the top. It had a ring attached to the roof and a chain for hanging.

"I thought you could hang it outside of your kitchen window," Helen said.

Geneva examined the birdhouse closely. "I love watching the birds. I have black-capped chickadees and yellow finches and little Carolina wrens—they are my favorite. One year a wren built a nest inside my back porch. They must have flown in while I had the door propped open. I had to leave the door open for weeks—until their little ones hatched. I have always envied birds. Can you imagine how wonderful it would be to fly?"

Geneva set the birdhouse on a table and took Helen by the hand. "Thank you so much. It will look lovely in my garden. Now, come, look what Joly brought me."

She led her into the dining room where a light blue hat with matching blue netting lay on the table. A slightly dusty peacock feather stuck cockeyed out of the banded side.

"It's to wear to the wedding. Joly says It is 'Prussian' blue. Isn't it lovely?"

"Oh yes. Very pretty," Helen said.

"I added the feather. My father kept peacocks, and I've always kept feathers in a large vase upstairs. Some say keeping peacock feathers is bad luck, but I don't think so. I don't believe in bad luck. Have you ever heard one? A peacock?"

"No," Helen said. "I haven't."

"They sound like babies wailing." She straightened the feather. "Do you think it's too much?"

"Oh, I don't know." Helen was diplomatic, not sure how to tell her the feather was indeed a little much. "What will you wear with it?"

Geneva paused. Her smile faded. "Oh. I don't know. I really don't know. I haven't had a new frock since Simmy died. I never learned to sew."

"There's a lovely little dress shop in town that lends on approval. Why don't you let me see what I can find for you?"

Geneva touched Helen's sleeve. "You're so kind. I am so glad John brought you with him. Sometimes things happen that are better than one can ever plan." She hooked her arm into Helen's and patted it. "Let me fix us some tea."

Like two old friends, they rustled around the kitchen. Geneva wrapped a towel around her hand and pulled open the cast iron stove to stoke the fire. On the top, a copper kettle steamed. She tempered a china teapot while she filled a silver infuser with loose tea, and then filled the pot. She pulled a cookie tin from a glass-fronted sideboard and held it up for Helen to see.

"My vice, I'm afraid. I love cookies." She set the tin on a small drop leaf table beneath the window. "I've been saving these for a special occasion. These were my father's favorites. Molasses and ginger with a pinch of rosemary. I grow my herbs out back—you can see." She pointed to the window.

Helen looked out to see knots of well-tended plants. As unkempt as the rest of the yard had been, this area—just beyond the kitchen door—was trimmed and clipped.

"You'll have to see my gardens in the spring. This time of year they look a little bedraggled. But in the spring, I have jonquils, irises, hyacinths, peonies—all sorts of flowers come up. Simmy helped me plant the garden after my mother died."

"Simmy was very dear to you, wasn't she?"

"She was everything to me. Like a sister. She was the most selfless person I have ever known—and the kindest. She learned it from her mother, Clarissa. She—Clarissa—told me once that kindness was better than beauty. I'm sure I had said something haughty—I was a handful as a child. I can still remember her exact words: 'Not everybody born pretty or rich—not everybody's that lucky—but everybody can be kind. Being kind makes you happy.' She was right."

"You grew up together? You and Simmy?"

"We were born the same month. Clarissa nursed me—that's what I was always told."

Geneva took Helen's hand again. "Let me show you something."

The two women stepped out the back door and walked through the yard until they reached another garden covered with a carpet of still-blooming alyssum. Beneath a crepe myrtle clinging to a handful of faded blossoms, Geneva pointed to a small headstone: 'Jane Simms Elias, beloved friend.'

"Her mama and daddy are buried somewhere out on the farm, but I never knew where. Zeph couldn't remember, either, so we chose this spot. Every spring, I think of the flowers as a tribute to Simmy. She was so dear. I am sure that's why it was easy for me to fall in love with Zeph. I loved Simmy so."

"When did she die?"

"In '23. It is hard to believe she's been gone five years. Her heart gave out. She had been getting weaker for a year or so. She never said anything, never slowed down, but Zeph and I could tell. She died leaning over a wash tub." Geneva paused and her eyes welled up. "It is the only time I have ever seen Zeph cry—he has always been so strong. But Simmy was special—his baby sister."

"Tell me about Zeph," Helen asked as they walked back to the house.

"Dear Zeph. He worked from the time he was big enough to haul a bucket of corn to the coop. He did not have much chance to be a child. Lightner—his daddy—put him to work as soon as he could walk, and then when his parents died, he looked after Simmy. Zeph takes care of everyone."

"Some things don't change, do they?" Helen said.

Geneva smiled. "I don't know what my daddy would have done without him, especially after the war. Those two got along fine."

"Even after Alice Lyford was born?"

"Not at first. That took time. My father was sworn to uphold the law, even unjust laws. We had put him in a difficult spot—an impossible spot. In his own way, though, he loved Zeph. I know it is hard to understand."

"I can understand you admired your father."

"Yes, I did. He taught me so much. To read. To write. I loved to learn—and my father indulged me. I did not have an occupation in the traditional sense, not like you—a librarian," she said, voicing 'librarian' with a kind of reverence. "But I might have. Daddy would have helped me. But I chose differently. I was a wife and mother."

Helen listened with growing admiration for a man she would never meet.

Geneva was quiet for a moment. "The most important lesson he taught me, though, was how to forgive. Conflict is inevitable in life.

But forgiveness—nothing is as noble or important. We will fight and disagree, but if we do not forgive, we die poor. Forgiveness was Daddy's finest lesson."

The air took on a sudden chill. Geneva shivered. "Our tea should be ready."

Geneva stood on the porch until Helen disappeared over the hill. The air was thick with the scent of rain, and the sky had clouded over. A brisk breeze was kicking up, and leaves fluttered out of the trees. The swing, nudged by the wind, squeaked and swayed. She thought of the hours she had spent there with her father.

Closing the front door, she started upstairs, her right hand gripping the curving banister. She was smiling. How long had it been since Geneva had talked so freely about her family, about life? Even with Joly she measured her words. But this afternoon—this conversation was different. This was the way women talked; this was how she had always talked to Simmy.

Geneva paused at a tall mirror in the upstairs landing and gazed at her reflection. In her eyes and brow, she saw her father, and in her mouth and the shape of her face, her mother. Hayes and Thomas and Grayson were there, too—and Alice Lyford's laughing eyes. She touched her cheek and stared at the faces of the generations stirred together and painted with the same brush. There, too, was her beautiful Joly.

She heard the rain begin, sheets of it slapping against the windows of the belvedere. She stepped into her bedroom. The yellow curtains billowed in the squally air. She lowered the window.

Lying on a table was Caroline Snow's bridal veil—delicate and perfect—as if hours and not decades had passed since it was last worn.

CHAPTER 59

1928

Breach & Loss

Had Zeph known Geneva was in danger, he would have protected her as he always had. But he didn't know. No one knew the sanctity of Cairnaerie had been breached.

In all her years, Geneva had never been afraid, even when her family was gone. She had been lonely sometimes, but never afraid. Time and topography had always guaranteed her safety. Cairnaerie was her sanctuary—an extension of her father's arms holding her. It had protected her, secured her, kept her. She felt as safe there as if she had been locked into a vault, so she thought nothing of it as she sat at her dressing table combing out her hair and heard noises in the parlor below. She smiled, thinking Zeph had arrived. He often came early to bring in wood for the stove or to start a fire for her, so they could spend a quiet evening together and a night of love.

She finished brushing her hair, which cascaded over her shoulders in thick gray waves. But when she stood to slip on her dressing gown, she heard a different kind of sound. This sound was not Zeph. Confused, she stood in the center of her bedroom as the noises escalated—sounds of drawers and cabinets opening and crashing. Panic gripped her. She blew out the lamp and moved silently out into the dark hall. As if her past hiding directed her, she found the attic stairs and escaped to the belvedere. Quietly she turned the key and listened, barely breathing, afraid to move.

Heavy footfalls moved from room to room. They crisscrossed the halls. Someone was rummaging through her sideboard. She heard metal clanking and wood scraping. Then footsteps were making their way up the stairs. She held her breath. When the heavy steps came within inches of her hiding place, she pressed her hands over her mouth. Without such precaution, terror might escape her throat. The doorknob rattled, but discouraged by the lock, the intruder moved on. Time disappeared as she stood paralyzed, afraid to move, while the intruder ransacked her house.

Suddenly, like a blow from an ax to her head, she was struck with an awful realization. *Zeph.* Her eyes widened as she stood trapped in the dark staircase. *Zeph.* She began to pray. *Oh, dear God. Keep Zeph away.* Over and over she whispered the words. *Keep Zeph away. Please, God. Please. Let them take everything I have, but keep Zeph away.* In sheer panic, she dropped down on the stair, consumed with this solitary supplication.

Finally, after minutes that seemed to her like hours, the house fell silent, but Geneva did not move. The moon passed out of the clouds and flooded the high, windowed room. She looked up as the comforting, soothing moonlight draped her in its heavenly raiment. But she still did not rise, listening intently for any chink in the silence below—a great chasm of quiet that kept her closeted. Her back and legs began to ache. Her hands shook. For the first time, she realized she was cold.

Outside, along the path from the chapel, Zeph ambled toward Cairnaerie, whistling, unaware that anything was amiss. When he stepped into the disheveled kitchen, he was instantly alarmed. "Geneva!" he shouted, lumbering through the house. "Geneva!"

He pounded up the stairs calling her name, and when he saw the attic door opening, his heart leapt. Geneva tried to speak, but her voice failed. When she saw him, she dissolved into tears. Zeph had come late, after all.

Zeph made Geneva stay upstairs while he cleaned up some of the house. As he righted tables and replaced drawers, he began to reassess his decision to stay at the chapel. He had always protected Geneva, and he believed Cairnaerie was out of harm's way. For the first time, though, he wondered if his confidence had been misplaced.

After he brought her downstairs, and she assessed the damage, she saw that most of her silver was missing from the dining room, along with candlesticks and bowls. To her great relief, she discovered her father's silver pocket watch, obscured by a vase of dried hydrangeas, still sat on a shelf in the library. The losses were considerable, but her gratitude over Zeph's delayed arrival was so overwhelming, it all seem trivial.

Only later did she realize the silver pitcher from her sideboard was gone—the pitcher holding her letter to Joly.

CHAPTER 60

1928

Epiphany & Separation

Geneva was winded when she stepped into the cemetery. She had forgotten what a climb it was from the house. It had taken her so much longer than when she had raced across the fields as a child with Simmy or Zeph. Stopping to catch her breath, she gazed out over Cairnaerie, a view she had not seen for years, not since 1903, the year she had lost Hayes.

But this morning, she had been strangely—and unmistakably—drawn here. She didn't understand why, but she recognized the same feeling she had as a child whenever her father called her. She pulled the moth-eaten cloak she had rummaged around for tight around her shoulders.

Geneva had not told Joly about the robbery. Nothing should worry her before her wedding, she had insisted to Zeph. She was convinced that the letter to Joly was lost, thrown away, gone forever. Surely a robber wanted things to pawn or sell. She refused to consider any other possibilities, but as brave as she tried to be, the robbery had awakened new fears.

The cemetery was overgrown with waist-high grasses. She pushed her way through to two ornate tombstones and tramped down the grass in front of them. It seemed disrespectful to have let it grow up so. *I should have come here more often,* she thought, wishing she had a scythe to cut back the weeds. Kneeling, she traced the cold, lifeless letters of her parents' names.

Learning of John's plan for the wedding had pleased her. It had also unsettled her because after all this time she was finally leaving Cairnaerie. Already she felt strangely guilty for bringing in strangers—as though she were disobeying her father. Even though he had been dead for almost thirty years, the pull of his will was still present, the need for his approval still lingering.

Here she was, the young woman who had hurt him, the errant daughter who had stubbornly insisted on her own way, now preparing to defy him once more. But she was a grown woman—no, she was an old woman—and yet she longed for her father's blessing, wished for his voice somehow to say, *Yes, my Little Bird, fly.*

Wind whistled through the orchard like a bagpipe's lonesome drone. A solitary blackbird cut the marble sky. Drawing herself up to her full height, she looked out over Cairnaerie, waiting for some small hint of resolution.

And then, with a suffocating swiftness, a new realization overtook her. It had been Geneva—not her father—who had prolonged her cloister. This epiphany struck her viscerally, and from deep within her a bitter cry rose. She gasped and clutched a tombstone to steady herself. Yes, her father had set up the arrangement. He had made her stay hidden. But in the decades that followed—long after he was gone—hiding had become *her* choice. It was *she* who had caused her cloister in the first place—and it was *she* who had continued it. Everything she wanted was within her grasp. There had been no need for her to leave. Suddenly she knew: This had never been her father's wish. The cloister that had protected her had become too secure, too comfortable. It was easy to be brave in seclusion—but seclusion weakened bravery. The courage of her youth had atrophied.

The wind whistled again. The clouds parted. September painted the sky as if a great artist were at work. The colors should have warmed her, but they stood in stark contrast to the fear that chilled her. She was trapped in a winter of the soul. As much as Geneva Snow wanted to believe she was the same courageous woman who had taken charge of her own life and married a forbidden man, she was not. Falling to her knees, she wept. *How can I leave now?*

She looked up as sun broke through. Leaving was no longer about her life only. It was about someone else's life now. It was Joly's turn to live.

The words came on the wind. *Fly, my Little Bird, fly.*

CHAPTER 61

1928

Bank & Bribes

Zeph headed toward town, walking in the field beside the road to avoid motorcars, which seemed to multiply daily as they rolled along dodging holes and horses. Carrying his mailbag, he was deep in thought. Although Geneva had dismissed the robbery, it worried Zeph, especially the disappearance of her letter to Joly. His best hope was that Geneva was right; the letter had been tossed away. His worst fear was that someone would open and understand it. Zeph was not naturally suspicious, but this nagging concern made him wary.

As he stepped through the post office door, he steeled himself, as he had done for several months. Tobias Jebson was boorish and uncouth, but Zeph had not thought of him as a real threat. Now he wasn't sure.

"Good morning, Mr. Jebson," he said as casually as he could. He slipped off his hat and held it at his side.

"How you, Zeph? You got you another boatload of mail." Tobias shook his head. "A damn boatload."

"Thank ya," Zeph said.

"How's that girl of yours?" He sneered as he spoke.

"Oh, she's fine."

"She sho is fine. A fine-looking girl," he said. "Who'd you say she was marrying?"

"Thatcher Oden."

"He's that tall nigra over at the sawmill, ain't he?"

"Yessir. A good man."

Tobias looked directly at Zeph, a sly smile on his face.

"I s'pose he knows your girl real good—to be marrying her and all." Tobias let the thought linger in the air. "He know her real good?"

The hairs on the back of Zeph's neck stood up.

"Guess he knows everything about her," Tobias continued, his disposition suddenly menacing. "A man's got a right to know who he's marrying. Ain't that right?"

Tobias caught Zeph's eye and gave him a strange look as he handed him a stack of mail folded into a large magazine.

"Thatcher's known her since she was little," Zeph said. "Knows her pretty well." He dropped his mail into the bag and stepped back. "Thank you, Mr. Jebson. I'll be seeing you."

"Now you go on and read your mail. You read it all. Real good." His voice held a malevolence Zeph had not heard before.

"Yessir. Be seeing you, Mr. Jebson."

Zeph left the post office shaken. As soon as he was out of sight, he found an old stump beside the road and sat down to thumb through the mail. Stuffed with the rest was a dirty, crumpled envelope with Zeph's name scribbled on the front in grease pencil. It had no postmark and no stamp. Zeph's heart sank.

He tore open the envelope. Squinting in the full light of the midday sun, he could just make out the words: *Keeping secrets is expensive. You pay me $100 and my lips is sealed.* Fear shot through him like a bullet. But he knew what he had to do—what he had always done. He would handle the problem and spare Geneva.

Without hesitation, Zeph withdrew the money from the bank. Normally, Betty Louise Perfader would not pry, but the nervous look on Zeph's face prompted her to ask him a question.

"Zeph, it's none of my business, but are you having some trouble or something?" she whispered across the counter. "Do you need any help?"

"Oh, no, Miss Perfader," Zeph said, making light of it and quickly inventing an answer that was truthful without being true. "You know—weddings. Trying to do it up right for Joly. Appreciate you asking, though. Right kind of you."

The wedding was as good a red herring as Zeph had. He smiled broadly to reassure the teller.

"Well, Zeph—it's easy bein' kind to someone who comes out on Thanksgiving Day to unclog my kitchen sink for me.

Zeph laughed. "I remember that. You had yourself a mess, Miss Perfader. A real mess."

"I sure did. And you rescued my whole dinner."

Zeph left the bank, thinking of the Judge—he had told one good lie to protect someone he loved. Now, Zeph guessed he had told one, too.

As instructed, Zeph left the money at a designated spot and walked away with little thought of the cost. With his hands stuffed in his overall pockets, he wondered: *Would it be enough? Jebson's a greedy man.*

Out of a gnawing uncertainty that the postmaster's greed would not be satisfied, Zeph resolved to do whatever it took to protect Geneva and Joly.

Whatever it took.

CHAPTER 62

1928

―――――◆―――――

Cousins & Covenants

It was raining when Geneva rose early to tidy her parlor and prepare for the cousin she had corresponded with for decades but had never met face to face. Looking out the kitchen window, she hoped her father's adage would hold true: 'Rain before seven, clear before eleven.' She smiled as she remembered how interested he had always been in the weather, how he had set up a weather station near the back door and for decades kept meticulous records of rainfall, temperature, and such. She thought of John—what a marvelous time he would have discovering her father.

After slipping bread left to rise into the oven, she sat down at the small kitchen table and re-read the letter.

Mr. Anderson Goodwin, Esquire
Goodwin, Keissel, and Sturn
42 Brass Rim Street
Baltimore, Maryland
September 15, 1928

My dear cousin,

I have received your correspondence detailing your requests concerning the dispensation of your estate. I am sorry that I must inform you that what you wish may not be as straightforward as you hope. There are several complicating factors, which must be addressed. I wish we could resolve these through letters as we have done in the past, but I am afraid it is not possible within the time-table you request. I do believe it would behoove us to sit down and discuss this matter at length. I have several potential solutions for you to consider. Would you be averse to having a visit from an old and slightly decrepit cousin?
Devotedly,
Anderson

Geneva laid down the letter and slipped her glasses from her nose. She placed her hand on her chest for calm. Anderson's letter had shaken her at first. What she hoped would be a simple legal transaction had hit one more hurdle. Nothing, though, would change her mind. She knew what she wanted to do.

She pulled a shawl hanging on her chair around her shoulders. *My hands are so cold this morning,* she thought. *I cannot seem to get warm. I must lay on another log.*

She expected Anderson by early afternoon. Zeph would meet his train and bring him to Cairnaerie. Joly had helped prepare tarts and pies, and she had collected squash and October beans from her garden. A pitcher of egg custard cooled in the springhouse. A smoked ham was ready to be sliced paper thin. Zeph had sharpened the carving knife. Everything was ready.

Earlier in the week, Joly had helped her prepare Hayes' bedroom for her guest. Together they had whisked away years of accumulated dust, washed windows and swept floors, freshened linens, and set out a cobalt vase filled with fresh yellow tansy.

While they worked, they had chattered about the wedding—and Geneva had savored it. Weddings had always been important in the South. They drew relatives from far and wide, and no one missed one—short of a death, a newborn, or a serious illness. It was a happy occasion, a gathering before God and man, a public declaration of all things good and glorious. It was social, yes, but it was much more. Once Geneva had overheard her mother say that her life began the day she married Bertram Snow. In many ways, Caroline Snow's life had ended at his death. Geneva did not want to die without going to another wedding—Joly's wedding.

She had not been able to see Alice Lyford marry Fulton Jennings a year after her father's death—a time when all the accumulated weight of hiding, of sickness and death, had begun to leach into Cairnaerie like a poison. As with Joly, Alice Lyford had known her mother only as a kind friend—part of the dwindling Snow family that the Eliases had always worked for. Out of fear, out of protection, out of her own uncertainty—it was all these things—Geneva had never told her daughter the truth. And she regretted it. Now she was determined not make the same mistake with her granddaughter. She would have to write another letter, but for today, she had other things on her mind.

Geneva put another log on the fire and went upstairs.

The longcase clock struck ten as she stepped into Hayes' bedroom to check it one last time. Soft light from a muted sun permeated the room. She tightened the bedcovers and straightened a vase of wildflowers on the side table. She brushed away a few dropped petals, slipping them into her pocket.

To freshen the room, she raised the window several inches. Outside, rain drizzled and a chill wind stirred the leaves of the pin oaks. They were beginning to dry and curl, but they were stubborn. The oak leaves would hold on until spring. They would not fall until new, emerging leaves shoved them off their branches. *How like life,*

Geneva thought, leaning her forehead against the windowpane, *one generation waits for the next. They hold on tightly—for as long as they can—until the young generation grows strong. Only then do they depart. It is sad, but this is the order of things.*

Staring out through Hayes' bedroom window, Geneva thought about death, about her mother and father, about the last time she had stayed in this room, tending her dying brother. It had been a desperately painful stretch of years.

It had also been a time of forgiveness.

1903

CHAPTER 63

December 1903

Farewells & Mercies

At the crest of the hill, Geneva faced east, standing in the mercurial darkness that amasses before dawn. Thick clouds obscured the mountains, and a great teeming fog lay across the landscape. In too short a time, the day would break with faint promise of some radiant heat to warm the raw autumnal morning. For months, colorless days had stretched in long pale ribbons from dawn to dusk, and fitful sleep had brought her little relief. Her spirit, so indomitable, suffered as if from a chronic sickness.

She had departed before light to pay her last respects to Hayes. Pneumonia had struck him quickly, killing him in less than a week. On Monday, he was healthy and strong, repairing fences. By Friday, fever had consumed him. He could barely draw a breath. And then, he was gone, her faithful brother. She had stood at his empty bed in disbelief, his room, lifeless and shrouded with the dust of winter. Blue light played sluggishly on the walls, casting breathless shadows—like death was still clawing its way in. The curtains drooped like ancient faces. His college books lined a shelf. His shaving implements rested on the dresser cloth. His coat and scarf hung on a peg by the door. His boots stuck out from under the bed where a faded quilt was thrown back. His wardrobe stood ajar, as if he had simply stepped away and would return shortly. But he would not.

And now, their mother lay dying.

Looking out across the farm from this high vantage filled Geneva with unspeakable sadness. Before her eyes, Cairnaerie was dying. The farm's demise had begun gradually after Bertram Snow's death three years prior. Hayes had given up his job and returned home to help, struggling to maintain some semblance of production, a difficult task. And then early this fall, two farm hands—the last ones left—had deserted them ahead of the first siege of snow. As winter prepared to settle in again, the farm—a shadow of what it had once been—withered like a lingering flower at hoarfrost. Without the relief of sunshine, a dry and quiet cold was slowly squeezing life from Cairnaerie. Zeph did what he could, but Geneva recognized the irreversible truth: Her father's beloved home, once a great and lively calliope, was falling silent. Now here she stood, seeing it all.

Death had drawn her out of the house to the cemetery. Hayes had no cortege or funeral procession as his father had had because the Snows had retreated from the community, wholly absent since the Judge's passing. After her husband's death, Caroline, in her whelming grief, had shunned all visitors. Absence and distance became conspirators and made Cairnaerie all but invisible.

As Geneva entered the cemetery, she ran her bare hands along the wrought-iron fence. The rusted metal, hard and cold, stood firm, waiting for another. The cool from the upturned dirt embraced her. The earth breathed and moaned, matching her sadness.

In the house below, vague lights flickered. Much of the house was shuttered, its former occupants few. Only Simmy and Geneva were left to tend Caroline, whose earthly life was closing. Vivvy had left soon after Bertram Snow's death, her obligation to the man who had always treated her as kindly as any man, complete.

"I ain't wantin' to be stuck here all winter," Vivvy had told Zeph after the Judge's funeral. "Nobody much to cook for no more. Simmy can do what needs be done. Nobody need me no more. Besides, they got you—and we knows you ain't going nowhere." Her words were sharp and true. "Briscoe's people. They be glad to have me." Vivvy's kindhearted nephew had not disagreed.

As Briscoe had ferried Vivvy away from Cairnaerie for the last time in his wagon, hauling a single trunk filled with all she owned, the old cook never looked back. Cradled on her huge knees, she held tight to a bag the size of a goose egg, tied with a leather strap. Inside were gold coins, payment from the Judge. He, a man of his word, had taken care of her.

Standing among the tombstones, Geneva thought about all those who had passed through her life. How she missed them, her brothers, her father—even Vivvy, as strange as that seemed.

Drawing her wool tight around her, she sat down in the damp grass and took a small book and pencil from her pocket. Shortly she would return to her mother's bedside, but she could not bear to let Hayes go without a goodbye.

> *My dearest Hayes, I cannot believe you have gone from us. You have been my comfort for so long, though I know it was a burden to you. I miss you and long to be with you again when—*

But she could not continue. The sadness blackening her spirit was a grief too great to assign to paper. She placed her pencil in the fold, her shoulders slumped toward the cold grass, and under the last covering of night, Geneva cried for Hayes.

Simmy carried a pitcher of water into Caroline's bedroom where Geneva sat beside her mother. Near the bed, a box of Beecham's Pills lay on the table, but it had been weeks since Caroline had been alert enough to take any kind of medicine. In her febrile delirium, she did not realize it was her lost daughter who attended her, who wiped her brow with a cool cloth, and who spent long days and nights at her bedside, more time than they had spent together in decades.

Simmy filled the basin on the washstand. Wiping her hands on her apron, she approached the bed.

"Her hands are so cold," Geneva whispered.

"Least she's peaceful. That's a blessin'," Simmy said.

Caroline had never fully recovered from the deaths of Thomas and Grayson, and after her husband died, sorrow tormented her. Slowly, a bitter wish that death would come to her as well consumed her. But it was not to be. Where once she gave to Cairnaerie a style and grace that brought life and beauty, she now brought the pall of death.

In the last few years, Geneva and Hayes had spent hours talking in whispers, often retreating to the belvedere to avoid the aging Caroline, whose decaying life rhythms made her ever present at night as well as during the day. She had found some solace in her painting, which took on a distorted darkness as if her pain, too great to bear, spilled from her, staining whatever she touched. Although living in body, Caroline Snow had gradually ceased living in spirit.

Geneva stroked her mother's hair. It was as soft as she had remembered when she was a child, and her mother's cheeks, though wrinkled, were still pale and flawless.

"Where's Zeph?" Geneva asked.

"Gone to get more wood. He took down that old apple tree. He'll be back before long. How is she?"

"The same. Sleeping."

"Are you hungry?" Simmy asked.

"A little."

"I've got some soup on. Go on and get some. I'll sit a while."

Geneva slipped out of the bedroom as Simmy took her place beside the bed and held Caroline's hand. The joints were knotted and the nails bluish, but there was a still a delicacy in her hands— the long, tapered fingers of an artist. Simmy looked at her own calloused hands and wrapped them around the old woman's. The room grew chilly.

Before long, Geneva tiptoed back into the room.

"I brought you some soup," Geneva said. "Come eat something." She set a tray on a small table near the fire and returned to her place beside the bed. Outside a dry winter wind blew, and an occasional gust funneled down the chimney, making a hollow sound like a child's penny whistle.

Zeph came in with an armload of wood. He crouched down next to the fire and added another log. One broke and fell into the ashes as the new log ignited, crackled, and flamed up. As he rolled it back on the andirons, a hint of wood smoke lingered.

Simmy, warming her hands on the soup bowl, smiled at her brother.

By the next morning, Caroline was gone. As Geneva had held Simmy when Lightner died, now Simmy held her grieving friend. For Geneva, it was a bittersweet parting. She had, lost her mother without knowing her, and her mother had never fully known her.

—

Geneva waited for Zeph on the porch. Wrapped in a heavy quilt, she pushed and pulled the swing, letting it float in the cold air.

When she saw Zeph coming, she stood up. He stopped in the yard and climbed out of the wagon that had borne Caroline's coffin to the cemetery for burial, a ceremony witnessed only by the three left at Cairnaerie. The wagon was empty except for a shovel and a mattock. He wrapped the reins around a low tree limb before joining Geneva on the porch.

"It's all done," he said.

"Thank you, Zeph." Her gratitude was impossible to fully express. "I sent Simmy on home to rest."

Zeph took Geneva's arm and they walked into the house. An uncommon silence gathered around them like clusters of welcoming children. A peace covered them as if they had finally slipped beyond the grip of time. They were at long last together and unencumbered. Geneva absorbed this breathless, waiting presence. Zeph took her in his arms and with his broad hand held her head against his chest. The sound of his strong heartbeat comforted her in a profound way. The family she had been born into was gone. Except for Grayson, they were all gathered in the small hilltop cemetery, a place of memories. She clung desperately to her belief in eternity, of life everlasting.

"Geneva." Zeph spoke quietly and lifted her face. He looked into her eyes with the tenderness she had always cherished. "I have something I need to give you." He stepped back and took an envelope from his pocket. He paused, the way one pauses before the last leg of a hard journey. "I been keeping this for you. Your daddy—he wanted me to give it to you. The year before he died, he gave it to me. Asked me to keep it till he and your mama were gone." He handed her the envelope.

Immediately, she recognized her father's bold, oversized hand and his personal seal on the back. She ran her fingers over the letters.

"You've kept it all these years?"

"Your daddy was a good man."

Her hands trembled as she broke her father's seal and opened the letter.

My dearest daughter,

I am a man of reflection who finds the law to be a good and suitable guide for one's journey through life. Yet over these past years, I have concluded man's law is frail and inadequate because who we are and everything coursing through our minds and bodies is far stronger than the laws of society will ever be—and far more important and enduring. I have concluded that God's law and love is nearer the perfection we seek.

I will not deny to you that I was shocked and disappointed by your marriage. Perhaps I was wrong, but I could not see past the dilemma your union with Zeph presented. My first reaction was as a man of the civil law. I was bound to societal rules and expectations. It was impossible for me to publicly sanction a marriage so contrary to what was considered proper and acceptable. Yet I struggled with the situation more than I could confess to you or to your mother.

In my heart of hearts, I knew you were right. As a young boy, I was orphaned. My sisters and I lived with my uncle in Baltimore until we became a burden to him. Another family took in my sisters. I never saw them again. I was ten, old enough to make my own way. I wandered Baltimore's streets with nothing more than a hungry belly and a heart full of the greatest sorrow a boy could imagine. Every morning I would rise, hoping for a job or some food. Eventually, though, I despaired. That's when Mr. Ezekial Coker took me in.

He was a Negro man and a widower who worked as the sexton in a Free Methodist Church. Mr. Coker could neither read nor write, but he helped me find a job in a law office sweeping floors. He taught me how to work and encouraged me to learn, and he never asked me to repay him. My single obligation was to offer to others the same kindness he had given to me. This is the reason I could not punish Zeph.

Hayes suggested I allow you and Zeph to live openly, that I by such a pardon might alter the prevailing custom. Your brother made a persuasive argument, which I considered, but in the end all I could think of was the awful ordeal your life would have become because those who break barriers suffer the harshest penalties. Perhaps Hayes could see further into the future than I, or perhaps he had more faith in the changes that will result from Mr. Lincoln's legacy, but I could not permit it. I also did not have the heart to put your mother through what would have been an awful trial for her. I was caught in the cruelest of traps. In my deepest soul, I knew you were right, yet I had to straddle the cruel line society had drawn. I did the best I could.

I feared for Zeph as well, and my arrangement gave him a measure of protection. Lightner and Clarissa were good people. I owed them an obligation to treat their son with kindness and to offer him mercy, something society would never have granted him. Although I knew Zeph to be an upright man, many people are unflinchingly devoted to their own opinions about Negroes and would never have accepted your marriage under any circumstances. Some believe justice is a rope and a tree—and I knew that fate would have been far worse.

And I feared for my granddaughter. For all the respect I have for the law and for the restraints society rightly and wisely casts upon us, I could not prevent my heart from being lost to your Alice Lyford. Yet I could not bring myself to love her openly, having lived for so many years in the bright lights of polite society. I loved your daughter as best I could from afar.

Therefore, it was with as much concern for Alice Lyford's welfare as for yours that I engaged your cousin, Anderson Goodwin, to set up the arrangement. With his help and a solemn oath of secrecy, I devised a plan to protect you and allow you to live your life with your husband and daughter because I came to understood that this was what you wanted above anything else.

As a father, I take seriously God's commandment to care first for my family, as I am commanded to do in 1st Timothy 5:8— "But if any provide not for his own, and especially for those of his own house, he hath denied the faith, and is worse than an infidel."

I have taken care of my house, all of it.

I will ask Zeph to save this letter for you and give it to you when both your mother and I are gone. He is also instructed to notify Anderson's establishment. At my request, he has agreed to continue as your legal counsel and benefactor.

And finally, my Little Bird, I owe you a wedding gift. It is long overdue. Although in life I could not sanction your marriage, I will do so at my death. On the occasion of our own fifty-fifth wedding anniversary, your mother and I agreed on a belated gift. Yes, your mother and I agreed. Time is a wonderful healer, and death and pain change us all, even your mother. Though it was difficult for her, she eventually came to understand the depth of your love for Zeph.

I believe our gift needs no explanation. You will find it at the center of our universe.

All my love,

Daddy

Geneva closed her eyes and repeated her father's words: "At the center of our universe," sweeping through the echoes of her memory, searching to understand. She was a girl again, blooming with youth, sitting with her father in the swing. In the bright shadows of her memory, she saw her young and handsome father holding her small hands and singing...

Little Bird, Little Bird, sing to me.
What is your name, my Little Bird, sing?
Little Bird, Little Bird, sing to me
Is your name blue, my Little Bird sing?

"No, Daddy. No," she said, laughing. "My name is not blue!"

Little Bird, Little Bird, sing to me.
What is your name, my Little Bird, sing?
Little Bird, Little Bird, sing to me
Is your name red, my Little Bird, sing?

"No, silly Daddy, no." She reared back and laughed, and then she grabbed his sleeves, shaking them. "Sing more, Daddy. Sing more."

"I have another idea," he said with a wink. Bertram carried his daughter to the foyer and deposited her on the star. He bowed deeply. "May I have this dance?"

"Yes, Daddy." She curtsied, throwing her skirt out at her sides. Then he swept her up in his arms, and they twirled around the room, her squealing, him waltzing. Around and around, they circled the star.........

Geneva opened her eyes wide and looked at Zeph. "He told me," she said. "The center of our universe. He told me." She dropped to her knees and drew her hand over the floor as if she were feeling for broken glass. "Zeph, give me your penknife." She opened the knife and inserted the blade tip at the edge of the star's center. The piece moved. She looked up at Zeph with fragile eyes. He had known every emotion Geneva had ever had. He had comforted her and rejoiced with her and grieved with her, but he had never seen the look he now saw in her eyes.

She lifted the circle of wood. Underneath was a tiny jeweler's box. With her hands shaking, she opened it. Inside two gold rings glowed, a smaller one nestled inside a larger one. She poured them into her palm and, taking up the larger, once again read the inscription: *To my beloved husband: Bertram, 1843.* Tears streamed down her face.

"I've come home, Zeph. Like the prodigal."

The air was still, and a long winter sun rolled through the open door as they knelt face to face at the center of the star. Never in her life had Geneva known such peace and forgiveness—they washed through her body and soul. It was complete redemption.

Geneva took Zeph's hand. "To my beloved husband, Zeph," she whispered. She slipped the ring on his finger.

Zeph lifted the smaller ring and said, "To my beloved wife, Geneva."

1928

CHAPTER 64

1928

Money & Means

"Dark night. No light," Tobias said to Cletus as they moved through the tangled underbrush. Under a slender curl of moon, the two men stepped cautiously, guided by the gurgle of the nearby creek. "Best kinda night to be runnin' the still."

"You got that right," said Cletus, who followed two paces behind.

The air was cool and moist as the two men threaded their way through the forest. Bugs flew around their warm faces.

"What'd you tell Mr. Proffitt?" Cletus asked.

"I tol' him I was making pickles for my Sunday school class," Tobias snapped. "You're an idiot, Cletus."

"You think he'd squeal on us?"

"Then who's he gonna git his best li-bation from? Mr. Calvin Coolidge? I don't think so. Besides, I always give him an extra quart. Keeps him happy. Keeps him quiet. It's how smart men do business."

"So he won't squeal?" Cletus said.

"Hell. He'd do that, and half the town'd have his hide. You listen to me—I know. It's a delicate balance. You scratch my back and

I scratch yours, and everybody's happy, you see? But it's all gotta be kept secret. Nobody talking."

"If you got you'n itch, jes git yourself a willow branch and stick it down your back. That's what I do. Works right good."

"Cletus, if you were any stupider...." Tobias adjusted his sack and put his hand up to push a small branch away from his face. "Watch yourself now. Ya see, it's all about secrets. Secrets—they's as good as gold. Maybe better."

"I'm good at secrets."

"Well, if you wadn't, I'd a been done with you a long time ago."

Tobias' still was in a hollow northwest of Hyssop, tucked between the north side of Brick Mountain and a sheer rock cliff cutting through the ridge. To reach it, he had to follow the creek up along a piddly waterfall that emptied into the Cleary north of town. It came straight out of the mountains, running clear and clean, the right kind of water for moonshine.

When they got close, they took off their boots, tied the laces together, and slung them around their necks to wade through the water.

"Damn, that's cold," Cletus said as he crossed the stream.

Cletus, his opossum-like face pushed out from his shoulders, carried a sack of cracked corn. Tobias lugged a sack of jars that rattled as he sloshed through the muck. Cletus got there first and dropped his sack on the ground next to a crude shelter—not much more than a lean-to—small saplings lashed together with bailing twine and fashioned into a wobbly three-sided structure. The shelter was a testimony to the secret location they had discovered. Most of their brethren had smaller copper pots and an apparatus they could break down and move at the first stirrings of trouble, but not Tobias. His location on the far side of the creek next to the waterfall was a gem.

Tobias laid his sack down next to Cletus' with a clink. Jars were too hard to come by to break, and he did not want to impose on the good nature of W.D. Proffitt any more than necessary.

"You get the fire going. And stir the mash," he ordered Cletus. "I'll hook it up."

Cletus ladled the mash into the copper pot hanging over the fire. For nearly an hour they worked to resuscitate the machine. Then they lay back, listening to the corn mash bubble and boil, watching the steam rise and anticipating the first drops of liquid gold to run out through the tiny copper pipe—the money piece, old timers called it. Tobias pulled out his newly acquired watch and held it close to his nose.

"What time's it?" Cletus asked him.

"Eleven forty."

"That's a mighty fine looking watch you got there."

"It is right fine, ain't it?" Tobias said. "That Mr. Lassiten was a good customer."

"What'd you get for them gold bobs off his sleeves?"

"Cuff links, Cletus. Twelve dollars. Them things was solid gold. Fourteen karat."

"I b'lieve you could've had the man's back pockets. You went easy on him."

Tobias stretched his legs out and smirked. "Well, you know, I'm pretty fair with my customers. I won fair and square."

"Sure you did, Tobias." They both laughed.

"Ain't my problem he couldn't hold his liquor," Tobias said. "College man like that. Man with that kinda upbringin'—that kinda edgy-cation."

The moon ran into the clouds and disappeared. Only the glow from the fire cut the darkness. Tobias poked at the embers.

"What you gonna do with all that money you been collecting?" Cletus asked.

"Goin' in my nest egg. Every red cent. For my old age."

"You gotta have you a right big egg by this time."

"Well, I tell ya, Cletus. When I get me enough money, I'm gonna re-tire to Hi-wa-ya."

"When's that gonna be?"

"Could be soon."

"How soon?"

"Well, that's gonna depend on my brown sugar daddy."

"Your what?"

Tobias spat into the fire. "Never mind, Cletus. Go get us another jar."

Cletus rolled sideways and grabbed another Mason jar.

"What'd you bring us to eat, Tobias? I'm gettin' right hungry."

"Look over there in that sack. I brought some eggs."

Cletus grabbed the bag and stuck his nose in it. "Pickled? I hate pickled eggs."

"Then go hungry. Hell, Cletus, you're as par-ti-cular as a skinny woman and jes about as useless."

Cletus tossed him the sack of eggs. Tobias shoved two into his mouth and downed them with a swig of his homemade brew. Cletus took another swig and closed his eyes.

The still bubbled along soothingly.

The next morning, Tobias was sitting in a stupor when Zeph came in for his mail. Zeph no longer trusted the postman, but he was dependent on him. He had no choice. Mail had always been Geneva's lifeline, so it was by necessity and sheer will that he kept coming. The threat to Geneva and Joly weighed heavily on him, making it hard to look Tobias in the eye, so he was glad the postman was out of sight behind the partition that separated the tiny lobby from the equally tiny mailroom. They both knew what the other knew; but it was to neither man's advantage to bring it out in the open. Tobias was biding his time—his own destiny within his reach—and Zeph was bargaining for safer days. Zeph and Tobias were, in a sense, racing the same horse.

As he stepped toward the window, Zeph braced himself. "Mornin', Mr. Jebson. I'm here for my mail." He could see the mailbag was half-emptied, and letters and packages were dumped haphazardly on the floor. Zeph heard Tobias grunt and stir. A chair scraped the floor and he appeared at the window looking disheveled.

"Be with you in a minute, Zeph," he said in a hoarse voice. He disappeared again. As Zeph waited, the post office filled with an offensive stench.

"If I caught ya at a bad time, I can come back."

"Naw, jes hol' on a minute, boy."

"Why don't you let me come back later?" Zeph said.

"No, you jes hol' on," Tobias said, irritated.

Zeph heard him leaf through the mail and reappear at the window with a package. The postman, in apparent distress, was the color of creamed lima beans.

"You feelin' bad this morning?"

"Jes a little under the weather. Something I ate," he said, and he handed Zeph a large bundle of mail before disappearing again. It was clear Tobias did not feel much like socializing. Relieved, Zeph slipped out of the post office.

Tobias hobbled back to his chair, his stomach bloated and his head pounding. Fighting nausea, he picked up a familiar brown envelope postmarked Baltimore and smiled menacingly. "You forgot some of your mail, boy." He turned it over in his fingers several times and then tore it open with his teeth. He folded the check and stuffed it in his pocket. "You go tell that Black Beauty of yours—you go tell her Tobias Jebson is a man of means."

CHAPTER 65

1928

Fatherhood & Provision

John stepped into the clearing at Swope Chapel and held back the branch of a sapling for Helen. They had had a pleasant walk—one, no doubt, made countless times by Simmy, Zeph, and Joly. Given the roundabout path they traveled, they now understood why the chapel had provided safe refuge for Zeph's family. Indeed, it was a secret place.

The building itself was poetic—as stately in its humbleness as any great Southern plantation along the James River. What it had housed was great: a family unwelcome in polite society but a family nonetheless.

Helen was instantly drawn to the quaint structure. Or was it that she knew its story? She tried to separate her thoughts from the lives of Geneva and Zeph, but she found it impossible. This cast-off house of God was too symbolic of their long-hidden marriage.

Zeph was sitting in a pool of sunlight that tumbled down through the trees. He had not heard them approaching, so John cleared his throat and crunched leaves underfoot to announce their arrival.

"Why Mr. Klare and Miss Van Soren, I was watching, but you kinda snuck up on me," Zeph said with a rumbling laugh. "Come on over. Take a load off your feet. Did you folks have any trouble finding us?"

"No trouble at all," John said. "Your map was good."

"It's hard telling folks how to git here since I kind of know the way without thinking."

"Thank you for having us," Helen said.

"My pleasure. Joly and me—we don't get too much company out here. We want to see people, we gotta go out and find some. But that's all right—we like it that way. Simmy used to say she was glad she didn't have to go dustin' up for company."

"Miss Geneva told us you made the chapel into a house by yourself," Helen said.

"I guess that's about right. But Simmy—she helped me all along, too. She always had good ideas about where things oughta go. It's made us a right fine home. Geneva used to love coming down here. She hadn't been down for a while, though. We're getting old, I s'pose."

Helen could see the appeal of Zeph Elias. Underneath his gentle manner was strength that needed no proving and a gentle charisma hard not to like. He talked about his family as if they had lived the most ordinary of lives.

"You two come on in here and let me show you around," Zeph said.

The vaulted chapel ceiling was crisscrossed with hand-hewn beams. Whitewashed beadboard walls met wide planks of soft yellow pine, grooved and stained where parishioners had once threaded pews. It was a large room scattered throughout with furniture, finely made and arranged for utility—a table, chairs, and one large sideboard.

Helen noticed the imprint of the women who had lived there: green-checked curtains, a large vase of summer wildflowers dropping petals, a large iron skillet on a shelf, and a maple rolling pin hanging with a breadboard. A simple and efficient kitchen.

"This is where you and Miss Geneva were married?" Helen asked.

"Yessum. Right up here," Zeph said, stepping toward the pulpit, still intact. "I left this preaching spot here with one pew. Seemed a little sacrilegious to do away with it all together. And besides, that way me, Simmy, and Alice Lyford had us a church when we couldn't get into town, 'specially when Alice Lyford was a baby. It's a right good hike to Nicodemus. It was closer when we were living at Cairnaerie—and 'course, it was a whole lot closer than the new church. We'd jes sit here and worship all by ourselves. We'd do a little singing, and then I'd read out of the Bible. It wadn't much, but it made us feel like we were doing right by the Lord." He chuckled. "Simmy would make us get all dressed up, and we'd sit here and have us a big time."

"Did Miss Geneva ever come?" Helen asked.

"She sure did. As Alice Lyford got bigger, she'd come down for days at a stretch."

"No one missed her at Cairnaerie?" John asked.

"No sir. She'd have moved out here for good 'cept we were always afraid somebody'd find us. The Judge, he'd warned me to be careful."

"He knew she was coming out here?" John asked.

"Not at first, I don't believe, but after a while he did. One winter we all got snowed in for going on a month. Snowstorm blew up so fast everybody had to stay put. The whole valley was snowed in. Snowed for three days straight and stayed on the ground till May. It was two weeks before the weather cleared enough for anybody to get out."

"She wasn't missed?"

"No sir. They knew where she was. And we had us a big time—jes like a real family. I reckon 'cause we weren't together all the time, we never did get tired of being cooped up like most folks might."

Helen pointed to a porcelain doll on a chair near the stove. "Alice Lyford's?"

"Yessum. That's Baby Bea. She was Geneva's favorite when she was little. Geneva brought all sorts of toys. Most of 'em are gone now—passed on to other young'uns. But we couldn't part with Baby Bea. Geneva also brought books. She taught Alice Lyford and Joly how to read."

"She must have enjoyed that," Helen said.

"Oh, yes. And those girls took to reading in no time at all, jes like Geneva. She taught 'em like her daddy had taught her."

With understandable pride, Zeph showed off the handcrafted tables and chairs he had made and the cradle where Alice Lyford and Joly had slept—even the root cellar he had dug out by hand. "This was Simmy's idea. The root cellar." He pulled up the heavy planks. Cool, dank air wafted up. "She figured it'd stay cool in the summer under the center of the chapel here—and wouldn't freeze in the winter, so we could keep apples, potatoes, salt pork, and such. Judge Snow would give us a couple of hams every year."

"So the Judge took care of you?" Helen said.

"He sure did. I kept on working for him like I always had."

"Did Geneva know? That her father was helping?" John asked.

"She figured it out after a while, but we didn't talk about it. Not talking made it easier on everybody."

Zeph replaced the heavy planks over the root cellar. "Now come on out here, and lemme show you my cistern."

The cistern had been Zeph's biggest undertaking, he said, dug by hand and plastered over the course of an entire summer season to catch rainfall for his family. He proudly showed them how he had engineered a system of pipes into the kitchen so Simmy could have running water.

"I can get water here at the pump," he said, turning the crank on the cistern and filling the cups inside. Helen and John watched the stream of water spurt, then gush from the cistern into a bucket hung on the spout. "There's a little creek—runs down over there, down across that little rise. But I didn't want Simmy to have to always be hauling water in, so I put in this pipe. Now, y'all come on inside. Joly made us some little honey cakes."

Zeph stood in the clearing until Helen and John disappeared along the narrow path back through the woods. All afternoon, concern for Joly had weighed on his mind, whispering worrisome prophecies that he could not shake. He looked up into the canopy of trees. "Should have told her sooner," he said to his leafy audience. "Shouldn't have waited this long." Zeph knew he and Geneva could survive whatever trampling the truth might deliver, but Joly was young. She had her whole life ahead of her. He could not let her get hurt.

As he strolled back into the chapel that had housed such happiness, he hoped he could protect Joly until after the wedding—until he and Geneva could tell her the truth. He hoped he had done enough.

CHAPTER 66

1928

Plans & Disruptions

Tobias tugged on the chain and a single naked bulb danced on the end of a wire. It cast a garish light over the mercantile's stockroom. Cluttered shelves and boxes and crates stacked everywhere were filled with apples, canned goods, Christmas balls, seed packets, and bundles of small confederate flags, the kind the local UDC put out on Veterans' graves every April. Cured hams hung in cloth sacks from the low beams and made the room smell smoky. Standing in collectives in each corner, hoes, pitchforks, shovels, and other implements waited for another spring planting to begin. Multitudes, varieties, assortments—every conceivable kind of tool or household item—were stacked and piled in the crowded stockroom.

"Look over on the left, toward the middle shelf," Tobias heard W.D. Proffitt holler from the front of the store.

"I'm a lookin'," Tobias yelled back over his shoulder. He squinted in the bald light. In the afternoon heat, the windowless stockroom was oven-like. He mopped his face with a dirty handkerchief and stepped toward the left wall, scanning the shelves. Cans of salmon, jars of hair tonics, cartons of cigarettes, and shoeboxes—plus boxes of mouse traps, work gloves, and matches—filled the shelves. He grabbed a dusty shelf to steady himself and stepped across two large boxes marked "fragile." Dust stirred along a row of cans. He sneezed, and then he saw what he was looking for.

"You find it yet?" Mr. Proffitt shouted. "You been in there a long time, Jebson."

"Yeah. I got it."

He pulled down a canvas duffel bag from the shelf and brushed it off. Dust and mouse droppings rained down on the oiled floor.

"This the biggest one ya got, W.D.?" he yelled out to Mr. Proffitt.

"That's all I got."

"It'll do."

———

Tobias was waiting for Cletus. He was sitting on his cot, dressed in his aviator jacket, dusty brown pants, and a faded pork pie hat squashed on his head. The duffel bag, stuffed with all his belongings, bulged beside him.

"You going somewheres?" said Cletus when he arrived with an emptied mailbag.

"You might say that."

"You coming back?"

Tobias sniffed.

"You ain't. Is ya?" Cletus sounded genuinely disappointed. "Where you goin' to?"

"You ask too many questions, Cletus."

"Well, who's gonna run the post office then?"

"Hell if I know. It ain't my concern no more."

"Maybe I will. I'd make a right good postman."

"You ain't smart enough."

"Sure I am. Them folks in Blast Holler thinks I'm right good."

"Suit yourself."

Cletus tossed his mailbag on the floor and pulled a chair out from the wall. He straddled it backwards, draping his arms over the back and crossing his forearms.

"I brung you something," Cletus said. He pulled a dead toad out of his pocket and tossed it at Tobias.

"What'n the hell's that?" he said.

"It's a flat toad. Found it in the street. Musta got run over. It'll bring you luck."

"Luck? I don't need luck. I got smarts." He tapped the side of his head and tossed the toad back. "*You* need luck. Keep your damn frog."

"It's a toad."

"Well, I don't want it."

Cletus looked sad. "You really leavin'?"

"I am. Gettin' outta this two-bit town."

"And you won't say where to?"

"Nope."

"Then what'd you want me for?" Cletus said, half indignant and half disappointed.

Tobias smirked. His frustrations with his sidekick aside, he understood that Cletus depended on him—actually liked him—and besides, Cletus was handy to have around. "You wanna go?" Tobias said.

"You mean go off with you?"

"Yeah. I told ya. I'm fixing to re-tire. To Hi-wa-ya."

"Tobias, I cain't go off to Hi-wa-ya. It's too far. I cain't swim, and besides, I ain't got money like you."

"I'll take ya anyway if you wanna go."

Tobias watched Cletus pick through the words and then break into a grin that split his pointed face.

"You joshing me?"

"Nope."

"You'd take me?"

"Yep."

"And I don't gotta pay?"

"Nope. Jes work fer me."

Cletus slapped his thighs. "I b'lieve I feel like celebrating."

"I thought you might."

Tobias tossed his hat on the cot and opened the dry sink while Cletus threw the latch on the door. Tobias pulled out two shot glasses and handed one to Cletus.

"I propose a toast to my good friend, Tobias Jebson," Cletus said.

"Why thank ya. And I b'lieve I'll toast my brown sugar daddy."

———

A ragged American flag—Moss McKinney's flag—whipped atop the rusty flagpole as a crowd gathered outside the post office. The front door was standing wide open, and four shiny black sedans lined the road. Whispers buzzed through the crowd. From the back of the building came a ruckus that sounded like a cockfight.

Tobias, tied to a chair, flailed and cursed as a cadre of dark-suited men tore through the contents of his room. Into cardboard boxes went his shot glasses and his supply of Mason jars and corn bags. The table was shoved aside, the rug thrown off, and the floorboards, upended, stood perpendicular. One skinny man lay on his stomach, his head and shoulders hanging into the hole. He passed jars full of the clear, potent liquid to another man kneeling beside him. Each wore a black fedora straight on his head, except for the man on the floor; his hat had been tossed on the edge of Tobias' rumpled cot.

"Looks like sloe gin to me," one man said.

"No. White lightning," said another. "It's got to be."

"Well, I don't know how'n the hell it got there," Tobias said. "I been set up, gentlemen. You can bet your granny's panties on that. Somebody's set me up!"

The men ignored him.

When the prostrate man stood up, his suit was covered with lint, grass, crumbs, and assorted dirt, some more odiferous than others. He brushed himself off and ordered the other men to take the boxes to the cars. They filed out, each carrying a clanking collection of contraband. The last two men untied Tobias, grabbed him under each arm, and led him out, leaving the door gaping.

The crowd was silent as they passed. Even Buster watched without barking. Ignoring his predicament, Tobias smiled at his customers, giving them little winks and strutting as if valets instead of revenuers were escorting him. W.D. Proffitt, his face burning, swallowed hard and averted his eyes. He, like half the men in the crowd, worried Tobias might not be above bargaining his way out of a jail cell with their decent lives as collateral.

After Tobias and his escorts rumbled away in the black motorcade, the crowd dispersed quietly in a mixed state of shock and fear. A few women wagged their fingers, and many of the men turned away troubled. Each one in the crowd had the same thought: Who had turned on Tobias Jebson?

———

It took a guarantee of substantial libation and several days for Jacob Lassiten to post bail for Tobias—but not before Lassiten extracted from him the promise of a favor.

"You have my word, Mister," Tobias told him on the steps of the regional jail. "I can do that right di-rectly. Soon as I get my own affairs back in order."

"You do remember the names?" Lassiten said.

"I most certainly do."

———

Tobias opened the door of the post office where, in his absence, Cletus had helped himself to his friend's accommodations. Buster was inside the post office, too, laid out on the floor like he owned it, and likewise, Cletus was stretched out on the cot. When Tobias came through the door, Cletus sat up and made silly excuses.

"I thought you'd be away longer," he said. "I was jes keeping your place up for you—knew you wouldn't want jes anybody coming along and moving in."

"Sure, Cletus. I bet you did," he said, ignoring him as he rummaged through a drawer.

"You're my friend, Tobias. You don't think I was moving in on you, do you?"

"Forget it, Cletus. Don't matter. I'm not staying."

"What do you mean you're not staying?"

Tobias jerked out the drawer. "You think I'm gonna let them come take me a second time? Hell no. Get up." He shoved Cletus off the cot and dumped out the drawer.

"Cletus, you seen a claw hammer around here?"

"Whatcha need a hammer for?"

"You seen it?"

"No."

"Ha," Tobias said as he spotted the hammer sticking out from behind the wood box. He grabbed it. "Come over here, Cletus." He motioned toward the pot-bellied stove in the center of the room. "When I say, you pull that back—and hold the stove pipe, so it don't come loose and crack me in the head."

Cletus gripped the edge of the cold stove. Tobias took the claw end of the hammer and slid it under the bottom. He levered it up several inches.

"Okay, Cletus," he said, straining. "Now pull."

With the stove tipped up and ashes spilling out onto the floor, Tobias reached underneath and pulled out a small strong box. It was covered with soot, which he blew off. He sneezed, rousting Buster. "Shut up, dog," he said, wiping grit off his face.

"What's that?" Cletus asked, eyeing the box.

"My nest egg."

"Well, I'll be damned. You outsmarted 'em, didn't you, Tobias?" Cletus was proud of his friend. He hovered while Tobias opened the box. "How much money you got in there?"

"Enough."

"How much?"

"I got me more'n three hundred dollars. I'm going to Hi-wa-ya." Tobias did a little dance.

"Who-wee," said Cletus. "Hey, I thought you said you'd take me."

"Cain't now." He pocketed his money and tossed the empty box onto the cot. "Lost too much merchandise. Them bastards. But you can keep the still. You jes keep it going—keep it producing—and you'll be joining me soon."

"When are you leaving?" Cletus said.

"Soon as I finish my business."

"You going to the still tonight?"

"Not tonight. I gotta tie up some loose ends," Tobias said. "Can't leave town without meeting my obligations to my customers. You know I always take good care of my customers. Pays off, Cletus. I'm a living example. How you think I got out of the pokey?"

—

While Tobias hung around most of the week keeping a low profile, he helped Cletus get the still running again. It was the least he could do.

"You make sure you don't go telling nobody I came back," he said to Cletus one night while the mash bubbled.

"I won't. I tol' you I wouldn't."

"Well, you make damn well sure."

"Your secret's good with me. You kin trust me, Tobias. I kept this still quiet, didn't I?"

Tobias grunted and threw back a drink. Payback was running through his veins. Revenge was not ordinarily a motivation for him. Money had always been enough, but his stint in the jailhouse had soured him. "I had me a good thriving business going here, and somebody snitched on me."

"You know who?"

"I got my suspicions."

"Well, who? You don't think it was me, do you?"

"Hell no, Cletus. You ain't smart enough."

"So who you think it was?"

"None of your business, Cletus. An eye for an eye, I say."

"What's that mean?"

"You ask too many damn questions, Cletus."

CHAPTER 67

1928

Bitterness & Endings

Midnight. The clock tower in the university's chapel struck. Cold fog swarmed and muted the sound as Jacob Lassiten stumbled onto a footbridge at the north end of the campus. The air, moving in a slow and ponderous animation, caught the light of the crescent moon's penumbra. Lassiten was disheveled. His coat hung crooked off his shoulders as if he had managed to put it on without using his hands. His collar, usually so neat and stiff, flapped at his neck. With one stay missing altogether, he had a mildly comical look. But there was no comedy on his face—no expression at all. No sadness, no joy—a body absent a soul. At the apex of the bridge, he stopped and dropped a bag, which landed with a clunk.

In the distance, the fog flowed in and around rows of columned brick buildings. At their center, barely visible from the bridge, rose the outline of a large and lighted hall where Lassiten's classmates had gathered to celebrate.

"Damn them all," he spoke to the night, his solitary companion. He imagined their boisterous conversations. Certainly, they were discussing him. The thought left a bitter, metallic taste in his mouth. He spat over the rail.

A featherlike wind stirred the maudlin gloom. Nearby, a street lamp glowed. The lamplight shimmered across the water, which appeared still, but against the quiet of the night, it gurgled peacefully. Somewhere, a dog was barking.

Lassiten opened his coat and unfolded the letter. As he did so, an empty flask fell from his pocket and clattered across the wooden bridge. With an angry kick, he knocked it off into the water where it splashed and bobbed and then floated away. Impassive, he watched it disappear beneath the bridge. Turning in the direction of the street lamp, he read the letter again, and then he tore it into tiny pieces and sprinkled them into the water.

"Damn them all," he said again.

Lassiten picked up his bag and got to work.

CHAPTER 68

1928

────────◆────────

Accusations & Complications

John tried to finish grading, but his mind kept wandering to the wedding and the plan for Miss Geneva. He had worked out the details, but Helen had insisted that he drive all the way to the house, and he wondered how the undercarriage of his Ajax would fare along the rough path. Nonetheless, that was the plan, and he had to admit that having Miss Geneva walk out to the road wasn't feasible. Fortunately, a dry month made him hopeful the swale would be passable. He jotted a note, "check spare," and stabbed it on his inkwell.

He had almost finished the last paper when the department secretary came to his door.

"The dean asked me to give this to you," she said.

"Thank you." He took the note, and though it was clear the secretary was lingering, it was also clear John was busy. "Thank you," he repeated.

When she left, he opened the letter casually, expecting a routine memorandum.

Mr. Klare,
   Please be in my office at three o'clock this afternoon.
Dean Albert Rollins

A vague concern washed over John, a sensation he had felt before. He shook it off. He had intentionally toed the line at Haverston College. Of that, he was certain.

At 3:00, the dean's secretary ushered him into Rollins' office to wait—a familiar tactic. John and his colleagues had decided the dean was an actor at heart who staged his meetings for maximum intimidation.

"Sit, Mr. Klare," Rollins said, striding into the room and closing the door.

His voice could unravel a rope, John thought.

Rollins settled behind his desk as John took a seat.

"I'll get right to the point, Mr. Klare. It has been brought to my attention that you and...." He adjusted his glasses and consulted a smudgy note written in grease pencil. "...And a Miss Van Soren, one of our librarians, have been spending a great deal of time together. Is this true?"

"Yes," John said guardedly. "At times. Yes. We have met." He quickly assessed his meetings with Helen—nothing but talk about Miss Snow. With a sinking feeling, though, he realized a casual observer might have thought otherwise.

"Privately?"

John's insides churned. *What is he talking about?* he thought. Wary, he made no immediate reply—even though hesitation might convey complicity.

"Privately?" the dean repeated. "Without a chaperone?"

"Yes," John said honestly but added "professionally." His mood plummeting, he wondered if someone had seen him at Helen's apartment.

Rollins drummed a pencil on his desk and fixated on a point in the room behind John.

"I see," the dean said. The room became uncomfortably quiet—except for the pencil taps. Casual voices drifted in from the hall. To John, a courtroom came to mind.

Rollins stopped tapping and set his jaw before saying: "Then I must ask you for your resignation."

Blindsided, John was suddenly back in Indiana. Back at St. Ballard. His sense of justice rose and indignation took over.

"Resignation! Without even asking for an explanation?"

Taken aback by John's boldness, Rollins looked up. He put down the pencil.

"Yes, Miss Van Soren and I have met together—that's true." John's voice was forceful, but he spoke carefully, trying not to sound defensive—or guilty. "We have a professional relationship. May I ask what prompted this?"

When Rollins made no response, John scrambled.

"We have been doing research. And I believe it could bring great notoriety to this college." It was the best he could think of quickly—and it was also a truth he was only just beginning to comprehend.

This piqued Rollins' interest, but he was still dismissive.

"Research? Everything at this college comes through me, and I am not aware of any such research—other than what you did with Smalley's student."

This gave John pause. The truth had betrayed him in Indiana, so he sidestepped. He summoned a voice he imagined Shackleton might have used with doubters.

"It's exploratory research. And I am not at liberty to discuss it yet. I promised my source secrecy."

Rollins looked dubious.

"And I intend to keep my word," John said, adding one salvo.

"I see."

"I can assure you, Dr. Rollins, that nothing I have done or Miss Van Soren has done is inappropriate—not in the least." *That,* John thought, *is the truth.* He looked defiantly into Rollins' shadowed face, knowing he had mounted his best defense, and now he was angry. *Let the chips fall.* But with frightening certainty, he also knew chips sometimes fell awry.

Rollins set his elbows on his desk and clasped his hands together. "Let me get this straight. You deny any inappropriate activity, but refuse to tell me what you were doing and expect me to believe you?"

"Yes," said John, sounding more belligerent than he had intended.

"You put me in a difficult position, Mr. Klare." The dean picked up the pencil and began to tap again.

"If you wish," John said, looking for compromise and knowing how academics reasoned. "I will talk to my source. If that individual will permit me, then will I explain more—but only with permission."

The dean was silent. All John could hope was that he had created enough question in the man's mind to get a reprieve.

"You have one week." Rollins put down the pencil, lowered his head, and began to work. "Good day, Mr. Klare."

John exited shaken—but with his sense of justice fully inflamed. He knew without a sliver of doubt that he had done nothing wrong. If anything, this new wrinkle affirmed his decision to help Miss Geneva. Injustices—like those suffered by Benny and his friends at St. Ballard—deserved an advocate. In an instant, the Elias story took on a broader and nobler theme. *If I have to repeat St. Ballard, so be it,* he thought firmly. *This is right.*

The timing, however, was anything but right. Joly's wedding was days away. He would have to tell Helen, but not yet. He had to put it out of his mind until after the wedding.

CHAPTER 69

1928

Waking & Wonderment

Geneva stood on the front porch in the darkness. She exhaled into the quiet night—quieter than she had ever remembered a night to be. Through the naked forest, through the crowds of bare-limbed oaks and maples, she watched the harvest moon glide weightlessly into the black October sky. It dwarfed the landscape, dwarfed Cairnaerie, and made her feel strangely sad, realizing this would be her last cloistered night. It was comforting to feel the moon creep alongside her on the darkened porch—a familiar presence she needed tonight. Tomorrow was Joly's wedding day.

Geneva awoke with nervous anticipation. All the fear, the regrets, the mistakes, the intervening years telescoped into one exquisite sunrise. She pulled back the curtains in her bedroom and lifted the window. She had made the decision to leave, and now she looked toward the wedding with more of a sense of purpose than fear. And as she had done on ten thousand other mornings, she opened her journal.

It is dawn, and I am wakeful—my spirit as restless as if I were a child again, waiting for the Christmas aurora. The air in my bedroom is moist and heavy, wrapping me like so many other autumns, so many Octobers. A thick fog hangs over the landscape, holding back the sun's full light like a bride's veil. I wonder if Joly is yet awake, sitting beside her window, waiting as I do for the light to rise like a celebratory banner above the mountains. She is not able to see the mountains—not yet, but she will soon.

The day of promise is here at last—the day she weds and the day I leave Cairnaerie. I wonder how an ordinary man would feel on the morning he was to walk free from a cell. I wonder about the soldiers freed from prison camps. How had they felt on their morning of impending freedom? It could not have been any less glorious, any less captivating—or any less intimidating. But months or even numbered years could never compare to my lifetime of seclusion. Soldiers would have walked out gladly into the familiar, into a world that would have welcomed them, into a world expecting them—even hoping for them. But the threshold I cross today is so different, my hermitage so long. I leave a life lived without ordinary expectations, without ordinary events—without anything ordinary.

I do not know whether I should think of this day as an end or a beginning. Is this the start of a new life of freedom or merely the concluding chapter of my confined life—or will it be a glimpse into a future that will escape me altogether?

This morning, as the mountains emerge from the fog, I will emerge from my hiding place. Part of me worries, but I am comforted by the sounds of the morning, echoing through my farm, my home. I wonder if I will still hear them against the bustle of a town, against the busyness of life, against the excitement of leaving—against the celebration of a wedding.

Today should be a wonderful day. This October has come gently, like a lazy, gliding blackbird. The air is mixed with currents of cold and hot air, the pine-scented, fall-scented air, swollen with the sensuous smells of the harvest, the fading honeysuckle, the goldenrod, the wind-brushed hay, and the flags of temperature foreshadowing another winter.

Cairnaerie is light and airy this morning. A breeze, ever so slight, slips in from the west. It is a crystal morning, a sharp, crisp, transparent morning—the perfect kind for Joly and Thatcher to begin their life together. And I will be there.

Geneva buttoned her dress and pulled on white gloves. For weeks, her outfit had been a significant topic of discussion. Helen had carried several dresses on approval from a local shop, telling the salesgirl they were for her Aunt Neva Hampton, who was not up to the task of shopping herself. Helen had worked hard finding something to match the hat Joly had given Geneva. She also had kindly—and tactfully—persuaded her that the peacock feather might draw too much attention.

Geneva had not been quite this dressed up since Easter Sunday decades ago and certainly not in fashions so modern, but it was important she blend in. She adjusted her skirt. Her hands ached, but that mattered little this morning.

She was ready more than an hour before they were to arrive, so she waited on the porch, rising periodically to check the time on her father's clock. Shortly before ten, she heard John's automobile making slow but determined progress over the rough fields and wholly inadequate pathway. The automobile looked exactly as it had in magazines—but the sound was unexpected. It made a riotous noise and smoked so that at first she thought it was on fire. Every bird perched peacefully took to the sky when the noisy contraption rolled into the yard. She was anxious about riding in it, and for a moment, wished she could join the birds, escaping to the sky.

Deliberately, though, she trained her eyes not on the rumbling car or the fleeing birds, but instead she focused on John and Helen's smiling faces as the Ajax stopped in front of two towering oaks and they stepped out. On their borrowed trust, she would marshal the courage to ride in into this mechanized carriage.

"Good morning," Helen said, her voice so full of comfort that Geneva knew she understood her apprehensions. "What a glorious day."

Geneva gathered her bag and stepped off the porch.

"You'll have the best view here," John said as he helped her into the front seat of his waiting car.

Geneva's stomach was curled up like a pig's tail. The automobile lurched forward and began to move, juddering so much she was sure her teeth would shake free of her head.

John drove away from Cairnaerie carefully. Even so, every hole, mound, and bump along the fields jostled the Ajax and its occupants until they reached the newer macadamized road. Then the ride became smoother. Before she knew it, Geneva was enthralled with landscapes she had not laid eyes on in decades.

Ned Turpin's barn was gone. She could see few signs of his farm except for the burned-out shell of the house where Ned and Addie had raised eleven children. *What happened to them all?* she wondered, remembering the brood of towheads. Passing the edge of Skunktown, she caught a glimpse of the house where Vivvy's people had lived. Chickens and geese overran the side yard, and rusted machine parts were scattered up and down the creek bed that ran beside it. She saw a new porch built on the side of the house, and next to it was a vehicle parked where she remembered Briscoe's horse and wagon sitting.

As they approached Hyssop, they passed enormous buildings. One, a brick structure along the river, was a new silk factory, John explained. They passed a school—a large two-story brick building. Nearly sixty children attended, Helen said. Geneva could not imagine seeing so many children all in one place. They passed Pascal's orchard where Zeph, Simmy, and Geneva had picked ripe cherries, pears and apples as children.

"Mr. Klare," she said, shouting over the noisy engine. "Could you stop here for a moment?"

John pulled the car to the side of the road and helped her step out of the car. Geneva walked a few feet into the orchard to pull off several apples hanging within easy reach. "These were the best in the valley," she told them, handing apples to her friends. "The Pascals used to have a little fruit stand somewhere along here. My daddy loved their apples."

Before going to the church, John drove through town, passing rows of stores and businesses where Geneva had remembered open fields. She saw crowds of people, long tree-lined streets, and new buildings—a town so different from the one she had known. She had never seen so many people—or the world moving so fast.

The college—once a triumvirate of small clapboard structures—now stretched all the way down Fisher Street in a line of perfectly symmetrical Georgian-style brick buildings. John drove her by W.D. Proffitt's Mercantile—the most modern of stores, selling everything from farming tools to ready-made clothing, and items shipped from as far away as Japan.

The town's gaslights were gone, replaced with electric light poles, strung together like high fences running up and down every street. John explained that at night the town was nearly as bright as midday, a concept Geneva could not fathom. The handful of buildings she might have remembered—the livery, her father's law office, the Baptist church—were either gone entirely or so altered she did not recognize them. Fires, floods, storms—but most of all progress—had made the town unrecognizable. Geneva was thankful for the regular delivery of magazines that had prepared her—at least in part—for such changes.

She put her hand to her thumping heart, wondering if she would survive the day's excitement.

CHAPTER 70

1928

Joy & Union

A crowd was already gathering at Nicodemus Baptist Church as John and company arrived. His Ajax had struggled a little coming up the incline at the top of the hill, but he was determined to take Miss Geneva as close as possible. He was equally determined not to let his own worry over the Rollins problem mar this happy day. He would deal with it later.

They made quite a spectacle arriving and drew a crowd when John parked and helped the women out of his car. Many congregants who had met John while he was assisting Lassiten greeted them warmly. This part of John's plan had been perfect. Any questions their presence sparked, John and Helen answered masterfully with their contrived story about Helen's aunt, Neva Hampton. Geneva, nervous and understandably reluctant to engage in conversation, smiled politely.

The church with its green windows, clean and sparkling, glowed in the freshly-cut yard, which was filled with people and horses and children all milling around. So many dark and lovely children brought to Geneva's mind her beautiful Alice Lyford, and she imagined her running with the other children—a sight she had never seen with her own eyes. She took a deep breath to maintain her composure. She had missed so much. But Geneva would not dwell on it. Today she would fulfill her granddaughter's wish—and soon she would tell her the truth. For perhaps the first time, she looked forward to this conversation.

Once they were seated in the church and Geneva had a moment to look around, she was especially glad for Helen's help. She had outfitted her suitably, which boosted her confidence. Helen, herself, looked lovely in a pale purple dress with a long, dropped waist, a cream-colored collar, and a low-slung belt. Two strands of matching beads and a stylish cloche hat completed her outfit. John seemed to take notice.

The church was crowded and the air close as the midday sun straddled the steeple. Fans of all shapes and inventions waved like butterfly wings while the men steeped in their Sunday coats. Just before the ceremony began, the deacons pulled up the windows on both sides of the sanctuary. Fresh air rolled in.

A great fog of joy filled the church. At the front of the sanctuary, the Galilee Songmen, their voices full and robust, swayed to the rhythms of a gospel song. It had been so long since Geneva had heard music, she thought surely the windows of heaven had opened. The sound, the music, the voices flooded her ears and washed away all her fears. It seemed fitting that Joly's wedding would begin with this lusty, heartfelt rhythm of the Gospel in song.

Thatcher, as handsome as Joly had claimed, walked in and stood with the Reverend. And then like a flock of birds, the congregation rose to see Joly, on Zeph's arm, enter wearing Caroline Snow's wedding dress and veil.

Geneva dared not look in Zeph's eyes. To be so close, so intimate—to be a part of their public lives for the first time—overwhelmed her. She had come full circle. Her mind overlaid one hidden ceremony on this newer, public one. She was floating, flying—one moment in Nicodemus and the next at the Swope Chapel—one moment with her young, handsome husband, one moment with her dear, faithful husband. When Joly passed by and saw Geneva, tears welled up in both their eyes.

"We are gathered here in the sight of Almighty God..." Geneva heard a mixture of voices, two men of the cloth half a century apart, intoning the same words. It was as if the voice of Reverend Hawkins had drifted across time. "...to join in holy matrimony, Miss Joly Jennings and Mr. Thatcher Oden. Who gives this woman to be married to this man?"

Zeph cleared his throat, and with a strong, clear voice answered, "I do."

Through tears, Geneva saw eddies of colored light.

The mood in the churchyard was festive after the ceremony. Geneva began to relax. John's plan had worked flawlessly. The trio moved easily through the crowd; Professor John Klare, Librarian Miss Helen Van Soren and Miss Van Soren's aunt from North Carolina, Miss Neva Hampton—an appellation conceding to honesty.

Zeph was relieved. The wedding had come off without a hitch. He was especially glad trouble was locked up in the regional jail— or so he believed. Soon, he thought with a considerable sense of relief, he and Geneva would sit down with Joly and Thatcher and tell them the truth. As happy as Joly looked today, he believed she would understand.

Rows of tables covered with sun-bleached cloths overflowed with celebration food—peach cobblers, sweet tea, rhubarb pies, succotash, and pan after pan of pork barbecue and ham biscuits— all so reminiscent of the church picnics of Geneva's childhood. Directing the event was a large, officious woman, attended by a small, crooked man with an endless smile. He took dishes from the nattily-dressed guests and placed them exactly where instructed. Geneva recognized him—it was Briscoe Robinson—and she could hardly believe her eyes. He had aged so, but he still had the same twinkle in his eye. Briscoe had never been handsome, and after all these years—even shriveled from age—he still looked like a little brown owl. But his voice had hardly changed—the same twitter she remembered teasing Vivvy.

Briscoe's laugh bounced above the crowd. Geneva smiled—until a sudden realization doused it: *What if he recognizes me?*

Geneva blanched and took a step back.

"Are you all right?" asked Helen, seeing her falter.

"Briscoe," she said faintly.

"Pardon?"

"Briscoe Robinson."

Hearing alarm in Geneva's voice, Helen took her arm and led her to the edge of the yard. They huddled beneath a chestnut tree. "Now, what did you say?"

Geneva could hardly speak. "Briscoe Robinson. He might know me."

Helen motioned for John. "There's someone here who might recognize her."

John, comfortable in the success of his plan, was reassuring. "It will be fine," he said. "Just remember that you're Helen's aunt."

"You're right, John," Geneva said half-heartedly, and she repeated several times, "Neva Hampton. Neva Hampton."

"I'll stay right with you," Helen said. "Don't worry."

Just then a timely diversion approached—a tiny woman wearing the brightest yellow dress any of the three had ever seen and a matching, crown-shaped hat, covered haphazardly with duck down.

"Why, Miss Gladiolus," John said. "How are you?"

Geneva, amused by the apparel, smiled in spite of her unease.

"I'm quite fine, Mr. Klare," said Miss Gladiolus, thumping her chest. "Fit as a fiddle. You've brought us some guests, I see. I thought I'd know everybody here, but I guess I was wrong. I don't believe I've met you two." She grinned at Geneva and Helen.

"Then let me introduce you," said John. "This is Helen Van Soren and Miss Neva Hampton, Helen's aunt. Ladies, I'd like you to meet Miss Gladiolus Tinker. She knows everything you'd ever want to know about Nicodemus."

"Oh, you hush." Miss Gladiolus playfully slapped John's arm. "It's a pleasure to meet you fine ladies. We're right glad to have you here. Idn't this a glorious day for a weddin'? Jes glorious. I don't think I ever seen a prettier day for a weddin'—and I seen a lot of 'em here. I'm sure it's a good omen for the bride and groom."

John stepped in, deftly took Miss Gladiolus' arm, and escorted her away. "Do you think anyone has brought deviled eggs today?" he asked her, heading toward the food.

Geneva gathered her composure.

"Thank you, Helen. I'm all right now," she said.

"Are you sure?"

"I'm sure." She patted Helen's arm. "We're missing the excitement."

Geneva could avoid Briscoe, but it almost seemed unnecessary. The ceremony was over—and if confronted, they could fly away at a moment's notice and disappear in a cloud of dust.

Helen and Geneva rejoined John, who was surrounded by a crowd of short ladies wearing colorful hats.

"Why Miss Delphenia," John said, addressing another member he had met during visits with Lassiten.

"How are you, Mr. Klare," she said, flattered to be recognized. "This is my great niece, Esther."

"It's a pleasure to meet you," John said. "And I'd like you to meet my friends, Miss Helen Van Soren and Miss Neva Hampton."

The scene was repeated over and over, John introducing the women and shaking hands. Helen noticed how much people liked John Klare.

"You got to try these." Miss Gladiolus was back again, this time with a plate of eggs. "These is Aggie Spurlock's deviled eggs. Well, her recipe at least. Best deviled eggs in the whole world. She gib me the recipe jes 'fore she died a dozen years ago, and I been makin' 'em ever since."

Helen and Geneva stood by watching as John ate one egg after another and listened with the patience of Job to Miss Gladiolus.

"You know, that woman never would tell nobody what her secret ingredient was. She was kinda stingy that way—when it come to sharing recipes—but she wadn't stingy about making 'em. I don't have near the energy that woman had—when she was in her prime—kinda dried up near the end, though. I'll bet she made a million of them eggs during her lifetime. Or maybe two million. It's all she ever brought, except for her ham biscuits. She'd make those out of her good country ham and beaten biscuits. They was a little dry, but right good. But not nearly as good as these eggs. I used to rave about 'em. I jes love 'em. And I'd tell her so, every time I seen her. I even seen the Holy Ghost one time after eatin' some. I ever tell you that story?"

John acknowledged her question with a wave of his hand because his mouth was full of the famous delectable.

"Oh, yes, I remember. I did tell you about that. Well, when Aggie took sick, she called for me to come over. By that time, she wadn't much more than a skeleton with a little skin stretched over her— had some kinda wastin' disease. Don't recall what they called it. Anyway, she called for me, and I come over and sat with her. It took her a long time to come right out and tell me, but finally she did. She told me what her secret ingredient was and made me promise—made me swear on the Bible—I'd never tell nobody. And she made me promise I'd jes keep on making and taking them to folks, like she done. Look over there. I still put her name right there next to the eggs. Aggie Spurlock's famous deviled eggs. I don't even put my name on 'em. 'Course everybody knows I make 'em now..."

John, Helen, and Geneva were so engrossed in listening to Miss Gladiolus they did not notice Briscoe leave his food duties and, with a plate in hand, drift toward them. He stood off to the side and listened, looking intently at Geneva. He seemed to recognize something about her. Finally, his curiosity got the best of him, and he sauntered over.

"Well, hello there, Briscoe," Miss Gladiolus said.

Geneva stiffened. Helen took her arm.

"How you doin', Miss Gladiolus?" Briscoe said in his high-pitched voice.

"Right fine. I been running my mouth like I always do." She chuckled. "You know these folks here? Let me introduce you to all my friends. This is Mr. John Klare. He's a professor at the college. He's the one writing down all the history for us. And this is Miss Helen Van Soren and Miss Neva Hampton."

"Pleased to meet you lovely ladies, and Mr. Klare," he said, and he tipped his hat. Then he addressed Geneva. "You live around here?"

Geneva's heart skipped. She opened her mouth to speak, but her alias flew out of her brain, and she stood without words, exposed. Just then, Zeph walked up behind Briscoe and collared him in a bear hug.

"How're you this fine afternoon, Briscoe?" Zeph said. Over Briscoe's shoulder, he winked at Geneva.

"Well, if it ain't my old friend, Zeph," he said, patting his captor's arms and grinning. "Your little girl's all growed up, and she's a beauty."

Deftly, Zeph turned Briscoe away from Geneva.

"I think I'm going to have to agree with you, Briscoe. And now, we need you around back of the church. Mrs. St. Clair's looking for you. Says she needs you to help her."

Briscoe looked deflated. "Oh law—that woman's a slave driver. Thought I'd slipped her. Well. Nice meeting you folks." And he walked away, his owlish face hanging.

After Zeph whisked Briscoe away, Geneva finally pried words from her throat. "I think we should be going now."

But it was too late.

CHAPTER 71

1928

Cruelty & Chasms

The first sound was a bottle crashing through a window of the church. Jagged shards of green glass rained down on the grass. The crowd hushed as a drunken Tobias Jebson stumbled across the churchyard. The festive mood vanished.

"Ladies and gen'lemen," he said. He was hardly able to stand, and his words were slurred as he wobbled through the crowd waving a fistful of papers. "I got me some information you people oughta know before you go on celebratin' this here union. It's unholy—unholy union."

The crowd stood in stunned silence. No one moved.

"You people thought you was rid of me. But I got friends. Important friends." Tobias Jebson was as drunk as he had ever been and as mean as he had always been. With every cruel word he spoke, the bitterness of his arrest intensified. "You people is fools. Fools! You better listen to me good."

From opposite sides of the churchyard, Zeph and John exchanged glances and moved toward Tobias, leaving Helen with Geneva.

"I got it right here in my possession. In-for-ma-tion y'all be right interested in," Tobias said as he lumbered toward the bride and groom.

Thatcher moved in front of Joly.

"You oughta know who you's marrying, boy. You know? Do you? You like little white girls?" he said to Thatcher. "How 'bout mixed breeds. You like them? Mongrels?"

"Stop. Get outa here," Thatcher said, and he stepped toward Tobias, his fist raised.

"Now you wouldn't hit me, boy? You better not. I got infor-mation for you. I'm your messenger—and I got the law on my side this time." Tobias snorted. "Yep, this time, by God, the law's on my side."

"Leave," said Thatcher, close to exploding.

Tobias mocked him. "You think you're something, don't you, boy. You don't know nothin'. But I do."

Quickly, Thatcher's brother joined him shoulder-to-shoulder— a daunting line of muscle. Still Tobias did not back down, his liquid courage rising—and armed with Geneva's stolen letter, he went on boldly.

"You think you got you a pretty little nigra girl—pure as coal dust. But you wrong. You wrong, boy. Wrong as you can be." He laughed and shook the papers at the gathering crowd. "I got some information you oughta know boy."

Pointing toward Joly, he said, "She ain't pure like you think she is. You got you a nice half-breed, boy. She ain't who you think she is. She's got her a white grandma."

Joly looked toward Geneva and when their eyes met, time stopped. Caught in Joly's gaze, Geneva stood frozen, exposed, and guilty as understanding struck Joly like lightning. All the questions, all the promises of secrecy, all the reasons why Geneva wanted to live alone fell away. Every eye turned toward the young bride. Geneva closed her eyes and crumpled against Helen. The only sound was Jebson's demonic cackle.

"Get out of here," John said, summoning all his professorial authority and shouting out of his own long pent-up anger. "Go."

Jebson spat in his face, but John didn't move.

"You want me to leave, do you? Whatcha gonna do? Call the law on me? You in this up to your lily-white neck—ain't ya, perfessor? You been aidin' and abettin'—that's good lawyer talk—aidin' and abettin.' Ain't it, perfessor? You guilty as all the rest." He slung his arm toward the crowd. "All y'all is fools. And this here weddin' is a fool's errand—lettin' this good, upstandin' nigra boy here marry a half-breed...."

A single shotgun blast shattered the air, startling birds and people and showering the gathering with leaves. While the crowd's attention had been riveted on the unfolding drama, Zeph had slipped around the back of the church. With a single blast, he grabbed Tobias' stage. In a voice booming with barely-controlled rage, Zeph pointed the rifle barrel at Tobias' chest.

"I'm not a killing man," Zeph said, his voice like a dam about to break against decades of accumulated anger. "But I'll shoot you right here and now if you don't go. I swear to my Almighty God. I will shoot you to hell."

Tobias was dazed, his white eyes bulging, and his liquid courage souring in his belly. With the concussion from the shotgun blast hanging in the air, blood and liquor drained from Tobias' face and fear jumped him like a wildcat.

"Go." Zeph bellowed. He cocked his rifle. "Go!"

Looking down the barrel of Zeph's shotgun into a face distorted with the rarest kind of wrath, Tobias sobered up. He ran. Zeph shot another blast over his head into the trees as Tobias fled helter-skelter down the hill like a headless chicken. One more blast and Tobias had disappeared.

Zeph picked up and pocketed the letter as everyone else looked for Joly, but she was gone. She had fled from the church, fled from Thatcher, fled from Zeph and Geneva, and fled from the truth. On the back of a horse tethered behind the church, she had fled, her great grandmother's wedding gown flowing recklessly in the wind.

Lying on the ground in the churchyard was Caroline Snow's wedding veil. Trampled.

CHAPTER 72

1928

Regret & Echo

Zeph opened the windows in the parlor. Off to the west, storm clouds gathered and distant thunder troubled the afternoon. Geneva's distress was palpable, filling the room with anxiety.

"He'll find her. Thatcher will find her," Zeph said, but his assurance was lost on Geneva. She hardly heard him over the echo of regret storming out of her past. Joly's pain was the same pain Geneva had caused her father a lifetime ago—exactly the same. She knew this with agonizing certainty. Once again she suffered the crushing guilt of knowing she had hurt someone she loved. Once again Geneva had destroyed a cherished relationship. And she knew she was responsible.

"It's all my fault," she said. "I should have told her sooner."

"No, Geneva. I'm just as guilty," Zeph said. He left the window to join her on the settee. "She was bound to find out."

"But why at her wedding? How could anyone be so cruel?"

"I don't know. I jes don't know. But no sense blaming yourself. I'm guilty, too." Zeph rubbed her hands. "We did the best we knew how. Blaming won't help."

All the agony of her broken relationship with her father washed over her in waves of regret. Even though he had forgiven her in his own magnanimous way and walked into eternity having granted her the great gift of mercy, it was of little comfort in the moment. Like Geneva's father, Joly was innocent, an unwitting player in Geneva's drama. Regret as potent as strychnine filled her, and it was a poison unlike anything she had ever tasted before. To wound a parent was heartbreaking; to hurt a child was excruciating. *Am I the most selfish woman on earth?* Her reproach was stinging and absolute. Nothing Zeph could say blunted it.

As he had always done, Zeph hid his own anger and donned the placid demeanor that had long shielded Geneva. Rain, soft as a child's tears, blew in.

"Geneva, I believe I'll jes stay with you tonight," he said. He took her hand and stroked it, and then he wrapped her tightly in his arms while she cried. Privately, he struggled with his own failure to protect their granddaughter. What he had done had not been enough. He had failed Joly. Zeph had failed them both. "She'll be fine," he said, determined to be reassuring. "Don't you worry. She's a sensible girl. Our Joly's a good girl. But you got to forgive yourself. We both do."

———

Joly moved around her new home, working, distracting herself, putting on calm as deliberately as a garment. A bushel of apples waited by the kitchen door, ready for her to make into sauce. Fabrics to sew were piled on a table. Every minute of her days that she could manage to fill was one less minute to feel the hurt.

After Thatcher found her and brought her home, two days elapsed before Geneva knew her granddaughter was safe. Her relief, though, was short-lived; Joly refused to see either Geneva or Zeph. Thatcher did his best to comfort her, but Joly's wound was raw and gaping. She was walking through hot coals. Except for Thatcher, everyone she had depended on had betrayed her. She shut out them all, even her grandfather. The power of betrayal and the weight of her own new truth suffocated her. It was not the facts as much as the dishonesty that drove her into seclusion.

Joly put a bowl on the table and set two places. She pulled an apple pie out of the oven and set it aside to cool. She was picking potatoes to peel when someone knocked. She opened the door to find her grandfather. Before she could refuse him, he stepped in and gestured toward the room. "You mind?" he said.

Without a word, she moved aside.

Zeph lowered himself into a straight chair, and with his elbows on his knees, he clasped his hands together and put his head down. He ached from the gulf that had opened between them.

"Joly, I...."

"...Why didn't you tell me, Grandpa?" she interrupted. "Why didn't you?" Standing near the door as if she were ready to flee again, she grasped the latch.

"We were trying to protect you, Joly."

"By lying to me? You told me she was a friend—and she was my grandmother? How could you? How could you lie to me?"

"Joly..."

"No, Grandpa. Don't say it. Don't tell me you were trying to protect me. I'm a half-breed. How can you protect me from that? You should have told me. All these years—and you never told me."

"We did the best we knew." Zeph's eyes were wet, and his shoulders drooped, making him look older than Joly had ever seen him. "If you'd jes talk to her, I believe...."

"...No." Joly, stone-faced, stomped her foot. She was, at that moment, immune to any sympathies. "I won't talk to her. I never want to see her again." She grabbed the locket around her neck and ripped it off, throwing it to the floor. "Never." She began to cry.

The room grew quiet, magnifying Joly's sobs. Zeph waited for her anger to dissipate, but it was stubborn anger, the kind harboring the deepest hurt. There was so much Zeph wanted to say to her—how much he understood her grief, how life had a way of stealing and hurting—how it could also heal. But she was not ready to hear him. Not yet. He stood up.

"I want you to think about something, Joly."

She glared at him, all her anger and dismay distorting her young face.

"You gotta think about forgiving," he said. "You jes got to. No other way, honey, to stop your own hurting."

CHAPTER 73

1928

Jeopardy & Equality

B y Wednesday!" Helen gripped her coffee cup so hard her knuckles turned white. Dean Rollins' deadline loomed like a thunderhead. "When did you find out?"

"Right before the wedding," said John, rubbing his forehead. He had a blistering headache. "Keep your voice down."

McClanahan's was crowded and noisy. The clatter of dishes and conversations made it hard to talk. Helen huddled her shoulders. "And you didn't tell me?" She was angry and made sure he knew it.

"Look, I'm sorry, Helen. I should have told you, but..."

"Yes, you should have. What were you thinking?"

"I was thinking about the wedding," he said defensively.

"What are you going to do in a week?"

"Well, I've been thinking."

"Great," she said with stinging sarcasm. "You've been thinking."

Her comment stung—but he probably deserved it, he thought.

"Yes. I have been thinking," he countered. He drank more coffee, hoping it would help his headache. "If you'll just listen."

Helen glared at him.

"First, I'm going to talk to Miss Geneva..." he said.

"...What good will that do?"

"Would you just listen for a minute?" He closed his eyes and rubbed his head again. Helen's reaction had surprised him, although it shouldn't have. Maybe he should have told her earlier. But he hadn't—and he couldn't change that.

"I'll ask her if I can tell Rollins," he said. "Maybe the dean will understand. It's all I've got."

"What makes you think he'd understand? He's as hard as a rock—and it seems a little unnecessary to ask her now, don't you think? Everyone knows."

"Not everyone," John said impatiently. "One community, yes. But not Rollins' circle of friends—I can't imagine how it would filter there." John's frustration kept him on edge, and his headache only exacerbated it. "Anyway, that's beside the point."

"It's not beside the point! It is the point," challenged Helen.

"I know, but it's beside the point for me—I made a promise, remember?"

"Secrets! There are too many secrets." Helen's bracelet clanked on the table.

"It's not just secrets, Helen, it's the law."

The din in the restaurant was beginning to ebb. The waitress offered them more coffee. "No," they said gruffly in unison.

Their conversation paused, and the anger between them began to subside. Helen calmed down. But for the moment, she conceded nothing because she still hated being left out.

"We're dabbling in something that's socially awkward," he continued, "but it's also dangerous. I know all too well."

"St. Ballard?"

"What else?" he said. "I'm an expert."

Helen ran a finger around the brim of her cup. She needed to change her tune—arguing would not solve the problem. Even though she was irritated with him, she admired John. Ambitious men were not always so principled.

"Okay. I see your point," she said. "But if she agrees to let you tell him, what do you think Rollins will say?"

John shrugged. "I have no earthly idea."

"Could you simply tell him she's been living alone all these years? Without explaining about Zeph?"

"Eventually, it would come out." Absentmindedly, John squared the salt and pepper shakers. "Think what her journals must say. I'm more inclined to tell the whole story up front and hope he's open-minded enough to accept it."

"Would he?"

"Who knows? As we know, educators can have strange convictions."

"Don't we!" Helen shuddered. "At least Lassiten's gone."

John drummed the table. "You realize your job is probably on the line, too?"

Helen stared down at her coffee. As John watched her, an unexpected wave of empathy swept over him. For her sake, he regretted ever hearing from Geneva Snow. *I can dig ditches, but what does a single woman do with no family, no fallback?* "I'm sorry I got you involved," he said.

"No, don't say that." She looked up at him and finally smiled. "I'm not sorry. I like adventures. And I wouldn't trade this one— even if it does turn out to be expensive. We're in this together, John Klare. Like it or not."

He smiled. He was not sure he had ever felt more grateful— or closer—to anyone than to her just then. "You're a real peach, Helen."

"And useful," she said, teasing.

Suddenly John brightened. "Smalley."

"What?" She laughed. "You're as changeable as the weather."

"No, really. Dean Smalley knows Rollins. Maybe he can advise us."

"But I thought you were going to ask Miss Geneva."

"I am, but Smalley might know something," John said. With hope rising, he reached out and grabbed Helen's hand. "Interested in a road trip?"

CHAPTER 74

1928

Love & Lamentation

Geneva stood by the window in her parlor and looked through the cold glass. Staring out in the direction of the cemetery, listening to her father's clock, she counted the seconds. *Strange,* she thought, *how comforting the sound—the minutes of my life counting down.* In the distance, shadows raced across the fields, and beyond the window, a cold wind rattled tree limbs like bones. A kind of defeat she had never known stalked her.

Winters had always unsettled her, but she dreaded the coming one more than any other. Without reconciliation with Joly, she knew it was more than she could endure, more than she would survive. Even with entreaties by Zeph and Thatcher, Joly still refused to see her. To Geneva, it was fitting punishment. Never in her life had she been so unable to mend what she had broken. She thought about the time Simmy broke the handle off her mother's wash pitcher and how she and Simmy had stolen hoof glue from the barn and pieced it back together. *Oh, if only hearts could be mended so easily.*

Hearing a car, Geneva rose quickly, hoping it might be Joly, but it was not. Instead, she saw John and Helen. She opened the front door and waved them in. She was glad to see her friends, but her thoughts were elsewhere.

Sitting in the parlor, John explained his own predicament—another problem added to Geneva's anguish over Joly. Helen watched her distress intensify, every bit as much as if an anvil pressed down on her shoulders. She hated to see her friend so burdened, but she knew John would not proceed without her blessing—and this she admired.

"I am so sorry," Geneva said when John had explained his dilemma. "I should never have involved you."

"No. No need for apologies. I know how much the wedding meant to you. I'm glad you contacted me—and frankly, I'm honored that you trusted me. Some things are right even though they are difficult." As he spoke this, he realized how much he believed this.

"So true," Geneva said. She wanted to smile, but it was not in her. Up until this moment, she had never felt accursed. Had she made another choice long ago, her life would have been so different, but then again, she would not have lived so happily with Zeph—and Joly would not be at all. "Everything we do has consequences," she said. "I have spent my life living with the costs of my own actions. Some good. Some painful."

Beyond the window, the blue sky beckoned her as never before, as if Heaven were waiting. She turned to John. "What can I do to help you?"

"I know this is hard," he said. "But I'd like to confide in my dean—tell him your story. I'd also like to talk to Dean Smalley at the university. My former professor. If I can persuade them, we may have a couple of advocates. But." John stopped, clearly marking his intent. "I will not talk to either of them unless I have your permission."

Geneva appeared frail, defeated, like life had wrung the last strength from her. She was, at long last, ready to let go and suffer whatever consequences came—the consequences her father worked so hard to forestall. Now here they were, finally coming to roost. She would pay whatever price her secret life required.

"I am so sorry for the trouble I have caused you. Of course, you may tell them. What can happen to me now? I have lived my life. Yes. Go ahead. Tell whomever you must." She looked wistfully at John, envisioning him as having the kind of courage that she, herself, had once had. Her trust in him was complete. "I will talk to Dean Rollins myself," she added, "if you think it would help."

"I won't ask you to do that," John said, although he knew her offer was sincere—and noble. But she was not strong enough to confront a man like Rollins.

Geneva sat back and sighed deeply. Tearing up, she said, "I have always exacted so much from my friends."

Helen moved to her side and put her arm around the old woman's shoulders.

"Do what you must," Geneva continued. "But please protect Joly any way you can. I do not want her to be hurt anymore."

Before John and Helen left, Geneva handed him a bundle of Grayson's letters and one worn journal—tied with a red satin ribbon.

"Take these—your passé-partout," she said, bravely finding a smile and patting John's hand. "If these do not persuade your dean, I'm afraid nothing will."

After John and Helen left, Geneva returned to the parlor to read. She lifted a journal from the table and opened it to November 10, 1903.

She was searching for air, for some peace of mind, but she could not quit a preoccupation with death. It followed her like a specter, hovering in the silent rooms, sparking remembered conversations that drifted ghostlike out of an unending silence.

It has snowed all day and now sleet is tapping against the windows. How mournful a snowfall can be. Mama lingers still, suffering. I feel wicked for hoping she shall soon be released from the pain of her earthly life, yet I am terrified at the thought of letting her go. I am comforted in knowing she and Daddy will soon be together, to spend eternity in uninterrupted happiness—and with the mind of God, she will come to understand my love for Zeph.... November 10, 1903.

I am alone now. Zeph buried Mama next to Daddy. If it were not for Zeph and Alice Lyford, I should wish to join them. But my family needs me, and I must find the will to go on. It is my duty. Duty. How many times did I hear Daddy say that? Strangely, I am at long last most thankful for the arrangement—his duty to me. Though to some it might seem cruel, I have been hidden away with those I love most in the world and protected from those who would harm them. I am a prisoner of my own decision, but I have never been locked away from love. I have been surrounded with it. How ironic it is that out of my father's deep heartache, I came to have the one person I so desired.... December 2, 1903.

I am eternally grateful for my father's forgiveness—the resolution that came so unexpectedly and that covers me so completely. It has made me whole, and I shall go into eternity knowing the sweetness of redemption, my father's generosity reflecting my Savior's gift. I am tempted to rush ahead, to sup the gift wholly, and to discover what lies beyond the grave.... December 4, 1903

Zeph closed the rest of the shutters on the north side and closed off Mama's bedroom and studio. I do not recall a winter so harsh. As I lie in my bed at night, I hear the windows rattling in the belvedere and the cold wind combing down across the roof and chimneys. I will insist Zeph and Simmy join me here for the duration of the winter. Surely, we are forgotten—and far enough removed by time and place not to be found out. Now with Mama gone, it seems unnecessary to keep up the charade." .... December 17, 1903.

Another storm gathers above the mountains. The temperature has plummeted, and the clouds assemble in evil striations as if they were writing for me another long snowy night of bitter solitude....
December 31, 1903

Geneva closed her journal and slid it onto the side table. For a long time, she stared into the embers of the dying fire. The room grew colder, but she did not notice. Except for the incessant tick of the longcase clock, the house was bereft of even the smallest noise, as if all living things had left and taken every other sound with them.

CHAPTER 75

1928

———————

Guilt & Truth

John Klare! What in the world has brought you here?" said Smalley, delighted to see his former student stroll into his office. "What a treat. How are you, my boy?" Standing and rounding his desk, he reached out with two hands and took John's hands in his.

"I'm well, sir. It's good to be back."

"And whom do we have here?" said Smalley, eyeing Helen with a speculative smile, which John quickly clarified.

"Dean, I'd like you to meet Helen Van Soren. She's a librarian at the college."

"My pleasure," he said. He gave Helen a little bow and kissed her hand. Instantly, she saw why John had spoken of Rufus Smalley with such affection. Open and amiable, he was the antithesis of Dean Rollins. Standing shoulder-to-shoulder with John, he had impish eyes and thick, unruly hair, both the color of tobacco. His appearance was altogether rumpled and unstarched. Had his name not been on the door, she might have mistaken him for a Fuller Brush salesman.

"Rollins didn't send you back to me, did he?" Smalley joked, sitting down behind his cluttered desk.

"Not yet," John said gravely.

Smalley frowned. "Has something happened?"

"I—actually we—have a problem," John said, glancing at Helen.

"I'm sorry to hear that." Smalley reared back, tenting his fingers at his mouth. "Why don't you tell me about it?"

The three spent the next hour locked away as John explained. Smalley learned about Geneva's extraordinary life and heard how he himself had played a pivotal role.

"I'm sure you see my dilemma. Miss Geneva and her husband— they're good people," said John, finding it difficult to articulate how he had come to feel about the family. "I don't want to jeopardize them, but I would also like to keep my job—if that's even possible."

"What can I do?" Smalley asked.

"I was hoping you could tell me if I should confide in Dean Rollins."

"You've discussed it with Mrs. Elias, I trust?"

"Yes. We stopped by on our way here."

"She offered to go to Rollins herself," Helen added, "but she's not up to it."

"I agree," John said. "Rollins intimidates me."

Smalley laughed. "It's mostly for show, John. Albert Rollins is not nearly as tough as he seems." A puff of air from an open window tousled Smalley's hair and rustled papers on his desk. He moved a book to anchor them. "What's your timetable?"

"Wednesday."

Smalley winced. "You are in a pickle, my friend. Albert is brilliant. I've known him a long time professionally. I'm racking my brain to think of anything he might have said that would give you a clue about how he would react. I wish I could give you an answer, but—in all candor—I can't. I simply don't know. Some academics are open-minded. Others are not so charitable."

"Oh, yes. We know," said John, exchanging looks with Helen. "Jacob Lassiten was certainly not."

Smalley pursed his lips and was quiet for a moment. "I'm afraid Mr. Lassiten is no longer with us."

"I don't understand," John said. "I thought he was in the law school."

"Jacob is dead, John."

"What happened?" John and Helen said in unison.

"Well." Smalley took a deep breath. "It's rather ironic. It seems Jacob was an octoroon—one-eighth Negro."

John and Helen were stunned.

"Jacob Lassiten? Negro?" John said. "An octoroon? I know the term, but..."

"Apparently, the board of the law school found out, and they rescinded his acceptance."

"How did they know?"

"I have no idea. Of course, the state uses all sorts of 'research'— as you well know."

"I do indeed."

"It is quite sad. He was not a pleasant person, but he was bright and had potential. No one deserves such a fate. After he was dismissed—the next morning—a groundskeeper found him under the bridge. He had hanged himself."

John groaned as the weight of injustice fell on him. Even for Lassiten, someone he had disliked, this was wrong. The afternoon took on a distinctly somber mood.

"Then why did he hate coloreds so?" Helen asked.

"Fear? Maybe self-loathing? I don't know," Smalley said. "All we can do is speculate. Maybe by coming down hard on them and by pushing eugenics, he thought he could shield himself. Or there's always the chance he didn't know."

"Like Benny," John said.

"Exactly." Smalley nodded at John and then stared out the window, musing. "Education *should* make us better. It is a poor commentary for academics that so many have bought into this rubbish. I keep thinking they'll come to their senses, but..." He looked back at John and Helen. "Well, we can't solve that today. Back to your problem."

This time, however, no miracles were in the offing, and even Smalley's optimism, which John had always depended on, was waning.

"I'm not sure you have much choice, John. If you don't tell the whole story, you're out on mere speculation—that would be a shame. But if Rollins is anything like some men, you're out for the same reasons St. Ballard fired you. Guilty by association. One thing I do know about Rollins—he lives for Haverston. He's as devoted to your college as I am to my wife. The lady's journals might be a windfall for the college. I'd love to get my hands on them myself."

"If they throw me out, Dean, I'll be on your doorstep."

"John," Smalley said, looking him straight in the eye. "A long time ago, Miss Lancaster was my third-grade teacher—but I still remember her best advice: If you tell the truth, you don't have to remember what you said."

"So honesty is my best policy? It's already cost me one job. What's one more?" John said flippantly. "But I've also jeopardized Helen, I'm afraid."

Both men looked at her.

"I agree with Miss Lancaster," she said.

CHAPTER 76

1928

Redemption & Amends

John and Helen waited together outside Dean Rollins' office, lambs ready for slaughter. The autumn sun spilled through high windows, making the anteroom stuffy. Helen nervously clasped and unclasped her purse, until he asked her to stop.

"Sorry," she said, stilling her hands.

"You're making me nervous," he said.

"You're not already?"

He shrugged and gave her a resigned smile. "I've been here before, remember?"

Over John's protests, Helen had insisted on coming and privately he was not sorry. In one hand, he held the bundle of Grayson's letters and the red-ribbon journal. He set them down, leaned forward, and twisted his grandfather's signet ring.

Helen gestured toward the letters. "Have you read them?" she whispered.

"Some of them."

"Will they convince him?"

"I don't know. They might—so long as he's not of the same ilk as Lassiten."

When the door opened and the secretary ushered them in, Rollins was already in his office. He was standing behind his desk, reading a letter. The draperies were pulled back all the way, and John could see the lavish office fully for the first time.

"Please be seated," Rollins said without looking up. He took his time as John and Helen settled into two chairs in front of his desk. Helen found him rude and was on the verge of telling him so, when he looked up and stunned them with a generous smile.

"Thank you for coming," Rollins said, sitting down. "Since I talked with you last, Mr. Klare, I have received a telephone call from Dean Smalley. He told me that I have misunderstood your actions—and would be wise to listen to your story. Therefore, if you would allow me, I'd like to make amends."

John was flabbergasted. Was this the same unapproachable man so fond of intimidation? Helen, unable to contain herself, unleashed a "Hallelujah."

"Do I presume you are Miss Van Soren?" asked Rollins, amused.

"Yes, I am. Helen Van Soren. Research librarian."

"It's a pleasure to meet you, young lady. Well now. We have much to talk about."

John, still speechless, nodded.

"But first let me apologize for jumping to conclusions. I hope you can understand why this issue is important to me—the reputation of the faculty affects the college's reputation. There are some things I won't tolerate."

"Yes, of course," John mumbled.

Rollins rested his arms on his desk, giving John and Helen his full attention. "Now," he said, "I would be most obliged if you would begin at the beginning."

CHAPTER 77

1928

Pain & Passion

Turnips and potatoes, spread on old newspapers, covered a shelf in Joly's modest kitchen, the smell of yeast bread was in the air, and a small pot of water simmered on the cookstove. The table was set. She looked out to see if Thatcher was coming down the road yet. Outside a frigid wind blew. After the wedding, the weather had turned, but it was not as cold as Joly's heart. Even though Thatcher had been tender and solicitous, her pain still invaded every hour. She was not yet willing to explore why she felt so torn. Her wedding day had joined her to Thatcher, but at the same time it had ripped her life in two.

It was some consolation that the revelation made no difference at all to Thatcher—but it made a great deal of difference to Joly. She was not who she thought she was, and the bitter affront of betrayal had shaken her. She was angry with Geneva, angry with her grandfather, angry even with Simmy—angry with all of them for deceiving her. She moved through her days pushing back pain, fighting emotion, and waiting for forgiveness to speak up and say, "Now is the time." But it had not. Instead, a strange and vicious grief consumed her. The old and the new Joly were separate, disparate people, and until they reconnected, any thought of reconciliation with her family seemed impossible.

She lifted a log from the wood box by the door and stoked the cookstove fire. The room was warm and comfortable as she waited for Thatcher, the single person she could trust. He had told her all he knew—what Zeph had told him—and she had absorbed it like a stone absorbs water, through small imperceptible cracks and fissures that from a distance are invisible. It was all she could manage as she protected her wounded heart and tried to understand her life, which was now bisected into a before and after. She would not let anyone, not even Thatcher, touch the tender raw portions. It was too soon.

Joly walked to the back room where she stretched out on their bed. She ran her hand along the nubby surface of the quilt. Outside the evening sky was purple with deeper shades blending into the mountain's ridges. She watched the room darken as one might watch ice melt, but nothing was melting in Joly's heart.

She spotted a pink calico book on the shelf. She had poured love into it before the wedding. Now she had a different emotion to dispense. She pulled it off the shelf, opened it, and read. And then she picked up her pencil.

When she heard Thatcher whistling, she closed the book and walked to the porch to welcome him home. Seeing her, he smiled and waved. Being alone with Thatcher, she could escape the ghosts of her past. She could live and try to forget—as much as forgetting can dull pain.

CHAPTER 78

1928

Life & Eternity

Until that day, John had scoffed at premonitions—nothing more than the mind's tricks to explain the unexplainable. But all day an uneasiness had dogged him, as if something were shifting in the heavens.

After teaching his Saturday morning classes, he had, as a favor to Miss Armenia, spent the afternoon raking leaves downed by a hard freeze and heavy rains. As he raked and the temperature dropped, he repeatedly checked the sky to see if a storm were coming, but it remained clear.

In the evening, he had settled down to read when someone knocked on his door. Opening it, he saw Zeph. Tears streamed down the old man's worn face.

"Zeph. What's wrong?" said John, alarmed. "Come in."

Zeph stood with his head down and his hands joined. For a moment, he could not speak.

"Zeph?" John said, taking his arm and urging him to come in.

"It's Geneva." His voice cracked. "She's gone. She's gone."

"Gone?" John said. "Gone where?"

"Passed, Mr. Klare. She's passed."

Disbelief flooded John's mind as Zeph's words sank in. John closed the door. "What happened?"

"I found her lying on her bed," Zeph said, unable to hold back a sob. "It's like she was waiting. She's all dressed up like she's going someplace. She must've known. What am I gonna do? Geneva was my life. My whole life."

"I'm so sorry," he said. Shocked and wholly unprepared himself, he had no idea what else to say or do. Without thinking, he looked around for Helen—and wished like heck she were there. "I guess we call the undertaker?" John asked clumsily as he grasped for something to say.

"No, sir. No need to bother him. I wanna take care of her. I can do what needs to be done. I was hoping you could help me."

"Of course. Anything," John said. "Sit down, Zeph. Can I get you something?"

"No, sir, but thank you. I got work to do."

"How can I help?"

"I walked down the mountain, and, frankly, my legs 'bout give out."

"Where's Claudine?"

"Back at the chapel. I didn't want to take time to go back. Would you mind toting me back out to Cairnaerie?"

"I'll get my coat."

It was fully dark by the time John and Zeph drove out of town. Above the deserted road, a cloudless winter sky—a black blanket decorated with a million seed pearls—shrouded the mountains. John drove fast along the winding road, although he didn't know why. Death was not something he customarily rushed toward. Morbidly, he wondered how long she had been dead before Zeph found her. He doubted it had been long, knowing how attentive Zeph had always been.

"She's cold, so cold," Zeph said.

"Have you told Joly?"

"No sir."

"Do you want to go by her house first?"

"That'd pro'bly be a good idea. This is gonna be hard on her." Pain showed on Zeph's face, the kind one feels for another, a doubling of one's own.

Joly was alone when Zeph and John knocked at her door. As soon as she saw them together, she knew something was wrong. She braced herself against the doorframe.

"Joly," Zeph said quietly. "Miss Geneva's gone."

"Oh, Grandpa. No," Joly said, and she collapsed to her knees, wailing. "Oh no. No." Zeph knelt beside her and stroked her hair as she wept. Unable to hold back his own tears, he cried with his granddaughter. The edge to Joly's hurt disappeared like a vapor, but where hurt and anger had lodged, remorse swept in and swallowed her.

John stood awkwardly in the doorway and clenched his teeth. He felt like an intruder and again wished Helen were with him. She would know what to do and to say.

"Why didn't I go see her?" Joly said. "I should have gone to see her." She buried her face in Zeph's chest and unleashed a guttural moan as regret and agony rushed out of her.

"Hush, child. Hush. It's not your fault," he said, offering all the comfort he had to give. "It's me oughta be feeling bad. I shoulda told you a long time ago. It's my fault, honey, not yours. We never meant to hurt you."

"I know, Grandpa—I never meant to hurt her, either."

"She understood—more than you know, honey."

Zeph realized death had once again intervened. He thought about Judge Snow and his posthumous forgiveness, how it had lifted Geneva and made her whole. Now he would help lift Joly. He would tell her the whole story. He would help her, but he also knew that the road to forgiveness was often the hardest one to travel.

"Was she alone?" asked Joly, peering into her grandfather's eyes with the look of a hungry bird.

"Yes. But I'm going to her now. Mr. Klare's carrying me in his motor car."

"I want to go with you."

"No, honey, you stay here. You need to wait for Thatcher and tell him. When it's time, we'll come fetch you. Nothing you can do jes yet." He turned to John. "Could you bring 'em, Mr. Klare?"

"Of course."

The moon, full and white, hung low in the heavens like a great open eye, as if God were watching. John motored along the dark road, heading toward Cairnaerie, toward the last chapter of Geneva's life. When the Ajax rolled into the yard, the house was completely dark and deathly still. A vacuum of cold winter air encased Cairnaerie and every living thing seemed frozen.

John brushed away fear as he and Zeph mounted the porch stairs. Death seemed to swarm around them. When they opened the front door, moonlight spread out over the star embedded in the foyer floor, and for a fraction of a second, John thought it was glowing. Zeph felt his way to a lamp and lit it.

They found Geneva as Zeph had described, lying on her bed. She was wearing the same dress she had worn the first time John came to Cairnaerie. One small, knotted hand lay on her chest, clutching a handkerchief. The other lay limp at her side.

"I'm not sure what we should do," John whispered.

"I know what to do. I'll stay with her tonight."

Zeph pulled a chair up beside the bed and laid his hand on her arm.

"Do you want me to stay?" John asked.

"No sir, you don't need to. But I'd be obliged if you could come by tomorrow afternoon. I'll need a little help then. And could bring the others with you?"

John put his hand on Zeph's shoulder. "Of course. What time?"

"About four o'clock."

John left Zeph and headed back down the mountain. He need-ed to see Helen.

Zeph pulled a chair up beside the bed where Geneva lay as if she were only sleeping, and he took her hand in his. Throughout the long night, he listened for its quiet rhythm, but this night had no rhythm, no heartbeat. Instead, seeping out of the silence, he heard the voices of Geneva and Simmy laughing and teasing him. He heard his own mother singing to him and his own father teaching. He heard the sounds of Cairnaerie when it was strong and produc-tive, running like a fine machine. He heard the wagons and hors-es moving hay, the farm hands swearing, the plows tearing open the fields. He heard the swish of fodder brushed by the wind, the whinnying of horses, and the cackle of brooding hens. He heard Geneva's father giving orders to haul hay out of the lower fields. He heard her mother yelling at Vivvy. He heard Simmy calling his name. He heard the sad muffled voices after Thomas and Grayson had died. He heard the babbling of Alice Lyford. He heard Geneva whispering to him in the chapel.

All night Zeph stayed beside Geneva, holding her cold hand, listening to the Judge's clock. At each hour of the night, it struck with a deep, sad tone, a monody from her father, an elegy marking one more hour of separation. But Zeph was used to separation, used to waiting, and used to taking what came his way and making of it what he could. There was no bitterness in the man. What hurt and anger had once stirred in him, he had thrown away, choosing forgiveness instead—a fertile ground for joy.

He thought about his life—in the beginning, one of servitude by circumstance and later, by choice. He had served his family well, the best he was able, and given them all the love and protection he could. He had fulfilled his promise to the Judge. He had taken care of Geneva, kept her safe and hidden. And he had loved her with every ounce of his being. Tears on Zeph's face glistened in the moonlight.

"I'll be coming on directly, Geneva," he whispered. "You wait by the gate for me."

When Zeph saw the first ribbon of sunlight fall across Geneva's soft, still face, he stood up and went to the shed. All morning he cut and carved, hammered and sawed. He worked like a vigorous young man, intent on finishing this one task. In the late morning, he took a shovel and walked out through the fields toward the family plot. One last time.

Late that afternoon, John arrived with Joly, Thatcher, and Helen. Zeph was waiting for them in the swing, his hands folded in his lap. He stepped off the porch to meet them.

"Come on with me, Joly," Zeph said, holding out his hand to her. She looked haggard and drained from a sleepless night. As he took her hand, he whispered in her ear. "She understood, honey. All she ever wanted in this world was for you to be happy." Joly squeezed her eyes shut to stem her tears.

"I want to see her, Grandpa," she said, choking out words. Her hurt and resentment were gone, replaced with other jumbled emotions and layers of pain she would have to peel away slowly.

Zeph opened the front door and led them into the foyer where Geneva lay in a simple pine coffin, hand hewn and lined with a faded double wedding ring quilt. Her face was colorless, and her mouth was drawn up in the slightest allusion of a smile. Thatcher held Joly close to his side.

Standing with Geneva's small band of friends in this immense house, Helen was overcome, and in a gesture both generous and spontaneous, John put his arm around her.

How did it all come to this? Helen thought as she fought back tears. *How senseless to have lived locked away for so long.* As much as she had tried, Helen could not understand the cruel society that had kept Geneva a prisoner. Neither could she understand the father's decision to lock her away. It angered her, and her anger mixed with grief undid her. *To die with only five people who knew you ever lived is a mockery of life.* She swallowed hard to stifle a rage she could barely contain and watched Zeph. He was smiling. He bent down and kissed the brow of the woman he had loved so long and so completely. Even if understanding could not break through to Helen, it had certainly come to Zeph.

Looking at the sky, Zeph gauged the remaining daylight. "We best go," he said. "I've got a wagon hitched around back."

The women dropped back for the men to close and secure the coffin. On the top was a familiar six-pointed star, carved skillfully and lovingly. John, Zeph, and Thatcher hoisted the casket onto the wagon. Zeph took the reins and led the procession out across the field toward the cemetery. No one spoke as the cold afternoon sun bore down into their souls. Helen felt like she was walking into eternity.

Zeph had dug the grave. The dampness of the opened earth sent a shiver through Joly. Thatcher pulled her close. Helen stood with John, her mind a volatile mixture of grief and anger.

Zeph spoke quietly. "I'm not a preacher, but I have to say a few words." He paused and raised his face and hands heavenward. "We're all here, Lord, to give you back a woman we've all loved. Her name, Lord—well, you know her name, don't you? It's in your book. Geneva here, she knew you, and she drew her strength from believing on you. She was a good woman, a good wife, a good mother who loved us all—and loved you, too. We ask you to take her and hold her close tonight. All of us here, we're gonna miss her something awful, but we know she's in good hands. We thank you, Lord, for lettin' us know her." He bowed his head. From deep within the man's soul rose the strains of a song, his deep voice like a thick balm. "Amazing Grace, How sweet the sound...."

In the west, the sun lay down on the mountains and pulled the dark over them all.

John drove the small party back to their homes, dropping off Helen, then Thatcher and Joly.

"Thank you for your help," Joly said to John as she and Thatcher climbed out of the Ajax. "Grandpa, you're staying here tonight. You have to."

"Sure, honey. I will. I'll be along directly."

Thatcher echoed her thanks, waving, as they slipped into the house.

Zeph stared ahead into the darkness. Taking a deep breath, he reached into his pocket. "Mr. Klare, Geneva left this for me. I can make out my name, but my eyes jes aren't strong enough to read the rest. She was always after me to get some spectacles. Guess I shoulda listened." He fingered the envelope tenderly. "I'd be much obliged if you'd read it to me."

John opened the letter. By the light of the full moon, he read the words, but it was Geneva's voice that penetrated Zeph's ears.

December 1, 1928

My Dearest Zeph,

Last night, I dreamed I visited the cemetery and a new grave had been dug. Above a black mound of earth was a headstone inscribed Geneva Caroline Snow Elias. Once before a dream stirred in me the same passion I felt when I awoke this morning. As you know, I have always believed in dreams.

I have lived as full a life as any woman could hope for—for I have had the company of a cherished husband. Though distance often separated us, we were one, were we not? My life has taught me to live beyond myself, to find happiness even if circumstances belie it. When Joly was married, I was nearly overtaken with the feeling that you and I were giving our granddaughter away. My last prayer for Joly is that she finds as great a happiness with Thatcher as I found with you—and that someday she will find a way to forgive me.

What happened at her wedding is not what I wanted, but I cannot change it. I am leaving you with the heavy burden of putting things right. Once again, even in my absence, I know you will take care of me. Just as my father entrusted you to help me find happiness in seclusion, I trust you to help her. Help her understand. Help her know how much I love her.

My beloved husband, I say goodbye for the moment. We shall surely be reunited in Heaven where our love will be celebrated— and never again hidden. I want you to put on my stone Geneva Caroline Snow Elias, daughter of Bertram Snow and Caroline Hampton Snow, wife of Zephyr Elias, mother of Alice Lyford Elias Jennings, and grandmother of Joly Jennings Oden.

And finally, my ring is enclosed. Please make sure Joly gets it. I will always love you.

Geneva

John's eyes were moist. He cleared his throat and handed the letter back to Zeph, who cradled the ring in the palm of his hand.

"She always said Joly ought to have it." The great and kind eyes of Zeph Elias were overflowing. He wiped his face with his sleeve and hung his head, though John could see him smiling, the same kind of distant, knowing smile he had first seen on the face of Geneva Snow when she talked of her family.

Distance, John thought, is no barrier.

1929 — 1930

CHAPTER 79

1929

Windfalls & Wishes

D ean Rollins was arranging chairs in his office when the door opened and a stately gray-haired man stepped in. He was carrying a large envelope.

"Mr. Goodwin. Come in," said Rollins as he walked over to shake the man's hand. "It's a pleasure to meet you."

"Thank you," he said. "But call me Anderson. It makes me feel young."

"Of course. Anderson. I am delighted you were able to make the trip. I know it is a long one for you."

"Indeed, it is. But this case has taken me far—and I do not mean only geographically."

Rollins nodded. "I understand. I asked the others to arrive at a quarter past so I could speak with you privately." Rollins stroked his chin. "Do I understand correctly that the college is mentioned in the will?"

"You must have talked with Zeph."

"Yes, I have."

"Well I can answer your question affirmatively; however, I would like to withhold the details until the reading."

"Of course," Rollins said. "How well did you know her?"

Anderson smiled. "For someone I met face-to-face only once, I suppose I knew her quite well."

"That surprises me."

"It's true. We corresponded for years—ever since her mother's death. You come to know a person when you handle all their affairs, especially those as peculiar as Geneva's."

Rollins gave him quizzical look.

"You're wondering how I ever got involved," Anderson said.

"You read my mind."

"Her mother was my second cousin, which makes her my second, once removed."

Rollins, shaking his head, chuckled. "Someday, I'll figure out how all that works."

"Yes, it is confusing. Our grandmothers were sisters," Anderson said. "When this all started, her father contacted me—it was a family obligation, at least at the beginning. He needed someone he could trust, and who better than family? Bertram Snow was a skillful lawyer—and a deeply caring man, I must add. He and I wrote the trust that was, shall I say, fireproof. I had some concerns, of course. In the beginning—certainly. But Bertram adored his daughter—and there were no easy answers. Sometimes situations arise one cannot change—but you still must walk ahead. That's what he did. Neither of us ever imagined it would last so long. I certainly didn't."

"It is quite a story," Rollins said. "She must have been a remarkable woman. I'm sorry I never had the privilege."

"Frankly, Dean, I was surprised—pleasantly, I assure you—that you were as open to this meeting as you were. We both know the Elias marriage is problematic."

"But the will and the trust are not, I presume," Rollins said.

"Correct. Bertram made sure of that. For a man who was heart-broken, he had an uncanny ability to consider the future."

"May I be totally honest?" Rollins asked.

"Of course."

"I do have some reservations, given the current state of things. As you might guess, some on my faculty are not quite so—shall I say—charitable toward Negroes. But I'm a realistic man, and I can see where all this is going. Society will change. It's inevitable. The question is when, and that's a question I can't answer."

"We do the best we can for the moment," Anderson said.

"Yes, we do. My decisions are based on what's best for the college and its future—and beyond that, on what will serve the greater good."

Momentarily, the dean's secretary opened the door.

"The others are here, Dr. Rollins."

"Send them in."

She held the door while they filed through.

"Good afternoon," Rollins said. "Let me introduce you all to Anderson Goodwin. John Klare, Helen Van Soren, Joly and Thatcher Oden. And I believe you've already met Zeph Elias."

"Yes, I have," Goodwin said. "Good to see you all. This is an important day."

Zeph was smiling from ear to ear.

"Please, all of you, be seated," said the dean.

Zeph and Thatcher flanked Joly, each holding one of her hands. John touched Helen's arm, a gesture she acknowledged gratefully. Rollins offered Anderson his chair, but he declined. "I prefer to stand, Dean, but thank you." Holding a crisp new document, Anderson adjusted his glasses and cleared his throat. "I trust you all know why we are here today." Anderson began to read:

I, Geneva Caroline Snow Elias, being of sound mind and body, do hence-forth instruct my attorney, Mr. Anderson Goodwin of Baltimore, Maryland, to dispense the full complement of my estate, including all real estate, the contents of my home, Cairnaerie, and seventy-five percent of the monetary value of investments he has made on my behalf, per my expressed wishes as I have directed herein.

To my granddaughter, Joly Jennings Oden, I leave all my earthly physical possessions, including my home, Cairnaerie, and the entire scope of my es-tate, numbering 1,578 acres, located due west of Hyssop, Virginia, in Vassel County. On the advice of my attorney, who has advised me that existing es-tate laws and the current social climate may encumber its full dispensation, the estate is to be placed in a trust to which Mrs. Oden, with the counsel of Mr. Goodwin and/or his agent, will have full and unfettered access.

Mrs. Oden is also to be given fifty (50) percent of the value of my invest-ment holdings, in an amount to be determined by the executor, Mr. Goodwin, at the time of said disbursement.

It is also a condition of this bequest that my husband, Zephyr Elias, be given full and complete care and support in whatever manner, at whatever cost, and in whatever measure he deems to be acceptable and comfortable for the remainder of his natural life. There shall be no limits on this condition. In addition, Mr. Elias is to be gifted with the purchase of a new car, the brand and style to be of his choosing.

To Haverston College, I leave the unrestricted custodial rights to all the extensive letters, journals, record books, and sundry ephemera contained within and related to my estate for the express purpose of cataloging, docu-mentation, and historic research. These include, but are not limited to: all the journals I have kept, as well as those kept by my father, Judge Bertram Snow; all the correspondence from my brother Grayson Snow while he was a soldier during the war; all the personal letters of my mother, Caroline Hampton Snow; and all of the business and personal correspondence and records that my father, brothers, or I accumulated.

As a codicil to this will, and a condition of the above clause, it is my stated desire that these documents be kept together in toto for future generations to study, that they may learn of the struggles and victories that have marked my life.

To Haverston College, I leave one quarter of my investment holdings, an amount estimated at the date of this will to be $155,000. This sum shall be combined with the funds resulting from the sale of my southern Virginia land, which conveyed to me, the last living known heir, at the death of my brother Hayes Snow. I have directed my attorney to undertake and complete this sale.

The sum of these two investments is to be used for one purpose, that being the construction of a new library to be named in memory of my father, Judge Bertram Snow. All the books in my personal library at Cairnaerie are to become the seed for the collection. The portrait of my father that hangs in the parlor of my home, Cairnaerie, shall be prominently displayed in said library. My mother's paintings also shall be displayed in a special gallery to be deemed the Caroline Hampton Snow Gallery. If the college wishes to accept this gift, the board of trustees must agree, in addition to the above restrictions, to the following conditions without exception:

John Klare is to be appointed curator of the aforementioned historical collection and Helen Van Soren is to be appointed librarian for the collection. Each is to be employed by the college, each drawing an annual salary that shall be equal to that of the dean. This employment will remain in force until such time as he or she chooses to pursue another line of work or to retire. At that time, a permanent faculty chair shall be established to oversee the collection in perpetuity.

One gift I wish to specify and highlight: It is my desire that my great grandfather's silver watch remain in my family, and that Joly, at the appropriate time, bequeath it to her children. The watch was once a small anchor of hope for my father. John Cairns, his maternal grandfather, my great grandfather, and Joly's great, great-grandfather, was the maker. Although *by its nature it marked the passing hours of his life, I hope it will become a tangible reminder of our eternal connection.*

Lastly, as a final and unalterable provision of this bequest, the Snow Library shall be open to all patrons regardless of their race or status in society. These are my wishes and with them I hope I leave the world a better place.

Signed on this date, September 10, 1928.
Geneva Caroline Snow Elias

Anderson Goodwin laid the will on the desk in front of him and lifted his glasses to rub his eyes. No one spoke. The room was utterly still, each absorbing this news. Beyond the window the wind blew, and students milled around campus as if it were any ordinary day.

Inside the room, however, the earth had moved.

CHAPTER 80

Spring 1930

Laughter & Legacy

Helen stood in the center of the foyer. Cairnaerie, open, fresh-washed and gleaming, surrounded her like a lovely, gilded frame. What a clamorous house this must have been, she thought. She imagined the Snow children bounding down the winding stair-case, laughing and barreling out the front door, their voices echo-ing through the halls.

"Remarkable, isn't it?" John said, leaning casually against the doorframe, holding a cup of coffee.

"How long have you been standing there?" she said.

"Long enough to read your mind."

"Oh? Then tell me what I was thinking, Professor."

"*Full* professor, Miss Van Soren."

"Oh, excuse me, *full* professor. What was I thinking?"

"You were thinking how sad it is this beautiful house is empty," he said as he walked over to her.

Helen did not answer. There seemed no need. Instead, she took his cup from him and had a sip. For more than a year, she and John had read and cataloged the contents of Cairnaerie. The house had become an office of sorts for them as they worked daily side by side. They had discovered a treasure of information—newspapers and documents, journals, letters. Old tintypes, ambrotypes, and daguerreotypes—an undisturbed trove of history evincing a world now gone. The history they uncovered had exceeded John's wildest estimations.

The gate had been cleared of brush and the path, made road-worthy. With the enthusiastic backing of Dean Rollins, John and Helen had been relieved of their responsibilities on campus to work at Cairnaerie. To Rollins' credit and to the consternation of some faculty members, he welcomed Zeph into his home, a gesture Geneva would have found as fine as anything he could have done. Helen had sensed in Rollins a genuine disappointment that death had prevented him from meeting Geneva Snow Elias.

"Is Zeph coming today?" John asked, taking back his coffee cup. "There's more on the stove."

She smiled. "I think so. He said Thursday."

"That's good. I'd like to dig around in the outbuildings."

With Helen's able help, John had pieced together the Elias story and chronicled the family with the meticulous and voluminous papers left behind by a father and daughter. Each book, drawer, and ledger he opened came with unspoken thanks for the remarkable gift of their words. Geneva's journals began in 1860. The five-year-old had written her name over and over and had recorded bits of her earliest years. Bertram's journals, started when he worked as a janitor in the law office, were filled with observations about life and commerce dating as early as 1833. Among the most touching entries John found were Bertram Snow's writings about his friend, Ezekial, and, hidden in his desk, a small stack of tender and heart-ful letters from Susannah Snow to her brother.

Through the keepsakes, heirlooms, field books, and documents, a family portrait had emerged every bit as detailed as Caroline

Snow's paintings. When John and Helen had first opened the door to her studio, they were stunned at the number of paintings that portrayed her life—from Richmond through her later painful years. If they had found Geneva's estimation of her mother's prolificacy exaggerated, they no longer did. It was as if the stories Geneva and her father wrote, Caroline had illustrated.

Reading Geneva's journals, John often depended on Helen to shed light on passages so personal that at first he was reluctant to show them to her at all. Yet he could not withhold them from someone so equally invested. How different this journey would have been without Helen! He had thought this often as they worked together, but he had never told her so.

"Anybody home?" Zeph's voice boomed as he came through the back door. He dropped a gunnysack in the hall with a thud.

"Hello, Zeph," Helen said.

"I brought some taters for you folks to take home. I got more'n I can eat. They're beginning to grow eyes—matter a fact, they've got so many eyes, I s'pect they can see better'n me." He chuckled and adjusted his new eyeglasses. "When my early peas and spring onions come in, I'll bring some to you."

"Thank you," John said.

With Joly married, Zeph came often to the house to fill in parts of the family's story, some even Geneva had never known. He told them the sad story of the senseless lynching of Joly's father, Fulton Jennings, outside Sulphur Hill when he had ridden to find a doctor for Alice Lyford fighting to deliver Joly—the struggle that took her life. He told them about the midwife who had carried the orphaned newborn on horseback to Hyssop to find Zeph and Simmy. He showed them the note he had kept all those years, written by his dying daughter, instructing the nurse where to take the child if she died.

They learned what it was like before and after the war—how it felt, looked, smelled, and sounded. They learned about local children during the war selling household goods and food to transient soldiers for stacks of currency that were only soup labels.

"One little girl," he told them, "when her daddy found out she'd sold some of his tools for soup labels, beat her right n'er dead. Little thing never did know what she'd done wrong. The children didn't know the difference."

As descriptive as Geneva had been in writing, Zeph was with his words, telling a broad history, nearly a century of stories. Helen recorded each one with the duteous bent of a librarian.

With Rollins' help, most of their work was closely held, a prudent calculation by the dean. He was discreet—a sentiment Geneva would have appreciated. Privately, Rollins brought John into his innermost circle, a select group of administrators who regarded the Snow gift as a kind of tontine with benefits for co-operation. John learned to know a side of Rollins never seen by ordinary faculty. His support allowed John, Helen, and Zeph to move about freely, to stop looking over their shoulders. Within the academy—given an overarching desire to stay in Rollins' good graces—no faculty members questioned the dean's decisions or John's meteoric rise in status, although some complained privately—out of the dean's earshot. This time, the dean's tight ship served a noble purpose.

The contents of the will remained secret, except to those needing to know. The world, after all, had not changed as much as Geneva had hoped.

Zeph tugged open the door of the empty cabin. A cool, earthy scent with a hint of stale smoke greeted them. "This sure brings back memories," he said. Decades of neglect had left it dusty and weather-beaten. Cobwebs anchored the walls, and dried-up insects littered the windowsill and floor. All the furnishings were long gone, but Helen could imagine where Zeph's cradle had first rocked his baby girl.

"The Judge built this for my mama and my daddy," Zeph explained. "Simmy and me—we kept Alice Lyford right here till we moved to the chapel."

"How long did you stay here?" John asked, looking around at the room, at the cold ashes from a fire, at the clouded window, flowing with age.

"Oh, maybe six months—while I fixed up the chapel. It was hard being so close to Geneva and not even speaking her name. I'd sometimes catch a glimpse of her at her window, but that was all. Hard time. I asked the Judge about it—if me and Simmy could move out to the chapel and take Alice Lyford. He said that suited him as good as anything."

"Who took care of Geneva?"

"Vivvy took up when we moved. Judge Snow—he told her if she would keep their secret, he'd take good care of her the rest of her life. I think Vivvy kind of enjoyed it. She never did like Geneva much, and keeping her kind of a prisoner suited Vivvy."

"But you still saw Geneva?" John asked. "After you moved?"

"Oh, yessir. Sure did. More than ever. We had to be as careful as chickens near a foxhole, though. At first, Geneva didn't understand why we moved, but when she realized she could slip out—be with us—she liked it. If we'd a stayed here, I'd never have seen her, 'cept through her window. After a year or so—when Alice Lyford was toddlin' around—Geneva would come for days at a time."

"Life went on at Cairnaerie?" John said.

"Yessir. Life went on."

CHAPTER 81

Late summer 1930

Promise & Forgiveness

The house was ready. Helen stood at the kitchen door looking out at her handiwork. Early in the spring, as Miss Geneva
had forecast, the flowers bloomed, and Helen had weeded the bed
around Simmy's grave. Now the yellow tickseed, fiery bee balm,
and lavender verbena once again marked the small headstone with
a floral rainbow. With a worn cedar-handled broom, Helen had
swept the flagstones and wiped away the thick pollen coating the
benches. An arbor of tangled vines awash with fragrant climbing
roses framed the far end of the terrace, and shaded violets, sweet
woodruff, and Galax leaves lined the well-worn path to the chapel.
The vague aroma of grapes tinged the warm air. Now it was all fading again toward another year's end, but this year was different.
Cairnaerie was reborn.

Helen left the door ajar and walked back through the house,
checking each room, each window, each tabletop, making sure they
were spotless. This would be a special homecoming. Helen would
make sure it was right—the way Miss Geneva would have wanted.

In the years since Geneva's death, Cairnaerie had been cleaned
out, cataloged, washed, and repaired—restored to a kind of glory

that only Zeph remembered. Legions of workers sent by Rollins had started work as soon as the will was probated, and a slew of documents were drawn up by Anderson Goodwin and signed. The overgrown shrubbery had been cut back, and what couldn't be salvaged with pruners was dug up and replaced. The yard and flowerbeds were raked clean, weeded, and replanted, and all the exterior trim was scraped, repaired, and painted. Even the swing sported a fresh coat of paint and a set of new, galvanized chains. The barn and outbuildings were restored, and several were re-roofed. The chimneys and brick walls were repointed, and the cisterns were replaced with modern water tanks. A new Delco plant, installed in an outbuilding, provided electricity to the house for the first time. The oil lamps were emptied and hauled to the attic. The road in had been graded and widened, an improvement John appreciated since he had replaced his old Ajax with a brand new 1929 Oakland.

Helen walked into the foyer. The freshly polished star shone, and the chandelier glittered as it caught the sun streaming in from the open and freshly washed parlor windows. How different the house was full of light and air. It seemed hard now for her to picture the house dusty and shuttered—the way she had first seen it.

She checked her watch and glanced at the stairs. Did she have time? She had put it off too long. This might be her last chance.

Carrying a dust cloth, Helen climbed the stairs, wiping the banister one last time. In the niche, the dusty peacock feathers were gone, replaced with bundles of wild flowers, their fragrance wafting. The house whispered as air rose through its heart.

She crossed to the back of the house and pushed open the small door. Hot, dry air washed over her as she climbed the stairs to the empty belvedere. She swept away cobwebs.

Helen unhooked a window and pushed it open. Air rushed up the steps as if the house were exhaling. She shielded her eyes. The sun glittered in a cottony sky above the mountains and meadows. How beautiful it was—and how far away it must have seemed to Geneva. She stood there alone—trying to see it through her late friend's eyes.

As she turned to leave, she spied an envelope tucked above the door. Stretching to reach it, she saw her own name written in the now-familiar hand of Miss Geneva. She sat down at the top of the belvedere's stair and opened the envelope.

My Dear Helen,

I knew you would come up here to my belvedere—this private place for thinking and feeling and discovering. I chose to write to you here, sitting on these steps, the vast sky above me, and my beloved Cairnaerie, below.

By the time you read this, I anticipate you will have discovered most of what there is to know about me. From the moment we met, I knew you were disturbed by the circumstances of my life, yet I saw how hard you struggled to understand. I hope you have learned from my journals what a happy life I lived.

I am so glad you came with John. Had I designed the circumstances that brought us together, I could not have chosen a more perfect companion for the last months of my life. In our short time, I found a true friend. I wish I had more time to know you better, but as my life has taught me so well, we do not choose all our paths. We do, however, choose how we travel them. Joy is in discovering love, but the best and truest love is making joy out of life in whatever circumstances we find ourselves. Of course, there is a traditional way to live, and we are drawn like rivers to the sea into believing one way is ideal. But that is not necessarily so. We cannot abandon our loves, and we cannot imprison them in expectations any more than we can draw with our hands the face of God. My father taught me God is love, and if that is true—which I firmly believe it is—then love has no boundaries, no limits. Love is timeless and eternal.

I am telling you this for I know you love our dear John. He may not realize it yet, but do not be discouraged. Men do not have our intuition, our ability to recognize love when it is a bud not yet broken. We see it and feel it—almost before it exists. In time, he will come to love you. I know he will.

I want you to have something special to remember me. You will find it behind a loose board in the back of the wardrobe in my bedroom. Push near the right bottom corner.

I am forever and devotedly....

Miss Geneva

She folded the letter and tilted her head back, letting the sun bathe her face. How could she miss so acutely someone she had known so briefly?

Helen opened the door to Geneva's bedroom, almost expecting her to be sitting by the window. Drawing back the yellow curtains, she opened the tall wardrobe and got down on her knees to feel for the loose board. She moved it aside. Inside was a small box tied atop a newly-made journal. She untied them and opened the book. Inside was an inscription:

To my dear friend, Helen,
Try Again.
Love,
Miss Geneva

Helen smiled. No more explanation was necessary.

"I will, Miss Geneva," she said. "I promise I will."

And then she opened the box. On a small piece of dark blue velvet lay a brooch—a china oval set in roped gold. Lifting it, she held it in her open palm and moved to the window to examine it closely. In the finest of brush strokes, she saw a landscape of rolling hills—it was the view from the belvedere—and at its center, a bird flew unfettered and free. As Helen stared at the image, a strange sensation swept through her, and something inside her broke. For the first time since their first meeting, she let go of the resentment she had held about Geneva's cloistered life. Closing her eyes, she clutched the brooch to her throat, letting the feeling of freedom seep into her soul.

Finally, she understood.

Helen stood on the porch as John's sleek, new Oakland trundled across the bumpy yard and rolled to a stop in a freshly graveled parking area near the house. John jumped out of the automobile and opened doors for his passengers before wresting two large sacks from the automobile. Talking and animated, John was clearly in charge. Helen smiled.

"Where's Zeph?" she asked.

"Coming from Swope," Thatcher said as he helped Joly, who carried a bundle in her arms. "He's up to something."

"He always is," said Joly, laughing.

As Helen waited on the porch, she heard a door inside the house open and close.

"Zeph, they're here," she shouted over her shoulder.

"Bring 'em on in here," Zeph answered, his voice echoing from the foyer.

Helen came down the steps and spread her arms wide. She said the words she had rehearsed—the words Geneva would have said today. "Welcome home, Joly. Welcome to…." but the words caught in her throat as her gaze met Joly's deep blue eyes—the eyes of her grandmother.

"Oh, Miss Helen," Joly said, laughing and crying. "Never in my wildest dreams…"

"It's your home now, Joly," John said. "The paperwork was filed Monday. It's all legal and official."

Joly tried to take it all in. The deed to Cairnaerie was not a wedding ring and had no letter of reconciliation, but it said to Joly everything Bertram's gift of the rings had said to Geneva.

Zeph came to the front door and stood with his arms crossed. He was grinning.

"Grandpa, what have you been up to?" Joly asked.

"I got something for ya. All y'all come on in here." He waved them into the house.

Thatcher helped his wife up the stairs. John set two boxes on the porch next to the sacks and walked in with Helen.

In the middle of the foyer, centered on the inlaid star, sat Alice Lyford's cradle. Without saying a word, Joly walked toward it and laid her newborn daughter on a blanket—one with tassels.

"Thank you, Grandpa," she whispered.

"You and me, girl—and Thatcher here…" Zeph's voice broke. He took a deep breath. "We got us a young'un to raise. And she's got such a pretty name. Geneva. Yessir, that's a beautiful name."

AUTHOR'S NOTES

The story of Geneva Snow and Zeph Elias is fictional, but the challenges they faced are not—and neither were they limited to the times in which they "lived." Prior to the Civil War, slavery acted as a deterrent against interracial marriage. During Reconstruction, however, the Virginia General Assembly passed legislation prohibiting such marriages to legislate what slavery had, up to that point, discouraged. Although marriages between "whites and coloreds" occurred, they were rare, and in 1880 constituted fewer than one percent of all white marriages. One notable union was the 1884 marriage of Frederick Douglass and Helen Pitts, a white woman, who said, "Love came to me, and I was not afraid to marry the man I loved because of his color."

In the early part of the 20th century, much of the impetus for anti-miscegenation laws found justification in the powerful eugenics movement—a "science" advocating racial segregation and the need for maintaining purity among the races. The movement, which drove passage of Virginia's Racial Integrity Act of 1924, put the powers of science, academia, and government—a daunting coalition—behind racism, and in doing so, prolonged the social stigmas associated with the crossing of races communally and especially matrimonially.

It was the mixing of blood that those legislators—and many of the nation's top academicians—found so odious. Eugenicists believed interracial marriage and the resultant progeny would cause the downfall of civilization. Relying on "science," speculative genealogies—sometimes based on gossip—determined an individual's race by their percentage of "colored" blood; an "octoroon" was an individual who was one-eighth African-American, a "quadroon" was one-quarter. When illuminated, such a report presumably inspired Theodore "Benny" Benwick's dismissal and Jacob Lassiten's suicide.

It is ironic that the allowance was far more generous for whites marrying persons of American Indian descent—a concession, no doubt, to the 1614 marriage between the Virginian John Rolfe and Native American Pocahontas. Many of their descendants populated the commonwealth's General Assembly. A white individual could legally marry a person who was one-eighth Native American. For African Americans, however, no such tolerance was lent. A single drop of "colored" blood was enough to classify an individual as non-white, a determination made by bureaucrats like Walter Ashby Plecker. Plecker was the first registrar of the Virginia Bureau of Vital Statistics and leader of the Anglo-Saxon Clubs of America, first organized in Richmond in 1922.

African Americans were not the only victims of eugenics. Perhaps the saddest part of the eugenics movement was forced sterilization, a state-mandated "service" visited on the most vulnerable—those deemed mentally inferior or morally lacking, and those who, if allowed to propagate, would presumably produce individuals with equal disability. Among those considered "lesser" were immigrant populations—and "science" once again "proved" it, based on the newly emerging field of IQ testing. Eugenicists preached that in discouraging propagation among these populations by preventing the "tainting" of better "stock" through anti-miscegenation laws, they would ensure the strength of humanity.

The movement was strongly endorsed by many biologists and sociologists of the time at prominent American universities, including Stanford, Yale, Harvard, Princeton, Berkeley, and the University of Virginia. Additionally, corporate financing for the movement came from the Carnegie Institution and the Rockefeller Foundation, to name a few. Likely because of its seemingly scientific bent, eugenics had many prominent proponents as well, including Margaret Sanger, George Bernard Shaw, Winston Churchill, John Maynard Keynes, Charles Lindbergh, Supreme Court Justice Oliver Wendell Holmes, and thousands of politicians and scholars. It was the lure of modernity, science, and the considerable weight of academia that resulted in the widespread acceptance of eugenics.

Thankfully, the eugenics movement was exposed for what it was, blatant and ignorant discrimination, after Adolph Hitler and his legions embraced it. Gradually the movement faded, yet eugenics remains a cautionary tale as society moves forward into such brave new worlds as the advent of human genetic coding, in vitro testing, and as new iterations of eugenics, encouraged by legalized abortion, begin to eliminate groups of individuals such as those with Downs syndrome, spina bifida, and other physical malformations. Creating preferred humans—as eugenicists believed noble and modern society deems desirable—is a potent temptation.

While Virginia's most notorious black/white relationship is that of Thomas Jefferson and Sally Hemmings, the marriage of Mildred Delores Jeter, of African and American Indian descent, and Richard Perry Loving, a white man, is the most consequential. The Lovings, who married legally out of state and moved to the commonwealth in 1958, were arrested and faced imprisonment under Virginia law. It took until 1967 when the United States Supreme Court finally overturned Virginia's anti-miscegenation law. It was perhaps, as one commentator wrote, the most appropriately named court case in American jurisprudence: Loving vs. Virginia.

And love won.

The name "Cairnaerie" is the author's invention. In fact, exceedingly few references exist to such a name, however, one discovery unearthed during the author's research was surprising and serendipitous: The first American watchmaker was a 'John Cairns.' The name, if nothing else, creates a bridge between the fictional Cairnaerie and the real craftsman of Providence, Rhode Island. John Cairns, watchmaker, died by drowning in 1809.

And finally. Along with John Cairns, Adam Wysor and Eve Turnipseed are the only real names in this novel. Adam and Eve do lie together—their tombstones hidden in an overgrown and cattle-trodden cemetery—somewhere in rural Virginia.

ACKNOWLEDGEMENTS

A book completed is art produced, and its measure as good or poor is highly subjective—as the measure of all art is subjective. A book, though, possesses a dimension that other mediums do not. While a painting may whisk one away for a momentary jaunt to another place or time, it cannot do so with the depth and expanse of a novel. A novel, thus, is art that becomes an adventure where a unique story is discovered—an amalgamation of a writer's words and a reader's experience and imagination. On this premise, I offer this novel. I do so with great trepidation and, quite candidly, with a solid nudge from some friends. Some of my trepidation stems from the subject matter with which I have no personal experience. I have seen racism from a distance only, therefore I ask readers for some grace because experience, though powerful, is not a requisite for empathy.

And those friends who nudged. I am savvy enough to believe (and old enough to know) that it is wise to trust those who have one's best interests at heart. Mine do. I am, therefore, persuaded to take this step. I am so grateful for their help. One of those friends is Jean Young Kilby, author of *Ten Cow Woman: An Ethiopian Tale* and *Freedom Riders.* She and I have shared a special writing journey, and her help has been indispensable. I am reminded, as I write this, that my own serious pursuit of fiction began about the time I meant Jean. Another friend is Luanne Brown Austin, author of the long-running and award-winning column, "Rural Pen," and *Stain the Water Clear,* a compilation of her columns. One more is Toni Ressaire, who lives in France, drinks fine wine, and sharpens the cutting edge of electronic publishing. I also thank Martie Smith, my friend and favorite librarian, whose encouragement helped me get back on track when an unhelpful editor caused me to lose my way. There are others—Donna, Cheryl, Jan L, Mary Kay K, Jeannie, Allison, and Fred—who encouraged me at critical moments, motivated me to strive for excellence, or pushed an always eager but sometimes unsure writer.

The two greatest gifts any writer can receive are honesty and a vote of confidence—and these friends have given me both. I am immensely thankful for their help and friendship.

I am also grateful to two who were there before everyone else: my mother, an author in her own right, who read to me (especially Rudyard Kipling's *How the Rhinoceros Got His Skin*) and gave me her consuming love of books and her talent for words. And my dad, who so often said, "Marthie, you're the best writer."

Above all others, I am grateful to my husband, Mark, whose work ethic is second to none and whose heart is for God and his family. Like my dad—and Bertram Snow—he has taken care of us all. Our children and I are the fortunate beneficiaries. He alone knows how much work went into this novel. His unending patience with my obsessive need to write and his unfailing encouragement have been my lifeline—and his belief in this novel has made all the difference.

And finally, I am grateful for those who take the time to read this book. It is my great hope that every person who touches it will be blessed.